RHYTHMS AND BLUES
VOL.1

I0674550

by

BRENDA FAUCON

LIFE BRINGS THE BLUES. THE BLUES BRINGS LIFE.

ISBN: 978-2-9557203-0-1
First edition: June 2016 (Print and eBook)
Second edition: October 2017 (Print and eBook)
10 9 8 7 6 5 4 3 2 1

Cover design: Saturn9 at 99designs.com
Front cover photography: Sasha Radosavljevic
Back cover photography: lanzeppelin0 via pixabay.com
Interior design: Price Hall
Author photo credit: Michel Goessens

Website: brendafaucon.com
Web design: webservices.dramat.is

Dedication

For Price,
whom I adore every moment of every day

Chapter I
Katherine

There were moments when Katherine Loch thought she might not make it to the next. Only five weeks ago, thirty-five days, just over one month, very much less than two…

"… you were alive."

She said it aloud. Every day was assigned its own hope-depriving number, and yet telling herself it hadn't been long at all made the weight of her loss less heavy to bear.

Katherine had a last look at the drab cottage that had been her prison for the last thirty of those days, locked the door, and dropped the key through the letterbox. It clattered on the floor, missing the doormat entirely. Remembering the trash, she rattled the door handle fruitlessly and sighed. To her annoyance, thinking about things out of turn seemed to be a new feature in her life.

The ocean wind toyed with strands of her dark ash-blond hair. Only this morning, after a nourishing treatment and the first decent blow dry in weeks, had she noticed it was streaked through with highlights—probably from having spent summer days outdoors with Norman, as they silently dreaded the moment a last shared sunbeam would sink behind the horizon, forever out of reach.

Resolutely, Katherine turned away from the cottage and the memory. She found an elastic band in the right-hand pocket of her windbreaker and, quickly twisting the wayward hair into a knot, made for the perilous path that ran alongside the cliff. Her jeans were carelessly tucked into a pair of green Wellington boots. Indifferent to the wind clawing its icy fingers into patches of bare skin, she slipped once or twice but otherwise left an even trail of tread marks in the semi-dry mud down to a desolate, rock-strewn beach.

The stunning chalk cliffs, eloquently named "The Seven Sisters," were just visible in the distance through their white luminescence. Gloomy weather kept the rest of the landscape tucked inside the previous night's shadows. Overhead, a vigorous gust took a large herring gull by surprise. He dipped sideways with a laughing call, as if amused by it, and made an elegant turn, flapping his wings in defiance against the wind. Katherine marvelled at the gracefulness with which dozens more gulls moved in and out of low hanging clouds, their wings beating brightly against a blanket of grey that threatened a torrent of rain.

She did not mind. Activity along the boardwalk indicated the morning was already in full swing, but the town's bustling noise could not breach the sound of waves as they crashed violently against the many large rocks piercing the surface of the sea. The scenery formed a natural cocoon against the world, and Katherine was glad for it.

In a final bid to avoid contact with the neighbourhood, she walked briskly towards water's edge and, burying cold hands deep in her pockets, observed her new surroundings. Having spent a restrictive childhood in London and having moved to the continent at the age of eighteen, being in England again was quite strange. But even after six years of connubial bliss in the Netherlands, and after going from wife and muse to widow in a dizzyingly short period of time… even if unwelcome circumstances invaded the experience, the magnificent coastline was undeniably invigorating.

Katherine took a deep breath, kicking a rock in her path. While this beach was sandier than Brighton's, it was littered with sharp rocks, making for a much less inviting spot to spread a towel or a picnic blanket than the smooth pebbled beaches of the neighbouring seaside city seven or eight miles west. In thirty days, the mornings had not yet been clear enough to see Brighton's pier, furthering the perception that Blackwell-on-Sea, as of today officially her new home, was an isolated village. With mist blanketing the gabled rooftops and Blackwell Castle looming protectively over the fifty-six half-timber dwellings that were the village's thriving heart, Katherine needed to remind herself that the year was 1983 and not 1577.

Moving here had been Norman's doing—or that of Katherine's mother, depending how you looked at it. He said the idea was hers, which was odd considering Tessa had died two years before Katherine and Norman met. She attributed the vision to the fact that he'd been drugged out of his mind when he mentioned Blackwell-on-Sea, but to his credit, he held on to the belief until the very end. *Her mother had sent a message.* Of course, over the years she'd almost certainly talked about her mother's dream to have a shop here. Yet despite her scepticism, through a perceived conspiracy from beyond the grave, the two of them were instrumental in getting Katherine to this unfamiliar place. So perhaps the more astonishing plot twist was that Tessa still seemed to have some influence on her life. Since having arrived here, the sense that she was being reintroduced to her mother would not let go.

Bracing muddy boots against the first breakwater one by one, she tucked her jeans more neatly into them. She'd given neither Mum nor Aunt Celeste, Mum's older sister, much thought these last few years. Life with Norman was powerful enough to have formed a boundary that couldn't be measured in distance. Circumstances had forced Katherine to mature faster than society would consider normal and she had been legally emancipated on her fifteenth birthday. Honesty demanded that when her mother died, grief hadn't been so gripping. But in recent months, as Norman's fate loomed over them like a hungry monster, the blurred images of *that life* slowly gained an unsolicited edge, and there seemed a gently bubbling need to put those relationships into a different perspective.

Katherine's life, so far, could be measured in chapters that encompassed the places she'd lived, to begin with a rather bizarre childhood in Battersea where from a young age she had nursed her mother through a crippling illness, leaving Katherine in a constant state dealing with life, working hard and... longing for freedom. As time dragged on, Tessa had become more and more trapped within the confines of rheumatoid arthritis, pain pills, and self-medicating alcoholism. Just before turning sixteen, after coming home from school, Katherine had found Tessa with her eyes wide open, the stench of vomit, mixed with that of alcohol spilling from an open bottle fallen from disturbingly twisted fingers.

She'd stared at the instruments of her mother's art for a long time. Those fingers had created so many beautiful things! Battersea was a small neighbourhood on the banks of the Thames in southeast London, where Tessa had been the go-to seamstress. Mostly she was commissioned to make ordinary household things, but sometimes a bride came along and for a while their kitchen would be the centre of the most intricate embroidery, the finest stitches, and life would gain an inkling of magic! Sadly, her mother's nimble fingers slowly deformed until they could no longer thread a needle. Painkillers were normal by then, and Katherine suspected alcohol was a way to compensate for an emotional pain that she'd always sensed existed but her mother never shared. The only hours Tessa did not wither in pain were the ones she slept through on a cocktail of pills and booze. There was little point in feeling guilty about being an enabler. It had fewer side effects than morphine.

Katherine protected Tessa from the prying eyes and vicious gossip their neighbourhood had no shortage of. Only two people knew the gravity of the situation: the ever-aloof Celeste and the doctor who treated her mother at home. The choices for medication and the possibilities for outside care were explained to them on more than one occasion, but despite a difficult relationship, mother and daughter vehemently agreed they wanted to stay together. Soon it was Katherine who handled repairs and created simple things like bed sheets, housecoats, and eventually pencil skirts and dresses. Doctor Feldman cared for Tessa every day around lunch time and, becoming a voluntary guardian of sorts, in the evenings helped the young teenager manage time and money. In many ways, he was the only father figure Katherine had ever known.

The idea of being legally bound to Celeste after going through years of hardship and learning to be independent became unthinkable. Ever encouraging, it was with Markus Feldman's support that Katherine filed for legal emancipation. Aunt Celeste hadn't cared much. She'd listened. She always listened. Then life continued to spin around the axis of her dignified back. Tessa consented to Katherine's legal separation on the premise that she would not leave. Somehow the idea that it was she who cared for Katherine, still lived inside of Tessa. For that reason her death just a few months later had brought a great deal of sadness, but mostly relief to Katherine's life. Finally, Tessa had been set free from a crippled body, and admittedly Katherine was ready to get on with it.

After that, she lived in the gabled attic of Aunt Celeste's B&B. The sisters had never been fond of each other. What had happened to them during the war and in their childhood that forged the siblings into the hardened adults they became was unknown. More than Tessa, Katherine had always thought Celeste incapable of affection. But while the relationship with her aunt was awkward as a result, a place to live seemed a comfort easy enough to offer

Katherine, who accepted entirely for pragmatic reasons. She'd sewn her teenage fingers to the bone in order to support herself and her mother and was left fairly poor if one didn't count the sale of their tiny Shaftsbury Park cottage. Living rent-free meant the freedom to pay for design and business courses.

Her first action as an orphan living in the more prominent neighbourhood of Wandsworth was to retire Mum's foot-pedal-driven Singer. A small amount of her inheritance was invested in the latest and greatest electric sewing machine, which allowed her to do more work in a shorter amount of time. With Wandsworth neighbouring Battersea, customers soon followed. Together with local business, this generated enough income to pay for the coveted courses, buy food, and squirrel away a little for a rainy day. Having the tools to become financially independent was the new goal.

The next two years were filled with school and work, an apprenticeship she'd found at a renowned tailor shop in the heart of London. It hadn't paid much, but bringing the experience to the neighbourhood proved invaluable. It wasn't until a handsome Dutchman named Norman appeared on the scene that life took an adventurous turn. They met as he busked near the corner of one of the city's busiest shopping streets and became immediately inseparable. Every day for two weeks he'd strummed the Blues on a battered guitar and waited for her to appear. Being at the beginning of a summer-long course at art and design school, she refused to accept his plea to elope to the Netherlands. He'd returned home.

At the end of term, under the surprisingly mournful eyes of Aunt Celeste, who knew better than to think she could change the mind of a girl so fiercely independent, Katherine had filled two suitcases and kissed her goodbye. Norman had waited for her at the ferry with a wilting bouquet of handpicked cornflowers the colour of her eyes. To *his* family's consternation, they were married just three weeks later.

Thirty-five days ago I was not your widow.

Norman now came to her nearly every night in the dream: a constant reliving of their first meeting. The dreams seemed so real that every moment of waking was a blissful one, euphoric with possibility. But the edge of consciousness stole it away and hope was replaced by tightness in her chest and a terrible ache in the pit of her stomach. With a quiver of her long eyelashes, the sensation of having him close floated out of reach. Each time was a new defeat that wrapped her cornflower-blue eyes in a blanket of tears.

Gazing out at the English Channel, she wished for a week or two in the company of Doctor Feldman. These days he lived in the Canary Islands where sunshine and a savagely injured toreador twenty years his junior made retirement fulfilling. Katherine smiled at the thought of them. On the rare occasions she could visit, the pair was exuberant in their welcome and Doctor Feldman's frequent embraces never ceased to be a surprise for a girl whose family was not outwardly affectionate. She missed him terribly and vowed to have a long letter in the post to him the next morning.

The incisive barking of a large dog penetrated her musings. She turned towards the sound and, to her surprise, found she'd walked past the gloomy castle without being aware. Bounding across the beach, dodging rocks, ears pushed flat against the wind, the dog wore an excited expression. She had seen the animal before from a distance and, unafraid, knelt down in the sand, holding her hand out to be sniffed. The animal seemed young and vigorous, and panted hotly in her face. It likely belonged to somebody nearby.

"Hello!" Her fingers disappeared into well-groomed black fur as she scratched the German shepherd's neck.

A quick glance confirmed the dog was female, and a nameplate helpfully dangled from a beautifully tooled leather collar. It was with barely contained excitement, thick tail wagging with an abundance of joy and energy that the dog sat long enough for Katherine to be able to read the inscription.

"Are you eager for a friend?" She half-smiled.

Seemingly happy to make her acquaintance, the gorgeous beast held her head to the side for better access. One side of the tag read simply "The Castle." Katherine threw a glance at the imposing black fortress. On this side, the walls were broken and looked like gaping wounds. Not even a ray of sunshine could put cheer into that facade, she thought and made a face. She turned the hand-tooled silver name plate.

"Billie!"

The dog barked triumphantly.

"Well that's a boy's name, isn't it... or at the very least that of a goat!" She mused, gently fondling the dog's ample, pointy ears. "Would you like to join me on my walk?"

With Billie the Dog bounding by her side, Katherine continued to the far breakwater, allowing the beauty of the surroundings to penetrate her musings. She was taken aback by the profound effect the sound of the sea had in just a few weeks' time. She came to expect it now, as if she'd been waiting for it all of her life. At times, she wondered if her mother, in the past, had been equally charmed by this village because of its beautiful beach.

The dog barked. Billie, full of pent-up energy, held a stick of driftwood in her mouth. Katherine looked from the dog's pleading eyes to the castle and back again. She shook her head in disbelief.

"Some would envy you for living there, you know,' she said, "but don't expect such foolish sentiment from me. I only look to the future. The past is not for me."

Even to her own ears, the statement sounded robotic. Billie dropped the stick at her feet. Her tail swept the air as vigorously as the wind that blew around them. Unable to resist, Katherine picked up the stick and hurled it away as hard as she could. The muscles in her face strained against a smile.

But the dog couldn't hold her complete attention long and she pictured Norman. In their final weeks together, when delusions of a future they would never have blurred with reality, Katherine was forced to admit to the fear she wouldn't want to make it through a day without him. With an immediate need for direction and no other avenue to pursue, Norman had then fuelled the idea of the shop with a passion that belied the pain in his cancer-ridden body. To the disbelief of Norman's family and their friends, and even Katherine herself, he'd quietly, and to the best of his weakening abilities, helped to begin making arrangements. He'd insisted on the sale of the ancient little house that had been left to him by his grandparents, to raise a down payment. In the face of their community, he'd been that brave. But privately Norman was devastated by the absurdity that he wouldn't live long enough to see the shop come to fruition.

Having had a good run across the beach, sometimes on a dare for the surf to touch her feet and running away each time it got too close, Billie the Dog seemed contented. She trotted beside Katherine, tongue happily dispensed from the side of her mouth as if it were something she could do without. Yawning, Katherine pushed memories of Norman back into their little box and focused on the thought of a first pot of coffee in the newly remodelled apartment above the not-yet-remodelled shop. She checked the time. People would arrive soon to unload a lorry full of her things from the Netherlands.

"Well then, dear Billie," she said looking at the dog, "how do you get to and from the beach?"

Billie didn't have a reply. Taking hold of the leather collar, she gently guided the dog to the top of the cliff. Katherine gazed at the castle with some reservation. Assuming someone would be there, the time to begin interacting with Blackwell residents had come. She and Billie crossed the drawbridge. For lack of a modern doorbell to ring, she regarded a big metal pull that looked like it might function somewhere deep inside. At first glance it seemed like too many centuries would have gone by for it to still work, but she grabbed hold of it and gave it a good yank.

Who in the world would ever have had reason to ring this bell voluntarily? Katherine wondered. The hundreds of wicked spikes jutting from the door were enough to send anyone packing. From the beach, sitting atop the lower ledge of the cliff, the castle was menacing enough, but to stand here with the wall above the gigantic front door reaching into the sky, even this approach seemed like a very bad idea. Billie sat patiently by her side, staring intently at the tiny door that was carved from the bigger one and when they heard the sound of a slide being manipulated on the inside, the dog leaped to eager attention.

"Good morning," Katherine said with as much of a smile as she could muster. She had given herself the space not to have to interact with very many people other than the workmen renovating the building she had bought on High Street, so she felt terribly out of touch. "I hope I'm not disturbing. Your dog was on the beach and I wasn't sure how she got there, but here she is, safe and sound. And thoroughly exercised I should say."

"Billie?" the man with gold-rimmed spectacles said, puzzled. "Everybody knows she goes to the green door."

"Oh. In her defence she was reluctant to follow me here but I'm new in town and unfamiliar with the goings-on. My name is Katherine."

"Yes, I've seen you on the beach in recent weeks."

His tone was not unfriendly even if his voice was so soft she needed to strain to hear him from the dark recesses beyond the massive door. Billie barked at her master and danced around as if to make introductions. To Katherine's relief, the master didn't have much else to say.

"Billie. In!" he commanded, and nodded to Katherine. "Thank you, young lady. Very kind of you to keep her company."

With a sorrowful backwards glance, Billie trotted away and hopped the ledge, disappearing into mysteriously gloomy depths. The old man slammed the small door with a loud thud. Was it possible to *slam* something of that weight, she wondered, staring at the thick wood for a full thirty seconds. What an abrupt encounter. She touched her face as if to wipe away anything that might have been offensive to the old man and looked around to make sure she was the only one there. An old green Triumph turned the corner with a roar in the direction of Brighton. The first-day tourists were grouped in small numbers at some of the galleried terraces for breakfast. She could have marvelled at their early arrival and did vaguely note the *Van Tours* bus parked in Blackwell's only car park. But her mind was on the notion of not being ready for having a lot of contact with neighbours, versus the eerie echo in the wake of a thousand-year-old door being abruptly shut.

"Too many historical influences," she concluded out loud.

In her imagination, this town in the Middle Ages would not have been quite so quaint and meticulously kept with flowers in every window box no matter what the season. Horse shit would have been the norm, and voluptuous, gummy women would have thrown slop from leaded windows onto the cobblestone streets with little regard for passers-by. She could almost hear the tortured screams and sounds of misery that must surely have bounced from the thick fortress walls. Rudeness would probably have been normal... *then*.

Raindrops started to fall in lazy spats. Katherine shook images of dire circumstances away and threw the hood over her head. *There's one of us in every town, Katrientje.* She had no trouble hearing Norman's quip in her mind. The urge for dialog too strong to resist, she replied before his presence could slip away: "It is perfectly okay to be eccentric without being rude!" The sound of her own voice again made her look around self-consciously, though not soon enough to realize she had stepped onto the street just as the green Triumph approached. Her heart very nearly jumped out of her body when it screeched to a halt not two inches from her knees. The passenger door flew open.

"Goodness, me, young lady! Are you all right?" And to a driver obscured from Katherine's sight by the glare in the windshield, he barked, "Damn, son, can you not slow down in the heart of the village?"

"Sorry!" Katherine heard from the car, a hand appearing in the window to give the apology credence. "Shut the door, Dad, I've got to go."

Katherine remembered the man. He was a handsome, sixtyish, long-time village resident whom people looked up to. His name was Ned Denison and he'd voted in favour of her buying the shop after the presentation she'd had to make before the village council. He was the type of man who was everybody's mate, and she had liked him immediately. He slammed the door shut. The Triumph waited patiently for Katherine and Ned to cross the road before it roared away. He shook his head in exasperation and put a hand on her arm.

"I'm fine," Katherine said. "I should have paid attention."

"Bloody kids!" he countered with a wave of an arm. "My son is late for the airport. My apologies. It's Mrs. Loch, is it not? Have you moved in to your place?"

"In mere minutes." She smiled.

"Does this mean everything is in working order?"

"I'm happy with the way the apartment has been restored, but progress in the shop is slow and quite frankly sapping my funds. I wanted to talk to you about that."

The statement amused him. "Is it a bank you're looking for?"

Katherine grimaced. "It's not as bad as that. Not yet anyway. It's always been my intent to buy what furniture is necessary, but having visited your place some time ago, combined with the sudden need to be frugal, got me thinking about options."

"What do you propose?" Ned wanted to know as they arrived at the renowned antiques shop with its tasteful window displays. He touched all of his pockets in search for keys.

"I need furniture to display my merchandise. Large pieces. How would you feel about displaying some of your pricier, bulky antiques in my shop? Perhaps even things that haven't sold in ages. I would not only advertise for your shop, I would sell them for you too. If the arrangement works, I'd like the opportunity to exchange the pieces for something different with every new collection, or at least twice a year."

Ned's first thought was that his shop didn't need the advertisement and, continuing to pat his pockets, considered refusing on the spot. Why would he risk the damage? Katherine's eyes were on him intently, blue, huge. She waited patiently, biting her lower lip. He cleared his throat. The entire village was supportive and wouldn't dream of buying outside of its own shops, but things like this had never been done. If they were, he would be aware of it. His hands stilled.

"Commission?"

A slow grin spread across her face. "It depends if you'd charge a leasing fee, doesn't it? If so I'd obviously like the opportunity to recover some of the cost. I know I'll be lucky to break even in the first couple of years and there will be a need to be flexible. For this, I'm even prepared to restore the stuff that hasn't seen the light of day in decades. Whatever. I know you're the best source around for miles. I've checked."

He nodded though it wasn't clear if he did so because he agreed or because he appreciated the pitch.

"Put together a contract," he said, fishing a key chain from a trouser pocket he'd patted at least twice. "I'll sign it."

"Just like that?" She frowned. "Right here on the street?"

He inserted a key and shrugged. "Seems a great way to get rid of my rubbish!"

They shook hands and she left feeling a bit victorious. To her surprise, a small crowd had gathered on the sidewalk across from her place. She found them speculating loudly. Katherine slowed her pace. The movers, dressed in white overalls, unloaded the familiar black leather sofa from a red lorry and turned it sideways to fit through the shop's door. How they would get it up two flights of stairs with a hard turn between them was anyone's guess, and Katherine tried not to think about the newly painted walls she had finished just yesterday.

"Have you seen the new owner around?" the mailman called to the group. He was thick around the middle and a leather mail satchel was slung over a shoulder, tapping against his leg as he walked.

Owner… bloody hell that's me! She thought.

God, I can't do this. How can I do this?

Thirty-five days ago… just thirty-five days ago my sole ownership was to take care of you.

"Morning Darryl, you're early today," a neighbour replied from the doorway of a porcelain shop. "Alders is the contractor. Don told my Harold she only ever meets them Monday mornings. She makes them fix things before they can move on and they work overtime when she's not satisfied."

"Ooh, what a lovely table. Is that Spanish, you think?" the newsagent's lady added as two different men carried out the Moroccan coffee table. "I heard she's on the picky side and she's doing all the painting to save on the cost."

Katherine had yet to be introduced to many of her new neighbours, but she'd visited each of them covertly, as a shopper. She wanted to see how they worked and what their attitude towards tourists was. At this hour of the day, most of them were dressed in dust coats, and the newsagent's head was wound in a dark-blue kerchief as she held a feather duster in her hand. The porcelain lady leaned on a scrub brush with a cigarette dangling from bright red lips. A steaming bucket of soapy water stood by her feet on the cobble stones.

"I believe it." A coiffed, blue-haired woman dressed in a raincoat twice her size jumped in as she dragged a red and green tartan grocery bag on wheels, one of which squeaked at every other turn. "Lorna was telling Mark a postal account was set up with a substantial sum, but it is dwindling fast."

Katherine rolled her eyes and managed to slip behind the gossiping quintet. Bloody right they worked overtime. The cost to rewire an entire house to bring it up to code was nothing short of staggering and the men seemed to have a habit of hiding bad things behind strategically placed tool boxes.

She ignored the moving van and made for the bakery where the proprietor cooed a young employee off to school. A bell sounded shrilly across the village square, announcing the imminent start of classes. The blond teenager smiled as they passed each other in the doorway and Katherine gave her a friendly good morning. The few times she'd been served by her, Katherine thought her too shy to handle the shop, but the baker's wife, Thelma, was always around and didn't seem to mind.

"Good morning," Katherine said as she eyed the trays full of miscellaneous pastries, wishing they could tantalize her taste buds. Toast and croissants were all she could handle, with loads of butter and jam.

"You again!" Thelma wiped her hands as she turned to the counter. "You're becoming a regular."

"Yes, I suppose I am." Katherine managed to return a smile. "I'll have a small muffin bread, sliced for toasting, and two croissants, please."

"Right-o!" She got to work. "You've a funny way of ordering your bread, like they do on the mainland. Do you live nearby?"

"Do I?" Katherine raised an eyebrow, thinking she had placed her bread order in much the same way for years. Then she realized it probably did sound different. Dutch in English. Backwards.

While Thelma filled the order, Katherine perused a corner shelf laden with colourful tea mugs and a few different kinds of specialty teas. A mug the colour of spring leaves on an apple tree at the back of the shelf caught her eye and she reached for it gingerly. In the light, its colour was reminiscent of Norman's eyes, and loving once-overs any time she'd walked into a room.

"You've certainly been here longer than any tourist I've seen. Would you like to get your butter here, fresh from the dairy farm?"

"Sorry? Oh! Lovely, yes." She coughed to get the lump out of her throat. "That will save me a trip to the grocers, thanks."

Pulling herself together, she snatched a box of Chamomile tea and deposited both items on the counter. Thelma was an efficient shopkeeper, Katherine knew. She'd had several opportunities to observe the baker's wife over the last few weeks and marvelled at her confidence. She worked swiftly, making few unnecessary moves, always cleaning up after herself or the help. The bakery was attractive, with stacked wooden crates filled with local artisan products, flour-filled burlap, and real sunflowers against walls painted as blue as the sky on a pleasant summer day. There were clear boxes with handmade marzipan fruit in a rainbow of colours, and another shelf held chocolate figurines with a medieval theme. The selection and prices were handwritten in white chalk on a narrow blackboard that spanned two walls, broken up only by exposed beams. Beautiful assortments of bread and rolls were displayed in baskets that lined the shelves behind the counter. The place was reminiscent of a French country bakery.

Thelma gazed at her expectantly. Katherine took a strawberry and a boysenberry jam, adding them with a deep mental breath for courage. She wasn't ready. Gossip combined with the occasional sighting in one of the shops might buy her another week or two of solitude. In a village like this, she thought, word probably travelled like a hummingbird in need of nectar, so maybe a physical presence wasn't necessarily required yet.

"You are right," she said, finally. "I am new in town and here to stay, I hope. Mister Tinker owned the place before me."

"Oh, right! Your shop is quite a decent size, isn't it? You have our good wishes. The mug is on the house."

"Thank you. That's very kind."

"What's the shop to be then? Something to do with fashion, I heard? Does it need a lot of work?"

"Ladies' fashion." Katherine nodded, trying not to have a panic attack. "And yes, the work is ongoing but the apartment is nearly done and I'm moving in today, regardless."

"We've a mass of fashion shops in Blackwell."

"I'm aware of that, but everything I sell will be my own creation. And I am flexible," Katherine continued. "I'm interested in making custom things for people, including wedding gowns, I think."

"So I could come to you with a magazine and say I want that?!" she said, adding the amounts on a small calculator.

"Well I wouldn't be allowed to copy, but we would use it as a starting point and work something out. Or you can bring a pattern and I'll make it happen, no problem. But to the day tourists, it will be off the rack mostly."

"That'll be eight and six, please," Thelma said, taking Katherine's cash. "What a brilliant idea! Like a neighbourhood seamstress! It's about time someone did something for us locals. Other than The Wicked Mule and the yearly Medieval Festival, nothing much happens for us here. It's all about the castle and tourism and Bert's sausages."

"This is not your typical British bakery," Katherine remarked, looking around again.

"We've been here just over a year, right after we were married. My husband, Sean, apprenticed in Paris and in Brussels for a number of years. The ingredients we use are local artisan and we bake in a brick oven."

Katherine thought at first they might not be accepting of her, but she realized during the presentation for the town council that the people of Blackwell-on-Sea were not shy to accept newcomers who had something to offer that was alive since centuries past. Katherine not only had cash in hand but it was her skill in embroidery that caught their interest. The town elders, Ned Denison among them, had asked for a demonstration on the spot. Having spent hours on a presentation about her vision for the shop, they found the three freehanded cats at the corner of a handkerchief using a needle and thread from the bottom of her purse, to be on par with the medieval spirit of the village. The stipulation to the sale was to include these sorts of accents in the shop, just as the silver artist's creations bore marks of the small hammer she used to form the jewellery and the baker's used stone-ground grains.

"That explains the fancy chocolate figurines and most definitely explains the exquisite croissants. I'm pleased we're neighbours," she said with a friendly nod. Not giving the conversation a chance to continue, she made for the door. "See you soon."

Someone else came in and Thelma's focus shifted. Katherine marched to the new house with as much determination as she could muster. The heels of her boots came down on the pavement like hammers. Every strike was as difficult as the next to achieve. The foreman of the crew called her attention straight away. They were done with the furniture, ready to unload boxes, and would she be available to direct the staging, the foreman wanted to know. The two remaining people who'd stayed around with unbridled curiosity received no more than a friendly good morning and her excuses in the same breath as she made haste through the door. With a sigh of desperation and a longing eye on the coffee pot sitting forlorn on the second stair, she followed him. She picked it up along with the suitcase she'd brought the night before and made a mental deal that a fresh pot would be the reward for braving the next hour.

Of course, it didn't work out that way. She staged, munching on a dry croissant while they carried things in and had seven boxes of books unpacked before they were through. But to their credit, when the men left, the double bed had been put together under the eaves of the house and the smaller bedroom beside it held cupboards and racks ready to receive the masses of clothes she'd made for herself over the years. The living room would be used as a work space with the dining room table serving as a cutting table. Every large piece of furniture was in place, including those in the sewing-room-cum-office off the landing. The only exception was the brand-new drafting table in its box underneath a leaded window. She wanted to assemble it herself.

Moments after they left, with the kitchen in complete disarray but with coffee brewing in the pot, she had a shower in the en-suite bathroom and dressed in a black silk nightgown. She eyed the bed as longingly as she had the coffee pot earlier, but there were a number of hours of daylight remaining and her need to have a semblance of a home far outweighed any hope of sleep. Nights were a strange mix of fitful dozing and wakeful loneliness, and the longer she could manage to be awake, the better the chance for a few hours of warding off the darkness.

With a first cuppa of the day, Katherine walked from room to room in her new home. The windows in the sitting room looked out onto High Street, and her shop was situated just about halfway between the town square and the castle. The street was only twelve feet wide but the leaded windows provided enough privacy from the neighbours across from her. Not a single building in Blackwell-on-Sea was very straight, which added to the charm of the village. Every window had a flower box filled with mums. Hers were sadly empty of the splendid colour that gave Blackwell its vibrancy and reputation as the place for a lazy afternoon shopping trip down by the sea, even in fall and winter time. Katherine had to admit that despite the town being an historical gem, without the flowers, the buildings and their interesting geometric monochrome half-timber shapes would lose some lustre.

She took a piece of paper and wrote down *shopping* with a line underneath. She added *dirt* and *flowers*, and threw the pen down, wandering to the next room. She was pleased with the apartment. It had been a toss between this property and one much cheaper away from the main street. To venture so close to the thick of things with every chance of failure was risky and she knew it, but for the first time in her life she felt there was nothing left to lose. Having turned twenty-four several months before, the future was entirely her own for the second time in her life. This kind of freedom would not have been her choice but no one had thought to seek her opinion.

Every relentless minute that went by, she missed Norman. The final moment, *that blasted moment*, was a memory so impossible to relive that pushing it away had quickly become essential to her survival. She struggled to understand how life could go on. How was it possible to feel as if she had died with Norman while still enjoying the scent of iodine in the air, and that of a freshly brewed pot of coffee? How could she enjoy any of it… any of this, without him?

The doorbell rang. Katherine didn't realize what it was until it buzzed a second time. She wanted to ignore it. Had this been the Netherlands she would have, but with pressure to become a part of the community and the risk that it was a neighbour being neighbourly after having witnessed her arrival, it would be quite impolite not to answer the door. Without the time to change into something less comfortable, Katherine navigated the stairs barefooted and bounded to the door. Pushing aside a corner of the newspaper that covered the door's window, she found a vicar on the doorstep.

"Bloody hell," she murmured as she took the keys from the floor and unlocked the door. She popped her head out. "Good evening."

"Good evening. I was told by the mayor just now that our new sheep has joined the flock."

"The mayor? Where does the mayor hold office at this time of the day?"

"Well… down the pub, of course. Why?"

"Oh, well, administration really. I've tried him during normal working hours four times and he's never in." She said with a half-smile. "It never occurred to me to try the pub."

"Well, you can find most anybody down The Mule at this time of the day. I thought I'd take a moment to introduce myself. I'm Robert Welch, otherwise known as Vicar. Or just Robert," he smiled.

He was dressed in a black shirt collar, topped with a black blazer over a pair of jeans. He wasn't a handsome man. Everything about him seemed averagely British. With salt-and-pepper hair and a pair of spectacles dangling precariously from a gold chain around his neck, Katherine estimated he was in his fifties. He wore a wedding ring, Katherine noticed as he moved his hands when he spoke.

"Can we expect to see you in church on Sunday? Services are at eight and ten thirty. I can ensure a formal introduction."

Katherine raised an eyebrow filled with scepticism. "What, to *God*?"

Her reply took him off guard but to his credit he recovered quickly. "Err… it's quite likely He already knows who you are, my dear. What I meant was to the villagers and the odd tourist that attends our sermon."

The vicar's exterior was as stern as his sense of duty was alive beneath it, and while Katherine appreciated such a trait in a person, and probably even more in a vicar, she thought ferociously of a way to end the conversation.

When all else fails, tell them you're naked, she heard Norman say off in obscurity somewhere and resisted the urge to look around, keeping intense eye contact with the man before her. *When even that fails, be naked.*

"I'm naked!" she blurted.

Katherine held her breath, and possibly even prayed a little for the man to disappear. *Tsk tsk tsk. Lying to the village father*, she heard Norman say. *Are you sure you don't want someone to talk to?*

Bloody voice.

Shutting away the world was as needed as it was dreaded. She missed intelligent conversation greatly, and the idea of having to turn around to face an empty, unfamiliar house was as overwhelming as longing to be alone with her grief. The latter overpowered the need to hide behind a facade of normalcy, the only way to function in the face of heartache. Her world had stopped. To rejoin it seemed impossible without having first figured out who she was meant to be in this new life.

"I was just running a bath," she thought to add.

The vicar seemed puzzled and Katherine realized belatedly her hair was quite damp from the shower. She kept her eyes steady, but her cheeks burned.

"What's your name?" he asked.

"The mayor didn't say?" She couldn't help but grin, and he tried to reciprocate because he knew he was equally caught.

Her resistance to his profession melted a little. "I'm Katherine. Katherine Loch."

"Ah," he said, suddenly pensive and failing to hide it. He nodded into empty air and studied his thumbnail for no real reason other than to rummage through his own thoughts, it seemed, and he shifted his weight from one leg to the other.

"Mrs. Loch, I really do like to get to know the people in this parish regardless of their faith or philosophy. It would be an honour to have a chat down The Wicked Mule sometime soon."

"That's kind of you. I've a lot of work to do for the launch of my business, Vicar, but perhaps… sometime."

"Eventually, everybody ends up at The Mule, Mrs. Loch. It's got the best pint, the best publican, and the best music south of London, and it's quite unavoidable. In fact, you could get that administration done now if you wanted to… might I suggest that I take it to the mayor for you now? I'm sure he will drop it on the doormat later."

Katherine couldn't hide the bewildered look on her face and the vicar chuckled a little.

"It's just the way of things in Blackwell, Mrs. Loch."

She shrugged a shoulder and leaving the door at no more than a crack, reached for the packet of paperwork where she had left it on a trestle table.

"That'll save me some time. Thank you." She said as she extended a slender arm around the door to hand it to him.

He nodded. "You'll find an engaged community here. Allow me to bid you welcome to Blackwell-on-Sea."

"You're very kind, Vicar. See you 'round."

He made a brief curtsy and turned in the direction of the village square. Katherine shut the door with a groan and leaned her forehead against it, aware of the weight of her choice to be alone. The room at her back was large, empty, and in a state of decrepit aging.

She turned around to face it. Her eyes filled with tears that rolled across her eyelashes onto her cheeks like wayward raindrops spilling from the leaves of a weeping willow tree. She balled her fists against life.

Chapter II
The Pub

At just after five o'clock on such a cold December morning, it was difficult to imagine that the village would soon come to life with the hustle and bustle only a small town could. Not abruptly like an eruption, but gently like a flower that opens itself to the first rays of sunshine after a long night of hiding within. The south of England at this time of year could be as mild as it could be stormy, but this particular morning, frost covered the town as if a thin layer of dust had settled silently atop the medieval buildings overnight. The centuries-old cobblestones in its heart glistened like silver beneath the "gas" lanterns that oozed charm even though they were electric.

The sweeping beauty along the coast of East Sussex with its sand and shingle beaches, steep sandstone and chalk cliffs, desolate moors, and lush green farmland all set against the blue-grey of the English Channel had offered a treasure of activity since before the Romans left and the Normans invaded. In modern times, traces of violent bloodshed long gone, what remained was Blackwell-on-Sea.

What used to be the Elizabethan half-timber homes of middle-class gentry hundreds of years ago were now the shops that sustained the town through the slow economy of the 80s. Overworked city dwellers liked to get away even from holiday spots like Brighton, Hastings, and Eastbourne, and this was a place they liked to get away to for a dose of quaint history as well as top-of-the-line shopping. But at night, as day tourists retired back to the nearby larger seaside resorts, it became an oasis of supreme calmness. There was a lone posh hotel in the town square, and the odd bed-and-breakfast, but they too drew the sort of people in search of tranquillity.

The day ahead promised nothing but low-hanging clouds with temperatures not much above freezing. Paul's irregular footsteps sounded loudly up and down the narrow cobblestone street, echoing against the medieval facades and coming back around, giving him the feeling as if he were inside a tunnel. Breath escaped from his mouth in even white puffs. His gloveless hands were buried deep in the pockets of his black wool overcoat. He despised the cold. His stump ached with it. Nine years had passed since he'd lost his right leg in a crash; he should be used to it, but he wasn't, and he cursed the day it happened for perhaps the millionth time.

Despite his loss, Paul was an eternal optimist, and, aching aside, the day ahead also held the promise of a glowing fire in the hearth and the warming sound of conversation. Unlike the shops the tourists came to ogle, his establishment catered to the villagers' craving for a well-drawn pint and companionship, and the fire was one of the reasons people were drawn to the pub. With the need for warmth to chase away the chill and the ache in his body, and with thoughts of the previous night's conversations still lingering in his head, Paul arrived at the front door of The Wicked Mule and turned the key in the lock.

A wave of stale air, reeking of beer and cigarette smoke, greeted him. He left the door wide open and proceeded immediately to prop open the back door as well, allowing the icy December air to rush through the large room. Paul leaned over the bar to flip a light switch or two. Without removing his coat, he continued to the hearth where he checked the embers of yesterday's fire. They were out, thankfully, and he set about the first task of the day, which was to scoop the ashes into an old metal bin, sweep the hearth floor, and prepare it with kindling and hardwood soon to fill the pub with a blissful aroma.

The Wicked Mule had been the beating heart of the village for decade upon decade and century upon century. Old yellowed photographs hugged the walls between amber windows, and while they were no testament as to precisely how old the place was, they certainly showed how fond the townsfolk were of a pint. Over the years, of course, some things had changed. While the bar structure was original, the old wooden top had been replaced by a new one made of a lovely thick dark teak. The walls, whitewashed over and over by previous owners, had also received a makeover. Paul made the wise decision to wash them in a warm ochre—a colour that came to life from the rays shining through amber windows during the day and the glow of the fire at night.

If one didn't count the bar, the hearth was the centre point of The Wicked Mule. The same stonemason who had built the bar had also worked on the hearth. Both were made of local beach pebbles, large and small, in all manner of colours. Legend said that they'd been hauled to the pub's location by an old man who earned his trade by carting heavy loads for townsfolk with the aid of a cantankerous mule hitched to a timeworn wagon. According to the legend, it was unclear which was older: the man, the wagon, or the mule.

The stonemason soon discovered that the only way to ensure the mule's cooperation was to reward him with a pint of ale for each cart full of rocks that was hauled from the beach. In fact, after that first pint, any subsequent offer of water is said to have been steadfastly refused by the mule. Upon completion of the job, whenever the beast was left unattended, he would wander his way back to the pub. Many a patron would amuse themselves by buying the mule a pint and roared when the old man charged through the door only to find his mule quite smashed again. No one knows the original name of the pub because since that time—1546AD according to the only flat stone in the fireplace—everybody referred to it as "The Wicked Mule."

With the doors still open, Paul filled two old metal buckets with hot soapy water in the kitchen. The chairs were already on top of the tables in the main room, something he forced himself do before he limped home in the evenings. It was his least favourite part of being a pub owner. Many people wondered why he came to the pub at five in the morning to scrub the floors, rather than hiring someone else to do it. Who really enjoys scrubbing floors? Paul certainly didn't. He was here because the pub was his life and he liked having it to himself a while. He needed these five or six hours of solitude to recharge his batteries and transform himself into the convivial publican that people had come to expect because the truth of the matter was that Paul liked to socialize as much as he liked solitude, and he loved his pub as much as he liked to get away from it.

Once the buckets were filled, he hauled one of them up the circular stairs to the loft area, which housed the snooker table and darts corner, along with tall tables and chairs along the walls. A sturdy railing allowed patrons to look down to the bar area and entryway. It was the most significant change he'd made to the place. It had taken letters to the historical society, architects, engineers, permits, and lots of money. These were the rooms where he and his parents had once lived, but he had chosen not to make this his home. Snooker was a popular sport, as was darts, and placing the table here was the only way to maintain the integrity of the fireplace area while adding a lot more square footage to the pub, which in turn brought in extra income on tournament nights.

Downstairs, rather than filling the place with just the standard tables and chairs—of which there were but a dozen—the area around the hearth was furnished with second-hand overstuffed sofas from the 50s and cushioned chairs, all of which had been restored and reupholstered by Ned Denison who owned the antique shop down High Street near the sea. It made for a lovely place where Paul could enjoy his coffee and paper in the mornings, but more importantly it was a cosy spot for people to have a chat and a laugh.

The joy he'd found came at an immeasurable cost He'd inherited the pub from his parents who'd died in the same car crash that took his leg, along with a pain-free existence. The settlement from the accident, and the inheritance, had left Paul quite well off. In moments of feeling sorry for himself, he'd considered selling the place. He was only twenty at the time of the crash. It was the Denisons, Ned and his wife, and their son Steve, who had nursed him through. Ned, who'd been a classmate of Paul's father, had pointed out to Paul that he could either piss away his parents' life savings or build upon what they'd left behind. He could feel sorry for himself or he could make them proud. Whether or not they had lived to see retirement, the pub would have been Paul's eventually anyway, and there was no sense feeling guilty about it or feeling guilty that he was alive and they weren't.

And so, at the tender age of twenty, with Ned's help, he'd become the owner of a business that he'd grown to love and that was lucrative enough for him to stash away a tidy sum for a nice retirement someday, somewhere warm, where the aching in his leg wouldn't bother him as much. He'd invested quite a bit to accommodate his own taste and comfort. He'd envisioned his ideal pub and created a haven that would draw its patrons back time and again. To keep the younger crowd hanging around, he'd also invested in a sound system, and the music that was played every night was carefully selected.

The plan had worked, and if The Wicked Mule had been successful before he took it over, it was a goldmine now. Paul thought his mother and father would likely be pleased with what

The Mule had become. He was proud of it and aware that he couldn't have made it happen without the support of the Denison family, which had been unwavering and complete. They were his family of the heart. He'd never asked Steve how much sacrifice it was for him to come home from University every weekend when he should have stayed to study. They had been best friends since they were toddlers. He owed them his undying loyalty.

By the time the floor was dry, the toilets scrubbed, and the kitchen spotless, Paul had a pot of coffee brewing for himself and a few extra logs on the banked fire. All that remained was to find some breakfast and a good read. Satisfied, he shrugged back into his thick overcoat and braced himself again for the cold.

The bakery, conveniently located on the opposite corner from the pub, was not yet open. The light was on but the blinds were shut. Paul consulted his watch and noticed it was several minutes before seven. He was normally the first customer anyway but hunger made him quickly cross the street and knock. The baker's wife unlocked the door and stepped aside to let him in.

"You're out early, Paul!"

"Morning, Thelma. I was just thinking that. It must have been the cold that made me speed through the chores faster."

"I noticed you had the door wide open," she said as she quickly moved to retrieve a tray of pastries from the back and drop it in the display counter.

Paul wiped his feet before he entered the store. He knew that Thelma had just finished scrubbing her floor as well, and being the first customer of the day, he didn't want to be the one to muck it up. The heavenly buttery aroma from the ovens drifted around Paul in waves of seductive temptation.

"What'll it be this morning?" Thelma asked in her usual brusque sort of way.

She wasn't a morning person, Paul thought, and yet she'd just married a man with a trade that would get her up well before the crack of dawn each and every day of her life. Love was something that fascinated him, but he preferred to be a spectator.

"Are the croissants out?" he asked and braced himself as she leaned back in the baker's direction. Paul could see him move about through the open door.

"Sean, are the croissants out?" she yelled to make herself heard over the sound of an industrial-sized dough-mixing machine.

"Not for about five minutes," her husband yelled back. "Is that Paul?"

"Who else would it be then?" Thelma asked but not loud enough for Sean to hear.

Paul smiled his lopsided smile. Sean was a good-humoured man in his mid-thirties who very often came out into the shop to have a chat with Paul. This morning, instead of the usual hearty handshake, his hands remained clasped behind his back.

"Hello, neighbour," he said with the huge grin that defined his spirit.

"Sean. Been up a while?"

"You know how it is, Paul. Unlike my lovely bride here, I live for the night."

The comment earned Sean a scowl from Thelma as she tried to move past him to retrieve more trays. He grabbed her bottom with hands covered in flour, leaving two distinct white handprints on her black trousers. He winked at Paul and quickly wiped his hands on a damp towel he kept tucked into his apron. Paul muffled a laugh.

"The scones are ready, but if you'd rather have croissants, I can run them across the street in a few minutes," Sean offered helpfully.

"You will not!" Thelma said, as she now filled the cash register with coins. "It's too early for beer."

"I've been working all bloody night!" Sean countered.

"I don't care. We can send Lettie over with them, Paul," she added, not wanting to seem unfriendly.

As if on cue, the girl who helped them in the shop every day walked through the door, and good mornings were uttered all around. She was young, in her final year at Blackwell Secondary School, and though Paul didn't know Lettie well, he knew her old man well enough to know the poor girl didn't have much of a father. She dumped a heavy rucksack behind the bakery door and prepared to work until the start of school.

"Scones would be lovely. I'll have two, please, and an éclair." Paul put some coins on the counter top. "Have you heard anything about Tinker's old place?"

"Someone said it'll be a clothing shop. Just what we need more of around here," Sean replied.

"Do shut up! Who tells you these things in the middle of the night anyway?"

Lettie prepared a small pastry bag with Paul's order and set it on the counter, making eye contact. She took the money and quickly made change.

"If you know so much more, why don't you tell us then?"

Oblivious to the handprints on her bum, Thelma made to open the shutters and turned to Paul as she did it. "It's going to be a boutique."

Sean threw his hands up in mock defeat. "Really!"

Paul laughed. "Well that makes all the difference!"

"No, there is a difference! I know you don't get out much after you open but construction contractors have been working in there for two or three months now. The new owner is throwing big money in to get it all done up."

"What's the difference between a clothing shop and a boutique, then?"

Lettie rolled her eyes. "It's just more posh, that's all."

"That's right, better quality and more expensive," Thelma agreed.

"I didn't think we lacked those sorts of places." Paul shrugged. "I will see you later today for my baguettes," he said and left waving, the bag with the warm scones tucked against his body.

He purchased *The Times* and a newly released sci-fi book he'd ordered some weeks before, but eager for his breakfast, he kept the chat with George the newspaper handler short. Leaving the shop, he threw a glance to his right where the old Blackwell Castle stood. In the mornings he never paid much attention to it even though he lived in its shadow in one of the cottages by the cliff. But as always when he took the time for it, the sight of the structure, dark and gloomy as it was, filled him with a sense of familiarity and pride. He and Steve had spent many a childhood hour there playing hero knights who saved the town from doom.

Paul made his way back to the pub. Most people up and down the street had begun their day. Even above the vacant store front, soon to be a purported boutique, a light shone brightly in the upstairs windows. He noted floor-to-ceiling bookshelves packed with books on the far wall, but that was all he could see.

Paul pondered the fact that there hadn't been a lot of news about the newcomer since she moved in and was quite curious about just what sort of person had moved into their midst.

Chapter III
Rafael

As a new owner in the shopping district, Katherine had decided that attending the quarterly merchants' meetings would be a necessary evil. Having the first under her belt, there was but one conclusion to be made: what an incredible waste of time. It was probably not clever to have been the first to leave. Ideally, she needed fellow merchants on her side to be successful. But after two hours of listening to people bicker about parking permits and one-way streets, she couldn't get back to her drafting table fast enough.

As the town hall's heavy door fell shut behind her, the icy blast of wind that met her was in brutal contrast to the heat in the grand hall. Katherine shivered. She tied the sash on her lamb's wool coat tighter around her body and found a pair of thin leather gloves in her pocket. Pulling them on, she jumped resolutely down the four steps to the sidewalk for a brisk walk home, where a mountain of work awaited.

The boutique's grand opening was just eight weeks away. The spring-and-summer collection counted thirty different ready-to-wear pieces so far, available in the three most common sizes. There would be a sample for most other sizes. Having assessed the entire collection earlier that day, she decided there was room to add a few complementing pieces. Ideas played at the edge of her brain. Sleep was elusive most nights but in the circle of light from a desk lamp, the world was reduced to a manageable size and time fell away. Katherine savoured being at the drafting table, with watercolours and concepts flowing freely.

It would be a challenge to get it all finished, but she didn't care. The work was so much more gratifying than making horrid flowered bed sheets or nylon housecoats! Of course, she'd been making clothes for herself and others for years but to be able to do so in a setting all her own was as novel as it was familiar.

The church bells struck ten o'clock. With an energy that belied the late hour, Katherine wound her way through the trees along the cobbled square. Numerous benches sat beneath them, and an illuminated fountain with the puzzling sculpture of a mule sitting atop a pile of beach rocks graced High Street just where it became traffic-free. The front of the stone Norman church, the town hall and the hotel were lit strategically, as were the goods in shop windows, all with the intention to entice evening strollers. Furthering the incredible quaintness of the square and the heart of Blackwell was the smell of wood-burning fires carried on the wind.

Her thoughts drifted back to the meeting. The chance to introduce herself to the other shopkeepers had been the best part. In particular, it had been interesting to meet the people she wanted to do business with. After the deal she hammered out with Ned Denison, he was great in making introductions. He was still sceptical that Katherine could sell furniture in a dress shop but wholeheartedly recommended that other shopkeepers strike a deal with her too. She had appointments with the owners of a shoe shop, the high-end leather goods store, and a local artist who created the most beautiful silver jewellery. They'd invited her down the pub for an after-hours drink. When she'd asked which pub, they had laughed out loud and collectively said, "There's more than one?"

Katherine nodded in response to a strolling elderly couple's "Good evening," and approached the pub in question, The Wicked Mule, where she turned right. A group of patrons was ejected from its corner doorway, on their heels a Led Zeppelin Blues song. She closed her eyes against the familiarity of every lick and chord, and skirted by the group as they bade each other good night. Her only focus was to unlock the door to the as-yet-unfinished shop and take the stairs two at a time to a snug sitting room warmed by a smouldering fire.

Making her way deeper into High Street, the sound of her boots was all Katherine was aware of, overpowering even the voices that lingered by the pub. The castle loomed over the village, secure on its cliff at the end of High Street. Against a crisp night, scattered with bright stars and a last quarter moon, only its dark silhouette was visible. Even after spending three months in its shadows, the emotion it invoked was still a toss between admiration and trepidation. It was an impressive sight, and she had grown to accept it as part of a daily routine.

A distressed wail penetrated her musings. The sound was so full of agony that she was immediately alert and slowed her pace in response. Any remaining voices now faded in the direction of the church, and it grew quiet. She noted with a sideways glance that the bloke on the opposite side of the street who'd separated himself from the group outside the pub, also slowed. She held her breath as if the sound might otherwise deafen the all-encompassing stillness.

But a lack of further distress calls and driven by cold feet, she continued to walk, albeit with less vigour than before. Almost immediately a low cry pierced through the night, stopping her dead in her tracks. It was only the fear that it might be a baby that kept her where she was, alone with a stranger on a deserted street. Closing her eyes to concentrate on her surroundings, she heard the surf but otherwise nothing, not even the wind so much because the street was protected from it by the bulk of the castle.

"Walk a few steps."

Opening her eyes, she turned to the man and realized he had probably addressed her.

"What?"

"Make that sound with your boots," he said, motioning Katherine forward.

He approached with hands shoved deeply into his pockets. Wearing trainers, he made no sound at all. Katherine took five deliberate steps in the direction of the boutique.

"Whaaaaaaawww."

"Someone's trying to get your attention," he concluded. "Whatever it is, it's reacting to the sound of your boots. It's crying for help."

Katherine walked forward. There was a private alley with a spiked cast-iron gate that she knew led to a small pleasant courtyard behind the linen shop. The cry was more alarming this time. Katherine's gloved hand flew to her mouth in response.

"That's not a baby, is it?" The man's voice was smooth as honey but held a tone of urgency.

Without looking at him, Katherine could feel his eyes as he searched for an opinion.

"The thought crossed my mind," she whispered, "but who would leave a baby on the street?"

"It wouldn't be the first time around here." The reply held a trace of bitterness, and Katherine regarded him with curiosity.

"It came from the alley," she said and resolutely stepped towards the gate.

The streets throughout the shopping district were lit by what appeared at first glance to be real cast-iron lampposts with old-fashioned gas lamps. Being Victorian in style, they added a strange touch of another century to the medieval and Elizabethan mix, and the softness cast an almost ethereal aura around the man, but they did nothing to illuminate the alley.

"Have you got a lighter?" he asked.

"I don't smoke," she said.

"Neither do I. I may have matches."

He searched his pockets and came up short. Katherine tried the gate. It wasn't locked, and it swung open with an eerie sound, stirring a chuckle from her mysterious companion despite their sense of urgency.

"Deep into that darkness peering, long I stood there wondering, fearing, doubting, dreaming dreams no mortals ever dared to dream before…," he quoted with surprising lyricism.

Katherine raised a sceptical eyebrow.

"I can appreciate *The Raven* at a time like this but could we get on with it?" she asked sweetly.

His face revealed surprise but he went through the gate. She followed. They walked forward gingerly as if they were afraid to step on something that was alive. Whatever had cried out had calmed until they heard a small whimpering about halfway down the alley where it seemed to be darkest. They crept along the wall. Katherine had the disturbing feeling that just ahead they would be swallowed by a large gaping hole.

The man stopped. Katherine ran into him.

"Oh… sorry," she whispered, quickly taking a step back. "I can't see a hand before my eyes."

"We need light. It's probably best if one of us takes care of that while the other ventures deeper into this trap. Paul will have a torch."

"Who's Paul?"

"Are you not familiar with The Mule?"

She debated a moment, ignoring the question, and determined the pub was closer than her place. "I'll be right back."

Moments later Katherine threw the door to the revered Wicked Mule open for the first time since having arrived in Blackwell. It took only a twinkling glimpse of the place to understand the complete picture. The glowing hearth at the far end of the pub immediately drew her in; a decade-old Queen song dominated the speakers, and with dim lighting and the low hum of small talk among people who knew each other, there was an energy of warm familiarity.

The attendant, a handsome bloke of around thirty with a blond widow's peak cut short, threw his gaze in Katherine's direction. In an instant everything, even the larger-than-life voice of Freddie Mercury, faded into the walls. Katherine felt a sudden rush to the head and there was no beginning, no end, and no depth to The Wicked Mule. Nailed to the floor with the doorknob still in her hand, she did a mental headshake and attributed the collapse of time and space to having had little to eat.

"Close the bloody door!" somebody yelled with a backwards glance.

Katherine, remembering her mission, complied. She approached the bar.

"Hi."

"Never is my day complete until a beautiful woman appears on the doorstep. I've a fresh pot of leek soup on the cooker, crusty loaves of bread. You look like you could use it."

His tone was pleasant, the smile that played on his lips genuine and reflecting in eyes that were icy blue and held an unmistakable twinkle of mischief.

"As lovely as that sounds, I don't actually need anything but a torch. Or matches. My name is Katherine. I live down the street."

"Ah, you must be the elusive new addition to Blackwell. It's about time you showed yourself."

"Are you Paul?"

"Indeed, I am." He threw the towel he'd been drying a glass with across his shoulder.

"Well then, Paul. Please hand me a book of matches."

"Just like that? Without buying a drink?"

"Yes. Just like that, no questions asked and 'please' being the only form of payment."

Keeping his eyes on her, Paul turned to reach into a gigantic glass bowl filled a quarter of the way with a hodgepodge of matchbooks.

"You must be in dire need for matches," he said as he threw one in her direction.

She caught it gracefully as a blast of cold air hit her in the back, "Indubitably. I really must run!"

"Katherine! Are you having a drink with us?"

Ned Denison put an arm around her shoulder as if they were long lost friends. At least five more council members followed him through the door and echoed the question.

"Sorry, everybody. Another time."

Katherine left in a hurry, and studying the matchbook in the little light there was, she noted it had come from Stockholm, Sweden, which caused her to wonder if the bowl was actually a matches collection to which any vacationing villagers contributed. The man who waited for her in the alley struck a match just as soon as she handed them over and held it to shed a bit of light on the source of the distress call: a tiny body that squirmed against the grate in which it was caught. The match extinguished.

"It's a kitten!" Katherine exclaimed with both relief that they hadn't actually found an abandoned baby and horror for the little creature's predicament.

"Would you mind handling the matches so I can try to get it out?" he asked quietly as if he didn't want to scare the kitten.

"Of course." She removed her gloves and took them.

She fell to her knees and struck the first match, holding it close. The kitten continued to whimper and squirm but was losing steam now.

"Shh. It's all right little one," he said, pulling the grate this way and that.

So intent was Katherine on the rescue that she forgot about the burning match. She dropped it with a gasp as it singed her fingers.

"Knowing Paul, those are not magic matches," he said, and she could hear the smile in his voice.

"Thanks," Katherine replied with a note of sarcasm as she lit two more. "He certainly has a large enough collection of them."

"He gets them from a friend who travels," he said, using force to bend the metal grate. "This poor little thing is freezing and starving," he added.

"Is it otherwise hurt?" she asked.

"Let's get back to the street for a closer look."

Katherine preceded the both of them and put the gate on the latch. They made for the nearest lamppost where he held the kitten towards the light. It was beautiful, all grey, and had such a sweet little face.

"I think it's a Russian Blue," he started, turning the cat this way and that with utmost gentleness. "His ear's been nicked but the blood is coagulating around the edges. Probably needs peroxide. He's malnourished and cold, so food and lots of cuddles. Look at him, he's shivering terribly. He could probably use a swaddle in your scarf."

Katherine's heart melted. It was so dark and cold, and the world must seem so big to such a little thing. If there was one thing she could relate to, it was feeling lost and alone. She reached out a gloved finger to touch him gently on the head.

"You'll take him home, won't you?" he asked, looking at Katherine as he held the kitten out to her.

She unwound the angora scarf from her neck and studied the stranger's face. An encouraging smile revealed even teeth, in a beautifully symmetrical face with an aquiline nose, square jaw, and thick eyebrows. She found herself struck by a pair of eyes that were as dark as the surrounding night, but with a gleam that revealed the depths of a kind, intelligent man. She took the kitten from him and their fingers touched, but two pairs of gloves prevented any real contact. She found it… regrettable and frowned. *What an odd thought to have.*

"What about you?" she asked.

The tiny grey ball of fur curled itself in the scarf, and Katherine held the bundle close to her chest. Realizing it must have sounded like a flirt, she looked down, flustered. He chuckled, amused.

"I wouldn't mind the company, I admit," he said, unable to resist playing on the double entendre, "but I haven't been home much lately. My girlfriend wouldn't like a cat, either. She's not the type."

"How is it there are people who don't like them?" Katherine said. "They are so regal and self-sufficient."

He removed a glove to rub the kitten on its tiny head. He wore a leather and sheepskin jacket with the collar drawn against the wind. A black beanie hat hid his hair. He hadn't shaved in a few days. His eyebrows were perfectly formed. She guessed he had brown or black hair by the looks of them. Not that it mattered. His hands reminded Katherine of Norman's. Perhaps because his fingernails were manicured.

"Indeed." He nodded.

"He is quite beautiful, isn't he? Oh, are we sure it's a boy?" She lifted the creature's backside gently towards the light, thereby displaying the evidence.

"Quite a lovely set of gonads, nurse!" The man grinned naughtily.

The kitten snuggled up to Katherine again immediately, shivering still. She bundled him in the warm scarf and he rubbed his tiny face on her chin. Tickling whiskers made her giggle and wrinkle her nose. His eyes seemingly cast her a hopeful gaze. The stranger's gentle laughter sounded warm in the cold of the night.

"Looks like he knows what he wants. I can't say I blame him."

Whatever will I do with a kitten? She thought of the expensive bolts of material and the battle that would ensue teaching him to keep off, but was immediately reminded that it was her boots the cat had responded to and perhaps it was a sign they were meant to be together.

"Well then, tiny fellow, would you like to come home with me?" The cat curled up against her in response and meowed softly. "What if someone is looking for him?" she thought belatedly.

"He doesn't look old enough to be away from his mother. Whoever didn't pay attention doesn't deserve him. Besides,"—he grinned— "look at him. You couldn't possibly let him go now, could you? It took all of two minutes for you to become completely smitten!"

The twinkling in his eyes seemed so genuine that Katherine chuckled, knowing she had been caught.

"Right," she said. "You caught me. Thanks for saving his life and for letting me have him."

"Take good care of each other." Smiling, the stranger walked a few steps back, turned, and picked up his pace again.

Puzzled by the bizarre circumstances of their meeting, Katherine clutched her new companion closely and watched the gentleman walk away. The kitten squirmed again, and she kissed its small nose.

"It's all right now, little fellow," she talked to it reassuringly. "We're together."

"Hey!"

She looked up at the sound of the honeyed voice that belonged to the stranger who, weirdly, hadn't seemed a stranger at all. She regretted not having touched his skin while harbouring the idea. He stood in the middle of the street, underneath one of the lights, legs apart, hands deep in his sheepskin jacket, breath escaping his mouth rhythmically like the flow of a song.

"Yes?"

"What's his name?" he asked loudly.

"Rafael," she said, too softly, as she glanced down at the little furry face that looked at her curiously and reached a tentative paw to her chin. The kitten's eyelids drooped and he purred loudly as he nestled deeper into his own contentment. She smiled, enchanted.

"What?"

"Rafael!" Katherine shouted back.

A light came on in the third-floor window of the porcelain shop. The stranger noticed but laughed anyway and turned again.

"Rafael," Katherine heard him say as he walked away. "You will sleep well tonight, Rafael." The voice melted into the shadows of the castle.

She couldn't have imagined leaving her home solo and returning mere hours later with a companion that would without doubt become a beautiful cat. Katherine could hardly believe it. Without removing her coat, they continued straight through to the kitchen where she deposited him on the floor. He meowed in protest at being left there as she opened the refrigerator.

"What would you like to eat, little one? There isn't much in the house, and you should not expect me to cook elaborate meals. How about milk, would you like that?" She looked at him and he edged nearer to her, craning his little neck as he sought eye contact.

"Yes? I'm quite sure this isn't good for you, but you've had a rough night of it. I suppose you've earned a bit of a treat."

She grabbed a small plate and poured some milk into it. Rafael lapped it up without prejudice. His eyes pleaded for more when he was done, but Katherine didn't comply. She had found a can of tuna, drained off the water, and forked a small amount onto the little plate. He sniffed the fish appreciatively and began to eat it. The rest of the tin was returned to the refrigerator along with the bottle of milk.

Removing her jacket, Katherine continued to the stove to drop more wood into it and switched on a couple of small table lamps in the sitting area on her way back to the kitchen. Rafael finished his meal as she put the kettle on. He meowed again.

"You're very small, aren't you? There are some things we should talk about. You should know now, not to get into my work. You might be cute and tiny, but I will swat your bottom if you mess up my fabrics! Come to think of it, I should close the door now." She followed suit. "I will concede that if I do leave it open, and you have an adventure in there, it will be my responsibility."

She left Rafael long enough to shut the door to the sewing room, but scooped him up as she returned to assemble her cuppa.

"Have you got that?" she continued as if she'd never left the kitchen. "If you don't mess with my work, we'll get along just fine. I'll get a litter box and we'll get a cat entrance in the door to the rooftop patio. You can choose to be inside or outside because you will be my friend and I want you to be happy. But you mustn't get your head stuck in a grate again. And you know, since you're here anyway, you can put your scent in the storage room downstairs. It's important to keep mice at bay. That can be your job."

Cup of Earl Grey in one hand, and Rafael in the other, Katherine made for the sofa. He regarded her with great interest, sniffing her face and her breath as she continued to address him.

"This isn't permission to bring presents in the form of dead animals to our doorstep, mind you." She sat down carefully and let go of him. "Lots of rules around here, I know. You'll get used to it, and so will I."

It was past eleven now, and the fire in the stove crackled as it caught dry wood. She had left the little door open and the light of the flames gracefully danced into the sitting room. Work would have to wait for the moment. As Katherine warmed her hands on the fragrant cup of tea, she looked into the flames without seeing them. The kitten had already curled into her lap, and she had the sense that he belonged there. It was a while before he stopped shivering, but he purred contentedly nonetheless, she hoped in the knowledge that he had come home.

The tea was hot and delicious and she finished the mug just as the doorbell rang. Puzzled by the late hour at which one would disturb someone, Katherine carefully set Rafael aside and quietly ran downstairs without turning on the stairway lights. There wasn't a soul by the door, but looking down to the doorstep, she noticed a paper sack. She opened the door. A piece of a baguette and something warm to the touch in a box with an ice cream label.

Soup. From Paul at The Wicked Mule.

Chapter IV

First Encounter

With a sigh of relief and a quick glimpse at the castle, Ned Denison locked the door to the antiques shop. He wondered for perhaps the fifth time that day why on earth he didn't just shut the place down. The shop was well established and ran like a train during the tourist season and the weeks leading up to Christmas. Between the holidays and the onset of spring, however, there was only the odd local in need of a fine piece of furniture or an extravagant gift of some sort, and they all knew where or how to find him. Having reached the pivotal age of fifty-five, frankly he could afford to retire and thought it time to consider when he might do that.

Beth, his missus of thirty years, was of the opinion that his grumblings—premature, she called them—had everything to do with an empty nest. With their youngest son in New Guinea visiting his older sister for the holidays, and their oldest son not only on his own but away from Blackwell a lot of the time, their house was filled with the fading echoes of children's voices.

It was true that life seemed a bit off centre lately. Beth was right, of course. She worked late several evenings during the week, and the telly was no remedy against having too much time to think. Not unless there was football on. Thankfully there was the one constant that could be counted upon: The Wicked Mule! With one last ensuring tug at the locked door, he resolutely began to walk in its direction.

Truthfully, with a successful business, a beautiful wife, and three good kids—ups and downs aside—he couldn't possibly be more complete than he was in this moment. Except for having a grandchild. He and Beth wanted a dozen of them, but Leah wasn't likely to start on a baby as long as she and her husband lived in Africa. David was only thirteen, and Steve.... Ned snorted without being aware of it. That would be the day!

As much as Ned loved his oldest son, what he did for a living these days was probably the only bone of contention in life right now. What sort of a father would Steve be given that he'd quit a good teaching job in pursuit of a dream to play in a band. A band! Utter waste of money spent on University for that boy, in Ned's opinion. What good did a degree in literature do him playing that freakish noise they called music nowadays?

Steve's mother had not entirely disagreed with Ned but, in true lioness-Beth fashion, continued to support her son in his musical endeavours anyway. That was the interesting bit of having married an independent woman. She was all for a terrific education and demanded it of her children. Steve had attended Oxford where he'd read music and literature. Leah had chosen hygiene and tropical medicine at the University of London. Both had graduated with high honours. But when it came down to it, Beth never wanted anything more than for them to be happy, no matter what their career choices.

Leah and her doctor husband both worked for Doctors Without Borders. Ned and Beth were proud that their daughter cared so much about the less fortunate though thankful that they were not in a country like Ethiopia. The situation there was so dire, he'd read in the paper, that something to do with music would be staged in July, to raise money. They seemed marginally better off in Guinea, but it was good of them to have invited David. Poverty was something their youngest needed to see in order to put his own privileged childhood in perspective. Being the latecomer had caused him to be more spoiled than the other two.

David had been what one would call "a surprise." After Leah's arrival just over twenty-three years ago, the career-driven Elizabeth had said "no more," and for several years they'd maintained vigilance. Until, in the heat of the moment, on holiday in bloody Marbella, Beth had remembered the diaphragm… in the bathroom back home. There was something freeing about making love without that barrier between them, and they'd done just that for as many hours as the children were mesmerized by the television, a novelty to them then. Beth had walked around dazed for weeks after a positive pregnancy test and even contemplated abortion. She'd asked Ned to think about it, but the request had fallen on deaf ears. A career might be a reason not to have them, but once the event had occurred, it wasn't a good enough reason to get rid of it, even for someone as progressive and modern as his wife. Fortunately within a couple of days, she had come to her senses but it had stolen away some of the happiness he felt about the baby and this caused another explosive moment in their marriage.

It was a testament to Beth's strength that they had made it to that point in their marriage at all. They'd hit quite a rough patch during her residency with long stints away from home. They'd had little money then. Steve, being only three at the time, had missed his Mum. As husband and wife they had failed to recognize each other's need for emotion and affection even when they were physically at a distance. For a brief period, they'd drifted apart and into the arms of others. They had made grave mistakes. They might not have made it but for a mutual belief that their love was worth saving. Ultimately, slowly, life returned to normal between them, with Leah as a result of their reconciliation.

Ned suddenly longed to have all the family around the dinner table for a delicious meal and a house filled with easy banter and laughter. But how would he ever accomplish it? Only David would be home after New Year's. The boy was the light of their lives not just for Mum and Dad but also for his siblings, who'd adored David from the moment they'd witnessed him popping out of their mother's womb. The thirteen years had not diminished their deep affection.

Walking briskly along the many shop windows, Ned waved to fellow merchants who were either closing up for the evening or soon would be. Those windows that were already dark reflected a stereotypical British man in his fifties, dressed casually but well, tweed cap covering a salt-and-pepper, slightly balding head of hair and a big conk of a nose that was sometimes the cause of much hilarity. He and Beth both had brown eyes, making that inheritance indistinguishable, but fortunately the children had inherited their mother's nose.

He marched by the always stylish Blackwell Tearoom. It was less than a quarter full, and he was happy he wasn't at one of those posh tables with pristinely starched white tablecloths, though admittedly the scone piled high with clotted cream, brought to a patron just as he passed by, made his stomach growl. He wondered what kind of soup Paul had ready for the after-work crowd. Come to think of it, what would it matter? A bowl of it and a pint or two shared in conversation with Paul, whom he thought of as a son, might be just the thing to chase away any deranged ideas about retirement.

Approaching the newest shop on High Street, Ned found its owner in the middle of the traffic-free cobbled road, staring at the facade. He followed her gaze and was surprised to see the shop's name newly installed. Beautiful, large black letters that looked like they were made of wood and antiqued with brushed gold were lit by fixtures with long, elegantly curved necks ending in curled petals. The fixtures cast such a warm glow it looked as if the name itself emanated light.

"Mon Chocolat," he read. He frowned, quite clearly remembering Katherine having said her place would be a ladies' boutique. Not quite making the connection, he joined the lovely young woman who, despite shivering with cold in her paint-covered shirt sleeves, smiled proudly.

"Katherine! Are you having a special moment?" he asked, smiling.

"Mister Denison!" she exclaimed. "I confess that I am. I feel as if I should pinch myself."

Behind the shop's windows, which had been covered with white paper for months, a glaringly bright light was on. In comparison with the rest of the shops, it looked like a spaceship ready for take-off. Adding to the illusion, the door stood slightly ajar, but not wide enough to be able to see anything. Everybody was curious as to what she had been up to in there but respected the secretiveness and waited patiently to be invited to the grand opening. At last though, a revelation!

"Explain the name to me, Katherine," he said. "I'm afraid I don't understand."

She laughed and it was a pleasant sound because he'd got the impression she was a bit sad and always hoped he was wrong in this assessment.

"Because you're a man, I'm sure," she teased. "I'll not hold that against you."

"Thank you, I think," he said dryly, hoping she'd laugh again, and she did have a good chuckle.

"Aside from the obvious, there are two things in life that please most women, Mr. Denison: fashion and chocolate. The name is a metaphor."

He nodded, thinking about it. George, who owned the newspaper shop, joined them in the street and made a similar comment about the odd name. His wife, Margaret, regarded him as if he were the greatest simpleton. Like Ned and Beth, they had been married for a long time and watching their exchange was amusing, like gazing into a mirror. When Katherine explained it to George, the latter continued to frown, and it earned him an unkind punch in the arm from Margaret.

"Think about it, George," she said and turned to Katherine in the same breath. "It's clever, my dear. Fortunately you're not catering to men, are you?"

"I might have had to go with 'Me Pint' or something obvious like that."

"Even then I'd have my doubts, dear. You better get inside as cold as you are! You're shivering and skin over bones. Come along, George! We're late for supper."

George gave Ned an incomprehensible shrug of the shoulders. With one last look at the lettering and a wink for Katherine, he dutifully followed his wife.

"Would you like to have a look inside?" Katherine motioned as if she'd been able to read Ned's earlier thoughts.

"I'd love to see what you've done but I was on my way for a pint and I think you should join me. Having the name on your shop deserves to be celebrated like a christening, and, besides, you still owe me one for the bizarre deal you made me strike with you."

"I am in the middle of painting," she tried.

"Come on! You've been working for months and no one ever sees you 'round The Mule."

Katherine, in no way wanting to leave her cocoon, and guilty of remaining distant from the neighbours, grimaced inwardly. There wasn't much choice but to consent. A look in the mirror would have alarmed her of a brown streak of paint on her cheek, but she ran inside only long enough to grab some cash and keys. She locked the door and they walked to The Mule, talking amicably. Ned ordered a pint practically from the doorway and promptly removed his jacket. Katherine was struck again by the cosiness of the pub, just as she had been on her first visit.

"This is Katherine." Ned pointed to her in the most nonchalant of introductions. "She's got 'My Chocolat' a few doors down. First round is on her."

Ned pronounced it "me chocolate," causing Katherine to wince. She dislodged herself from the door and slowly covered the distance that separated her from the handsome publican behind the bar. He turned a pair of curious blue eyes on her, and she was drawn into them so much that it rendered her speechless. It took the last notes of a Cream song through the second verse of a Deep Purple one before he said anything.

"Nice to finally have you, Katherine," he spoke. "Tell me, why do you hide from the world?"

She wasn't taken aback by the question. She suspected nothing that happened in this village escaped him and that it wasn't just the pub for the sake of itself drawing people, but because it felt like a womb the second you stepped over the threshold and Paul himself was doubtlessly a part of the balanced equation.

"I've been in an introverted mood and, not to mention, working non-stop," she replied honestly. "I'm sure you've heard it mentioned."

"The signs are clear everywhere we look." He winked at Ned, who chuckled, shaking his head. "You're by the window with your head down when I walk home at night and again in the morning on my way in. Do you sleep at all?" Paul grabbed a glass and threw it around, catching it ready to be filled from the tap. "Or just by the window?"

"Sometimes." Katherine's eyes were on what he was doing if his weren't. As he tapped the pint, he never took his eyes off her face and, to boot, seemed to be able to tell exactly when it was time to move the glass to top off an appropriate layer of frothy head.

"Nice advertisement in The Argus this morning," he said as he set Ned's drink down on the bar. "Now, gorgeous, reveal to me what is your drink of choice."

"The same, please" she said, managing a friendly smile that she hoped would erase any lingering sense of awkwardness between them. "And maybe some soup if you've got any."

"There's always soup. If one pot grows empty, another is put on the stove. It's as simple as that."

He handed both drinks to her on a round tray and, with a naughty wink, moved to serve another customer. Ned had made himself comfortable near the fire. Katherine hadn't realized how tired she was until her bum met with the sofa. She sighed and removed her jacket, eying her glass, taste buds prickling expectantly. She hadn't had a beer in ages; for Ned it hadn't been quite that long, probably not twenty-four hours, but after clinking glasses they savoured the amber liquid with equal and tasty abandon.

Katherine took the interlude to look around. She could picture the locals spending many a pleasant evening here and wouldn't mind becoming one of them. Norman would have loved it here, she thought and, just like that, her eyes brimmed with tears. She wasn't one to go "pubbing" on her own. She looked away from Ned, hoping he hadn't noticed.

"That is bloody tasty after a boring day!" Ned said.

"Well I can't say I've been bored, but I'll agree to the ale's effectiveness on the soul. Oh, here comes food, I think, and I am hungry!" Katherine smiled bravely.

Paul carried a large tray with two steaming mugs of soup and two more ales. His eyes sparkled in curiosity about the world and probably varied in colour from blue to grey depending on his mood. He was dressed in jeans and a light-blue button-down shirt, and was of average build, not short and not tall. Katherine took note of the limp as he walked.

"Pea soup," Paul said as he set the tray on the coffee table. There was a basket of baguette and some small packets of butter. "It will make Ned fart."

Ned winked at her by way of confirmation, as if he looked forward to it. Katherine laughed out loud. It sounded strange to her own ears. Paul grabbed two spoons from his back pocket and dropped them unceremoniously into the soup, which was fragrant and thick.

"Paul is quite famous for his soups around here," Ned explained. "There's always something available, summer or winter."

"It smells amazing," she said as she dunked a piece of bread and eagerly took a big bite.

"How is it?"

"Lovely! Who taught you?" she asked.

Paul pulled up a chair. He kept the leg that was painful straight, and Katherine saw the irregular shapes beneath his jeans as if he wore a brace. It piqued her curiosity about him even further. He was interesting. One could see that at first glance.

"Me Mum," he said, without further elaboration. "What brings you to this part of England?"

"Me Mum," she replied, and he gave her a lopsided grin. "She always said this was the ideal place to start a business, so here I am," she said as she spooned the soup with little pause.

"It depends on what sort of business. You were lucky to find a place on High Street for starters. I just hope you know what to do with it."

Ned frowned at his friend. "Now Paul, you may be right about that but that's no reason to scare Katherine. She hasn't even started!"

"Should the truth be hidden? This is the sort of place snobs from London visit, or older people with money. If, as a shopkeeper, your target is a teenage crowd, you might as well forget it."

"I did my homework. I am working for women who want quality things and can afford to pay for them."

"Then you might do well," he said. "And I want you to, don't get me wrong. You're much nicer to look at than some of the other geezers around here. You and Thelma both." He nodded as if to give his own statement more credence.

"Do you ever have private parties here?" Katherine wondered, looking around again.

"I'm open to anything. Have you got something in mind?"

"Yeah, the reception for my opening. I should really get off the fence about that."

"Would it be by invitation only?"

"Yes." She nodded, savouring the last spoonful.

She wiped her mouth with a paper napkin and had another gulp of beer to wash the soup down. She belched behind her hand.

"How much rearranging would it take?"

"Some. Take all but a few tables out. Make it standing room only."

"That can be arranged. When?"

"In five weeks. I was going to do it at my place to save money but I don't know anymore. It's probably not a good idea for the sake of my merchandise." She spoke to nobody in particular, as if working through a problem she'd been saddled with and finally coming to a conclusion. "So, the printer eagerly awaits a location. Are you in? I've got to know."

Paul threw an amused curl of a smile in Ned's direction and shook his head. The innocence that shone through her cornflower-blue eyes was a terrific camouflage for determination, she knew, and Katherine had become even more intensely focused since the start of this business venture, but they didn't know that.

Ned grinned. "She doesn't mess around, this one. Clearly unafraid to make last-minute decisions... that makes her already one of the blokes, doesn't it?"

"I would never claim to have it all figured out," Katherine snorted.

"You see what I mean?"

"How much would you charge?"

"Do you eat breakfast?" Paul asked.

"Yes, of course."

"Come over in the morning and we'll work it out."

"What time?"

"Seven." He grinned. "You're buying."

"Hey Paul, are you on break?" someone yelled from the bar.

Paul looked their way and waved. "No. Hold your horses."

Katherine told him she'd be there. He limped back to the bar with empty plates, and she turned her full attention back to Ned.

"Ambition isn't enough to build a successful retail business if it's not backed by hard bloody work. Paul is right that we've seen those who make bad decisions fold quickly. It's good to know we have a hard-working young lady like you in our community. You ought to be proud of yourself," he said.

"Can we get over the flattery and down to some business?" Katherine asked sincerely. "There are a few things I need for the shop and for the reception."

Ned laughed, drawing Paul's attention away from making change. From then on, he kept an eye on the pair as their heads were bent together in conversation. Before long, Katherine signalled for two more drafts and, knowing they were striking another deal, Paul shook his head at the informality of it all. Only in Blackwell-on-Sea! Of course, he'd heard through the grapevine that she'd made arrangements with several other merchants. He could hardly wait 'til morning to see what the blue-eyed mogul had in store for The Wicked Mule. And, in the long term, for his and everybody's lives.

***

DARRELL THE POSTMAN carried a heavy mailbag down Haskell Street, throwing post in letterbox after letterbox with the confidence of someone who'd done it for years. If he'd weighed his bag this morning the scale might have tipped over, but he whistled a Roy Orbison tune he'd heard on the radio, happy to be outside, happy to be employed, and happy at the prospect of a generous tip at the end of today's particular round.

Turning around the bend of Haskell Street, he focused immediately on a house halfway down, nearer to the beach. It had a black-lacquered garage and front doors on the ground floor with a spacious apartment above. It was the home of Blackwell-on-Sea's second most famous inhabitant, the first being Bert, who delivered sausages to the royal family. Steve Denison played in a band Darrell knew little about but every once in a while, there was a picture in an obscure music magazine that he delivered to a young man living on Castle Avenue. Darrell's missus balked at blokes with long hair, but he had spoken with Steve on several occasions when he asked Darrell to hold his mail. He seemed like a decent chap. Unlike the ice queen who lived with him, Steve tipped well. Of course, he'd heard through the Blackwell grapevine that she had left.

By the time he reached the house, he noted a light was on in the large upstairs windows. Steve had told him when he'd be back and, true to his word, he was. Four weeks out of the country to play music, Darrell supposed, not unlike Roy Orbison. Happily, he dropped four weeks' worth of mail, among which were dozens of forwarded letters held together with a rubber band by the thirty or so, through the mail slot. Later on, after the round, he would come back and ring the doorbell to ask if his services had been satisfactory. He'd considered spending his tip on the missus but came to his senses. After all, what she didn't know couldn't come back to haunt him! There was a horse by the name of BabyCake, and the palm of his hand itched to place a bet.

***

THROUGH THE DENSE fog of a beer-induced sleep, Steve became aware of a repetitive and persistent beeping. He moaned in protest, confused about where he was. The bed was too comfortable to be in a hotel. The noise didn't stop. With a deep sigh, his eyes still closed, he turned on his back and pulled a pillow over his head to muffle the sound. The pillow vaguely carried the scent of Anne's perfume. It triggered memories of arriving home the night before and, with the last of his wits about him, moving the alarm clock to the kitchen so he would have no choice but to get out of bed to switch it off.

The bloody thing screamed louder and louder. Much like his girlfriend lately, he couldn't help but think, and he almost smiled at his own little analogy. With a sense of dread, he wondered if she was home or out working a modelling job somewhere. He hoped for the latter. Steve threw his legs over the side of the bed and planted his bare feet on the floor. With a pathetic moan, he dropped his head in both hands to try to keep the room from spinning. He hated being hung over, and for that reason rarely got sloshed. He forced himself up, if not to shut up the damned alarm, then to get some aspirin down.

With eyes barely cracked open, Steve reached into the refrigerator in his American-style kitchen for a bottle of Perrier. Grateful for the salty taste of sparkling water, he thirstily drained the bottle and belched loudly in appreciation. He turned to shut up the relentless hollow shrill. It was just after seven. Only then did he dare brave any light. He reached for the switch, and the view of the rest of the apartment met him head on. He did a double take.

It was empty! All of the furniture except for the bookshelves, books, and the upright piano, was gone. Because he was not yet capable of complex thought, he fell down on a barstool, head leaning heavily on his arms. After a few minutes, despite the incessant hammering against his temples, which continued no matter how much pressure he applied, the peace of silence became unmistakable.

Hang on. No music, no voices, no audience, no woman…

Before long he managed to loosely plait his hair, find his trainers, and suit up for a run. No matter how difficult it was to roll out of bed when jet lag tried to keep him there, the first run after coming home from a trip was an event that he looked forward to. There was no place like home. That philosophy was renewed every time the wind from the Channel met his face and the vision of the castle loomed ahead as he pounded across Blackwell's sand-and-pebble beach. This morning it would feel more like a punishment to venture into the grasp of cold air and chase the beer out of his bloodstream.

He hopped down the stairs. With his foot, Steve shoved aside the stacks and stacks on the floor by the front door. It would be much later before he sorted through it and carried any letters from very young fans to his grandmother. That she loved to occupy herself reading them and typing replies with one finger, staccato, on an old manual typewriter endeared him more than anything she had ever done for him. It had started when he'd asked management to forward any children's letters that were addressed to him personally as opposed to the band. They were fun and they weren't so many that it became unmanageable. Her devotion to the task was not only for the sake of love, but also for the part of Granny that would always remain a teacher.

Dawn was free of clouds. Steve walked to the boardwalk doing a few stretches along the way. He would be witness to the sun casting its warm luminosity over the village. The prospect gave him a jolt of energy, and he made his way through the cluster of cottages quickly, resisting the temptation to knock on Paul's door. It was Monday and he would not likely be up at this hour. He took the path down to the beach instead. The sun had just started to edge its way over the horizon and he turned left towards it, away from the castle. He'd just begun a slow jog along the surf when the distant sound of joyful barking reached him. Steve smiled. Billie would be crazy excited to see him. In the next moment, she barked alongside him, hopping up and down.

"Good to see you too, gorgeous!" He gave her a quick scratch on the head without breaking his stride.

The sound of the water was steady and soothing, the air crisp. He filled his lungs with deep, even breaths. Increasing his pace a little bit at a time, his headache slowly dissipated. After the first mile, he found that he could let this thoughts roam to Anne. Since the last string of overseas gigs began, the excitement of spending time with her had diminished with each break in the band's schedule. They'd been together for nearly two years with severe ups and downs, but lately they couldn't be together for two hours without having a fight. He'd known it was a waste of time from the beginning, but her fiery passion and beauty had suited what he was prepared to give a relationship, and she'd wanted him for her own reasons. He had allowed it to happen.

They hadn't spoken since the day before he left for Asia. Taking his furniture, he assumed, was supposed to make a statement. It didn't surprise Steve. He knew Anne well enough to know that it was a ploy to forestall his breaking up with her. If she thought it would make a difference, obviously she didn't know him at all.

Steve turned, Billie following at his heels. Pounding on the hard, moist sand beneath his feet, he breathed deeply and rhythmically. His ears hurt from the cold, but he could hear the steady repetition of an easy bass riff in his steps, and in his mind, he played along. The beach was a very musical place if people would but care to listen and find its rhythm.

Billie barked a couple of times and took off as if she'd been hurled from a slingshot. They were near the castle now. At first he thought she must have been called back to home base, but she ran past the green door. Following her around the jutted portion of the castle, he was surprised to find another lone figure on the beach. Steve smiled when he saw the warmth with which the dog was greeted.

Upon approach, his solitary companion appeared to be a woman who, as he watched, went through a set of stretches with Billie panting patiently by her side. Even at this distance she seemed pretty. She looked vaguely familiar, but he saw so many people traveling around the world these days that faces seemed to blend together. He rarely spent enough time in one place to get to know anyone or trust his own judgment when it came to remembering whom he'd met and whom he hadn't.

She threw him a brief glance as he jogged by her. He uttered a breathless "morning," and she replied with a minimum politeness. Her eyes were red-rimmed. He wondered if she had been crying or if it was due to the wind. Steve increased his pace. He continued in peace down the beach towards his turning point which was the breakwater with the red mark up ahead. His mind turned back to Anne.

With his parents' long-lasting marriage as an example, and now that his career as a musician had reached a comfortable threshold of success, a good relationship seemed a higher priority. He had reached a point where he longed for what they had: a family of his own. The more time he'd spent with, and then without Anne over the last two or three months, had convinced him that their relationship was at a dead end. She was right in sensing that it was over.

He was realistic enough that it might not be easy to find a girl who was strong enough to deal with his absences, and see beyond what he did to who he was long enough to trust that he would always be a good provider no matter what his profession. Trust would have to be complete and mutual. Steve loved women and respected them, and the mother of his children would be the only one for him. He wanted someone with whom he could be Mummy and Daddy, as well as husband and wife, and be able to separate the two. He had quite put himself beneath the microscope enough in the last few years to know it was what he needed in a partner.

It looked like Tornado Wave's starving days were over. This last tour had been more lucrative, even for the band. It was just one of the reasons why they'd partied so hard the night before. Immensely tired from the long flight after a stressful tour, the band, roadies, engineers, everybody who'd been involved, had descended upon an unsuspecting pub to celebrate its success. Getting into the back of a cab, with their manager bribing the driver to take him all the way to the south coast at that late hour was a vague memory.

At the breakwater he turned around in a short bow and, with the sun to his right, retraced his steps in the sea-hardened sand. Gus was high atop the castle's keep. Waving would be futile. From the beauty of the sun shimmering in the water this morning, it was easy to see that Gus would be engrossed in painting the scenery. Steve too enjoyed the splendour of gold dancing atop gentle waves. It was so good to be home.

As he and the woman approached again, Billie left her side to join Steve. He smiled at the dog. He was quite fond of her. Apparently she'd found a new companion during his recent absences, and he was happy about it. The shepherd's decision to divide her time between the two of them, as though not to slight either one of her friends, was sweet. This time as they passed each other he noted the streaky blondish hair and striking blue eyes. He liked that she had no makeup on to cover the freshness of her face. The effort of jogging, in combination with the morning's crisp air, had sent a healthy blush to her cheeks. Again he sensed that he had seen her before but still couldn't place her.

In the last mile, Steve reduced his pace to a slow jog to wind down before the final half-mile walk. This regimen was routine for him. Next stop would be the supermarket, followed by the reward of a very long, hot shower to wash the tour away, and large amounts of caffeine in the company of a good book by the fire. That he had nothing to sit on didn't bother Steve in the least.

The sun climbed over the horizon at a much slower pace than a few miles of running took to complete, and Steve smoothly slowed to a walk in tune with Billie's new friend. Billie barked, running in circles around the both of them seemingly in an effort to bring them together. The woman pushed her hands against her sides as if to contain the pain. Steve couldn't help but grin.

"Painful?" he asked, abandoning any previous need for solitude.

When she glanced at him, she seemed a bit startled. Steve wasn't entirely surprised by that sort of reaction from people. These days he was recognized more than he cared to be. It just wasn't normally something he had to deal with at home.

She nodded, out of breath. "I've only just started doing this but I'm already questioning my own sanity."

Billie brought a stick and dropped it at his feet. He stooped to rub her ears and threw it. She brought it back before he could think of anything else to say.

"I'm sorry if this seems forward but haven't we met somewhere before?" she asked.

The question was posed so innocently that it convinced Steve of its genuineness.

"I had the same feeling actually," he said politely.

They were too winded to talk much and continued on in silence, heading towards the path that led along the cliff to the cottages. She was only about half a head shorter than he was, but somehow it felt as if he towered over her. Turning his gaze towards the sun, he concluded that it would not reach much warmth beyond its watery yellow colour. Its rays played on the water with the tenderness of fingers stroking piano keys. He could almost hear the notes. It would be a lovely winter day.

His attention was drawn away from the scenery when Billie took off for the green door and disappeared through it. No doubt a large bowl of fresh water and a hearty breakfast awaited her beyond the thick blackened walls.

"If I'm not mistaken, you're the man who rescued my cat. Do you remember?"

He remembered the name of the kitten, whose wailing had very nearly stopped his heart that night. "Rafael?"

She reciprocated his smile, and it quite took his breath away.

"That's right." She nodded enthusiastically.

"Did he survive the adventure?"

"He's recovered quite nicely, but there's a little triangle missing from his ear. He seems to always find something to get into trouble with, whether for my entertainment or his own I don't know, but he's quite fun to have around."

With a smile like that, it was clear the little creature had found a safe haven where he would be treasured. Their eyes met briefly. He forced himself to look away. The smile wasn't quite reflected in hers, he noticed, and in fact they were still a bit red. He surmised she'd been crying. He wondered why but still allowed a moment to consider what it might be like to stare into that blueness for more than a few seconds at a time. He must have momentarily lost his marbles, he thought, as he started the climb to the boardwalk.

"It's nice to know he's being cared for. It's nice to see you again as well," he turned. "Are you new here in the village?"

"You must be a local if you've noticed that!"

"We get the occasional long-term tourist."

"Everybody seems to have been born here." She laughed. "I hope you won't hold my being an invader against me. I feel quite at home actually."

"I doubt you would have been looked upon with kindness several centuries ago, but I think you're quite safe these days except perhaps from those who thrive on gossip. They are brutal."

They had reached the top of the cliff and Steve, having no idea which way she would go, stopped there. They were out of breath again. The climb was like torture after an already exerting run.

"Oh? Should I stick to the shadows like Rafael?"

Steve laughed. "I hope not, but you might want to avoid Bunco at The Wicked Mule."

"I think I'm safe then," she said. "I'm really not the type."

He nodded as if he'd already reached the conclusion on his own. "Do you run here every day?"

"Heavens, no! About three times a week if I have the time. Hopefully more as the days become longer and it isn't so bloody cold. You?"

"When I'm home, yes, I do. Billie could attest to it."

"Does she really live in there?" She pointed to the fortress behind them.

"Yeah, she belongs to the caretaker. Have you not met him?"

"Briefly, but he did not say much and nor did I. It's always just Billie and me here, until now."

"Gus is one of Blackwell-on-Sea's most colourful characters. In fact, if you crane your neck you can just see him up there."

She gazed in the direction he pointed but couldn't make anything out.

"If you climb on the wall you could probably see him better," he said. "Just don't look down."

Curious, she climbed on the wide ledge built from large, uneven rocks and cement without hesitation. Steve resisted the urge to hold her by the knees.

"I see what you mean. What's he doing?"

"Painting. He's a well-respected artist," he explained.

"He must have quite a view up there. Thanks," she said as he helped her down. "And it looks like Billie will have twice the exercise."

She took a few steps in the direction of High Street and wiped her brow with a sleeve of the fleece sweatshirt. Some part of him felt a strange, almost cosmic tug, as if he shouldn't let her go just yet.

"Not if we run together."

Was he flirting?

"I wouldn't call what I do running." She smiled back. "And it'll be twice the fun for Billie. Enjoy the day."

Steve stared after her.

Chapter V

Grand Opening

Katherine locked the front door to the shop and flicked on the lights. In the last week it had become a ritual for her to turn slowly, in order to fully allow the beastly hard work of the last few months to be a gift. The shop's stunning interior still caught her by surprise; the rich textures, deep colours, and lush fabrics instantly offered a feeling of luxury and guilty pleasure. Tomorrow would be the first day for the lights to be on, for the windows to be uncovered, and for the sign on the door to read "open." And in that regard, perhaps the bigger shock when turning on the lights was to be face to face with a dream that was now reality.

She'd left The Wicked Mule satisfied that Paul had a handle on preparations for tonight's reception. Neither he nor Ned realized what a tremendous beacon they had been in recent weeks, when exhaustion, and the fear to lose all that she had invested, threatened to paralyze her determination to see the launch through. Not that she displayed it, quite the contrary. That they made her laugh fuelled Katherine with the gumption to keep going.

Ned had stepped up to his side of their agreement and found just the right pieces of furniture. A hand-carved Italian church pew, circa 1800, made of solid fir was positioned to the left of the entrance, its back tucked against the window display. A monastery table that could have seated sixteen hungry monks—and probably had once upon a time—now served as the display for tees and sweaters, neatly stacked. Just on the other side, against the left wall, stood an enormous French Empire double corps buffet in solid oak, the doors of which were open to a neat row of skirts in the bottom partition and blouses in the top one.

Along the wall on either side of the buffet stood chrome clothing racks with more designs waiting for buyers in serene enticement. The cosy corner at the back had a dais in the middle of three dressing rooms and two strategically placed full-length mirrors. The dais had clever drawers to house the tools of Katherine's trade. An oversized painting in hues of blue married the two areas of sale. Early reproduction Louis Quinze armchairs upholstered with dulled gold- and silver-accented brocade, and small tables with books and magazines, offered the shopper's weary companion a place to rest while remaining a part of the shopping experience.

On the right-hand side of the shop and behind the 19th-century register counter Ned had found, was a wall-to-wall and floor-to-ceiling glass-fronted built-in that housed accessories like high-end purses and shoes chosen to match her collection. A small portion also displayed modern, handmade jewellery by a local silver artist. There was no room to house an inventory of shoes and purses, but to guide the customer to other shops in Blackwell, cards were organized beside the register. All accessories were part of the deals she'd struck with other merchants in the village, much as she had with Ned.

The chandeliers were the crowning pieces of Katherine's vision for the boutique. They had been Paul's idea. She'd thought modern lighting was just the thing but as soon as he'd entered the shop for a sneak peek, there was vigorous disagreement. Katherine smiled at the memory as she admired them.

"Chandeliers," he'd said, "not the sort that have no meat to them either... something large and baroque. Can you find something like that?"

He'd turned to Ned and they'd conversed about it for the next ten minutes as if she weren't in the room at all. Fortunately, the choice of lighting was the only objection they had. She and Ned had set off on a search and settled on opulent neo-baroque driftwood fixtures that added yet another layer to the texture of the shop. Paul, upon second inspection, had patted her on the head as if she were an obedient dog.

The final piece of the puzzle, a brand-new stereo with an impressive new gadget called a compact disc player, had been in its box by the stairs. When Paul found out what she wanted to do with it, he'd suggested a good friend to install it properly.

"Paul, you've been so kind to me. I couldn't possibly impose on your friends as well."

"Don't be daft! Aside from the fact that he's really good at this sort of thing, he could use the cash."

Katherine, thinking she could be helped while helping someone in need, had relented. Other obligations on that morning meant that she'd given a key to Paul to let the bloke in. She'd been completely surprised upon her return to the shop to find that this friend was none other than Rafael's rescuer. He was the only man she knew with a braid, let alone one that reached the middle of his back, and she recognized him even as he operated a drill with his back to her. Not having heard the door, he'd nearly jumped out of his skin when she said "Hello, there," after the drill stopped going.

"Bloody hell, I didn't hear you come in at all! Hi!"

He got up from the floor, wiping his hands on his jeans. Neither of them could hide their surprise to see the other. They shook hands in greeting.

"You must be Paul's friend." She smiled.

"Katherine," he said with a smile. "At last we meet."

"So it seems. This is my place."

He glanced around with renewed interest and nodded. "I'm impressed. Paul says it's a boutique."

"Yes," she said.

"Nice. I'll tell my mum and Granny to stop in. And all seven of my aunts. And my sister."

"Thanks. How is the stereo coming along?"

"Slower than expected, I'm afraid. At a glance I figured you wouldn't want to mess things up with cables in plain sight. Paul confirmed you'd have my hide."

Katherine laughed. She draped her coat across the counter. "That's true on both counts."

"You get the best sound by mounting the speakers in all four corners. It took a spool of cable but they are all hidden in the ceiling, as you can see. To make a long story short… you will have music in half an hour or so."

"Thank you."

"No problem." He smiled, picking up the drill again.

"Would you like some tea or coffee?"

He shook his head. "No thanks. I've got a flight to catch this afternoon. I want to finish this."

A while later, musical sounds met her in the sitting room. She went downstairs for a listen. Verdi had the honour of being first for a spin inside the new device. He played with the bass and treble until it was just right.

"That sounds really good!" she said.

He looked at her and nodded. "Yeah, it's quite a bit better than records, isn't it?"

"There is no comparison from what I've read."

"No, but it's a bit of a shame, really. I'll miss the ritual of cleaning a 33 and setting the needle down with utmost care."

"Do you think records will disappear?"

"I hope not. You have a good collection of classical here. Is that what you like or is it because it fits the setting?" he asked curiously as he bent over a small toolbox, tucking things in their proper place.

"Both, actually."

Unplugging the drill from the wall, he grinned mysteriously, as if he had made a bet with himself about what the answer would be and got it right.

"How much do I owe you?" she asked.

"Nothing!"

"That can't be. This took hours and not to mention the spool of cable."

"I'm happy to have been able to help." He waved a hand as if to wipe a debt clean.

"But..." She bit her lip, not wanting to insult. "I can't accept that. Paul said that you take odd jobs like this because..."

Paul's friend lifted a suspicious eyebrow. "Because?"

"Please, you must let me pay you for your time and for the cable. It's absolutely the least I can do," Katherine tried and sighed when his expression continued to demand an answer. "Okay. He said you needed the money."

"He said *what*?" Both caterpillar eyebrows were pushed to great heights in disbelief, but in the next moment he threw his head back with hearty laughter. "That bastard"—he shook his head— "is just taking the mickey. Whether with you or with me remains to be seen, probably both. Paul can be a scoundrel."

"But..."

"Katherine," he interrupted, "may I call you that?"

"Well, of course."

He smiled, tucked the drill under his arm, and picked up the remainder of the cable and the toolbox. "I'll settle for a run on the beach when I get back."

"You never did mention your name." Katherine nodded as she led him to the door and opened it for him.

"Steve."

"You've been so kind. Thanks, Steve."

"When do you open?"

"On Saturday."

"Good luck. And give the little Riff-Raff a cuddle for me."

Memory dissipating, Katherine did a last, slow 360 to take it all in. Despite a huge sense of pride and accomplishment, she remained afraid. Having reached the point of no return, from one minute to the next and one thought to the other, confidence and insecurity fought a terrific battle in her mind. She made her way to the bedroom, where Rafael greeted her from the bed, and after giving him the forgotten cuddle from Steve, she took a long hot shower and prepared for the evening.

***

THE MODELS ARRIVED on schedule and the moment they did, Katherine's home was transformed into a chaotic mess of beautiful, cackling girls without any semblance of modesty whatsoever. They strutted about the apartment bra-less and in thongs the size of Band-Aids. The hairdresser, Sandra, was holed up in the bathroom doing simple styles that didn't require much work, while Katherine handled makeup and dressing in the bedroom. As they finished, they were sent downstairs to wait in the sitting room. The process was systematic until incessant ringing of the doorbell penetrated the noise.

"Can someone get that?" Katherine yelled from the stairwell, and an undefinable voice said that she would.

Sandra met her on the landing for a moment to confer. The bathroom door was shut. Sandra, in her thirties, owned a less well-frequented salon away from High Street. Katherine had chosen her to do the work because she had fresh ideas and was a talented stylist. She had an eight-year-old son and a husband who worked shifts as a nurse at Brighton Hospital.

"Are they always like this?" she asked. "Andy will be green with jealousy when I tell him I had ten naked women in my hands this afternoon."

At about the same time a voice yelled, "man in the house!" which made the girls who were left in the bedroom squeal, not with an instantly gained reserve, but in anticipation of the typical male reaction.

Sandra and Katherine rolled their eyes and smiled at each other.

"Does that answer your question? Why did you need me?"

"The blond. Her hair may be too heavy for what you want."

Katherine gazed into the bedroom, but she didn't see a blond.

"She's using the loo."

"Oh, the tall one?"

"Yeah, with the body I'd kill for."

"And the disposition of Gollum in *Lord of the Rings*? Yes, I've noticed."

"Which one was Gollum?"

Katherine waved her hand. "Never mind, don't listen to me. Errrr… pull it all together at the nape of the neck. It will have to do. It's fine."

She excused herself and thundered down the stairs where she found Norman's half-sisters standing about on the landing. They were the last people she had expected to appear, and the shock of it stopped her in mid-descent. The girls broke into beatific smiles of recognition and reunion, radiance breaking through Katherine's armour.

"Oh my God…," she said. "I can't believe you've come! What a surprise!"

The girls—Marlies was the elder at eighteen, and Fiona, sixteen, —burst into giggles and hugged her fiercely when Katherine stepped onto the landing. A man had lugged in a rather large black box and a black guitar case which she did her best to ignore. Without proper pound sterling to pay for the taxi ride from the station in Brighton, they asked her to pay the driver. They kissed her heartily when she did.

"How are your mother and father?" Katherine was reluctant but polite to ask.

Norman's mother had never liked nor approved of their marriage and at his insistence Katherine had stopped trying to get along with her years ago. Any "good-to-see-you" greeting was always relative to their relationship, and she didn't speak enough Dutch to have complicated conversations with her.

"What is this?" she asked, pointing to the guitar and amplifier.

"You know what it is, Katherine. It's a gift, from our brother." Marlies said.

Katherine's eyes filled and she inhaled deeply through her nose to fight the tears. "But not the Gibson?"

"No. Not the Gibson. It's a gift for the launch. We ran away to bring it to you."

"You what?!" she asked incredulously, but the girls only giggled.

Katherine looked at her watch. She needed to get the rest of the girls ready and herself dressed in something other than the old pair of sweats and tee she had on.

"Come with me," she said, resolutely pushing away any thought of a gift from Norman. "First, you call your parents to let them know where you are and that you're safe. Then hair and makeup for the both of you, and we'll find you something to wear from the collection. I'm so glad you're here. I wasn't expecting anybody from the family."

"Mum is still very cross with you for selling the farm."

"It wasn't mine to sell! Norman arranged all of that, and it was his to decide what to do."

"She knows that, Katherine! She's just... grieving. None of us are over it yet. Are you?"

She shook her head, pulling them close as they went upstairs. "No. Not at all. The truth is, he was right, you know, without this I'd have probably thrown myself off a bridge somewhere."

"Katherine, you wouldn't!"

"No, but the weight of the work has been... life-saving, I suppose. That's all."

Merchants in the shopping district, fabrics and other materials suppliers in the industry, and a few press people had received an invitation to the grand presentation of what Mon Chocolat had to offer. With graceful calligraphy letters, the cream-colored parchment paper announced the arrival of a "New and Unique Gateway to Affordable Couture & the Latest Ladies' Fashion Designed Exclusively by Katherine Loch." Just over two hundred of the three hundred RSVP cards that had been included were returned marked *attending*.

The Wicked Mule had been transformed under Paul's direction. The hearth's fire was kept to a minimum, but only just. Tables and chairs had been removed; sofas scattered against the walls flanked by low end tables. A dozen illuminated daises had been situated throughout the pub. How Ned had managed, Katherine had no idea, and she was told not to ask. He and Paul too were stunned to have pulled the rabbit out of the hat in just five weeks' time. The only thing Paul would admit to was that he'd bribed the Bunco troupe to make finger sandwiches by setting aside five bottles of Sandeman Port for them to consume at the next game night.

"Okay?" Paul asked upon her last quick inspection.

"Yes. And even if it wasn't, I don't suppose we could do anything about it now."

"Right. Have you had anything to eat since breakfast?"

"No."

"Have a sandwich."

"I just brushed my teeth."

"So what?" He poured two glasses of decent champagne and put one in front of her.

"God, I need that."

"Eat or it'll knock you on your ass."

"Have we gone over budget?" she asked when she tasted smoked salmon. "I don't remember signing off on salmon."

"That's my treat. I was going to send a plant or two in congratulations but thought you'd be better served making a lasting impression. People always remember the food before anything else."

Katherine smiled. She couldn't disagree with that.

Paul pointed to her mouth. "Parsley, just there, on the left."

"Bloody hell!"

She ran to the nearest mirror to check. There wasn't any parsley in her teeth, of course. But it gave her a moment, just a few seconds by herself in the loo. Enough time to see the woman in the mirror, to breathe a sigh of relief at her reflection, and to watch herself knock back the entire glass of champagne as if it were courage in a glass. The moment of truth. No way back now.

"I should have known!" she said to Paul, who filled glass after glass carefully with champagne and set them down on waiting trays.

Katherine took one of them and knocked it back as well, allowing the bubbles to send a feeling of temporary bliss through her body. Paul grinned. Someone called her name, one of the models, and she waved in her direction to indicate she was on her way.

"Katherine," Paul said, forcing her to turn back.

"What?"

He stopped mid-pour and had a serious look on his handsome face. "You look stunning tonight. I'm excited for you."

Her heart skipped a beat. "Thank you."

He nodded. "No problem. Now, tell me… which one of these models is available for me?"

She snagged the nearest thing from the bar and pointed it at him. "You stay away from them until they are done working for me tonight, understood? After that, take as many of them home as you think you can handle."

"You're threatening me with a spoon, Katherine," he said dryly. "I'm not impressed."

She wore a flowing chiffon *décolleté* dress that reached the floor and matched her eyes. It was part of the collection, though hers was the only one in cornflower blue. She looked magnificent in it and worked the room tirelessly as her guests were shown a total of thirty-six different designs by the twelve models. Their mission was to look like mannequins, and not to interact with the guests, not even with eye contact. The only time they left their dais during the course of the evening was to change at mind-boggling speed with Katherine and Sandra's help in the back room.

Katherine might have been occupied explaining her designs and answering questions about fabric and colour choices, but she never lost track of the details. The models did beautifully when Paul didn't try to catch their attention. On a couple of occasions, she threw him a dirty look, which he acknowledged only with a wink wrapped in mischief. She guessed he'd be successful with a number of them, while he gave the leggy blond a very cold shoulder, causing Katherine to wonder if there was a history between them.

At the end of four hours of non-stop talking about her work, Katherine was exhausted. Arriving back at the shop shortly before midnight, she made for the stairs without looking at anything else, afraid there might be things that still needed to be done. Enough was enough. Norman's sisters had offered to tidy up in the morning. Tired from their journey, the girls had asked to be excused from the reception rather early. Katherine accepted it, hoping to be able to sleep a little bit longer if she could manage to sleep at all.

Her lips twisted into a grimace as she kicked off her heels and stooped to pick them up, stretching her aching back in the process. The soles of her feet burned as if she'd walked barefoot on a hot pavement for miles. The cold floor sent prickles of relief through her legs. The exhaustion of her body as she climbed the stairs was a perfect echo of what raged through her weary soul, but in a way, the physical pain was a welcome distraction from the mental one.

The shoes weighed a ton in her hand. A loud thud, followed by another, cut through the house when she dropped them one by one. Remembering the girls asleep on the sofa, Katherine flinched. She waited ten seconds before stripping off her dress. It fell on the landing with barely a rustle. The coolness on her skin was merely a prelude to the symphonic sensation of what the handmade Egyptian cotton sheets on her bed would feel like, she imagined, longing for bed.

But in her bedroom, she stopped dead. The feeling of panicked insecurity that had been such a plague in the last couple of weeks rushed through her stomach with the velocity of a stray bullet. A sudden, hurtful sob found freedom on her lips. The music gear was carefully deposited at the foot of the bed, and Katherine's sisters-in-law had thoughtfully tied a red bow around the neck of the guitar case.

Rafael yawned and stretched. He jumped down from the bed to greet her, and she hurried to cuddle his little body close. She dropped to her knees before the gear. Katherine was overcome by memories of a house filled with music. There had been times when she was unable to get away from it even though she wanted nothing more than silence to hear herself think. Did she miss the noise? Not particularly… sometimes. Rafael leaped out of her arms to the floor and went in search of the litter box in the bathroom.

The guitar didn't surprise her because Norman would have sensed that music would be the most dreaded to re-introduce into her life and therefore he would have done something to tempt her into playing. With a tender touch of the case, she experienced an unexpected jolt of excitement. The clasps released easily. She drew up a knee and rested her chin on it, sighing deeply in anticipation. Raf wormed himself back on the bed after a drink of water, still too little to jump but quite capable of using his claws. He peered over the edge as Katherine gently lifted the lid.

She gasped in surprise, instantly thrown into the memory of the last visit to their favourite music store together en route to a gig. They needed to buy string for Norman's beloved Gibson. He'd been so very thin and frail. It had pained her to realize that he seemed tired of fighting a losing battle. She had wanted to take him home, but he'd insisted she try a much lusted-after guitar and looked on from a wobbly, used drum stool. She remembered Norman's smug look of pride when, after the first few bars of a song, she'd sent him an approving smile. It was the first time Katherine had asked to venture away from the Gibson.

Now, here she was. Tucked in a luxurious bed of black velvet, shone the beautiful candy-apple-red 1957 Fender Stratocaster. Reissue, of course, not a real one. Running her fingers gently over the fret board, the strings felt taut with the need to be played. Had Norman gone back to the shop without her? Or had he sent someone on a mission to do it for him? Katherine decided he would have wanted to test it for himself, even if Fender would never have been his first choice.

Katherine lifted the instrument gently as she rose to sit at the foot-end of the bed. Its weight and shape felt unfamiliar as she placed it on her thighs. It was much lighter than the Gibson had been. Rafael hissed at it and jumped into the case where he promptly arched his back and played with a couple of picks. There was a long white envelope addressed to her in Norman's terrible handwriting. It had been trapped beneath the guitar. She supposed it shouldn't have come as a surprise, but it caught her off guard anyway. Touching a fingertip to it, she opted for a pick instead.

For months now, the acoustic guitar had been in a cubbyhole beneath the stairs. She had no desire to play. But this… proved indeed tempting. Strumming silent strings was quickly deemed unsatisfying. She released the amp from the other box and plugged it in. While it warmed, she got ready for bed, and when she hit an accidental chord picking up the guitar, the loudness of it nearly made her jump out of her skin.

"Bugger!"

Rafael shot out of the case and down the stairs with his fur up and ears back, hissing loudly. With a firm twist on the volume knob she was certain the noise level would be reduced to the confines of her bedroom, and she touched the string gently to make sure. She closed her eyes and took a deep breath, right hand poised over the strings while the left was clamped around the fret board. In her mind's eye she flipped through a Rolodex of songs. It stopped at one she disagreed with.

"No, not that one!" she said aloud.

The next one that came to mind, she played from memory, but being out of practice, she gave up quickly. Much more quickly than Norman would have allowed his pupil. The envelope stared at her, crisp and white against the black velvet. With a furiously beating heart, Katherine reached for it and was puzzled by its lumpiness. She turned it over and over in her hands before she slid a nail beneath the seal. Carefully, as if it might otherwise fall apart, she lifted a note out of the envelope. Her hands trembled and tears appeared uninvited on her cheeks. She took some deep breaths, bracing herself to read it.

Rientje,

If you're reading this, it means that where I am is nothing other than I'm no longer with you. It also means that you have soldiered through. Thinking of you as I am alive for the next hours or days but probably not much longer, stirs feelings in me that I wish I'd had before. Words could never do what you are to me justice. But you know, don't you? I see it in your eyes. Wherever I shall be when you read this, I hope I'll be nearby somehow. I shall likely want to paint you and be frustrated that I can't. I cling to the belief that in death nobody can take my heart because you are my heart and I love you. Because of you, my muse, I became a better artist, a better musician. And you! I am proud of your skill. I may have been your teacher, but I am not your talent. That's you. You practically melted for this guitar, so it's yours to enjoy now. You will have a need to play your heart out even if you think not. Perhaps after a while, you will even want to.

Forever yours,
Norman
P.S. Hope you forgive me the little sentimental nonsense included here. Thought you might like to have these things to remember me by.

She reached inside the envelope and touched something soft. When she realized what it was, she whimpered, and was again faced with another memory. She'd come home from the supermarket and noticed immediately the change.

"You've cut your hair," she'd said, arms full of groceries, as if informing Norman about something of which he was not aware.

He'd only smiled. "It will fall out anyway. I wanted to take control while I could."

He ran a hand over a closely cropped head, insecure about the result. She read in his eyes that it had been a difficult thing to do. He'd looked so healthy still, before the surgery, and it had been so difficult to grasp how serious his illness was.

"I like it," she said, with an honest stab at genuineness.

"You're a terrible liar, Katherine," he said.

She'd skirted the table to where he leaned against the kitchen sink and he'd pulled her close hard, and kissed her, harder. There had been something very desperate about the gesture. His hands had trembled as they grabbed fists full of her sweater, tearing at what was left of his life in a moment of despair.

Katherine lifted Norman's short blond pony out of the envelope. It was kept together with his wedding ring, which she thought he'd lost in the end because of the extreme weight loss. She was in near hysterics about it, and he'd had to console her, convinced it would be found eventually. She recognized the gold band with its inscription: *Carpe Diem* and their wedding date. He'd had six small onyx gemstones added to represent their years together. It was a sweet thing to have thought to do. She slipped it on the middle finger of her right hand, vowing to always wear it.

Hugging the instrument close, she began the song anew, allowing Norman closer tonight than in recent weeks. Like the sliding pointer on a Ouija Board, Katherine allowed her soul to be led. Through the sound of the Blues she was guided through the chords like water beneath the gravity of the moon into an ebb and flow of heartache and joy, forming a dreamy connection between heaven and earth.

Chapter VI

Counselling

If the night before was a blur of voices and questions and soft classical music, the next morning left Katherine little time to believe the moment of truth was upon Mon Chocolat. Even with help from Norman's sisters, it was a rush to get every trace of the models erased, the apartment back in order, the floor in the shop mopped, every last speck of dust and fingerprints wiped away. Finally, about five minutes before opening, they stood around looking at one another. Katherine felt that she should say something.

"It means a lot to me that you are here. You need to know that." She tried to smile but her voice broke at little. "But you must never, ever run away again to do it. If you want to visit, ring and I'll talk to your parents."

"Our brother told us in great detail how to get here. We felt safe."

The girls hugged her in their beautifully spontaneous way. They were giddy with an excitement that Katherine wished she could share wholeheartedly. But the price she'd had to pay wouldn't allow it. Not yet.

"Oh my God." Her hands shook. "I can't believe it. I'm about to open our shop. My mother is probably turning 'round in her grave."

"Do you want to turn back?" Fiona asked.

"Yes, all the bloody time."

"Did you like the guitar?" Marlies asked quietly.

"Yeah. It was a good surprise."

"More importantly, did you play it?" Fiona asked with the curiosity of a sixteen-year-old.

"Yes." Katherine admitted.

Fiona clapped her hands, filled with delight. "He said you wouldn't be able to resist it!"

Katherine laughed through her tears. She wasn't yet sure if Norman was right about the music, but the shop... How thoroughly ludicrous was it that it took the death of two people she loved most in this world, to make it happen? They had done it by giving her so much to live for. She was grateful, and yet, it was such a tremendously insane responsibility and the scariest bloody feeling she'd ever experienced, and if she could be quite honest, a small feeling of excitement had finally succeeded in sending a few butterflies through her stomach.

Thinking of her mother, she inserted what she remembered had been a favourite selection by Giuseppe Verdi. The music was as dramatic as the moment. With a deep breath to summon courage and an all-day-lasting smile, she walked to the door. There had been defining events in her life: her mother's funeral, getting married, being told of Norman's diagnosis, his death. As she listened to her own footsteps on the hardwood floors, a hand encircling her mother's locket, she experienced another. With Marlies at the ready to snap a few pictures, Katherine turned the key and deadbolts and turned the sign to "open."

Darrell the postman pushed through the door just seconds later.

"Well, well, well, boys and girls! Look at all this! Congratulations, my dear."

"Thank you, Darrell."

He handed over an envelope. "Here's your mail. Good luck with the business."

"It's not addressed." She frowned, turning it over.

"Oh no, sweetheart. Paul just gave it to me."

"Oh."

As he left, the florist, who had her shop on the town square, carried in a beautiful artsy bouquet stuffed in a modern etched crystal vase.

"Good morning!" Katherine said with a welcoming smile.

"My dear, what a big day for you, isn't it?! I thoroughly enjoyed the party last night." She looked around curiously. "It's lovely in here."

"Thank you. What have we here?"

"An order that came in a week ago; I was asked to deliver first thing this morning."

"Mrs. Shirley, you are an artist! What a lovely bouquet!"

"We each have our things that we're good at, don't we, dear. There's a card, and the vase was included as a keepsake," Mrs. Shirley added mysteriously. "I must run back to me shop now, dear. I'll be by later to have a look 'round. Good luck!"

Mrs. Shirley dashed away, and Katherine carried the vase to the counter. Marlies, by her mother's influence a connoisseur of everything that was a knickknack, commented the vase was black crystal. Katherine opened the small envelope tucked within a beautifully monochrome assortment of peonies, hydrangeas, and roses. The creamy white and light-blue colour scheme contrasted with the chocolate walls perfectly.

"They are absolutely gorgeous," she said, breathing in their scent.

"Who sent them?" Fiona wanted to know.

The card was a generic one from the flower shop, the handwriting almost too neat to be a man's. She read:

Congratulations. Best of Luck! Steve.

And Paul's card, which said congratulations and showed a photograph of a stupidly grinning mule with gigantic ears:

Just down the street if you need anything. Break a leg. Paul x

Katherine added the cards to the big fish bowl full of well-wishes and business cards. In the course of the next week she allowed herself a break from sewing, only working on the strictest necessary things like alterations and replenishing the things that sold out quickly. She took the time to create a mailing list for future advertisements, promotions, and other announcements from the collected cards. That done, she wrote some thank-you notes. Most of the cards were pre-printed and all she had to do was sign her name, but to the people who had worked with her, she wrote a more personalized message.

To Ned, she wrote:

It may be treasures you sell in your shop but, really, it is you who is the true treasure and I know exactly the amount to put on your tag: priceless. Thank you, Ned. From the heart. ~K.

To Paul she wrote:

This is the only thing I can think to say aside from thank you for everything:

The Road goes ever on and on
Out from the door where it began,
Now far ahead the Road has gone,
Let others follow it who can!
Let them a journey new begin,
But I at last with weary feet
Will turn towards the lighted Inn,
My evening-rest and sleep to meet.

The launch was second to none and I do so hope the model twins were
suitable to your needs! ~ K.

The note to Steve was trickier. For one, she had no idea how to
address it or where to send it. And they'd barely spent any time
together, at least not enough to form a solid opinion as to who he
was. In the end she wrote:

Steve,

Of the kindnesses you've shown, it would be difficult to say which one
means the most. The stereo system lends my shop its air of class and I'm
grateful for your meticulous work each time I power it on and off. The
flowers were a very lovely surprise and... there's Rafael; how can I ever
thank you for my inseparable companion? He is quite the source of
sweetness and entertainment in my life. Your generosity has touched me
in so many positive ways. They say a lot about the kind of person you
are.

Katherine

She stuffed them in her purse with the intention to deliver them
in person at some point.

As word about Mon Chocolat travelled, the curious kept
Katherine busy. She was nothing if not realistic, however, fully
expecting the mad rush of the first weeks to fade. Neither she nor
the bookkeeper had a true understanding of what to expect, but, for
the time being, her days were filled with customers and the evenings
were divided between alterations, making special orders, developing
the next collection, playing guitar, reading, and crying. Some nights,
restless beyond measure, she managed to make it through the list in
the space of an hour.

Despite having pulled herself up by the bootstraps and bringing
to fruition what she and Norman had created on paper, it became
increasingly more difficult to draw from that willpower. Katherine's
reservoir of determination depleted with each irrational thought he
might yet walk through the door to see it all for himself. She
recognized the day of reckoning loomed ahead and that running
away from it was fruitless. The last time she had kissed his lips, they
were as cold as the marble he was buried beneath.

Norman was dead. But she had not yet gained the strength to be
able to face that he'd never walk through the door.

Having honoured the promise to go through with the plans for
the shop didn't seem enough anymore. As if he had known this

would happen, the guitar had seemingly been sent from the afterlife. The letter demanded a second promise, another lifeline: to continue to play. She read it over and over, trying not to smudge it with tears, frequently smoothing away the creases that had become as permanent as permanent could be having been sealed beneath the weight of the Fender. It had been dated just three weeks before his death. It was a treasure. Not the guitar. The letter.

Playing, especially before an audience, would no longer mean that she had to do it because he no longer could. It would seem as if what she'd accomplished was for herself alone. Like an acceptance she knew was a lie.

Being down to earth enough to know not to count on the boutique's initial revenue, she was also realistic to recognize the looming razor-toothed jaws of depression. Denial was a safety net, but a breakdown was financially not an option. There was only enough left in savings to survive for a year with some extra in case of an emergency. Otherwise Katherine and her sewing skills were once again on their own.

To kill the life-sucking monster in whose shadow she wandered without direction and without much aim, she considered the idea of professional help. Among the many business cards that found a way into the fishbowl during the launch reception, Katherine had discovered one for a Doctor E. Ramsey, psychotherapist. The solution to the problem waited patiently beside the cordless phone on the coffee table for several weeks until early one dreary morning, Katherine dialled the number for an appointment.

Doctor Ramsey's waiting area was a haven of tranquillity, with muted shades of white and greys brought into relief by large Ficus plants. The sound of Native American music flowed non-intrusively from inconspicuous speakers. The furniture was Swedish modern, white, and sparse, with no more than two arm chairs, a table, and a small cabinet. Instead of magazines, the table was strewn with books of poetry.

Katherine tried to read a bit but found it difficult to concentrate. Silent though it was, the song reverberating through the room had begun with a slow and steady flute, swelled on a wave of percussion, and ended with the addition of turtle-shell rattles penetrated by passionate shouts. Her leg moved up and down much faster than the beat, and she heaved a sigh, realizing she was on edge.

Katherine wanted very much to connect with this therapist. Doctor Ramsey came highly recommended by Paul. When she'd asked for his opinion he'd replied to her question without the usual wit and said that Doctor Ramsey was someone who took the time to listen and was a master at seeing her patients through. He'd confessed that she continued to help him to overcome the tragedy of having lost a limb.

The door swung open, revealing Blackwell's psychotherapist. Katherine's resolve deflated like a balloon stuck with a pin.

"Oh," she said. "You're Ned's Elizabeth!"

Doctor Ramsey's sweet smile shone through a pair of kind, intelligent eyes.

"Yes, but not to worry," she said confidently, "the white coat acts as a protective shield between the outer world that includes my husband and the inner sanctum of insanity that is my office."

The smile of welcome never wavered, and there was a naughty twinkle in her brown eyes. Katherine met it with some trepidation. The woman whom Ned Denison had introduced as his wife Beth, reached a hand out in beckoning persuasion.

"Why don't you come in and have a seat? We'll talk."

If the reception area bordered the clinical, the office proved quite the opposite. The sofas were enormous, white leather, but the walls had been painted a lovely shade of stormy grey that had a calming effect. There were more plants. The wall without windows or cabinetry held nothing but two magnificently framed diplomas. One indicated a medical degree and another highlighted further education in counselling and psychiatry. Katherine was not unimpressed, but it did nothing to alleviate her initial discomfort. She took a seat at the edge of the sofa.

"I understand your reluctance, but truthfully I am a doctor and therefore bound by the laws and ethics of my profession. To whom I am married is of no importance, nor is the fact that this is a small community, relatively speaking, where everybody knows one another," she finished with a casual wave of the hand as she approached the floor-to-ceiling cupboards.

"I suppose you get that all the time?" Katherine marvelled at the tiny, cleverly hidden kitchenette.

"Blackwell-on-Sea is quite gossip-prone, have you noticed? There's a great desire for the juicy bits on the street, to be confirmed or discredited. Personally, I'm not a participant in the game. Not by law and not by my own ethics. Tea?"

"No, thanks. You're right, of course. I don't see why we can't give it a go at least. My apologies."

"Not at all." Elizabeth Ramsey smiled broadly as she returned with a sturdy mug of fragrant mint tea. "I hope you don't mind. I'm absolutely parched. It's been a busy day."

"Really? In Blackwell-on-Sea? I'm not sure that's comforting."

Beth Ramsey chuckled into her teacup. She took a couple of sips of the steaming liquid, seemingly not at all fazed by its temperature, Katherine observed that despite the cleanliness of the space and the crispness of her doctor's garb, Elizabeth Ramsey's hair was a mess of unkempt brown curls streaked with strands of grey. It was that touch of unruliness that she found disarming. She was a very lovely woman, in her early fifties, with a touch of crow's-feet from years of heartfelt laughter.

"Comfortable?"

Katherine nodded. She shivered ridiculously against the chill of the leather and held her hands clasped together between her knees to keep from trembling. Doctor Ramsey seated herself in the oversized chair. The sizable armrest held a clipboard with a notebook full of scribbles and doodles, a cheap pen at the ready to add more.

"Good. Now, tell me why you came to see me, or rather, why you seek my help."

"It's difficult to know where to begin. I have recently achieved something quite major, as you know. It's been like a dream. But... I'm not happy."

"Is this something recent, this unhappiness, or has something happened to bring you there?" The question was stated as if the answer were already encompassed within.

Katherine hesitated and said, "It hasn't been a terribly easy life."

"I want to hear everything you'd like to tell me, and the rest, I will get out of you with or without the torture devices I've got stashed away." Doctor Ramsey smiled.

Comforted not to have to carry the grief by herself anymore, relief flooded through her. Tears burned her nose and Katherine dug her fingernails into the palm of her hand to have something else to think about. She revealed the boutique stemmed from an ancient dream of her mother's combined with the tragic desperation of Katherine's dying husband.

"That's quite shocking. You are much too young to be a widow."

"I have an intense dislike of that word," Katherine said quietly, looking away. "I hate it to be honest."

"Why is that?"

"Because it's a dreadful thing to call someone, isn't it? Age has nothing to do with it. It makes me feel... I don't know... weak in a way. No longer complete."

"'Weak' is an interesting word to refer to your marital status. Tell me what it means."

Katherine thought about it.

"It's not as if I was able to do anything for Norman. It all went so fast. One day he suffered eye-splitting headaches, and six months later, he was gone. In that time, it seems all I could do was to stand by in absolute shock. It was exhausting. Frightening. I can't seem to remember much of it."

"Nothing?"

"No, well, yes, I do remember the special moments that we shared, of course. They are burned into my heart forever. But the horrific days of chemo and radiation, the surgery, the vomit, the pills, the seizures, and the tears, the fear, it has all sort of blurred together. It seems like one long, very long day."

"How do you feel about death, in very general terms?"

"It's a part of life. I understand that." She hesitated. "It happens to people who have lived a lifetime. It makes me sad for them and for their families, and yet it's acceptable."

"Now apply it to yourself."

"My mother's deterioration took years; four or five I think. Her suffering was not a constant at first. When it was, she started to drink to ease her pain. I admit having been relieved after years of caring for her. She was a prisoner in a crippled body. Her soul needed to be set free. At the time her death was liberating. But since Norman... I struggle with the why of things. Of life. I feel rather guilty about it now. My mother and I didn't have the best relationship. Not what I envision a mother and daughter should be. Of course, that might be an ideal that only exists in my mind."

"You didn't feel loved by your mother. How long ago was her death?"

"My mother was a great mystery to me. She still is. She died eight years ago."

Beth Ramsey quickly glanced at Katherine's chart, noting her birth year. She refrained from making a comment for now, but added to the scribbling on the notepad.

"And your husband?" she asked.

"Last August. About eight months."

"That's not long at all. And look what you've accomplished so far."

"That's just it, Doctor Ramsey. I am proud of Mon Chocolat. But at the end of the day, when the doors are locked..." She swallowed hard. A tear spilled from her lashes. "When I lock the door and I look around... what I see is that I have my dream without them. I find it... quite cruel."

"Do you have support from your father or siblings?"

Katherine shook her head. Tears flowed. She was unable to stop them. Doctor Ramsey quietly moved a box of tissues within reach and made another note.

"It's a nightmare inside of a dream that should be sweet. Norman pushed for me to have the shop because he knew it's what I would have done eventually and... as a way to keep busy, and he was right. Without it, I don't know what I'd do. Or my cat. I've adopted a kitten recently."

"Keeping occupied makes you forget reality."

"No, it's not about forgetting exactly. How can I? But the more I work, the less time to think about it, and when I don't think, I can't feel the pain."

"Reality is pain."

"I try to escape my thoughts. I try to keep busy so I don't feel how alone I am. And that's why I came here. I need help. I don't know how to move on from this, and I feel bad that perhaps I moved on from my mother too... easily. In spite of our relationship, she probably deserved more than what I gave her."

Elizabeth Ramsey nodded. The older woman leaned forward with her elbows on top of her knees and her hands together as if in prayer, searching for the right words.

"You did well to come to me and you ought to be proud of yourself for having done so. You will overcome these difficulties. Mourning consists of an array of emotions; some of them are straightforward while others make no sense whatsoever. Processing the death of your husband is also very different from that of your mother. He was your friend and your lover; she brought you into this world. It's different. I feel we must dig into each issue separately."

"It seems like such a mountain. I'm tired actually. The thought of digging into my soul is not an appealing one. But I understand it's necessary."

"That tiredness will lift as we proceed. As will the fear. Are you sleeping at all?"

"Off and on. I suppose I'm used to it. It's been that way since Norman became ill. I've learned to function."

"I'm never one to force medication upon my patients. For now, I don't know enough to determine if you need it. There are healthier ways like long walks or some other form of exercise. Meditation is a wonderful method of contemplation. If you need a prescription to sleep, however, you must tell me."

"I run when I have the time."

"Good," she said. "In that case, I would prescribe time."

It was a feeble joke but she was rewarded with a smile from Katherine. Doctor Ramsey returned it. They agreed to meet twice weekly in the beginning. It wasn't Doctor Ramsey's normal way of treatment, but as Katherine seemed to have no support system, the extra sessions would give her something to reach for.

Chapter VII
A Light Begins to Glow

The Wicked Mule was as thick with smoke as it was with people. Laughter and music co-existed in a tight battle for survival. A flyer on the door announced dart tournament night. Excited roars spilled from the loft, across the wrought-iron balustrade into the main room. Katherine weaved her way to the bar. As if it were meant to be, a patron settled his tab with Paul just as she approached. Smooth as Chantilly cream, she took his barstool. A group of five teens dressed in miniskirts and jean jackets decorated with music pins, and with enough earrings between them to supply a jeweller, sent her a collective dirty look.

"We've been waiting for that chair!" one of them said with menace.

Katherine levelled her gaze at the girl whom she thought to be no more than fifteen beneath the black eyeliner, hair spray, and atrocious teenage wardrobe.

"Prove it," she bit.

It earned her a once-over from the ringleader, who otherwise appeared to be the surveyor of the room. When the door opened, barely audible over the din but felt by a blast of cold air, they turned expectantly, hoping to see someone in particular judging from five disappointed sighs.

She turned away. Paul had moved to serve some others. She settled in, arms folded on top of the bar, and looked around with interest. It had been difficult to leave her cocoon. She was down. In therapy, Doctor Ramsey had discussed an exercise to get Katherine out of the house instead of the endless list of activities with which she kept the demons at bay. They had argued the point with Katherine questioning why she should go out when she had never been one to do so on her own.

"A change of scenery. Also, you don't know anybody here and never will unless you make an effort."

"I talk to people all day long!"

"Tell me, Katherine, where is the depth? Where is the range? Where is the laughter? Where are the friendships?" The questions painted a clear picture of Katherine's reality. "You have a clearly defined role to play in this community, in your job, but without any sort of emotional exchange, don't you?"

She breathed in the courage to keep the feeling of panic at bay long enough to order a drink. She focused on Paul, who pulled a glass of Pale Ale from the draft as he exchanged conversation with the person who'd ordered it. Rolled-up shirtsleeves revealed a pair of strong forearms. The comfort with which he moved about the bar, though with a small grimace at times, was something that would take some time for her to achieve. He seemed as much a part of the bar as the pub and its patrons seemed a part of him. If the people of Blackwell-on-Sea formed a quilt, she wondered, would Paul be the square in the centre?

Katherine sighed, pushing her hair away from her face. She hoped to at least have a chat with him if only for the sake of the exercise. After closing time and a can of tuna she'd shared with Raf by way of dinner, standing at the kitchen counter, she'd quickly changed into a pair of denim overalls and a crisp white long-sleeved tee-shirt, brushed her hair and teeth, applied some eye shadow, and run out the door before she could change her mind.

Perched atop the barstool, she allowed The Wicked Mule to embrace her. She had but to observe the place to understand why this was deemed the pub to be on a Saturday night. From the balcony came a loud "1... 2... 3," followed by another roar. Couples shared intimate conversation and the occasional snog on the sofas by the fire. A few tables were deeply engaged in card games. *Smoke on the Water* with Deep Purple's heavy guitars curled its way around the room. Many a head bobbed up and down with the music, but conversation never wavered. The girls next to her kept on about whomever they expected to see. She tried to tune out their giddy teenaged voices.

"Katherine!" Paul said knocking on the counter, yanking her out of her musings. "I'll be right with you."

He carried a full tray to a makeshift dumbwaiter and deposited the tray in it before ringing a small service bell. The mind-boggling contraption seemed quite primitive, but it served its purpose well. Paul pulled it up by a rope until it reached the balcony. A beautiful mane of long brown curly hair attached to Steve's head appeared over the balcony to receive it. He waved to Paul.

In the next instant, the group of teens beside Katherine caused a commotion. Steve's eyes flew from the tray to the teenagers. For no apparent reason whatsoever, Katherine and her barstool were brutally shoved aside. The inevitable way down to the floor was broken by something soft, an ample beer belly as it turned out. She apologized to the man as he helped Katherine to her feet and righted the stool.

"What do you think you're doing?" She turned to the girls with blazing eyes, but they barely acknowledged her anger, squealing and giggling as they did.

The angry voice of Paul demanded their attention. "Where are your parents?"

The pack's leader waved a vague hand towards the back of the pub.

"Join them or leave the pub! Now!" Paul demanded.

The teenagers scoffed, but the ample man who'd assisted Katherine loomed threateningly close, and they disappeared with regretful glances to the loft.

Katherine climbed back on her stool. An upwards glance was met by a pair of velvety chocolate eyes wrapped in a veil of concern. Having no idea what happened, she shrugged her shoulders and threw Steve a reassuring smile.

Those whose attention had been drawn to the commotion, returned to their respective activities. Paul gathered the posse's glassware and rapidly applied a damp cloth to the gleaming wood of the bar, as if to wipe away the fact they had been there at all.

"Bloody teenagers." He winked and asked if she was okay.

"I'm fine. I'll be even better when I have a drink," she said and meant it.

"What will it be then, beautiful?" he asked.

Steve popped up beside her. "Are you all right?"

"My drop was cushioned," she replied, pointing a thumb over her shoulder. "I'd love a cognac, please Paul."

"Put that on my tab, will you?" Steve said.

Katherine started to protest but Paul interrupted. "Let him. He owes you," he said.

"Nonsense!" she said. "I owe you for installing the stereo."

Steve shook his head. "Give her the kind you keep in the back for Gus," he said to Paul.

"As if I could waste an opportunity to put a dent in your wallet." Paul grinned mysteriously.

Steve discretely showed his middle finger. Katherine smiled, intrigued by the easy interaction between the two men.

"I don't see your drink. Do you want another ale?"

"I left it upstairs, so yeah. I'm sure it won't be orphaned long."

Before Paul could disappear through a door in the corner to what Katherine assumed was a kitchen, the chocolate eyes focused on her. He smiled and held out his hand.

"Hello, Steve." Katherine shook it. "At last I get to say thanks for the flowers! That was very thoughtful."

"Don't mention it. It's good to see you! You don't come here very often, do you?"

"No. It's quite a hopping place though, isn't it?"

Steve looked around before answering. The smile on his lips reflected in his eyes which, up close, were the colour of smoothly molten chocolate somewhere between milk and dark, maybe with a dash of butter to add the sheen. He wore black jeans and a black tee-shirt with a football on the chest. Loose from the plait she'd seen before, his hair covered the small sideburns and reached halfway down his back. He was attractive enough unkempt, but without the plait and recently shaved, he was positively handsome.

He turned attention back to Katherine and nodded. "You always leave here feeling good at the end of the night. But it's got nothing to do with drinking. Mostly."

Just at that moment, Led Zeppelin's "Immigrant Song" sounded through the speakers.

"Case in point." He smiled. "In other places, one relies on the jukebox and the taste of someone with a coin in their pocket. At The Wicked Mule, we're forced to listen to what Paul likes and thankfully he's got excellent taste."

"Excellent taste in what?" Paul, coming in on the tail-end of the conversation, deposited Steve's beer on a cardboard coaster. "Beautiful women?"

"Definitely," Steve said, throwing Katherine a telling wink that sent a warm blush to her otherwise pale cheeks.

"Something you could take a lesson from," Paul snorted.

"I was making a reference to your taste in music, actually."

With the utmost care, Paul set a wooden device down on the bar and said, "You lot are fortunate I don't subject you to German *Schlagers* night after bloody night," adding, "here's some lovely fifty-year-old cognac for you, gorgeous."

The snifter was cradled in a beautiful holder carved like a pair of hands, allowing it to hover sideways over a tea light. Paul demonstrated turning the glass over and over by the stem for the heat to release the smoothness of the cognac evenly. He poured the cognac in the snifter and ceremoniously lit a tea light. Katherine became warm inside just thinking about the golden liquid, smooth as caramel.

"That's gorgeous! I've never seen anything like it before," she said, admiring the roughly carved fingers. She brushed her fingertips lightly over the incredible detail.

"You wouldn't have. There's only twelve of them and they were a gift from Gus up at the castle," he said, putting the cork back in the bottle. "How is business?"

Steve took a draught from his pint and regarded her with interest.

"Busy. More so than I thought it would be," Katherine said.

"Let's hope it stays that way. Has your mum been, Steve?"

"I don't know. Dad said Uncle Benny complained about something my cousin commissioned for a wedding. He said the chocolate had left a bitter taste in his mouth."

He and Paul laughed, seemingly an inside joke about Uncle Benny. Katherine smiled but didn't really know what to say. Now that she was here, she wasn't in the mood to talk about work. She turned her glass over and over in the cradle until she thought it had been heating long enough. She blew out the flame, lifted the snifter from its cradle, and took a blissful sip. The amber liquid flowed smoothly down her exophages to the pit of her stomach and didn't stop until it reached her legs.

"Mm-mm," she moaned. "Wow."

"Nice?" Steve asked, as Paul's attention was needed elsewhere.

"Good God! That's the best cognac I've ever had. It will knock me on my bum, I think."

Steve's name was called from the balcony. He waved at a well-endowed woman in her fifties and turned to Katherine.

"That's my Aunt Rebecca. It's my turn to play darts. Are you here alone? Would you like to come upstairs with me?" He shook his head, grinning. "That didn't come out quite the way I meant it."

"I've got good company," Katherine retorted, indicating the cognac.

"Would you mind if I return?" he asked.

She shook her head. "Of course not, but don't mind me. I don't mind being alone."

Steve registered the array of emotions as Katherine scratched at something invisible on her jeans. Assertion and vulnerability seemed to battle it out behind the cornflower-blue eyes. He wanted to put his finger on what it was that he found so utterly irresistible about her and decided he would rather spend time to find out than to play darts.

"Give me two minutes. Don't let Paul take my beer."

As soon as Steve made for the spiral staircase, Paul wiped the bar down again, first with a damp cloth and then a dry one. The Wicked Mule must be the cleanest pub in England, Katherine thought. He reached for Steve's glass, but she stopped him with a motion of her hand.

"How's the cognac?" Paul asked, leaving it.

"Lovely. Is it always this busy on Saturdays?"

"Sure. Snooker and darts tournaments alternate and Bunco night is on the last Wednesday of the month. Ladies only."

"How on earth did you come up with Bunco?"

"My mother started it back in the day. The club consists of around fifty women who like to nip at my sherry and my port while they roll the dice. You should hear the things they talk about! It's bloody hilarious, and they flirt when they've had too much. Stop by sometime. Since you're a lady I'd be allowed to let you in."

She shook her head. "I doubt I'd blend. I'm a bit of a loner, really."

"So is Steve and I assure you he blends quite well. Give The Mule a chance to entertain you. Let me show you something," and he limped away pointing to someone at the end of the bar to indicate he'd heard their call for a Guinness.

Katherine looked on as he slowly lowered the volume on the stereo, paused the tape, and quickly pushed play on a second tape deck, re-adjusting the volume higher than it had been before. With the first riffs of heavy guitars, a collective roar blazed through the crowded pub. In the next moment a great number of people broke into a spontaneous sing-along. Katherine drew an amused eyebrow as Paul filled the drink order. He grinned in her direction.

"Why aren't you singing?" he asked over the noise, making change at the register.

The music was of the heavy metal sort that was so popular these days. Though she could probably admit to having heard this song before, the only thing on the radio she could tolerate was U2. The types of music she really loved would never be caught in the Top of the Pops and come to think of it, neither would this, probably

"Observe," he said when she shrugged.

He turned the volume almost all the way down for the chorus, and the crowd carried on confidently. Katherine laughed. Her mood lifted solely by being witness to the spectacle. When the song came to an end, Paul quickly switched back to the other tape.

"Was that the pub's official song?" she asked.

"There are others. You didn't know it at all?"

"No, not at all my cup of tea."

"What is your cup of tea?"

Katherine looked away. "You've been to my shop. I like classical and some other things. Steve seems more the sort of person who likes this kind of noise."

"Are you stereotyping?"

She laughed. "Yes, I think I am. He seems like a bit of a metal head."

"Steve is definitely first and foremost a head banger. And my best friend, a good chap."

"He seems nice. What does he do?"

With that, Paul confirmed that Katherine really hadn't the foggiest idea that she'd been chatting with the one and only composer of the song he'd just played. He never talked about Steve with strangers and hardly with people who weren't. It wasn't his place.

"He's a teacher, English and music." Paul smiled, content not to have to lie. "Here he comes now."

"Hi." Steve smiled, taking a stool and wedging it in between her and the next one.

She moved hers aside a little. "How did you do?"

"I lost."

"You lost?" Paul threw Steve a suspicious look.

"I did!" He raised the beer to his lips with a conspiring wink at Paul. "It's about time for your tea, is it not?"

Paul consulted his watch. He nodded. "Give me ten minutes," he said and moved to ring the big cow bell that hung from the loft. Several people immediately gathered around the till.

"What's he doing?" Katherine asked.

"Telling everybody he's about to take a break to eat. He's giving them a chance to order another or to settle their tab in case they want to leave in the next thirty to forty-five minutes."

"Interesting. You know I was sort of wondering about something earlier."

"What's that?"

"If the people in this village were a patchwork quilt, would Paul be the centre square?"

Steve laughed. "That's a brilliant metaphor," he said, "but not quite accurate."

"Who would it be then?"

"Gus."

"The man at the castle?"

"Yes, definitely, but you're right; Paul would be the next square, even before the vicar."

"Why?"

"The Wicked Mule may be Blackwell's beating heart, but the castle is its lungs. And the church is probably less frequented nowadays. Confessionalism, it seems, is held only in the church pews or in front of a pint, not both."

"That seems to be on par with my one and only encounter with the vicar," she said. "The first night I moved into my place he rang the doorbell to invite me to church and short of that, to The Mule for a beer and a chat."

Steve smiled. "Exactly. He's all right, the vicar, but the political and economic circumstances in England and in Europe as a whole tend to drive Paul's revenue up and that of the church down. Quite the battle for a man of the cloth."

Katherine refrained from letting sarcasm get the better of her. She too found more solace at the pub and in her drink than she could ever find in a church. But a more intriguing question burned in her mind.

"Where would you be in the quilt that is Blackwell-on-Sea?" she wanted to know.

"Me?" Steve smiled, amused. "Probably in the spot that is the least conspicuous."

"Really?"

"Yeah. Inconspicuous but accessible."

"How can you not stand out with a mane of hair like yours?"

"The hair used to be quite scandalous, but I'm relieved to say the town has moved on to other things to talk about."

"I'll wager it makes many women as jealous as can be."

"Bloody hell, I hadn't heard that one before," he said sarcastically.

"Don't think it's not true!"

"Would you two like to join me?" Paul dropped a concierge bell on the bar along with a sign that said *Ring bell for noise*.

Fascinated, she finished her cognac and followed Steve through the door in the corner. Behind it was indeed a kitchen, quite recently updated. Three of the walls were fitted with beautifully made white cabinets. There were two dishwashers, a washing machine, and a dryer. Along tall shelves that were meant to hold a dinner service, were a surprising number of apothecary jars neatly labelled with the name of the dried herb content. Behind the divided pane-glass doors of a cabinet stood a collection of interesting art-deco Japanese teapots and matching cups. Another held the white bowls and plates that Paul used for pub nosh. A half-full pot of creamy tomato soup was being kept warm on the Aga cooker. The aroma sent a hungry rumble through Katherine's stomach.

A woman in her thirties with shoulder-length black hair pulled precariously into a ponytail busied herself washing an endless stream of glasses while a dishwasher stood open, holding the rest of the washing up. Katherine had never seen her before. She worked rather efficiently, and there was just enough time to take note of the ugly yellowing bruise around her eye and on her cheek before she hastily released her hair from the elastic, in an attempt to cover her face.

"Your sandwiches are in the fridge," the woman said quietly and without making eye contact.

"Thanks, Susan. Will you keep an eye out?"

"No problem," she said. "Did you put the bell out there?"

"Yes."

"Hiya, Susan," Steve said. "How is Lettie?"

"Fine, Steve, thanks."

"Doing well in school?"

"Some things don't change, thankfully."

"Star pupil. Give her my regards, will you?"

She nodded, never wavering from her work. "She'll be sorry she missed seeing you."

Steve followed Paul and the tray of tea things out the back door, seemingly oblivious. Katherine needed to keep from asking about the bruise, not wanting to believe that Paul had delivered it. She said hello and continued on, hoping she hadn't stared. Another surprise awaited outside. The right-hand side of the narrow courtyard, with a gate to the town square, was littered with kegs and crates and kept in the dark. The left-hand side was like a small outdoor den complete with colourful lights, comfortable garden chairs, and a small fireplace! Enclosed by brick walls on three sides, a corrugated metal roof kept it dry.

"This place is full of surprises, Paul," Katherine said.

"Welcome to my office. Have a seat." He motioned to one of the chairs and lit a cigarette.

"Before I do, I'd like to ask a question."

"About Susan?" His retort came quickly.

"That's not your anger expressed onto her face, surely," she said.

Paul stiffened visibly. Steve, who'd taken the chair furthest from the fire, leaving the one in the middle vacant, scoffed. Katherine lifted a challenging eyebrow in his direction.

"I'm sorry." Steve held up his hands as if to shield himself, "It's just that you don't beat about the bush, do you?"

Paul calmly proceeded to pour tea from the pot. There were bits floating around in the liquid, but the aroma was strong and fragrant. The tray was balanced precariously on two small towers of upside-down yellow crates. A proper coffee table, its glass busted, sat on its side against the far wall, out of the way.

"Did you happen to see the man at the corner of the bar as you walked in?" Paul asked, selecting a sandwich from the stack. Steve followed suit.

"No."

"That's Harry. He's always there, which makes him invisible. He is Susan's husband. He beats her. We all know this, and we don't do anything about it because she won't leave him anyway. It's not my business except that part of her wages cover my expenses for his alcoholic tendencies." He went to take a big bite out of his sandwich, changed his mind, and said, "At cost, mind you. Have a seat."

Katherine quickly let her eyes take in Paul's profile as the flames from the fire danced across his face. He was quite handsome and his eyes, as he stared back at her, stood honest. Even in the semi-dark they were as icy-blue as the sky on a winter day.

"Do you honestly think I could have done that?" Paul asked incredulously, his mouth full and handing her a cuppa.

"God, I hoped not," she said. "I was just starting to like you."

"Just?"

Steve laughed again. "Are you always that forward?"

Katherine shrugged her shoulders and sat down gingerly on the rickety chair between the two men. "I don't fancy injustice. What sort of tea is this?"

"It's medicinal. My leg hurts. It takes the edge off."

"It smells vaguely familiar," she said and took a sip. It was hot and strong and sweetened with honey.

"Help yourself to a sandwich."

Katherine did. If the tea and sandwiches were delicious and nourishing, listening to Steve and Paul talk amiably about this and that fed her soul. Beneath a wad of colourful Christmas lights, these two strange men let her into their circle and succeeded in making her laugh.

***

PAUL WORKED HIS way through the meal, keeping a close eye on his companions. He had a growing feeling of anticipation each time he saw them look at one another in conversation. There wasn't anything other than polite, amiable discussion among them, but even as they carefully avoided the subject of anything too personal, it was comfortable to have Katherine share the space where he and his best friend invited few others. He couldn't be certain about Steve until they talked it over, but for Paul it felt as if he'd known Katherine a hundred years already. Something that was further confirmed when she produced two envelopes from the huge satchel she called a purse.

"What's this?" Steve asked.

"I sent thank-you cards to everybody but thought it more appropriate to hand yours in person because you were such a great help to me." She poured more tea into each of their cups.

Both men ripped open the envelopes with equal carelessness. Paul read his card, and while he laughed out loud at the pun on the models who had eagerly shared his bed that night, his heart did a small tumble when he read the poem Katherine had put down for him. Without a moment's hesitation, Steve and Paul exchanged their cards. Steve laughed a little too, but more than anything was taken with the lyric as well. They exchanged glances.

"Did you tell her?" Paul asked.

Katherine frowned. "Tell me what?"

Steve shook his head and regarded Katherine with even more curiosity. "Did you have to look that up? The poem?"

"Not at all. I know it by heart. I thought it was appropriate to my intentions. Why do you ask?"

The men grinned at one another.

"*The Lord of the Rings* is our favourite book. We've shared the same copy, which we bought together, for what..." Paul looked to his friend.

"Twenty years, I think."

"Really?"

"Yeah." Steve smiled.

"I read it every year or so."

"So do we."

"That's a terrific coincidence," Katherine said. "Don't you think?"

Their mutual smiles had turned to appreciative laughter, and Paul thought about the moment long after he arrived home, going through a nightly ritual of resting the painful stump in a hot bath and drinking more medicinal tea. He thought back to the first time Katherine had entered the pub. His world had tipped on its axis for the briefest of moments. Through experience, he had learned fate was something to be trailed and that, if one but cared to look, there were signs pointing in its direction.

Being halfway accused of beating a woman had shocked him and could only have been made by someone who had little experience of his character. Anyone else he would have turned out on their ear, but mysteriously, the memory of that first clash of his and Katherine's eyes had touched Paul like the prick of a needle. It had diffused his retort in such a way that he immediately trusted she was meant to be part of his life.

After the accident, he'd been consumed with so much anger that he was unable to express, that Doctor Ramsey had pursued him to keep a diary. She'd gone as far as gifting him one: a beautiful leather-tooled cover that held a brand-new notebook. He'd touched the relief of the beautiful images that had been hand-tooled, knowing without doubt that it was the work of Gus. Bizarre as the man was, he was a true artist and advocate in keeping the trades of the Middle Ages alive. Eventually, the blank lined pages had enticed him to write with a fancy silver pen, because to touch the pages with something as cheap as a biro wasn't good enough to complement the old man's craftsmanship.

He'd been doing it for nine years now. It took soul-searching to discover that he enjoyed committing thoughts to paper, and it took writing about his experiences to fulfil soul-searching. He could have reused that first cover and bought refill notebooks, but he still commissioned a new one every year. The diaries held his innermost thoughts. They held his triumphs, anger and disappointment like a cup, a sacred vessel… the things not even Steve knew about.

Paul's only entry that night was a very casual observation about the future.

Chapter VIII

Father

Katherine borrowed Ned's van for a trip to London to buy supplies for the shop and to Wandsworth where she removed several boxes from Aunt Celeste's storage shed, the last of the lot. With a stroke of good luck, she was saved from the usually awkward but mandatory luncheon with her aunt because Celeste happened to be absent, but no sooner had she arrived home than she realized there was simply no room to store everything. Spatial and emotional necessity on a collision course, it was time to go through it all and toss what could be tossed.

She'd discussed the difficulty of this task with Doctor Ramsey. It was an opportunity for cleansing, she was aware of that. But without remembering what was in the boxes, there was a distinct fear there might be things she wasn't ready to see. She went as far as to consider burning the lot or perhaps stuffing it in a rubbish container far away from the village. But it would be impossible not to wonder about it or question what she had done, which meant there was nothing for it. The job needed doing, and to ensure she was thoroughly annoyed by the mess, she precariously dumped the cardboard boxes in the middle of the sitting room and went upstairs to practice the guitar.

Following a fairly good day of business and a cup of instant soup over the kitchen sink while Rafael ate his tuna supper by her feet, Katherine deposited herself on the floor near a crackling fire and pulled the first box close. Rafael was most eager to help. His eyes were big and round with naughty curiosity. He was a terror in his need for attention. As soon as she sliced through the tape, he grabbed Katherine's hand and brought it to his nose for a whiff.

"You are a true Riff-Raff, aren't you? Steve is right, you know. Ouch! Stop it!" She mock fussed, unable to contain her mirth. "How can this possibly be of interest to a cat? Does it smell funny?"

Raf's tail twitched back and forth as if he were insulted by being called a name. They swatted at each other for a moment until she patted his tiny head and shooed him away. She opened the flaps of the first box, and then another and another. There were some old jeans and boots, and terribly cheap knickknacks gifted to them over the years by neighbours or friends. It wasn't difficult to take distance.

Box after box was quickly put aside, marked either "destroy" or "charity." Much harder was a small metal box filled to the brim with guitar picks, and a box of string. Norman was a good teacher and she had been an eager student. Every day for six years, they had played together. Eying the colourful picks, her nostrils burned with tears. She rooted through them and found a wrinkled and frayed piece of paper. Discovering it was something she had written to Norman years ago, her heart made a flip:

Just gone to the bakery. I'll want more of last night in return for nourishment. K

"Damn."

Katherine tried to breathe to keep tears at bay but quickly abandoned the idea and reached for the box of tissues she'd had the foresight of having nearby. It was a long-ago memory. Just after they were married, they'd ridden their bicycles to a nearby farm to pick strawberries and brought home kilos of them in their bicycle baskets. They'd had the most intense conversation after their outing as he attempted to make a strawberry tart while she fixed the plumbing in the bathroom.

They'd been equally frustrated with their projects and Norman had taken the wrench from her hand, peeled off her clothes, lifted her onto the kitchen table, and used the berries to make a paste with which he finger-painted her body. They had sprayed each other with the bottle of whipped cream intended for the tart. They had tasted sweetness on each other's skin, made love, and, for lack of anywhere to bathe, they'd showered in the pouring rain with a bar of soap. They'd made love, played guitar, made love again… a day-long and night-long embodiment of the spirited connection that existed between them. Why had he tucked the note among the picks, she wondered? Had he looked at it every time he needed a fresh supply? To remember?

"Damn it all!" Katherine shouted to the air. "*Damn you!*"

Resentment was never really in her nature but these days it had a habit of sticking its nasty head 'round the corner, and Katherine was terrified of what might be unleashed if she gave into it. Norman certainly wasn't there for a good fight. She kicked the box with an air of disgust and reached for the next one. Rafael, sensing her mood, jumped on his mistress's shoulder, and caressed his face against her cheek. The show of affection had an instant calming effect on Katherine.

"Hello, Raf," she said.

He purred in her ear. She dabbed her eyes and blew her nose loudly.

"Just two more of these and then we'll have a cup of tea by the fire as a reward. How about a book? Perhaps Jane Austen is just the author to chase the demons away tonight. I think *Northanger Abbey* might do... just the right balance of romance and drama. What do you think? Are we in agreement?"

The cat stepped with both front feet on a new box and stretched, resigned to the plan. Katherine cut it open and found thick reams of computer print. She frowned.

"What is this?" she said to herself. "Does this belong to us?"

They were stacks of what appeared to be financial records, year upon year. It was not something she had ever seen before. She shifted the heavy cardboard around and around, examining the handwriting on all sides. She couldn't say it was recognizable. *Deliver to Katherine.* The contents appeared dustier than any other so far.

She climbed onto her knees and heaved it on its side, and on its head. The paper plopped to the floor in a cloud of dust, causing her to sneeze four times in a row. She blew her nose, interested in a note card lying on top, or rather, stuck to the bottom of the paper. She peeled it away, sinking back to the floor. The front of the card was a lithograph depiction of a village square... *Blackwell?* She opened the card. Firm handwriting, as if what was written had been emotionally heavy at the time, it read:

Have you considered the consequences of your actions? It was signed R.W.

Katherine's heart very suddenly raced! She dropped the card like it was a hot potato. Reaching for the bottom page of the paper stack, she turned it over and read the last amount that was there. Seventy-thou—

"What?" she breathed.

This couldn't possibly be her mother's. Only Aunt Celeste had gathered that kind of wealth from her many beaus and late husband.

Surely! Why would someone have left this with Mum's things? Why was it to be delivered to Katherine specifically? Was it an accident? Or deliberate? Why was the card stuck to the bottom, and who was the author? And what about the cryptic message? Rafael's curiosity got the better of him, and with a feral sound he hopped into the empty box. Puzzled but intrigued, Katherine wrote *investigate* on its side. There was a time that she might have obsessed about it, but not now. She could cope with an assault on her emotions only so long.

The next box was one of the heavier ones, and she scooted closer to it on her knees instead of moving it. She sliced open the top with her Stanley knife and hid the blade to keep it from the kitten. This time a true surprise awaited her. It contained some of Norman and Katherine's significant Blues record collection, which he'd told her he had sold for a fairly decent amount of money. They'd arrived by mail to Aunt Celeste's address. Her heart made an involuntary tumble in her chest, and the beginnings of a smile curled around her lips.

"Rafael," she said, "I think it's time for our tea."

***

STEVE CURSED HIS answering machine for the umpteenth time. In the first weeks after breaking up with her in Amsterdam, where she had joined him with her usual seductive ways void of tenderness, Anne had been unusually silent. He had told her it was over and that in his heart and mind it had been for months. The obscenities she'd screamed only worked as an affirmation. She would not see they were not right for each other and the relationship was nothing but destructive. They fought stridently. He'd tried to convey they both deserved more than what they were to each other. She had cried and tried to seduce him. It did nothing to his concrete heart. He'd been more than ready for his story to continue without her. He didn't mean to be cold, but it was over.

The calls had started some weeks later and, since a week or so, had become incessant. It drove him insane. The messages on the answering tape were never more than a bid, plea, or curse to ring her, to come back and get back together. Today it was dejection and crying pleas. He listened to it with hands braced against the kitchen counter as if to brace himself against the onslaught. Before the message could reach the end, the telephone rang again, and the next plea came.

"Shut up, shut up!" He raised his voice to it, as if expecting it to reply.

Steve pushed the eject button, yanked the cassette from the machine, and with the force of anger, tore the ribbon from it and aimed it for the rubbish bin in the kitchen, which he missed entirely. It landed on the floor with a soft clatter, and he paced the empty living room to walk it off. When that didn't work, he reached for one of the guitars lined up on stands near the picture window and peered out to the pouring rain. After a few moments, he felt calm enough to play a tune.

Guitars were sacred in his life. Music had been his greatest love so far, the deepest and the most passionate. He longed to feel that same passion for a girl. A deep yearning had taken hold inside lately, to love and to be loved in return. In the latter part of his twenties, he longed to find the mother of his future children. He had sensed since long before the breakup with Anne that she was just beyond his reach.

The phone rang again, and in a fit of rage, he answered it.

"Leave it be!" he said angrily. "Why can't you see this is for the best?"

"Err... well, son, I can't be entirely sure, but I do see it's for the best you stop by this evening or your mother might serve my bollocks for supper, tossed in a cream of shame sauce. I should have called you two days ago but it slipped my mind. Someone will be here, though for the life of me don't ask who."

Steve snickered, his anger diffused. "Yeah, okay Dad, as long as we're not having bollocks, especially yours."

"Really? Feels like you've been nipping at them for years!"

Steve tried not to let the old man through the thick skin he'd been growing since he was a teenager.

"Is something the matter?" His father tried to sound casual. He wanted information, so he kept himself from pushing Steve's defiant buttons.

"I broke up with Anne a few weeks ago."

"You don't say. It's about time."

"Yeah, I know."

"You do?"

Steve ignored the chafe. "She's been bothering me increasingly, so don't be surprised for her to try 'round yours. If you do answer the phone when she does, tell her I won't change my mind if hell freezes over. I don't want you to have to be involved, but her behaviour is becoming erratic. I'd rather you be forewarned."

"Sure. I'll tell Mum and David."

"How is my brother?"

"He's got a game tomorrow night. In Brighton. Do you want to come?"

"I've got to work, but if I'm at a stand-still, swing by to pick me up. I'll let you know."

"If what it is you do is work, fine. Mum has a late patient this evening so come 'round about seven-thirty for drinks."

Steve scoffed and dropped the receiver on the countertop. Remembering his thoughts before his father's call, he shook his head. The old man would never believe he was capable of having such a need. The need for a family. He took up the guitar and lifted the strap over his head, taking care his hair wasn't tangled.

He walked around the empty room, strumming it with gentle fingers until he heard himself play the first notes of *Stairway to Heaven*. He stopped, hand resting on the strings to keep the sound from hollowly reverberating through the bare space. Thinking a large area rug was needed for the acoustics, he tried to remember where he'd last heard a Led Zeppelin song. Sending his thoughts on a journey through the last week, he arrived at dart night. *The Wicked Mule*. Of course.

"Immigrant Song," he said aloud.

His fingers found the strings again. He resumed *Stairway to Heaven*, picking up from the exact note where he'd left off earlier. It was one of the first songs he'd ever learned, and he could play it back to front. Steve smiled. The band Steve worked with had a long way to grow musically and a lot to prove before they would ever reach the cornerstone of musical history that Led Zeppelin was to heavy metal.

"The Wicked Mule," he said aloud, continuing to play thinking of the mysterious girl. "Eyes the colour of cornflowers."

The telephone book lay forlorn on top of the stereo where he'd looked up a number to get the needle on the turntable replaced. Abruptly, he picked it up, turned it to the second page, and got the number to the telephone company. Anne, he knew, would be in Japan for a job in the next few months. Without another thought, he had his number changed.

***

"TELL ME ABOUT your father."

"I was around eleven years old, I think, when I broached the subject," Katherine said. She was tired and tempted to lie down on the white leather sofa; only the fear that she might fall asleep kept her from relenting. "We were learning about anatomy at school."

"Anatomy?" Doctor Ramsey asked, smiling.

Katherine had come home from school, dripping with rain, to find her mother in one of her better moods. It was perhaps one of the most interesting events that had transpired between them, to begin with the good mood which for her mother, who spent most of her days brooding in faraway thought, was rare.

"Hiya, Mummy!"

"There you are, dear."

"Is there tea?"

"Of course there is, child. Take off your jacket and wash up," her mother said as she finished sewing a button to a housecoat for Mrs. Barker down the street.

"I'm famished," Katherine announced.

"Hang it up nicely, Katherine. It'll never be dry by morning otherwise."

"What's the point? It will only rain again," she retorted even as she did as she was told.

"Mould is the point, sweetheart. Fabric must be cared for as you well know. What did you have for lunch, then?"

"Disgusting grub! It's Wednesday, Mum, that stuff *they* call fish and chips. Ugh!"

"Oh. Do you want a sandwich and some crisps?"

"Yes, please! With loads of ham."

"We don't have loads of ham, but we do have some."

Katherine felt bad immediately, knowing they were short of money until her mum was paid for the job she was working on now. She hadn't been able to sew much for a few days. Her knuckles were swollen and painful.

"Sorry, I'm so hungry. I just can't stand the vast amounts of grease, Mum. I didn't eat it."

"I understand, Katherine. There is no need for you to apologize."

Katherine's eyebrows involuntarily shot up to her brow, a questioning look bouncing off her mother's back as she prepared the tea. No reprimand for not eating the school food which had cost money? Wisely, she kept her mouth shut, instead digging up a book that she would need for homework.

"How was school, then?"

She smiled. "Oh, it was quite interesting… and funny."

"Oh?"

"We learned about, you know… boys and girls and that." Katherine blushed and bent deeper over her rucksack to hide it. She found a biro she'd been looking for and reached for it, wiping off a bit of fuzz.

"What's so funny about that?"

"Well, Mrs. Terrence explained what happens to a boy when he becomes… aroused, I think was the word she used," she continued.

This time it was Katherine's mother whose eyebrows raised a fraction or two. She set the sandwich down on the kitchen table. Katherine attacked it with the gusto of a growing kid.

"I can imagine it was cause for much hilarity," she stated, reaching for the crisps. She counted ten on Katherine's plate and closed the bag with a clothespin.

"Susie asked Mrs. Terrence about what happened when the boy wore trousers. I've never laughed so hard in all of my life." She giggled into her next bite.

Tessa suppressed a smile in a sip from her cup. She poured some tea for Katherine, unable to resist asking more.

"Why?"

"I don't know. It just strikes me as quite a funny situation."

"Indeed," she agreed. "What else did you learn?"

"How things work when you have sex, and what can happen if you're not careful." She tried to sound matter of fact about it, popping a crisp into her mouth. "Oh, and that we mustn't allow ourselves to be touched inappropriately."

"That's right. Don't forget it, ever. Eat your sandwich."

For a minute or so, Katherine chewed together the courage to address what had been on her mind ever since the class. She had become aware of how things might have happened to bring about her own mysterious birth. It was a possibility now to ask, and she was too curious not to.

"Is that what happened with you, Mum? Were you touched inappropriately?"

She met her mother's eyes with her little heart thumping against her ribcage. Her mother stared, cup frozen in mid-air. As she came to a decision, she sat up a little straighter. Perhaps she had anticipated the question.

"No."

"What happened?"

"That's not something I want to talk about. It happened. Details are not necessary."

"Did my father abandon us?"

Katherine, on the opposite side of the table, sensed that the window to her mother's good humour would shut in her face any moment now, likely before she had finished the rest of her tea. The subject was off-limits normally. But somehow, somewhere, driven by an invisible force of courage to push against her mother's boundaries, Katherine was amazed that she was only eleven and yet understood this.

"We abandoned one another."

"Was that before or after my birth?"

"What does it matter?"

"Did he love me?"

There was a pause, but her mother's eyes never left Katherine's. "Yes."

"But not enough," she stated without catching a breath.

Tessa refrained from responding and gathered the dishes to have something to do.

"Is he dead? My father?"

"How should I know?" Tessa said, but she'd hesitated just a fraction, and Katherine didn't so much notice as sense it from her mother.

"If he isn't, may I write to him?"

"Enough!"

For Katherine, even at this tender age, there was a door between courage and fear, and it was called anger. And she kicked it hard, that door. It flew open so hard, that it banged against the wall in her mind.

"Why?"

Tessa closed her eyes. Frustration, regret, and sadness fought for power in her facial expression. Suddenly, she seemed a great deal older.

"It's complicated," she said quietly.

"Does he have another family?" Katherine stuck her chin out, bracing herself for the possibility that he might have chosen other children over her.

"Katherine, your father was not able to be that for you. Let it be."

"I have rights," she said even though she had no precise idea what that meant.

"He had no right to you."

They stared at each other, tortured souls together in a kitchen, yet locked in separate spaces. Katherine felt something happen between them. She knew that she would never ask about her father again, but somehow didn't see it as defeat. It was much more an acceptance of fact.

"I shall do my homework now." She took her book.

"Good." Her mother's relief was apparent.

"In my room," she added stubbornly, knowing it was not usually allowed but having a great urge to be further defiant.

"Wear your warmest cardigan," Mum had said with her back turned and the tea towel crunched into a ball.

KATHERINE, WRAPPED IN the memory, stayed a moment longer in the company of her mother. Regarding her as an adult, longing to trace the lines of fatigue and pain in Tessa's face, indeed thinking the outcome of this conversation might have been different had it taken place now, Katherine tried to drink it all in.

"There is one thing that I sensed even then," she said.

"What's that?" Beth Ramsey asked quietly.

"I was stronger than her," Katherine blinked away a tear. It rolled down her cheek slowly, as if reluctant to be released. She made no move to help it along.

"Why?"

"We lost something important between us that day, I think." She paused. "Or rather, she lost something of mine."

Practically holding her breath, Doctor Ramsey opted out of encouraging Katherine. She was in a trance-like state, as if she weren't in the room at all.

"She lost the little girl in me. My innocence…. It might as well have been my virginity. It would never come back either."

Doctor Ramsey remained silent for a moment, letting Katherine think it through. It was an important realization for her, a great step forward.

"You disrespected your mother's decision to stop where she did."

Katherine calmly walked out of the memory and focused on the current time. She shifted in her seat and pushed against her eyes with the palms of her hands.

"I resented her for thinking that I wasn't ready. I was. Even now I know that I was. Nothing could have been worse than to think he didn't want me, and I had already thought that for years. Perhaps if I knew more, I might respect her for why she never told me."

"You said it was never mentioned again."

"No. It was the only two-sided conversation we had about my birth."

"Did you ever get the sense that she might have wanted to tell you more about your father, as she became more ill?"

"No. The subject was the divide between us. It was like a lead curtain that was shut in a very palpable way. It was always there, on the good days and the bad."

"You said you went to your room."

"I didn't cry." She smiled. "I remember distinctly not crying. I knew exactly what I had to say to him, and I wrote a letter. I asked the questions I felt the most… urgent about. The things my mother would never tell me."

"A letter you never had the chance to send."

Katherine's eyes sought Doctor Ramsey's. She blew her nose loudly. "The next morning my mother announced going away for the weekend. Perhaps it was hope or intuition on my behalf, I don't know, but I tucked the envelope in her bag when she was having a bath, something she only did on those occasions. I addressed it *To My Father* and tucked it between two layers of clothing."

"And you think she delivered it."

"She never mentioned it so I can't be sure."

"What does your gut tell you, Katherine?"

Katherine closed her eyes. Her eleven-year-old lacquer shoes waited to be stepped into. She regarded them, the sting in her heart as intense as the sting of a little girl's tears. She thought about crossroads and choices. She stepped into the shoes, one foot clad in a crisp white sock frilly with lace applique, and then the other. The little girl threw her cornflower-blue eyes at Beth Ramsey.

"She gave it to him."

Chapter IX

Bartending Hazards

The truth about bartending is in the relationship patrons have with their favourite pub and its proprietor. Life was certainly no different for The Wicked Mule's publican. Many considered him a friend, but from his side of the bar Paul felt more the heathen parish priest and the pub his wicked confessional. If someone had a heavy heart or good news to share, sooner or later, they would gravitate towards The Mule to talk about pregnancies without fathers, weddings without a bride or other life-changing events. Even the vicar was no exception! It was the opinion of many that Paul was the other psychiatrist in town.

The customer most often in Paul's confessional was Harry Luvack. He was what one might refer to as the town drunk. Unemployment was high in the UK and Harry was one of the self-proclaimed victims of the new Conservative leadership, a leadership that did not believe the state was responsible for the individual. Mrs. Thatcher ruled from the almighty Number 10 Downing Street with little regard for the proletarian. Everybody fought inflation one way or another.

Harry didn't agree with the new political direction and refused to participate. Instead he sat on the barstool closest to the front door of The Wicked Mule day after day for a minimum of seven hours, having increasingly senseless conversations with nobody in particular about how the aristocrats and the government had screwed him over. He saw everything wrong with society, blamed it for his being out of work, and saw no need to pull himself and his family out of a dire situation.

It was as infuriating as it was disgusting. He played the victim part so well that he'd become lost in it. Other places around town had stopped running a tab for him. As a result, Harry had demanded what little money Susan had or simply taken it from her purse. Harry was a mean drunk, but meaner when he wasn't. Susan had begged Paul not to cut him off, saying that she would work for it when Lettie could stay with the boys.

Paul saw Lettie at the bakery every day that it was open, six days a week except Mondays, accepting responsibility where her father wouldn't. She was a terrific kid whose childhood was being stolen —and violated, even if her father never laid a hand on any of his children. It was difficult to understand why Susan not only allowed the situation, but sought to accommodate it. Now that she was old enough to understand that, it was hard to believe Lettie kept out of the claws of anarchy growing up in that family.

Until a better option came along, he contented himself with keeping a watchful eye on how much the man had to drink rather than sending him home dry and angry. He safeguarded Susan, ensuring she had the means to feed the children either by giving her a little extra money for doing his laundry, or by sending them home with leftover soup that he felt she'd earned. For the rest, Paul wasn't sure what to do and could never shake the feeling that he contributed to Harry's demise.

Even publicans have to make a choice.

"How's it going today, Harry?"

Paul set the first pint of the day in front of him. Every morning as he did, Paul attempted to get through to him. Harry mumbled something under his stinking breath and set the beer to his lips for the first greedy gulp of the day. The man looked as dilapidated as an old bicycle tire. His hair was combed back, still wet from a splash of water in the face. It made Paul sad to see that his clothes were clean and ironed by a wife who still took pride in her husband, even if he'd lost it for himself.

"Same old, lad," he said when he set it back down.

"I saw your daughter at the bakery this morning."

"So what?" He took a stub of a cigarette out of his jacket pocket, one he'd likely found on the street on his way over, and indicated that he needed a light. Paul handed him a book of matches from the big bowl, but took it away again immediately.

"What's her name, your daughter?" he asked, testing him.

"Uhhh… bah… not sure which one's at the bakery, lad. Can't keep 'em apart anymore."

"How many do you have?"

"Four. Four mouths to feed with sixpence from the state, if you can believe that."

"You must be proud of her for helping out. It's probably not easy, what with school and helping Susan to take care of the little ones."

"Fucking waste of time, school. They should all go to work."

"How's your job hunt going, then?" Paul liked to push his buttons, almost cruelly so. He couldn't help himself.

"Don't even start with me, lad," he coughed.

"I can't keep supporting your habit, Harry. Sooner or later, you'll have to take care of your tab. Not today, mind you. But soon."

"Yeah, all right."

"You don't see your Lettie wasting away like you are, do you, Harry? Remember your daughter? You could learn a thing or two from her. You should be proud."

Paul wished silently for something to happen, anything, so that the man would pull himself together. But he feared it was too late. Harry's skin seemed grey and his eyes yellowish. Liver disease had taken hold of his body. He wished that whatever the outcome, it would be the best one possible for Susan and her children.

Paul shook his head and went to tend to another customer who wanted a cup of coffee. Harry went back to puffing on the stump of a cigarette and mumbling to himself.

"What's wrong with him?"

The blond-haired man at the other end of the bar was someone Paul had never seen before. He pointed at Harry. Sensing the man wanted company and conversation, Paul carried over the stool he kept behind the bar and sat down. He liked to talk to new people, to find out what they were about. This one had the air of a tourist about him.

"Every day of drinking is one too many for him now, I'm afraid. I just wondered how much longer before something claims him to the netherworld."

"He's a regular? He seems lost to himself." There was a heavy accent in the slowly spoken sentence. Paul thought it might be Dutch.

"I was just thinking that actually. You know the sort then?"

"Sure. I have a bar in Holland. No matter where you go in the world, there is one or two for each café. One goes, and another takes his place, like cockroaches."

Paul chuckled. He introduced himself and shook hands with the man who said his name was Rick, who was indeed a Dutchman.

"What brings you here?"

"I'm looking for someone. Just passing through on my way to Cornwall."

"Summer would have been a better time."

"I can get by closing my place just before the beginning of spring but I'm too busy in the summer. Otherwise, I work most of the time without a day off. When I'm not behind the bar, I play drums in a band. At least—I used to," he ended, with a note of regret.

A group of young head-bangers came in and chose a table by the window closest to the hearth. It wasn't too cold for the time of year, especially near the smouldering flames, but the youngsters kept their jackets on nonetheless. They had preened them with buttons and spikes as was so popular these days. One ordered three colas. Paul set to work quickly.

"One pound," he said to the young man.

"One pound. Here you go. Hey, do you know where Steve lives?"

"Steve who?" Paul asked, pretending oblivion.

"Denison. You know. We heard he's from around here."

"If I knew where he lived, I wouldn't tell you, would I? What do you want with him anyway?"

"Just to have his signature and a picture. Would he do it, you think? Does he come here?" The kid seemed much more polite than his sociological status might otherwise demand. He looked every bit the cool and tough part and had a Blackpool accent. Blackpool was a long way to find an autograph.

"Sure he would; he's a nice guy," Paul said grudgingly and thought to add a little lie to get them out of his hair and away from Steve's. "But he's on tour, you know."

"Fuck, we heard that was over by now."

"They are getting more popular by the day it seems."

"Fuck, mate. They're unreal! Thanks."

The kid left with drinks and more information than Paul had ever doled out first-hand before. Paul put the money in the cash drawer, shaking his head.

"Who is he talking about?" Rick asked.

"Just a local bloke," Paul said, wary because Rick had also mentioned he was looking for someone.

It was true that Steve was happy to meet with fans, but he considered Blackwell-on-Sea a sanctuary where batteries were recharged and where he found inspiration to write. This was not the road; it was home. At any opportunity Paul would protect his friend from the prying eyes of people who felt they owned a piece of Steve because they'd bought an album or a concert ticket. Even from youngsters who had driven several hours to get here.

"You said you were looking for someone? Do you need help?" Paul asked casually.

"Sure. I am looking for Katherine Loch. She has a shop around here somewhere. I thought I'd have a coffee and begin my search with the person who should know everything and everybody."

"Mon Chocolat is where you want to be," Paul said, curiously. "That's just down High Street about twelve or so shops, on the left-hand side." He pointed. "Beautiful place. I'm not a woman, but even I can see that."

"You've met Katherine?"

"You can't be a merchant in this small a town and not know one another. We're all part of the same guild. She stops by for a chat and a coffee sometimes." Paul smiled fondly. "How do you know her?"

"She's my best friend's wife."

Paul did a double take. There was always a sense of sadness behind that fabulous smile of hers, but with their friendship being in its beginning stages, he hadn't pried about personal things and nor had Katherine. He'd only noted the absence of a ring. This complicated things for the prediction he'd noted in his diary.

"She's married?" he asked incredulously.

"Depends how you look at it. He died some months ago."

"Shit!" Even worse.

"Cancer," Rick casually added, as if it were a logical conclusion to the demise of his friend.

"I'm shocked!" Paul looked away, remembering the moments Katherine gazed off into the distance, seemingly deep in thought, apparently going back to a time that only she knew about. Of course, he understood all about tragedy and having to get a grip on life in the wake of it… or not at all. He regarded Harry as he did so often. It could have been him on that barstool, in the midst of a life lost in pity and booze. He thanked his lucky stars to have had the strength and the support not to drown in the vortex of his own tragedy. He admired Katherine. It was clear to see what she had managed to accomplish in the last several months. He remembered how difficult it had been for her to accept help from anybody. They seemed to have a lot more in common than what first glance would allow.

"I'm very sorry to hear it," Paul said, heartfelt. "I'm sorry your friend has died and even more so for Katherine. Our community has really come to respect her."

"I'll drink to all of that," he said as he lifted his coffee cup in salute.

"Katherine is well. She works too hard, but we understand the shop is doing fairly well." Paul smiled reassuringly.

"She always was a hard worker, and good at everything she does. Except for cooking. Whatever you do, if she invites you to a meal, know there will be tears involved. Not necessarily hers."

Paul laughed.

"Norman didn't at all deserve her you know. It was always she to put food on the table. His dreams and ambitions always came before hers. I loved him as a brother, but he took that from her."

"What did he do?"

"He was an artist, a painter... refused to make his hands dirty with anything other than oil and turpentine. And we had a band, a Blues band. Do you have live music here?"

"Not often enough, I'm afraid."

Paul topped off Rick's nearly empty cup. He reached over to the tin of biscuits underneath the bar and dropped a few of them on a small plate. The three head-bangers left without as much as a by–your-leave.

"We have so many other events that it's difficult to schedule. You said you play the drums?"

"Yes, Norman played lead guitar. When he was too ill to do it, Katherine would replace him. It allowed us to fulfil what obligations we had."

Paul's jaw dropped. "*Katherine?*"

Rick lit a cigarette. Harry, down the bar, turned his head and looked at the cigarette with obvious longing, sniffing the air as if he were a dog in search of a bitch in heat.

"Is she any good?"

Rick laughed. He slid off the stool as he shook a few cigarettes out of the pack. He put them in front of Harry and offered the one he'd just lit. Harry snatched it out of his fingers and inhaled deeply by way of gratitude. Rick returned to finish his coffee.

"I suppose I should find Katherine. How much do I owe you?"

Paul waved. "It's on the house. You didn't answer my question."

"You'll need to find out for yourself one of these days." Rick smiled mysteriously.

"Do you still play? As a band, I mean?" Paul asked curiously.

"We would if we had a lead guitarist, my friend... but she's moved away."

Rick winked and pushed out of the pub with a friendly wave, leaving Paul to stare after him, mesmerized by the things he'd just learned.

***

KATHERINE WAS UPSTAIRS rooting for a needle to make an alteration when the sound of the front doorbell distracted her from it. She ran down the stairs energetically, ready to greet her customer with a smile. The sight of Rick stopped her in her tracks. It took but a moment before she threw herself into his embrace.

"Oh my God, I've missed you!" Katherine said.

"You look fantastic!" He held her at arm's length and took her in from head to toe. "Well no, you're too thin, and you look tired. But look at this place!"

Rick released Katherine to take in the boutique. She was genuinely happy to see him. They'd become friends talking and rehearsing together in the back room of Rick's café. Rick had lied to Norman about being supportive of "the plan." He had lied because it was more important to him that his friend die with peace of mind, but he'd spoken with Katherine privately about it, had begged her not to leave for the sake of the band. They were very hurt that she would leave them for a new life. The conversation had been awkward. Katherine had turned a deaf ear while quietly respecting Rick for giving Norman what he needed so desperately in the end.

"You really did it, didn't you?!" He took her in as she stood with her hands in the pockets of a short black skirt, leaning against her counter. She smiled a little.

"Did you not receive my invitation to the opening?" she asked, quietly folding her arms. "What did you expect? What else would I have done? Join Norman in the eternal flame?"

Rick ignored Katherine's cynicism. He didn't know anything about fashion but had always recognized that Katherine was an artist in her own right.

"I can't believe you've displayed the painting here. Does it shock people?"

He admired the floor-to-ceiling nude oil, the colours of which were a blend of blues, greys, and pale greens melding with the pale transparency of a woman's body.

"It's too abstract for anyone to recognize me," she laughed. "It really pops against the brown walls, don't you think?"

"I love it. Do you live here too?"

"Yes, upstairs." She smiled. "How are things with you?"

"Can't complain. We all miss you."

She nodded. "I miss you too. It's very quiet in the house," she said seriously, "not at all like it used to be. It was difficult at first, hearing the silence. It was... really loud."

"Did you get the guitar? And the records?"

"I did."

"Have you done anything with them?"

"No."

"Are we ever going to be a band again?"

"You are a band. Just find a new lead."

"We already have a lead. As far as we're concerned."

"When will you stop asking?"

"When will you give an acceptable answer?"

"You're still angry with me." She sighed, shaking her head. She moved behind the counter, in need of a barrier.

Rick took note and rolled his eyes defiantly. "For fuck's sake! What do you expect from us?"

"I can't help you," she said. "My life is here. This was our choice together."

"That isn't completely true. Norman never wanted you to quit the band. You know that. You made this choice. But we need the band, Katherine. The silence engulfs us too."

The door opened again. Katherine turned. She found her distracted and agitated half-smile caught by a pair of eyes she wasn't at all expecting to see. The immediacy with which her senses sharpened, sending messages to parts of her body that had been in a state of involuntary hibernation was an even further surprise. Steve.

And he very tenderly carried an elderly lady with an impeccable hairdo and a face full of wrinkles on his arm.

"Steve, hi!" she said nervously.

"Hi, Katherine."

She turned to Rick. "Listen, we'll have to finish this conversation some other time. Do you want to meet me for dinner tonight?"

Rick stared at Steve before he replied. "I haven't got time to hang around. I'm on holiday. I just wanted to see you for a few minutes on my way through."

Katherine couldn't be anything but relieved. "It was sweet of you to stop by."

"Think about what I've said. Please."

"There isn't anything to think about. The answer is no," she said firmly.

"Katherine…"

"I've got customers."

Rick kissed her on the cheek and left a cassette tape by the register.

***

PAUL FOUND RICK from Holland back in the pub a few hours later, this time in search of a lager. He came in with the after-work crowd for whom The Wicked Mule was a daily routine they wouldn't live without, expert at getting an allotment of pints down in minimum of time, knowing they needed to be home for dinner and whatever mundane evening routine was expected of them. Paul enjoyed this time of day, listening to office and factory stories. Being busy, he was unable to chat for some time. But when everybody seemed to have been served to satisfaction, he made himself an espresso and put a new tape in the deck, a compilation of late 60s and early 70s rock 'n' roll.

"How do you like Blackwell-on-Sea?"

"Very nice. We have similar towns, you know, tourist traps. I enjoyed the castle. It's quite magnificent."

"It is; we're very proud of it. How was Katherine?" Paul asked.

He grabbed the barstool and carried it to the end of the bar where he could have a conversation without losing his vantage point. His leg bothered him, and he stretched it out to take the pressure off. People knew him well enough to leave him be when he took a moment to sit down.

"We had a brief chat. I'm proud of her. She appears to be okay on the surface. I'm just not sure if she's really okay."

"It probably helps to be busy."

"Does it?" Rick countered, lighting a cigarette. "I suppose you're right. Steve Denison was there."

He folded his hands before him on the bar, pensive and worried, cigarette dangling between his lips. Paul noticed the deep grooves in the man's forehead.

"At the boutique?"

"Yeah. He had an elderly lady with him. That was nice, what you did for him earlier," Rick said. "Keeping those kids away."

"We're all a bit protective."

"I couldn't help but notice a... tension between them."

"His Gran? Temporary, I'm sure. He's her favourite of all the grandchildren. She probably bullied him into taking her there."

"Don't bullshit me. You're skirting the subject." Rick smiled. "He and Katherine."

Paul drew an inquisitive eyebrow, getting an inkling of why he might have come back to The Wicked Mule. The protective shield was in place again immediately, and this time it included Katherine.

"I haven't heard of a person in this village who doesn't like Katherine, my friend," Paul countered.

"It's not my place to judge Steve Denison, but you do know him and you also know her a little bit, though I suspect you've a lot yet to see. So here we have our individual friends whom we've known for a number of years, your friend being the rocker and mine being the vulnerable widow. She hasn't got anybody to protect her from his world."

Paul pursed his lips. He had been thinking about this. "I know there is a lot about Katherine we have yet to discover. She's proved quite the intrigue. But if there is one thing she doesn't hide, it's her values. I've known Steve for nearly twenty-nine years. We grew up together, literally. I've never met anybody so perfect for him."

"That's what I was afraid of." Rick nodded and had a long drink from his glass.

"Why?"

Paul took a few quid from a customer who'd walked up to the bar and put his empty glass down. Having made the change, he marked the name off the book where he kept track of tabs. "See you later, man. Give my best to the Mrs."

"Norman and I had long conversations before he died, you know, when he was well enough to hold a thought together. He knew the treatment was futile but he gave it a shot because of her. She was his muse from the first moment, I think, but during the illness she became more like the ray of light that he knew he'd never be able to grasp. He painted furiously, with an inspiration and energy he'd never had before. His best work actually, which I'm sure she's still keeping under wraps somewhere. Anyway, my point is that he was concerned for her future."

"He knew death was imminent?"

Rick casually waved the hand holding the cigarette. "Of course. Katherine is the sort of person who will say, 'Okay, we've got this problem so let's tirelessly do what needs to be done. We will take care of it.' I'm not sure if she is an optimist or if she just forges ahead like a bull on a red... uh... shirt or something. In the end, of course, she stood by, helpless, just like the rest of us. I can't begin to tell you how devastating it was to watch them lose each other."

"He wanted you to keep an eye out for her?"

"Yes. He even suggested that we be together." Rick laughed without pleasure. "It must have been a moment of delirium. The thing is, I'd love to... who wouldn't? But I know when I'm out of my league."

"I'd wondered why she seemed so unapproachable."

"That's a quality band he's with, Steve Denison."

"Yeah, they just wrapped up a world tour. Of course, he hasn't been home much lately. The band's management isn't allowing them much of a break. They're getting ready for the studio again. Katherine doesn't even know who he is, which is pretty cool. Steve keeps himself to himself. Katherine gives me the same impression. If a single person in this town was aware of the fact that she is a widow, I would have heard about it."

Lettie pushed through the door to fetch her father for supper. Paul had been watching out for her. Her eyes met Paul's, and he motioned her to come 'round the bar, something she was reluctant to do, being shy.

"Come on!"

As she approached, he took note that she had changed of late. She wore a minimal amount of makeup, which was new, but it was more than that, and difficult to pinpoint. When he tried to envision Lettie as an adult, it was nearly impossible, but puberty had been catching her with cruel but magic hands.

"Hi Paul," she said.

He smiled at her until she blushed. "Do you read?"

She frowned. "Of course, I read. What do you think it is I do at school all bloody day?"

"Sarcasm from a fifteen-year-old," he said dryly, making her chuckle a little. "That's terrific. What I should have asked was, do you read books? For fun?"

"When I have time, which isn't often."

"I've got something for you," he said as he reached in a cupboard where he kept paper and beer cards and a stash of books.

"What's this?" she asked as he gave her a brand-new copy of *The House of a Thousand Lanterns*.

"I saw it at the newspaper shop today and thought of you. My mum used to love her stories. Have you ever read Victoria Holt?"

"No. You bought this for me?" she asked as if it was hard to believe.

"Yeah! Let me know if you like it. I've got loads of the stuff in boxes somewhere. If you don't like this one, I won't bother digging for them. I figured this was easier."

"Thank you." Her hazel eyes, which always stood a little bit hard as if braced against a world that judged her, softened and it did something to his heart.

"It's a reminder to read for fun once in a while." He smiled broadly.

Harry left almost meekly with his daughter, just the right amount of booze traveling through his bloodstream to keep calm. Paul shifted in his chair and moved his leg into a different position. Sitting had taken some of the pressure off, and he felt the muscles in his upper thigh relax a bit. He was aware he would have to return to his customers soon, and Rick, being a publican, probably knew it too.

"Cute kid." He pointed to the door as he finished the pint.

"Yeah. And clever!" He cleared his throat and got back on the subject of Katherine. "What are you concerned about?"

"Norman may have wanted nothing more than for her to be able to find love again but she deserves to be…"—he searched his mind for the English word— "cared for… eh… nourished?"

"Nurtured?" Paul offered.

"That's it. Let somebody take care of her for once and not from a distance with groupies in the mix."

"Hang on! He's not the type for that sort of nonsense. But he wouldn't give up his music. Not even for a girl like Katherine. I'd stake my life on that."

Rick nodded and got his wallet out of the inside pocket of his coat. Leaving two quid on the bar, he put the wallet back and produced something from another pocket. It was a cassette tape which on a whim, he'd retrieved from his car after visiting Katherine. He put it down on top of the cash.

"Don't tell her I gave you this. It was recorded during one of our gigs, about a year and a half ago. It's not the best recording, mind you. Norman plays on most of it, but at one point he asks Katherine to take over." The memory sent a smile to his eyes. "He wasn't ill yet but he had the shits that night. Probably her cooking."

Paul laughed.

"The difference between them is quite clear. I had something more recent, but I gave it to her, hoping she will continue to practice. My phone number is on the inside cover. And Paul…"

"Yes?"

"If you tell her I gave this to you, I'll personally come from Holland to ram a drum stick up your arse," he said, without even the smallest hint of humour. "I came here to convince her to play with us again. She said living without music was loud at the beginning, but she doesn't know just how loud it is to us every day. She's on the stubborn side. Call me if you think she needs a friend."

Paul nodded. He'd met some interesting people and listened to interesting conversations in his day. He'd even been asked an opinion about things that should have been private. He viewed it as part of his job. He had never been recruited to keep an eye on a girl he thought was someone who should be with his best friend. That could get complicated.

"You're saying he, Norman, wanted to see Katherine cared for all the way? He said that without any notion of jealousy?" Paul asked curiously because he wondered how the psyche of a dying man was different from a healthy one when it came to his wife with another man.

"Without jealousy, but not without pain."

"This may not be easy, you know."

"Nothing that's worth anything ever is, Paul."

"True." He nodded.

"Give me a ring."

They shook hands fondly.

"Did he know Tornado Wave's music?"

Rick nodded.

"What did he think about it?" Paul held the tape pressed against his heart as if it were a priceless treasure.

"He despised metal."

"Seriously?"

"Seriously. They lived on an old farm where the only thing that ever functioned right was the record player. It was all Blues all the time. Morning, noon, and night."

Rick left Paul with some measure of admiration for a man whom he would never be able to meet, but whom he might get to know a bit through the beautiful woman he had left behind. But he now worried whether or not Katherine would be open to a new relationship. Would they respect him if he interfered by giving one or both of them a subtle push towards the other?

Later on, during his nightly bath and last pot of tea, Paul listened to the tape with headphones on. He loved music and loved those musicians who threw themselves behind every note with every emotion they held within themselves. He understood from Rick that Norman had been Katherine's teacher. But passion couldn't be taught. One had it, or one didn't.

Norman ripped his heart through the strings of a guitar. He was passionate and fluent, the instrument an extension of himself. Katherine wasn't yet as technically savvy at the time of the recording. Yet to hear her play the Blues really moved Paul. So did what she had been living through. There wasn't any way possible he'd be able to sleep without having reached out to her. Despite it being very late when he got to bed, he dialled her number from memory.

"Hullo?"

"It's Paul."

"Shouldn't you be in bed?"

"Are you?"

"No. I've got some things to finish."

"I met your friend today."

She sighed. "I was afraid of that."

"Why didn't you tell me?"

"We've only met five minutes ago, so I'm not sure why I would have shared anything so private. Do you feel sorry for me now?"

"Shouldn't I?" The energy that reached him through the phone was anything but good. Defiant. "You're angry," he concluded. "Why?"

"I fiercely dislike anybody discussing my life freely behind my back."

"In that case, just so there are no misunderstandings between us, I think you should know that I know. About the music."

"Paul, look…" She paused. "I like you a great deal but it's not a topic of discussion between us. I don't want to talk about it."

She rang off.

Chapter X

Manipulation

It was a quiet afternoon at The Wicked Mule. Tuesdays usually were, particularly when it rained cats and dogs as it had all day. Paul had his well-worn copy of *Lord of the Rings* at hand and sat by the fire reading. He wanted to be home with his book. It didn't happen often, and he gave into such a whim even less, but tonight he preferred his bed over the hearth. It also didn't happen often that he missed having a girl in his life, but he did now. Perhaps he was a bit nostalgic. As he flipped over a page, he glanced at the only customer, who seemed not to need anything. Harry was nothing if not predictable.

Paul turned back to the novel he'd read so many times over the years, he'd lost count. Having turned the volume on the stereo to low, the most prominent sound in the room came from wood popping and hissing as it was penetrated by heat and flames, and the sound of rain pelting against the windows. Eventually, at around six, Lettie popped in.

Her demeanour, at least towards him, had changed since giving her the book. The smiles with which she greeted him were still rather shy, but they were more open and, in the mornings, at the bakery, Lettie actually spoke to Paul as opposed to depending on him to begin a conversation. He felt immensely drawn to her, he suspected, because of her circumstances. Any tiny glimpse of who Lettie was behind the usually brooding facade he considered a small victory, and the simple gesture of the book had certainly pushed the door to the girl's soul ajar.

Without giving her father the slightest glance, Lettie's eyes searched the empty pub. She fell down on the sofa next to Paul and removed her plastic raincoat. She was dressed in a pair of tight jeans, a plain sweatshirt that she probably shared with her mother by the size of it, and a pair of green Wellingtons. Again he got the feeling that she was in the midst of a major growth spurt and not just in height.

"Splendid that you're so early," he said.

"I was at the library and I wanted to have a word with you. Why?"

Because her eyes stood more frank than he had ever seen in her, Paul dog-eared the page he was on, something Steve really hated, and put the book down on his thigh.

"Because I want your old man out of here. I'm going home."

"Mum will be quite cross if I bring him home now. You know there will be a fight. Are you ill?"

"I don't know. The usual aches and pains and maybe the onset of a cold. What did you need me for? Are you hungry? Do you want something to drink?"

She shook her head, looking down.

"On me, Lettie."

She settled for an orange juice. Paul limped away to get it for her and added a packet of crisps. He paid the till out of his pocket.

"Thank you. I've come to ask if you have a job for me. A proper job."

Paul frowned. "Did your mum send you?"

"No. I just want to make some money of my own. She doesn't give me any of what I make at the bakery."

"Why here?"

"Because I like it here and"—she shook her head— "because, well, you treat me normal. I've asked for jobs. At the newspaper shop they called me 'poor 'arry's daughter.' I don't think I should have to put up with that. I can't bear it."

"You're too young to work in the pub. I'd lose my license."

"I've checked the laws. I can do things before you open, and on Saturdays when I'm not at the bakery. If I stay in the kitchen it wouldn't have anything to do with the pub, would it? I could even clean your house and do your washing."

"What do you need the money for? Clothes?"

"I just want to save some money, in a proper account, for when I can leave."

"Where are you planning on going?"

"Sixth Form for starters. I want my own life and my own money. Paul, please... please let me work for you. By law I'm allowed nineteen hours a week, and I'm only getting ten at the bakery, at most."

There was a tone of desperation in her voice. Paul's heart went out to her. She was cute now. She would be adorable in a year or so. With that, he predicted, would come another set of problems for

Susan. He hoped that Lettie would keep her head together and not end up like her mother. The very notion helped to bring him to a decision. If there was anything he could do for Lettie, it was to become a mentor of sorts, and he could do that best if he had her close.

"You're not sixteen yet. We would need to get a permit, and one of your parents would have to sign it. You wouldn't be able to work after seven either."

"I need to be home before Mum leaves, to watch the little ones." She shook her head and looked away. She was frustrated. It was easy to see and even easier to understand.

"How much?" He sneezed.

"Five pounds an hour."

"Five?! Are you insane?"

"I knew you would say that," she said with a twinkle that shone a rare light on her wit and her smarts. "Can't blame me for trying."

"How much do you get at the bakery?"

"Two. But all I do is sell bread. I want more to scrub piss and shit off of toilets."

"Perhaps I ought to employ you to drive bargains with the wholesalers for me." Paul grinned. "Okay... I'll give you nine hours, five here and four at the cottage. You'll get two-fifty until you turn sixteen and if I'm happy with your work, I'll increase it to three. During exams, I don't want to see you and I'm not obligated to pay you for time off until after you turn sixteen."

Lettie gathered her coat, shrugged into it, and tried to put the packet of crisps, which she hadn't opened, in her pocket, but it wouldn't fit. She resolved to hold it. Paul guessed she'd treat her brothers with it. He followed her to the bar and got behind it as she put her glass down for him. He dropped it in the wash basin.

"Get Harry to sign the permit when he's good and drunk," she said. "And I have rights. I don't want my wages discussed with my mother. That's between me and you."

"Thanks for reminding me of your rights," he said, giving her a look that made her blush.

He grabbed three more packets of crisps and four *Peperami* sausages off the shelf and found a sack to put them in. He also reached for four bottles of ale in the cooler and added them. He said to tell her mother that should top Harry off for the night and to return the empty bottles to him. She took the sack from the bar as he paid the till for the lot from a twenty-pound note he kept in his billfold.

"Have you thought about how to keep the money away from your parents?" he asked.

"No…"

"Set up a savings account. They have the highest interest. Give me the account information and I will deposit your wages directly into the account."

"Is that possible without a parent?"

Paul nodded. "You're old enough."

A terrific smile spread on Lettie's face.

She managed to get her father down from his perch at the corner of the bar and off to their home. The rain had slowed to a steady drizzle. Paul was grateful for getting an early release. Just as he wanted to lock the door, Katherine ran up the three steps and inside without missing a beat, holding her massive shoulder bag over her head.

"Hiya, Paul."

"Hi. What are you doing out?"

"I don't want to be but I'm famished. I'm going for a bite at Costas' place," she said, referring to the Greek restaurant in the shopping district. "I thought I'd drop by this book you wanted to borrow. You're probably slow as snails this evening."

Opening the purse, she took out a rather thick book: a photographic history of the Blues. She handed it to him with her ever-present smile. He gave her a fond rubbing over the head. She really was a terrific girl and he wondered why in bloody hell he didn't woo her himself. What was wrong with an "every-man-for-himself" approach? But of course, that wouldn't be at all the correct thing to do. She belonged with Steve. Anybody who knew them could see that, even if they themselves didn't.

Yet.

"How long has it been since you've had a decent meal? Do you even remember?"

"Were you about to lock the door?" She ignored him, artfully dodging his jab about her eating habits.

"Yes, I was. Nobody out in this dog weather anyway, so what's the point?"

"Would you like to join me?" she asked.

It was tempting. But Steve was in town. Carpe diem, he thought to himself. It took all of his willpower not to grin like a Cheshire cat.

He sneezed again. "Are you asking me to go out with you finally?"

"Paul, I don't want this to sound as horrible as it will, but that's a really frightening thought." She kept a straight face. "I mean, you've only got the one leg."

Paul couldn't even pretend to be insulted. His laughter bellowed through the empty pub. Katherine grinned wickedly.

"Pass, if you don't mind, love. I'm going home to soak in a hot bath, try to get the pain to subside before I go to bed... with my books if I can't have you."

She gave him a kiss on the cheek. "I'm sorry about your leg. It must be the rain. But Paul, I do wish we could have a meal together sometime. We never seem to have a conversation after ten o'clock in the morning."

"Let's do it another time. Soon."

"Promise?" She gave him a sideways squint, not believing it.

"Yes, I promise. Now go before someone else barges through this door."

He shoved her gently backwards out to the street and resolutely locked the door. She waved and, holding her bag over her head again, hurried away. He would have to buy an umbrella for her one of these days, he thought. As quickly as his painful leg allowed, Paul turned towards the bar and reached to switch off most of the lights. There was just enough light for him to see the dial on the telephone. He rang a number from memory. It rang and rang. It would be awfully disappointing to have an opportunity such as this and not be able to make something happen.

"Denison," a burly voice answered.

He could have collapsed with relief. "Ned, it's Paul."

"Paul, old chap. What can I do for you?"

"This is about what you could do for your son, actually," Paul said seriously into the phone.

"Which one?"

"Katherine's gone to eat at the Greek's just now."

"What of it?"

Paul could almost visualize the old gears begin to turn in Ned's head. They'd only briefly talked about the breakup with Anne, and concurred that Steve deserved to find a really nice girl in his life, someone to love and respect him for the man he was. Steve worked hard and brimmed with principles and ideals. He reached for what he wanted out of life. Any woman who didn't meet him there would never be good enough for him. Ned didn't see eye to eye with his son much, in fact they hadn't for a number of years, but even he knew that.

"I believe this presents opportunity to...," Paul started, losing patience.

"Yeah, all right, you meddling sod!"

Ned broke the connection without further ado. Paul smiled, dropping the horn back in its cradle. He set about to bank the fire for the night.

***

STEVE ENTERED THE Acropolis just as Katherine's appetizer was brought to her. His first view was of her profile as she gratefully smiled at the waiter. Steve's heart made a small, joyful leap. The rest of the restaurant was empty, likely because of the weather. Katherine was about to dip some pita into the olive oil-drizzled hummus, when his shadow fell across her newspaper. Her eyes struck him in the face like a whip when she looked up.

"Did you ring ahead for them to clear the place for you?" Steve grinned.

A section of her paper slipped to the floor. The musical harmony of lutes, bouzouki, and toumbeleki filled the air around them, but the music and the stab at an authentic atmosphere could hardly create the illusion that they were somewhere other than an English medieval structure. Rain dripped from the tips of his hair onto the carpet and the sports pages as he bent to retrieve them.

"Hi," she said, taking him in.

His eyes demanded attention in a way that made Katherine feel self-conscious. He could tell. She tried not to run a hand through her hair, but somehow, it did anyway. Warmed by the thought that he might actually have an effect on her, Steve's smile broadened.

"Fancy seeing you here," he said.

"What are you up to?"

"I'm to meet my father for dinner. Mind if I sit down until he arrives?"

"Of course. Do you want to share?"

She moved the plate of hummus to the middle of the table invitingly. The waiter, probably the owners' son by the look of him, asked Steve if he wanted a drink. He pointed to Katherine's glass of Retsina and said he'd have the same.

"What's in the paper?" Steve asked.

He'd already read three of them that day, and it wasn't as if he didn't want to say a thousand and one things to her, but he didn't know where or how to begin.

"There's a perpetual Cold War," Katherine said casually as she pulled apart a triangle of pita bread, "other than that, same shit, different day, as they say. The economy stinks, the price of oil is high, the threat of nukes persists, and people are starving in Africa."

She dipped the bread in the hummus and popped it in her mouth. It made Steve laugh.

"I've only heard such an expression in America," he said as he accepted his wine and took a sip. It was horrible and he made a face.

"That's where I picked it up."

"Oh? Where did you go?" he asked, finding common ground and running with it.

"Rented a car for a couple of months starting in Miami but mainly in the places where any sort of music is rooted like Nashville, New Orleans, Memphis, Austin, and ending in Chicago."

"Nice. What did you enjoy the most?"

"The Austin Blues Heritage Festival in Texas; it was 1981 in the spring."

"Yeah? Who did you see?"

"Loads of bands but mainly I remember Stevie Ray Vaughan and his band. It was brilliant! An outdoor gig with stars ablaze in the sky, the lights of the city sparkling everywhere, and a beautiful temperature. We heard a lot of good music in those two months, but that night was magical. Otherwise I loved driving along those huge roads and suddenly running into a giant statue of a lobster or something ridiculous like that." She turned away, confronted with the memory of the silly pictures they'd stopped to take at every single one of them. She squeezed her eyes shut against it.

"I haven't had the privilege to see them."

"What, the lobster things?"

He watched her eat. She made it look so delicious that he reached into the basket finally, and joined her in the appetizer.

"SRV. Double Trouble."

"You ought to when you have the chance. You know guitar players like him don't come around often, and when they do, they die."

"That's rather a pessimistic statement," he countered.

"I have a feeling about him, that's all." Katherine shrugged.

Steve craned his neck towards the entrance. He consulted his watch and decided that his father should have arrived by now. Steve lived nearby and he had walked. His father would have driven, as his parents lived on the outskirts of the village.

"Worried about your father?"

"He should have been here by now. Excuse me just a moment."

"Sure." Katherine dipped another piece of bread in the hummus and returned to reading the newspaper, but it wasn't long before Steve returned.

"It seems my mother has come home, and now my father doesn't want to eat out. Would you like company for dinner?"

She pointed to the chair he'd just vacated. "I haven't ordered yet. Thought I would read the paper and take my time."

Her smile was as inviting as her gesture.

"Great." He reached for Katherine's menu. "What are you having?"

"I want an enormous Greek salad with everything possible on it and extra olives."

"I thought I might have the same as you but I'm in the mood for a bit more meat than that."

He opened the menu and decided on the chicken souvlaki. They ordered and continued their conversation amicably. Steve was more relaxed now that he wasn't waiting on his father. He sipped wine while contentedly listening to her talk about this place and that. As much as he had travelled in the last couple of years, including in America, he had not visited the many places she had seen. It seemed her trip had been mainly about art and music, Blues in particular. Interesting. He helped her clean the plate of hummus.

"Do you love music?" he asked. "I mean,"—he beat a clenched fist against his chest, encompassing not only the heart, but the soul — "here."

Katherine wanted to consider her answer but, caught by the heart with which he presented his question, found herself speaking truthfully. "I do."

"Music is my life." Steve said intensely.

"I suppose, from the looks of you, you're into the heavy metal youngsters love so much these days."

"Well, yes, if you must put me into a box." He smiled. "I love many sorts of music."

"What about disco?" she asked, comically wiggling her eyebrows, making him laugh for the second time.

"I admire any well put-together piece of music. Disco is not exactly my cup of tea, but it's nice that it makes people dance and feel happy. Is that a good answer?"

"That's as diplomatic a description as I've ever heard." She smiled.

"I did read English, you know. One learns to express things properly at Oxford." He paused. "How is business?"

"I suppose I can't complain. I can afford to eat and pay my bills, but with absolutely no hope of recouping my investment. I've been working on the fall/winter collection."

"It's not even summer yet."

"I'm a bit late actually," she said, "but I will catch up."

"Rome wasn't built in a day. This town doesn't fully bloom until the weather is warmer. You will be able to find a rhythm in the seasons."

"What is it that you do anyway?"

Oh God, here it comes, Steve thought. The moment of truth, and he still wasn't sure that he wanted her to know that he was a professional musician. He knew from experience that a thousand questions would follow, none of which he wanted to answer. What if it scared her off? He found that when people got to know him, the questions were not necessary and he could talk about his job like any other person did. Then again, "musician" could mean an array of things. He decided on truth—some truth at least.

"I was a teacher up until about two years ago, here at the local secondary school."

Katherine relaxed against her chair, wine in hand. "That's what Paul said. What did you teach?"

"Did he?" Steve grinned, appreciating Paul's intense loyalty. "English and music. Year seven, eleven-year-old boys and girls." He grinned. "I made them learn their notes, recite poetry and write essays like there was no tomorrow."

"Did you like it?"

Their meals were delivered. Katherine picked up the salt shaker and was liberal with it on her salad. Steve watched her with interest. He hated salty food.

"That's not good for you, you know." He couldn't help himself.

"It is if you have a low blood pressure," she said as she did the same with the pepper.

"Do you?" He sipped from the wine again. The taste was barely tolerable.

"I haven't the foggiest," she said dryly. "But I don't discriminate at least." Her salad had a thin layer of black.

"There is that!"

He watched as she tossed her meal about a bit and stabbed at an olive that wouldn't cooperate. Finally, she picked it up with her fingers and popped it into her mouth. Steve shook his head and attacked his own plate. The chicken was tender and juicy, and he took another sip of wine.

"I loved it," he said, resuming their conversation. "I still teach on occasion. But I had a dream. I must have been the only man in this country with a stellar education and quite a good job, who left it for a career in music."

"Oh? Did it rub your family the wrong way?"

"My father still hasn't quite recovered. I doubt he ever will."

"But you didn't care?"

"I wouldn't say that. We may not see eye to eye at times, but at the end of the day we love each other. He likes to jab me about it. I thought he argued his points rather well, actually, except for one."

"What was that?"

"It's my life." He shrugged.

Katherine grinned. "Was it a wise decision?"

"I make a decent living. I'm happy."

"You can't ask for more than that. Show me your hands."

"Sorry?"

"Show me your hands?"

Katherine held out hers. Steve dropped his knife and fork and, while continuing to chew on a piece of meat, did as she asked. She began to feel around his own fingers with her eyes closed, kneading them this way and that. Her fingers were warm but her touch, innocent as it was, gave him chills. He was in fact in danger of swallowing the piece of souvlaki whole. She found his calluses effortlessly.

"Bass guitar," she stated, letting go of his hand to turn her attention back to the salad. "You don't seem to be using a pick at all." Her conclusion was a casual one, and he was surprised by her ease.

"Do you have calluses from your needle and thread?" he countered.

"Of course," she said. "I'd like to hear you play sometime."

"When the time is right that can be arranged, I'm sure."

Steve decided to throw the conversation in a different direction and asked about Rafael. Katherine's smile was immediate and complete, touching her eyes even.

"Most of the time he is an angel. That is after I got him to leave my bolts of material alone. I made a very cosy bed with leftover pieces. That's where he sleeps now, when I'm working. At night, he sleeps with me. I'm so relieved you didn't take him. I can't possibly thank you enough for that."

"How could I after seeing the love in your eyes?"

"Was it that obvious?"

"You were an open book," he assured her. "Do you want to take some of this chicken home for him?"

"Oh no, thanks. He doesn't get that sort of food."

"No? What does he eat? Mice?"

"He caught one in my fabric room and brought it to me like a prize. It was good of him to get his scent down there I suppose. But I don't let him outside except on the rooftop patio."

"Why?"

"I give him very healthy cat food, organic things, and tuna. And I don't want him to go out, because he might get hurt or worse. I want him to live a very long time."

"Every living thing dies in the end."

He was focused on his plate when he said it. Before he could lift a fork full of rice completely to his mouth, he could sense the change in Katherine's demeanour. There was hurt in her eyes and possibly the shining of tears, but she turned away too quickly for him to be certain.

"Yes, it does." Her tone was clipped. She got the waiter's attention. "Check, please?"

He wasn't quite sure what had just happened but guessed it probably had little to do with the cat. She was wounded. It wasn't the first time he was struck by it. He wondered why. When she turned back, she had herself quite under control, smiling even. She appeared to be quite good at putting on a brave face. She finished off her salad and her wine as Steve pushed his plate away. He worried that he might have said something that triggered a memory which upset her.

"Are you all right?"

"Yes, fine. Did you walk?"

"Yes. I live nearby."

"Would you like to walk with me?" Katherine asked, quite unexpectedly.

She assumed his dwelling was in her direction, Steve realized, when in fact quite the opposite was true. He allowed the assumption. The thought of spending some more time with her was too attractive. He nodded once. They paid their bills individually, and Steve left a generous tip on the table. On the way to her apartment, they walked side by side in silence. It had stopped raining, at least for the moment, but the air had a chill to it that kept Katherine's arms folded over her chest and his hands deep in his pockets. Dusk still touched the clouds, albeit faintly. The days were getting longer.

"Would you...?"

"Well...?"

They smiled at one another.

"You first," he said.

"I was going to say that it was good to have companionship for dinner. Nice coincidence we ran into each other."

"I quite agree and was going to suggest a nightcap or a coffee at The Wicked Mule to bring the evening to an end." Steve coughed.

"Paul shut his doors early tonight."

He frowned. "Did he? Is he ill?"

"His leg bothers him, he said, and he's got a cold."

"Oh."

"If it's a coffee you want, you are in luck. I may be rather useless around the kitchen, but one thing I can do is make a very good cup of coffee."

When he thought of all the times the vision of Katherine had walked across his mind since the night they rescued the kitten together, it was absolutely countless. Something had happened when her eyes met his beneath the streetlight that had haunted him ever since.

"It would be nice to see Rafael. He must have grown quite a bit."

"He's not so frightfully little anymore. I hope he's not afraid of you."

Katherine let them in, and he followed her up the stairs. The grey kitten, a small cat now, met them by the door to the apartment. Katherine swooped him up and kissed him profusely. For a moment Steve wished he were the cat.

"Make yourself at home." She disappeared.

He played with the kitten for a minute or two and then let himself take the time to look around. The small place was very cosy. The wood-burning stove did not generate a lot of heat, and while Katherine made a lot of noise in the kitchen, he took the liberty of throwing a large piece of wood on top of the smouldering embers, poking the fire until flames licked the bark.

Satisfied, he turned to the duo of paintings on either side of the double glass-paned doors and was lured by their subject. While the one downstairs showed more of Katherine's backside, the mirror images here were full frontal, and she was beautiful, though more full in the paintings than her thinner self now.

A splash of red on slightly parted lips gave one the impression that she had just been kissed. From the fullness of her breasts and erectness of her nipples, one would dare to assume the woman had been interrupted in midday lovemaking. One arm rested against the side of the painting and picked up in the next canvas. If the left-hand painting was slightly more conservative, the other image revealed largely the same, except here, the woman's slightly parted legs left little to the imagination. He could picture them having made love and the artist jumping out of bed, wanting to capture her beauty in the moment. She was like a flower with its petals open to the sun.

Steve moved on to the many books. A lot of them were English; some were Dutch. He found that trying to absorb a Dutch book was an appropriate way to calm the fire raging through his privates. Still the woman in the paintings tried to get him to turn around for another look. He fought the urge. He had not been with anyone since Anne. The paintings, despite their sensual subtlety, exuded eroticism.

Hearing a noise behind him, he turned to find Katherine marching towards the sitting room carrying a coffee tray. She was barefoot, still dressed in tight black jeans and a black turtleneck. She'd tied her hair back loosely, revealing big silver earrings he hadn't noticed before. Despite their size, they did nothing to detract from the loveliness of her face. His gaze met the woman's in the paintings again. Her eyes were honest and inviting, but sultry too, the wings of seduction lifting her lips into a smile of great intimacy.

In that instant Steve's gut was filled with collywobbles. There wouldn't be another woman until there was her. He thought back to the night when he played with Tornado Wave for the first time. Even though he was hired on paper and had endless rehearsals with the band in the months leading up to it, he'd had the feeling that the gig was the only real audition. Those collywobbles had sent him to the loo over and over, to great hilarity among the band.

The idea of Katherine sent a more subtle nervousness through him. It was unexpected. It was beautiful, like seeing his little brother born and being acutely aware that this was someone he would love forever. An instant and profound acceptance of what already was. And like the birth of his brother, the wondrous feeling was overwhelming.

Katherine.

The invisible hand of fate held his throat in a choke hold. He tore himself out of the moment by turning away to put the book back on the shelf, inhaling deeply in and out through his nose and mouth.

Katherine. Steve mouthed her name soundlessly.

"Do you take cream and sugar?"

Steve coughed the lump out of his throat, forced himself to the sofa.

"Cream, thanks."

They sipped coffee in a silence that was not quite comfortable, tension rooted in an unmistakable attraction that already lived between them. Perhaps it had been a bad idea to get together without the social safety net that the pub provided. Steve's heart beat erratically, heavy with fear, as if he were a fox trapped in a hole.

"These paintings of you are quite stunning," he said suddenly, unable to contain his curiosity as to whom she would have posed for with such obvious openness.

"Thanks. You've seen the one downstairs, of course."

She said it casually, not in the least embarrassed by her nudity. Their eyes met. He nodded. God, they were so fucking blue.

"I wouldn't want to have to choose between them. These are obviously a pair, but I like the one downstairs because it's so…"

"Leaving something to the imagination?" She smiled.

"Yes. Sensual as it is, there is something innocent about it. It's also massive, which is probably meant as a compliment to both sides of your character. These two…" He looked at them, but didn't quite know how to express how they affected him without throwing her over his shoulder and carrying her to bed—something he would not do without serious consideration.

"I'm surprised you recognized me. Not many do. Do they shock you?"

"Not shock. I'm mesmerized." He looked at her again, the real one. "The artist did a brilliant job capturing a gentle seductiveness as well as that boldness you possess, a fire that I think only he knew and had probably just experienced."

Katherine took a sip of her coffee and put her cup down on the small table. A tinge of a blush crept into her cheeks.

"You're quite perceptive. Do you like art?"

"At this moment and in this light, I can completely see your reflection in them, that's all. I would buy them in a heartbeat, but I doubt they are for sale."

"They are not and never will be. I'm quite flattered that you think I have a fire in me."

"I think you're quite wounded at the moment. Beyond that, I have little doubt. I can only hope that one day I will get to see for myself."

Steve was sincere. Intuitively, he knew that Katherine had been the love of the painter's life and for some reason this was no longer the case. He didn't think she was capable of any relationship until she worked through it. In a way it was a relief. A respite.

"You have already seen it," she said. "This entire operation stems from the fire in me. Had it not been there, it wouldn't have happened."

Steve put his cup down. It was time for him to go. The sensation he'd had earlier in too close a proximity to Katherine, threatened to obliterate any semblance of sanity he possessed.

He needed to go home.

To be alone.

To think.

"I must go, Katherine," he said with more stillness then he felt.

"It is rather late. I hope that Paul is okay."

"I'm sure he's had a couple of pots of his tea by now," Steve said, making Katherine laugh. "It's nice of you to be concerned. You see, there is that softness."

She commanded his eyes for what seemed like half of a minute, an eternity, offering a voluntary glimpse into her soul. In reality it was only a few seconds. She stood resolutely and preceded him down the stairs. There were no lights on, but for a small lamp in the store, casting it in a hue of mysteriously feminine luxury.

Before they could reach the door, she stopped abruptly. He nearly ran into her backside and made a step to the side to keep from knocking her down. She turned around slowly. He could smell her perfume and the scent that was Katherine quite clearly. He could also sense that profound sadness.

"What's the matter, Kath?" Steve heard himself say. He spoke softly as if afraid someone might otherwise hear the intensity of his need to comfort her.

A strand of hair had escaped the loose knot at the base of Katherine's neck. It hung in front of her eyes as she leveled her gaze at his chest. Mesmerized, Steve reached out a hand to tuck it behind her ear, capturing the sensation of touching her. Her eyelids fluttered against the lightness of his fingertips.

Without the reluctance he had come to expect, her eyes melted into his, innocently so. Still she said nothing. The sound of rain against the large shop windows had no beginning and no end, like music in a single, uninterrupted chorus. Life out there continued while in the small circle of light, the moment lingered.

"Thank you," she whispered.

"What for?"

"Sometimes you hear words or sounds, or you smell smells when you least expect them, and they cause you pain. But once you've had some time to process, you realize that it came right in the moment you needed it most. And instead of being painful, it becomes uplifting because it helps to give a little more meaning to the why of things."

"What things?"

She lifted her shoulders and said simply, "Life."

She sighed deeply, and when she looked away, the strand escaped its temporary restraint again, in slow motion. It slipped out, as if tipping over. Steve resisted the urge to catch it between his fingers.

"You also reminded me of things about myself that I'm in danger of forgetting. You were quite honest, I think. I appreciate it."

Ignoring his need to get away from her, to be alone with his thoughts, to be physically far away from her, Steve gathered Katherine in his arms. It was not the sort of embrace you'd want to be the first perhaps, but he remembered that he should savour it nonetheless. Her arms slipped tightly around his waist. She felt slight against him, but not fragile. Despite being sad, Katherine did not strike him as someone fragile. He kissed her cheek. The touch of his warm lips made her shiver.

"Katherine, I must leave now, I think."

"Yes," she said as she stepped away from him.

***

IN THE STREET, Steve watched as the lights went off one by one and the lights beneath the roof were switched on. He was able to breathe out here on the sidewalk. He sucked the fresh air through his nostrils as if they were his first breaths. He rubbed at his burning eyes and found them moist. His heart slowed. He wondered how it was possible in the flash of a nanosecond, to have a new sense of existence, a future that was different from the one in the moment before…

Whether to check on Paul or because he needed to talk about what had just happened, he wasn't sure, but he turned towards the sea and walked to the cottages near the promenade. This sensation… to fall in love was something he had always been curious about, but had never really felt. The urge to follow through with complete abandon raged through him now. He would have to put a leash around his own neck to keep from doing so. If feelings could be that unexpected and that strong—if indeed they were legitimate feelings—caution might be the best collaborator.

Paul's cottage was one of the few in which a glass wall offered a stunning view of the sea. Steve knocked on the front door, which was actually in the side of the small house. Rain had slowed to a drizzle. The surf threw itself on the beach and against the rocks with the most pleasant of sounds. The castle was beautifully illuminated against the dark cloudy sky, and wind played with his hair as if it were being toyed with by invisible fingers. There was no answer.

Steve walked around the front to see if the telly or any lights were on in the living room, but everything was dark. He frowned. It wasn't like Paul to close the pub so early. The bathroom window was dark, meaning he wasn't in the tub either. His watch told him it was just after nine thirty, which would be ridiculously early for Paul to be in bed. He decided to walk around to where he knew his friend's bedroom was located and found a shimmer of light behind the curtains. Steve almost called out Paul's name, hand ready to knock on the window, but there was a slit in the curtain.

Paul was quite alive, his hands around the naked bum of a black-haired woman who had straddled him. Steve was in the middle of a grin and about to turn away when she flipped her hair aside. The gesture was cause for the second shocking moment of Steve's bizarre evening.

"Susan!"

"HULLO?"
"It's Steve. Did I wake you?"

"No, not at all, I was reading."

Katherine lied. She shifted the weight of the Stratocaster and put another pillow against her back. Rafael, no longer afraid of the guitar and its peculiar noise, got up to make a bed against her leg.

"What are you reading?"

She looked at the unopened, but well-worn book on her bedside table. "*The Hobbit.* It's been a while."

"Nice. I thought I'd let you know he's fine."

"And yet, you don't sound at all relieved or unconcerned."

"I suppose I should work on my phone voice."

Katherine frowned. She wasn't fooled by the smile in his voice. "What's wrong? What was he up to?"

Steve remained silent a moment, debating what, if anything, to say. All those times that Paul had his back walked across the surface of his memory. What could he possibly say or not say, to give him that same honour. But, being met again with the vision of what he hoped Katherine would mean to him, Steve could never be anything but honest or else not say anything at all.

"Shagging."

Katherine burst into a fit of laughter. It sounded to Steve like a hundred bells ringing all at once.

"What a rat! Good for him!"

He smiled because of her reaction but found it difficult to agree. Walking home, he'd thought about how much it bothered him that this was a situation where, had it been somebody else, it would have been Paul he would have called to discuss it. Despite many friends, including his bandmates, Paul was the only person, other than his immediate family, in whom he was comfortable confiding.

"You're not pleased for him?"

"As far as the act of shagging, of course I am," he said.

"Did you see the other... person?" she asked, trying to be tactful.

Steve grinned. "Very smooth, Katherine. If Paul heard you say it like that, he might put you over his knee."

"He wouldn't dare!"

"I think he quite likes you enough to do it with absolutely no remorse."

"What's bothering you? Or do you not want to tell me?"

Steve got a bottle of water from the fridge and carried it to the bedroom. He'd prepared for bed before dialling Katherine's number and he fell into it now, utterly knackered. There were entirely too many things fighting for attention in his mind, not the least of which the person on the other side of the line.

"Paul and I have been best mates since we were born, practically. He was an only child, as you probably know, and he was part of my family even before my sister came along. Paul was either at our house or I was at the pub with my father, who went to school with his father and with Gus. We played, we ventured out, and we grew up."

He paused.

"Our lives are very different now, of course. I went to University, and he stayed here to take over the pub after his parents died. But none of that mattered. Our friendship is as strong as ever. Paul, because of his job, knows a lot of things about a lot of people. When you think about it, it must be a bit of a burden to be in his shoes, wouldn't you agree?"

"Sure."

"Anyway, through it all the one thing that has probably grown the most is our mutual trust. I suspect there are more like me in this town who feel that way, but I can only speak for myself when I say that Paul's got my back as much as I've got his."

"I understand."

"Do you?"

"Do you remember when you came to the shop with your Granny and I had a visitor?"

"Yes." Steve cleared his throat. "Was he the painter?"

"No." Katherine waited a spell before she went on. "He shared things about me that are quite private apparently. Paul rang later that night to tell me. He thought I should be aware he knew about it. I was rather upset. But since then I've spent a good bit of time with him. I trust that I will not walk into the pub one day for all heads to turn because of something he knows about me. I think he's probably quite clever at skirting a sensitive subject in conversation."

"He's borderline cunning in the art of getting information without giving it." Steve smiled.

"I can see that. Can't you talk to your parents about what's bothering you now? Or just go to him directly?"

"No, and yes, of course."

"Then what's the problem?"

"I suppose this is one of those situations where I struggle with where my responsibility as a friend ends and interference with what's not my business begins."

"Then it sounds to me like you ought to sleep it over; figure out if it's really Paul you're worried about or if it's your principles getting in the way. If it's the latter, then it's none of your business, is it?"

Steve remained silent. How quickly Katherine had arrived at the inevitable conclusion. He took a swig of water and told her as much.

"You're unable to be detached at the moment," she said. "If anything, it shows how deeply you care about Paul. You are fortunate to have a friendship like that, both of you."

"You're right. Thanks."

"Not at all."

"Are you going for a run tomorrow?"

"Only if you join me."

Steve smiled. "My alarm is set for half past six."

"God, that's brutal! See you on the beach."

Chapter XI
25th Year, Day 1

At 10:37am on the first day of her twenty-fifth year, the Box arrived. Katherine flipped through a new swatch book of fine varuna wool with the help of Lettie, who wandered into the boutique almost every Saturday while on break from her shift at the bakery. Lettie's intelligence was evident when she asked surprising questions about fabrics that went straight to the heart of fashion, how they were chosen for a season and how they were designed and who designed them and how long ago. Katherine liked her and found that she looked forward to these visits as she looked forward to the next time she might spend some time in the company of Paul and Steve.

"If you call out the numbers, I could write them down for you," Lettie offered.

"That would be a great help. Are you sure you've got the time?"

She checked her watch. "I've got fifteen more minutes."

"Okay... 4612 and 3656," and taken with a particularly striking shade of teal, added, "definitely 7858. Mark it with an asterisk or something."

Their attention was drawn to the door when Darrell pushed through it bottom first with the mail. He lugged a bulky package awkwardly in his arms, chubby cheeks flushed with the exertion of its weight.

"Morning, ladies." He plopped the package on the glass serving counter none too gently. It earned him a disdainful look from the teenager.

"Is that for me?" Katherine was puzzled. "I wasn't expecting any deliveries."

"It is. And I'm glad to be rid of it. I do need your signature here, love."

She complied. "There you are. Thank you."

"See you next week! Oh... nearly forgot! Here's a card. From the Canary Islands. Happy birthday, love!"

Darrell breezed out of the door again. As he marched by the shop's window for a delivery next door, his cheeks puffed in a show of relief to be rid of the day's heaviest load. He mopped his brow with a handkerchief.

Katherine rolled her eyes. "He's so bloody discrete that one, don't you think? Reading my bloody mail!"

"Is it today?"

"I'm twenty-five today which is absurd because I feel two hundred."

"Why do you say that?"

Katherine waved her hand through the air in a show of nonchalance. "Don't mind me. I didn't sleep well last night."

Lettie smiled and wished her a timid "happy birthday." Leaving the swatches to the teenager's curious fingers, Katherine carried the package to her desk. "See if you can find something that has nuances of grey but with a hint of red. I'm looking for something that is subtle but makes a statement at the same time. That should do it for now."

She set down the Box and took five pounds from a small strong box in the drawer. She locked both and gave the money to Lettie, who couldn't quite hide that she was happy about being given some cash.

"What's that for?"

"You've earned it by helping out."

Lettie bit her lip hesitantly.

"What?"

"I... don't want anyone to find it. Would you mind giving it to Paul? He would keep it for me."

"Sure." Katherine had a vague idea what the girl was on about... protecting her own interests. Clever.

She returned to the package, too curious to wait for after-hours to examine it. It might be a present from Celeste or her old mentor, or Norman posthumously. She scissored through the twine and wrappings very quickly and stripped some of the paper away. Her eyes fell on the lid of a brown cardboard box.

Wilson & Wilson Solicitors

She stopped cold. Goose pimples walked across her arms.

It could be anything in the package. Anything at all. But Katherine's intuition curled an iron grip around her heart. She needed to remember to breathe. She calculated the chances of the package having anything to do with Celeste or Doctor Feldman and arrived at none. The odds that it had something to do with her mother got a much better return. But...

What if it wasn't her mother at all? *What if...?*

Katherine's scissors clattered to the floor, making a significant scratch that would have normally dismayed her. She didn't notice. The sound tore Lettie's attention from the swatch book. She looked at the source of the sound and then to Katherine whose face went bloodless with shock before Lettie's eyes.

Chapter XII

25th year, day 2

Being at home, keeping his nose to the fret board, gave Steve some time to think about what he wanted to say to Paul regarding Susan, or rather, how he wanted to approach the subject. They hadn't spent any quality time together for a good long while, so he'd invited Paul for Sunday dinner, knowing they could talk the night away without the burden of having to be at work on Monday. Around three in the afternoon, he put the kettle on and tea things on a tray. The first rough cuts for the new album played on the stereo, filling the large open room with noise that would have upset the neighbours terribly had the volume been any higher. To give Paul his full attention and keep from being tempted to pick up any of the seven bass guitars that were normally within reach in the sitting room, Steve had carried them all to the guest room.

Paul announced his arrival by shouting from the front door downstairs. He was the only one with free access to Steve's home and vice versa. Not that they abused it. It was only for emergencies and to keep each other from having to come to the door. He clattered awkwardly up the flight of stairs, thumping loudly.

"Wow! That is brilliant!" Paul entered. He dropped a bakery box on the kitchen counter.

"Not bad so far. I've been instructed to compose six more songs but I've been having a difficult time concentrating. Have you locked the door?"

"Of course. It sounds harder than the previous record."

Without missing a beat, Paul produced a large bag of medicinal tea mixture from his pocket and set about filling the tea ball. He dropped it into the empty pot, and Steve smoothly followed it with boiling water from the kettle, instantly sending fragrant steam to his face. Paul regarded a multicolour, haphazardly crocheted tea cosy with some measure of scepticism.

"Did your Granny make that?"

"No, my brother did. A present." Steve laughed. "Granny taught him."

"Fantastic! What's it supposed to be then?"

"A tea cosy was all I was told. It seems to do the trick so I'm completely on board with it. What's in the box?"

"Strawberry tart."

As Steve put the box in the fridge, Paul removed his coat and dropped it over a kitchen stool. He took note of the two cups on the tray, alert to the fact that Steve would participate in his tea ritual when he usually didn't.

"Are you feeling all right?" he asked.

"Yes, of course. What about you? Sounds like you've got a cold."

"It's getting better. You haven't got your furniture back yet?"

"Anne has probably burned the lot on a stake by now."

"I hope she threw herself on top of it."

Steve grinned. "I should be so lucky," he said. "I bought some arm chairs, finally. Have a seat. There's a footstool for your leg."

"I'll take it off if you don't mind."

"Suit yourself. Is it that painful? Katherine said you'd closed up early the other day."

"Ah, the lovely Katherine! I did, yes, but I was coming on with this. Just wasn't up for it. How did you run into her?" Paul hid a grin as he unbuckled the prosthesis.

"We had dinner at the Greek's."

"Oh my God! Really? As in a date?"

"Of course not."

"What do you mean, of course not?"

"I just ran into her, that's all. We were the only people there. Would have been awkward not to."

Paul fell down in one of two comfortable brown leather armchairs that looked as if they had been lifted from a traditional gentleman's club. The tea tray stood on an oversized lamp table between them. It was a bright day, but as the afternoon stole some of the sun's intensity, a Tiffany lamp cast a warm glow. Aside from the built-in bookcases, the hi-fi unit with its state-of-the-art stereo system and an upright piano that belonged to Steve's Granny, it was the only furniture in the large, L-shaped room. The walls only bore neutral beige paint and some sad, empty hooks where pictures used to be.

"She's quite something, isn't she? Bloody gorgeous and doesn't even realize it."

"I get that impression too."

"Are you going to have a go?" Paul asked carefully.

"Will you pour or do you want me to?"

"Go ahead."

"Do you know she was worried about you that night?" Steve mentioned as he poured tea.

The concoction was such a blend of herbs that it was hard to define any one in particular. The aroma that drifted from his cup was reasonably inviting, and Steve sat back with it.

"She was?"

"Yeah, so after I walked her home, I decided to come 'round to check on you."

"Was that you ringing the doorbell?"

"It was."

Paul sighed. He slurped from his tea but replied without looking at his friend. "Sorry, mate. The evening took quite a bizarre turn."

"You would do well to check if your curtains are shut next time."

"What?"

"I did a turnabout the cottage when you didn't answer. I suppose Kath's worrying had an effect on me."

Paul sat up. "Are you bloody serious?"

Steve rubbed his face with his free hand, a feeling of frustration creeping into him. "It's been too long since we've really talked. I'm not as good of a friend to you anymore, I don't think."

"Bollocks! You knew life would be different when you signed up for stardom!"

Steve swatted the word out of the air with an angry gesture. "Stardom, my arse. I come home less than I want to and more than is strictly needed. But you're right. And I'm right. It's not enough. I miss being home."

"You don't have to justify yourself to me." Paul shook his head.

"Likewise. However, I can't help but wonder how and why someone else's wife was riding on top of you, with a bruised face, no less."

"Good God! How long were you standing there?"

"Not long enough to see the grand finale. I wouldn't have even known it was Susan, but just as I turned away she threw her head back, and my jaw hit your dead rose bushes. What did Harry do, break her nose?"

"I don't know." Paul sighed, massaging his stump.

"You seem on edge."

"Harry was furious because I'd closed up so early. I sent him home with the right amount of beer to top him off. Of course, something set him off—the kids making too much noise. Who knows?"

"And she came to you rather than hospital?"

"Steve, I tried pleading with her. If I understood her reason for staying, perhaps something could be done. Feeding it is not working, that much is clear."

"She's got to get out. You can't do that for her. Nobody can."

"I know," Paul relented.

He was relieved to finally talk about it. Keeping a journal was great, but it didn't talk back. Steve sensed Paul's need, and he was encouraged to press on.

"What happened?"

"She wouldn't listen, says she can't bear to leave a sick man, they need his unemployment money, she can't afford a sitter for the little ones and therefore can't work until they go to kindergarten, et cetera, et cetera. All legitimate reasons probably, but they don't add up to bruises and broken bones."

"There are benefits for women in her situation, and women's refuges! At the very least while Harry is sucking from your draughts, she could get some legal advice somewhere. Mum would help given the chance."

"I know," Paul said, irritated. "What if one day she isn't there to protect the kids? We had a tremendous argument when I mentioned that sort of thing escalates."

"It didn't so much look like arguing you were doing!" Steve grinned wickedly.

Paul couldn't help but return it.

"It'd been since Katherine's opening night. What's that, two months at least?"

"The models? One would think the memory of a threesome could carry you for a while."

Paul smirked now, devilish as the memory of that adventurous night spent between two gorgeous women marched before his eyes. He laughed.

"One would, yes. Until a deprived, abused wife comes along."

"God, what an awful thing to say!"

"I've never been one to beat around the bush, have I? You love me for it."

Steve laughed.

"She wanted to know if I wouldn't mind putting a sleeping pill or two in his last beer of the evening."

"What?!"

"Honestly, I asked if she had bloody got one too many blows to the head. That's when she went off. Bloody biggest tirade I've ever been subjected to in my life!"

"She must be out of her mind!"

"Apparently, because she opened her purse and threw a packet of pills in my face, which of course I wouldn't have. The odd thing is that she seemed to have this... need to fight back for once. We were shouting back and forth, emotions heated, and that's what sort of led us to what you saw through the window, you bloody peeping tom!"

"I know bloody well you don't shut the pub down unless you're either really ill or on holiday."

"Speaking of which, are we going to Morocco this year?"

"Let me have a look at my agenda. More tea?"

"Yes."

Steve leafed through the next months and found a window at the end of May.

"Perfect."

"I'll have the travel agent book it tomorrow," Steve said as he made a note.

"Let me know how much or else I can give you a blank check now."

"Whatever."

They chatted about last year's trip and what they might do this time around, which books they would take, where to eat, but before long, conversation returned to Susan.

"Do you have plans to continue this liaison?"

"God no! I was stupid to have let it happen. I haven't seen her much, except at work and only briefly. We haven't talked about it. She'll be in for a surprise when she finds out that I gave Lettie a job."

"You're not considering using the pills, I hope?"

"I'm not stupid! What were you doing at my place anyway?" Paul countered. "The Greek locks his doors at nine or sooner."

"Yeah, that…" Steve sighed.

Paul regarded his friend, comfortably slouched in his chair, legs resting on a large ottoman with bare feet crossed towards the fire. As was the norm, he was unreadable.

"Let's ask her over," he suggested.

"Have you not thought to ask her out?" Steve countered.

Paul sensed his friend tiptoeing around the subject. It wasn't as if they had never shared before. As boys it had been books and toys, and later on it was the odd girl or two who hadn't minded breaking up with one to be with the other. They'd always been respectful of one another in that way, knowing how easily the tender perils of love could ruin a friendship, and understanding that as young as they were, it was probably not worth it.

"Katherine is a lot like you but in female form. I wouldn't dream of shagging you, would I?"

"I'm not that attracted to you," Steve said wittily.

"There you have it. You don't like her?"

"She's lovely."

"Damn right."

"I don't know what it is, but something tells me to be cautious."

"Her husband died less than a year ago. August, I think."

Steve sat up, spilling tea. "Are you serious?" He put the cup down and wiped his shirt.

"I don't know much except he had a brain tumour and it all happened rather quickly. He helped her plan for the shop, wanted her to move on, even have a new relationship."

"He thought it would be that easy? No wonder she's so bloody sad."

"She doesn't know anybody here. Yesterday was her birthday, you know. Lettie told me."

Steve didn't reply. He was dragging his feet, Paul thought, refusing to come out and say it. Katherine didn't leave him completely cold then, though it seemed further push.ng would be necessary to make him talk about it.

"Can you imagine talking about shagging a deprived, abused wife in front of someone like Katherine?" Steve broke through Paul's thoughts all of a sudden.

Paul almost laughed, but he understood what Steve was getting at. There had been lots of girls over the years, but they had never let anybody into their circle of two before. Not *really*.

"You haven't spent enough time with her, mate. She's just like us. Sometimes it feels like you and I should have sprouted from the same womb. You're like my twin. We're the same and opposite at the same time. You can't have that with just anybody, and it probably happens once in a blue moon at that. Katherine is the exception. She's a third of triplets."

"I've never met anyone more feminine," Steve said, looking in the fire, Katherine's face dancing upon the flames.

Paul smiled. He sensed victory. "You fancy her, don't you?"

Steve jumped out of the chair and took the few steps to the fireplace. He gripped the mantle as if it might otherwise fall over. The flames kept hold of him. He realized that Paul was doing as he himself had done before… prying emotion out of him.

"Might as well.throw in a log; it looks like it might be dying."

Steve leaned in to the fire as if he were on autopilct, and when the flames flared happily, he returned the poker to its hook, focused on formulating his thoughts.

"Spit it out, Steve."

"The first time she and I met and every time since then, my life has flashed before my eyes," he said, surprisingly. "I'm falling like a demolished building."

Paul's eyebrows shot up. "What? As bad as that?"

Steve returned to his chair. He poured some more tea before he continued. "Do you remember when we were boys making fun of girls who talked about *the one*, but when it was just the two of us we would philosophize whether it might be true?"

"I don't remember ever having reached a conclusion. Do you?"

Steve shook his head. "Not until now."

This time it was Paul who was taken by surprise. "Are you quite serious?"

Despite the distinct gut feeling that they should be together, to hear Steve talk about a lifetime commitment was another matter altogether. In Paul's take on love, he had a difficult time believing it could be done.

"I'm going to marry Katherine. When I realized, it made me break into a cold sweat. It was that overwhelming."

"In what way?"

"I don't know. I suppose the shock of *understanding*. But the thing is, while it seems an inevitability, I haven't the foggiest idea how to get her to the altar."

"You're scared! What is it that you're afraid of?"

"Look at how I treated Anne! That was the longest relationship I've had, and when I saw it was time to move on, I turned away." Steve snapped his fingers. "What Katherine is going through, Paul, is… new to me. I'd like to think I have the integrity to support her but am I around enough? Am I good enough?"

"You've got the one attribute that you need to make a start…"

"What? Patience?"

Paul nodded. "You're one of the most patient people I know. Even when you're pissed off, you're patient."

"Why do I feel like we're fifteen again?" Steve said. "If we invite her, we should have a present. I don't want to make it look like it's anything other than good mates wanting to surprise her."

They put their heads together and came up with a plan that took them no more than an hour to bring about.

IT DIDN'T TAKE Katherine long to follow directions to Steve's place, even in near darkness. She'd been working and didn't bother to change out of her favourite overalls. She had only applied a bit of lip gloss, brushed her hair, put on something warm, and grabbed a bottle of wine on her way out. Rafael, asleep in his colourful basket, was oblivious. When she arrived, the door stood ajar.

"Hello!" Katherine called.

"Up here!" Paul yelled as he heaved himself out of the chair and used Steve's ancient crutches to meet her at the top of the stairs. He was shocked at the sight of her. She looked tired, and her smile wasn't what it normally was. "You've got to close your eyes though, before you come through the door."

"Where am I going?" She complied, and Paul shuffled her forward into a room where cooking was in process. "God, it smells good in here!"

"Just a couple of big steps. There. Okay, open."

She did.

"Oh!"

A couple of dozen balloons were strewn about. In the middle of an empty floor, a blanket had been spread out with large colourful pillows and trays and an open basket set for an impromptu picnic. Soft Middle Eastern music played on the stereo. The room was lit with candles and white Christmas lights, and it looked festive, as if she'd arrived in a Marrakesh market. The breath she tried to take became utterly stuck in her throat. She could hardly believe her eyes. She bit her knuckles in a fight for control.

"You did this for me?" she managed to whisper.

"Happy birthday," Steve said, wanting for his heart to quiet down.

Paul broke the heaviness of the moment, the way only Paul could. "I've got to take a piss. I'll be right back."

Katherine kissed him on the cheek, and he pulled her close, banging one of the crutches into the wall in the process.

"This is so lovely!" she said, removing her hand-knit cardigan and scarf. "Thank you for inviting me. How did you know it was my birthday?"

Steve smiled wide, and when she reciprocated it, he allowed his heart to jump wildly about in his chest. She had a crazy effect on him.

"Haven't you heard there's a tremendous grapevine in Blackwell-on-Sea? It's a bit late notice but we thought you might be working, and were of the opinion that you ought to have a bit of a party!"

"You were right, I was hard at work. Where shall I put this?" She indicated her clothes and the wine.

Steve took everything from her. As he did, she puckered her lips to give him a kiss as she had Paul. He put an arm around her shoulders for a cuddle.

"You look cute!"

"Thanks," she said against his neck. "What's cooking? It smells wonderful!"

"Have a seat! It's a Moroccan *tagine*, of sorts."

Paul returned. He dropped the crutches on the floor and nestled in some pillows. "We'd have invited more people but as you can see, there are only so many places to sit. Help yourself to some wine or tea. Steve isn't likely to serve you." He winked.

"I've been bloody well serving your one-legged arse all afternoon, haven't I?" Steve countered without the least bit of remorse.

"Up yours!" Paul said.

Katherine laughed. She had never seen Paul without the two legs of his jeans intact. It was rather odd, and yet feeling sorry for him would never have crossed her mind. She fell down crossing her legs beneath her bum. Steve opened Katherine's bottle with a hearty *pop* and brought it to the makeshift table where he kneeled on the bright-red pillow. He filled a glass and gave it to her.

"This is a great apartment. Have you just moved in?" she asked.

"My ex-girlfriend cleaned it all out. She's holding it hostage. I finally bought the club chairs this week."

"Interesting that someone should think material things could be a bargain against the heart," she said, sipping wine. "I assume she's a shallow sort of person?"

"Ooh!" Both men looked at each other, grinning.

"I think Katherine should become your answering service, Steve," Paul said.

"Why?"

"I've changed my number twice in the last week. Somehow, she gets people to give it to her. Which describes exactly her character, doesn't it?"

"You don't want to talk to her?"

"No. She's unreasonable. A bitch, really," he said but promptly held his hand in the air. "Sorry."

"Don't hold back on my account."

"You must remember her from the launch party," Paul said.

"Oh?"

"The long-legged model named Anne…"

"… with the blond hair down to her bottom?" Katherine finished, remembering.

"The very one."

"Damn. She was bloody gorgeous!"

Steve snickered. "If she were a quarter as nice in character as she looks, I might consider answering the phone."

"How long were you together for her to run off with your furniture?"

"About two years, off and on."

"I don't understand," she said, frowning at Steve.

"What?"

"If your opinion of her is that low, why did you waste that much of your energy?"

"Bloody hell, how many times did I ask you that very question?"

Steve studied Katherine over a sip of wine. Their eyes were locked in place, and if he thought she might turn away from his gaze, he was wrong.

"Shagging was an entirely new experience with her. Is that a satisfactory answer for you both?" He turned to Paul, eyebrow raised in question.

"At least it's an honest one," Katherine said.

"Well, there you have it. Furthermore, we were a convenient answer to one another's lack of caring."

"Wow, Steve. You have been introspective!" Paul raised his empty cup in salute.

"It caused a lot of anguish. I'm rather emotionally exhausted now. Tea?"

Paul chuckled. "There's another bag in the right-hand pocket of my jacket."

"Jesus, Paul, how much of that stuff do you carry around with you?" Steve said, shaking his head, beginning to question his friend's refusal of Western medication.

They sat around until it was time for Steve to return to the kitchen.

"I'll help you with the tea things," Katherine volunteered.

Paul, a master in knowing when to disappear, announced another trip to the loo. Katherine gathered the dishes and carried the tray to the kitchen where Steve busied himself preparing couscous from a packet.

"Shall I do the washing up?"

"You're my guest. Of course not," he said.

"May I watch?"

"I suppose I can't stop you." He smiled.

She looked on as he measured the water. He turned the gas burner on and put the pot with the water over it. He added some spices. Sensing that she was following his every move, he smiled.

"I'm glad you're here," he said as he whacked a small cube of butter in.

"It's sweet of you to invite me. Unexpected, I must say."

"We wanted to see how well you can party."

"I don't do it often enough to be any good at it I'm afraid. At least, not anymore."

"Paul mentioned...," he started.

Katherine stiffened. Her eyes drilled his with such precision that for a split second he had to concentrate not to avert his own. She didn't move, and it seemed an eternity but only for as long as a moment's moment could last.

"Do you remember in the restaurant when...?"

"Yes," she interrupted.

"I'm sorry for what I said."

"You didn't know," Katherine said and took a towel to the teapot. "It's not as if I'm vocal about it; in fact, I don't want to talk about it at all." She moved aside when Steve indicated he needed to get into the oven. "And anyway, you were quite right."

"It's not like me to be insensitive, despite the impression you might have after what I said about Anne."

"I would have to concur after only four hours of working with her. You must have the patience of a saint."

Steve grinned. She had great perception. "How is it that you have people figured out so quickly when you yourself seem a complete mystery?"

Katherine shrugged. Steve stirred the traditional stew of chicken and carrots, turnips and potatoes. She leaned back against the counter and watched intently. The conversation may not have been her taste, but her mouth watered. She hadn't had a home-cooked meal in ages, let alone something as exotic as a *tagine*.

"How patient should I be to ask you to have dinner with me?" Steve's voice penetrated her thoughts quietly.

"We've already had dinner," she said, matter of fact. "We're about to have dinner again."

"Not officially," he said.

Katherine searched Steve's face, detecting only the most serious of intentions. She folded the tea towel in half and draped it over the oven handle, taking a moment to control the unexpected surge of joy that took hold of her. Or perhaps it was to hide the shock of being asked at all, but in particular to be asked by Steve, which affected her. Apparently. The feeling was entirely foreign after six years with Norman. She took an almost tentative step closer and embraced him. He enfolded her in his arms, held her tight.

"Officially, there isn't anything I've got to give." She stepped back. "But unofficially we can have dinner any time you want. I would love to get to know you."

"What if I wanted to kiss you?"

"Then I'd say you might have a monster on your hands because I haven't been kissed in a really long time."

"I do love a good monster! What if I asked you now?"

"Then I would say your water has been boiling and the pot is likely to crack at any moment."

Steve's attention snapped back to his tasks and she made her escape. The piano beckoned. It was similar to the one Katherine learned to play on in the cold front room at her mother's house. She touched the lid and closed her eyes. It even felt the same. Unable to resist, she flipped it open and tried a key or two. It was perfectly tuned. As Paul and Steve chatted in the kitchen, the rattling of plates and flatware between them, Katherine pulled out the round stool just far enough for her to sit. It had been a while since she'd played, but gazing at the keys, she was able to see the notes to a favourite Mozart composition.

Katherine played Concerto No. 21, from memory as she had so many times as a child. It was one piece that her mother had insisted she learn. She'd been thinking a lot about her as she always did around her birthday, filled with the same questions year after year. The details of her birth, how long it took, who was by her side, if anybody. Why had she chosen to have a baby alone rather than an abortion?

And inevitably…

Who was her father?

At the first sound of the piano, both men became still. Their gaze moved in the direction of the music, but the piano was around the corner and they couldn't actually see Katherine. They listened. Their eyes met.

Paul leaned close to Steve. "I give you six months. If you two are not together by then, I will handcuff your wrists together in a room and throw away the key until I find you shagging like dogs," he whispered in his best friend's ear.

"Make that a promise," Steve countered.

Very quietly carrying plates to the improvised picnic spot, they listened until Katherine played the final notes. She was surprised when they applauded. She curtsied, put the stool back, and kicked a balloon out of the way as she rejoined them. Steve wanted to know how long she'd been playing.

"It was somehow very important to my mother that I learn to read music and play the piano. She loved classical music. We had an upright just like this."

"She taught you?" Steve asked.

"God, this is so lovely, thank you." She had a bite. "Delicious! Honestly. She did not; she hired someone. I remember having piano lessons before food on our plates."

"You were poor?"

"My mother managed to make ends meet, but not much more. As a child, it's difficult to understand why you can only have ten crisps with your sandwich, but the piano teacher takes precedence. As an adult I appreciate it more, and I do understand the importance of music in one's forming years. That is, until yesterday…"

Katherine sipped wine and looked around again. The room had a magical quality, like Paul's outdoor sitting area but cosier. She regarded both men as they ate and was overwhelmed with fondness for them. New friends. A true gift.

"What happened yesterday?" Paul paused to drink tea.

"I received a message from my mother."

"Oh?"

"She'd told me years and years ago that a small trust was set up when I was born, a small inheritance from her parents or whatever. It was in her will, but I wasn't to receive it until my twenty-fifth birthday."

Katherine shifted. They listened intently. Steve filled her glass and his own.

"Last week, I received a letter from a solicitor in London, asking to verify my identity. I'd been expecting it. It was a relief because, frankly, a bit of extra money to spike my emergency fund is quite welcome at this point in time." She ran a hand through her hair, pausing. "I was expecting a check. But yesterday, Darrell carried in a large parcel. There was a letter attached."

Both men had stopped eating.

"What was in it?"

"What did it say?"

"The parcel was a large Box. It may be an antique; I don't know. It's very dirty. There is something inside, but it's locked and there is no key."

Her memory went back to the night before, when there was finally a moment to examine the Box more closely. It was a metal strongbox, the old kind with a handle at the top and a lock at the front. It was rather heavy. The items inside shifted whenever she moved it. There was no evidence of a key and she'd sat back, blowing out air in defeat and relief at the same time.

"Could I force it?" she'd asked out loud. She was certain that it was possible. The Box appeared to be old, however, with heavy scroll work embedded into the dull metal. If this had indeed belonged to her mother, she didn't want it damaged. She'd made some room for it on the bookshelves and regarded it, hands covering her mouth, contemplating the implications of what might be inside.

"Take it to my father. He would be able to help." Steve pulled her back into the moment.

"Your father?" She focused on him. "Who is your father?"

"Why Ned, of course!" Paul exclaimed.

Katherine regarded Steve, hardly saw the resemblance because he looked more like his mother... *her therapist*! She rolled her eyes.

"God, this is a small town!" she said. "It's beginning to feel like *The Twilight Zone*."

"But there was something else, Kath? You said there was a letter?" Steve asked.

She sighed. As if the Box hadn't been enough of a shock, the letter had nailed her to the chair she'd fallen down on. She finished the glass of wine again, not realizing she'd had a need for something to calm her nerves about the news until Steve had handed her the first glass. The room was silent. Both men waited with unbridled curiosity.

"There was a check... for ninety-four *thousand*, two hundred and seventy-four *bloody* pounds."

Chapter XIII

The Box

"Katherine! Where have you been? I take it the shop is keeping you more than busy?"

Steve's mother. Damn. Katherine ignored the urge to press a fist against the headache that persisted behind her brow. She had resisted the need to keep the standing appointments and stressed about whether or not to continue. Any objection against the doctor's help could be argued away as being silly. Despite her son's sweet friendship and romantic pursuit, the need for treatment should take precedence.

"Not bad." Katherine entered Elizabeth Ramsey's office with lingering trepidation.

"Wonderful!" Beth smiled. "Tea?"

"Not at the moment, thanks." Katherine quietly shut the door, exchanging whimsical music for absolute silence as if turning a switch.

Beth kept the smile on her face, pouring hot water from the electric kettle over an herbal tea bag. She added milk from a glass bottle considering that Katherine had taken tea with her every time since the second consultation. In and of itself, it might not mean anything, but she had missed three appointments and wondered if there had been some sort of change.

Katherine fell down on the sofa and immediately lifted a parcel from her oversize purse. "I don't mean to be rude, but I've got some stitching that must be finished before I return home because..."—she rooted for the small needle box, continuing—"this is for a baby that isn't getting any younger apparently."

Beth laughed. "I have missed our sessions. There's a baptism, I hear, this Saturday?"

That's why I'm here, Katherine thought to herself. "Little Mary Stephenson. She will be the belle of the church."

Katherine did her best to sound conversational. Placing Beth Ramsey in each of her roles in addition to that of therapist had given her a good deal to stew over. The decision to return had been because the need for a therapist had been greater than the effect of Steve Denison, although one might be directly related to the other.

"I suppose I shouldn't be surprised, you know, about the baptism," Katherine said as she lifted a piece of delicately embroidered damask from brown paper.

"Katherine, that's a work of art! The baby is my neighbour's granddaughter, and as you said, by the time the vicar finally convinced them to have her baptized, she was already five months old." Beth sat back, cup in hand, and her focus went from the baptism dress to Katherine. "Is there anything you would like to talk about?"

"I've been working a lot," she said in earnest, and it was true. "We can pick up where we left off."

"Have you been working too much perhaps? You have dark circles beneath your eyes." Doctor Ramsey observed Katherine's face as she threaded a needle with swift and expert fingers. "Tell me about your progress with the exercise I suggested you do."

"Getting out?"

"The very one."

"I'm working on it." Katherine smiled into her work.

"The operative word."

"Yes. The operative word. But honestly, I have done my best to get out, difficult as it is sometimes, and there are others when I'm ready to be away from the chaos of my own thoughts, but there isn't anywhere to be. A few days ago, I went to the cinema in Brighton."

"Which film?"

"A Passage to India."

"Did you like it?"

"Very much. I enjoyed it."

Doctor Ramsey nodded with a smile. "Me too. Did you go by yourself?"

"I did, yeah. I made sure to arrive late."

"To keep from having the time to run?"

"Right. It wasn't easy to keep my eyes from the empty chair beside me, but the story swept me away very quickly, and in the end, I didn't mind so much."

Beth shifted, part of her mesmerized by the fine applique Katherine stitched into the material. The needle moved smoothly and steadily in through the damask, and out, in again and out. "People were meant to be a part of this exercise, Katherine."

"I've made a few friends. Not many. But a few."

Taking note of Katherine's careful smile, laced with fondness, Doctor Ramsey determined aloud, "It feels good."

"Well, it feels... strange. I haven't had a decent conversation in so long, I can't even remember. But of course, I do remember exactly how long it's been. My new friends are quite engaging and whether or not I participate, the conversation and banter always flows. It's nice."

"Conversation is important."

"More than anything... strong conversation. I really miss that."

"Good!"

"I don't know about that," Katherine replied.

"Conversation hasn't been intimate with your new friends?"

She shifted. "I wouldn't say that. There is banter and debate, certainly. They listen. They are interested and I am too. They seem like fascinating people."

"But it's not the intimacy you had with your husband and your friends abroad."

"No, not the friendships. It is quite different... better, actually." She focused on Doctor Ramsey. "You're going to get me to tell you why, aren't you?"

Beth Ramsey affirmed it with an encouraging gesture and had a sip of tea. This was an interesting session. She sensed Katherine was nervous. There were things on her mind. Her sewing hands fell still in her lap.

"I don't know who I am yet, in this incarnation," she said with a shrug. "In a way they are getting to know me as I'm getting to know myself, really. I mean, of course I'm who I am, but I also feel quite different. Everything is different, and it's sad and it's definitely hard, but it's... it sparks my curiosity."

"Tell me how you are different."

"I've got entirely different things to think about from before. My home is different, where I live is extremely different; my work, definitely, because it's on such a much grander scale and entirely tied to my future now... Everything is different but my experiences. I haven't quite reconciled how the new things fit into the overall puzzle. I suppose it all comes down to it being *my* puzzle. I'm aware of that."

"You are sensing a need for interactions that will help to make you whole again."

"I miss the people from before, but I don't really long to spend time with them. Not that I don't care. But they are a part of that life, the one that's too hard for me to think about. I have no need to share anything with them. But having rather isolated, I've lost track of the fact that I do *want* to share. One takes for granted something as simple as sharing a meal or asking someone about the day they've had or having a hearty political debate. Yet I'm not ready to share too much of myself or what I've been through."

The baptism dress elegantly draped across her legs, Katherine studied her hands. The fingers on her left hand were taped, and she squeezed each of them lightly, barely conscious of the pain. Doctor Ramsey took it in, having seen that sort of taping in guitar-playing hands and vaguely trying to reconcile it with needles and thimbles.

She trod on, sensing momentum. "You must get through this grief, Katherine. Building a new life will help you get there, but not including the devastation of your experience, would be a step back, not forward."

Katherine shook her head.

"You're reluctant for these new friends to get too intimate with the old you?"

"I am. I've had fun moments in recent weeks. I find myself looking forward to the next but…"

"But?"

"I'm not sure I ever want the two to converge. How do I get there? Without feeling immensely guilty towards one group or the other?"

"Are you concerned that life will move even a step further, towards love?" Beth Ramsey concluded by the way Katherine looked away uncomfortably, and added, "You feel that way already."

Katherine nodded. "My body and my curiosity are waking up to it, despite any emotional resistance. I really don't know what to do with it, Doctor Ramsey."

"You're an attractive young woman, Katherine. Someone is bound to be attracted to you and hopefully it would be mutual."

"I've never been with another man."

"You want to avoid it altogether, despite how your body feels about it and despite the emotional need we all have to be intimate with another person?"

"I don't want avoidance. I need respectful distance. Friendship is more important, I think. Much more important than my being so… incredibly bloody randy."

Beth tried to hide her smile in a terribly fake little cough. But she made the mistake of making eye contact with her patient, who reciprocated wholeheartedly with a sense of humour that would probably never be killed even in the deepest grief, and in the next moment both women laughed out loud at the expense of Katherine's awakening body.

"HIYA, NED."

"Katherine! There's a sight for bored eyes." Ned removed his reading glasses and dropped them on top of *The Argus*, the Brighton newspaper he'd been perusing. Next to him, none too neatly folded, were *The Times*, *The Daily Telegraph*, and one of the gossip rags.

"Business is slow, is it?" she gathered from the depth of the stack.

"This time of year, it ought to be better. But who wants to get out and wander leisurely through Blackwell in this bloody weather? Given the choice, I wouldn't!"

Despite the early afternoon hour, the area was blanketed in darkness. Rain streamed diagonally from a sky that skimmed Blackwell's rooftops, seemingly with no beginning and no end. The top of the castle lay hidden within the clouds, giving it a storybook illusion of doom. Miniature rapids of water flowed furiously along gutters that could barely keep up with the accumulative effect. It had been this way for two long days, leaving the population's mood barometer on miserable. The weather report predicted no end in sight, at least through the next day. Not a good prospect in early spring, when longing for sunshine walked hand in hand with the need for a bigger till to count at the end of the business day.

"I've made one hundred and twenty quid today," Katherine volunteered.

Ned whistled. "That's sixty-seven more than I've made, love. Have you come to spend some of it here then, to even things out a little? Who's minding your shop?"

"If I sold two blouses every day, I would be in the poorhouse. I wanted to catch you before you left, so I locked my door early." She blew her nose on a tissue she found in her pocket.

Ned noticed the pack on Katherine's back, a red one that appeared to hold the shape of something that didn't quite fit. Katherine shrugged the rucksack off her shoulders and carefully set it down atop Ned's glass countertop beneath which were countless cheap and not-so-cheap knickknacks displayed for sale.

"Have you got something for me?"

"I do," she said as she unzipped the side of the contraption and began to wiggle the object out of it. Ned helped by holding the rucksack. He was curious but it was still wrapped in large plastic sack with advertisement for Mon Chocolat.

"Steve and Paul suggested you might be able to unlock this," Katherine said as she produced the thing outright.

"Ah, you've met my son," Ned said, feigning ignorance. "I call them the Two Stooges, you know."

Katherine laughed. "That's not very nice, is it? They had a lovely little party for my birthday, with dinner and a tart with a candle. It was very sweet."

"The boys were always thoughtful, I will give them that," he said with fondness.

Ned turned the Box this way and that, and recognized the antique immediately for what it was even as its beauty lay hidden beneath years of tarnish. He'd sold one or two like it over the years.

"It's a lockbox. Back in the day, they were made to store documents," he said, admiring the intricate lace-like scroll engravings.

"There's no key for it. Would you be able to pop the lock mechanism?"

"Where did you get it?" A number of things shifted about inside. It was quite heavy, in fact. Probably more than two stone, he guessed.

"It was left to me by my mother."

"Well isn't that intriguing?"

"I only just received it. For all I know, it may have belonged to my grandparents or my mother's great-aunt."

Katherine's attempt to be nonchalant was betrayed by the edginess in her voice. She dropped the rucksack on the floor against the counter. Ned regarded her with interest. He was always struck by the notion that she reminded him of someone. perhaps a customer, long ago. He was terrible at remembering faces. Keeping his tone neutral, he asked if she just wanted the Box opened or if she wanted it cleaned to possibly sell.

"Sell?" Katherine was startled by the question.

It told Ned she hadn't even considered it. He couldn't be completely certain of the origin or value of the Box without a good polish, but he turned it over to search for the hallmarks. Its contents fell upside down with a dull thud. Katherine winced. Not knowing what was inside, the racket caused her an almost physical pain. She felt protective of the Box and realizing what Ned was looking for, her eyes widened.

"Is it silver? Do you think it might be valuable?"

He regarded her pensively, reached for his jeweller's monocle blindly, found it beneath the haphazardly folded newspapers, and moulded it to his left eye socket. For a moment life was propelled forward only by the ticking of many clocks standing or hanging about. It was seventeen minutes past four according to most of them. She still held on to the plastic sack, but abandoned it when Ned asked her to lock the shop. As she did, he turned the Box right side up, and again she cringed. He concentrated entirely on the lock now.

"I considered forcing it with a screwdriver but thought better not. I rather like the way it looks, tarnished as it is, and if it did belong to my family, however distant, then I wouldn't want it damaged, would I?"

"Certainly not. But I have a feeling that we wouldn't want it damaged regardless. Are you sure there's not a key somewhere?"

"I can't be absolutely certain, but I've checked everything that I know belonged to her."

"I might be able to pick the lock. Do you want to leave it with me? I could give you a ring...?" Ned asked, knowing it was a stupid question before he finished asking.

"I'd rather not." She regarded him with big blue eyes.

"You don't trust me?" he teased.

"Yes, of course. I don't mean it offensively." She blushed a little.

He smiled and wiped his hands. "Cuppa?"

She nodded appreciatively. "That sounds lovely."

"Let's take this to the back before I have need to beat my customers away from the door," he said with not a small amount of sarcasm in his tone.

Katherine grinned. She shrugged her rain jacket off as she walked to the small room behind the shop that served as both workshop and kitchen. However it had started its life, the room quite obviously hadn't seen a cleaning hand in years. Every surface was covered with discarded "someday-I'll-be-able-to-use-that" bits. Mismatched cupboards, most of them light blue while others had been painted many times by the hands of children, covered the walls haphazardly. To open one of its doors would very likely mean to risk one's life.

She dropped the jacket over the back of a rickety chair as Ned cleared the corner of a kitchen table of miscellaneous debris with a careless swoop of the arm. He placed the Box on the table with utmost care and pulled up another old chair. He opened a drawer, rooted through it, and with a curse of frustration, he slammed it shut again.

The thought of a fresh cuppa, quite forgotten by her host, sent Katherine on a search for tea things. She filled the kettle at the sink and lit an eye on the Aga with a match. She plunked the kettle over the flame. About a week's worth of cups were in process of sprouting new life in the sink, and quickly, she scrubbed all surfaces using the few means that were available. Muttering under his breath, Ned walked back and forth looking through things as forcefully as he had slammed the table drawer. Katherine thought he had the remarkable nature of a giant bear, gentle at times, cross when he needed to be. Greying hair stood in every direction, temperamental as his character.

Ned made her smile. She dried the cups and her hands, wondering if perhaps these were the sounds of having a father. With that thought, the Box assumed a larger-than-life presence. The kettle's whistle saved her thoughts from tumbling further along down an obscure path of hope.

"Where's the tea?" she asked.

"What?"

"Tea?"

"Oh, top left. I'd prefer lemon if th—"

Loud knocking penetrated from the front of the shop. Ned and Katherine regarded one another, startled.

"Someone in dire need of an antique?" Katherine said, when the knocking became the sound of a fist meeting the window.

Ned frowned.

"Your till might well get ahead of mine if you open that door," she teased.

Ned waved a hand through the air, uncaring. Katherine wondered if it was his age bringing that kind of attitude or the job at hand, or the tea, but thought it likely to be all of the above.

"If you don't mind, see who that is and tell them I've gone home."

Katherine nodded and left the room.

"Unless it's one of my boys," he yelled.

She walked through the abyss of someone else's discards only to find Steve absolutely drenched, standing by the door. He was clearly annoyed, but his face transformed into a look of surprise when she opened the door. She stepped aside to let him in and redundantly said the store was closed.

"I can see that. It's a bit early isn't it?"

Katherine experienced a genuine feeling of joy. She really liked him, but the leap in her chest and abdomen was still very unfamiliar, if not entirely unwelcome. Steve's hair and clothes were soaked through.

"You're dripping!"

"Who's that, Katherine?" Ned yelled from the back.

"It's me!" Steve yelled back, and he shook himself, not unlike a dog, sending raindrops everywhere, and to Katherine he said quietly, "Hi."

It had been a number of days since the birthday party and that run on the beach. If he rang her as often as he wanted to, it might be considered offensive in some societies, but he had only done it twice and very briefly, forcing himself to remain distant. But now, encouraged by an inviting smile, Steve leaned in to kiss her cheek.

She locked the door. "We've got tea on."

"I'd love some and a towel," he said as he followed Katherine to the back.

"Did you forget your keys?" Ned asked without being diverted from his task.

"Hi, Dad. I didn't think I'd need them."

As she set about gathering tea things on a tray, Steve reached by her to yank the tea towel off a hook. Uncaring that it was already damp, he wiped it over his face and used it to squeeze the excess water from his hair even before shedding his jacket.

"Do you know where my set of lock picks might be?" Ned asked, regarding Steve over a pair of reading glasses that balanced precariously on the very tip of his ample nose.

"I haven't been here in months!"

"I can't find them."

Steve shook his head. "I see you've cleaned the place."

Katherine looked on, amused, as he went straight to the table, opened the drawer, fished a brown leather pouch from it, and threw it to his father.

He caught it neatly out of the air. "Bloody hell!"

"They're always there! How many times have you told me to put them back over the years?"

"Wasn't that the first place you looked?" Katherine asked with a most angelic smile.

Steve grinned, happy to have someone with a daring spirit in his corner. He drew a questioning eyebrow in Ned's direction, unable to hide a good measure of smugness.

"Shut up, young lady! What kind of friend are you, making me look bad in front of my son?"

"I don't think you need Katherine as much as that, Dad. What are you doing anyway?" Steve's attention went to the item on the table, and he remembered the conversation at his place. "Is this your mother's Box?"

They all sat down, Steve dropping his jacket over Katherine's as hers was the only chair with a proper back.

"Yes," she said, taking a bite from a Jaffa cake. She made a face. It was quite stale.

"It's lovely… or it could be. Is there something inside?"

"You see, that is just like my Steve. Not curious as to the value of something, only for the mysterious content. In a nutshell, my dear Katherine, that is why I am still running this bloody shop instead of being retired."

"You've got David!" Steve countered.

Ned snorted. "He was born with a football attached to his 'ead. None of you lot are any good to me! I ought to send you back to where you came from, all three of you."

"I'm not sure Mum would sign up for that."

Steve regarded his father with amusement and affection. Ned winked at Katherine but kept his gaze as serious as serious could be.

"Would you mind, my dear, if I cleaned up just the bit over the hallmarks? I am curious as to the origin of this."

"Sure," she said and popped the rest of the cookie into her mouth, trying not to spit it out again.

With a small amount of silver polish on an old rag, Ned flipped the Box upside down once more and rubbed a tiny circle over the stamps. With a different corner of the cloth he wiped until it shone like a mirror. It was a simple thing to do, but Katherine noted the gentleness with which the task was performed. It held a passion that reflected in the small smile around his lips.

Ned revealed the small marks that would help him to decipher the birth of the Box. With the jeweller's magnifier in place, he examined them closely. His smile remained in place. Frozen. Antiques were something he never forgot, even if he hardly ever recalled the faces who'd purchased them over the years. Someone had walked across his grave. His body gave an involuntary shudder. What Katherine took for passion was an attempt not to drop the Box like a piece of burning coal.

Katherine and Steve conversed soundlessly, no longer noticed. He missed the energy between the two entirely. He was only aware of his own heartbeat and the rushing of blood through his ears. Willing himself to remain calm, Ned downed the rest of his tea wishing it were something stronger. In the short period of time he had to think the matter over, he found that all he had to do for now was to open the Box. A simple task.

With the utmost care, as if not to disturb what lay in the past, Ned inserted the most delicate of picks into the lock.

Chapter XIV

Tentative Step

Management had given Steve just two weeks to work on material for the band's new album. Typically, when an idea struck while being on tour, it was his habit to withdraw to work out a melody and bring it back to the others to work with as a band until the song was pre-production-ready. This time, with six songs that needed to fit into an already agreed upon structure, Steve thought it would be easier to do it at home, with room to think and to find inspiration. Instead it proved more difficult. Since Katherine, he seemed to have the attention span of a butterfly, and composing was in constant battle with pacing around or doodling meaningless poems on the sheet music, without any conscious awareness of having transitioned from one activity to the other.

Steve was irresistibly drawn to Kath. Not in the infuriatingly infatuated way he had been with Anne, who knew the spell to keep him coming back for more even when he knew it was pointless. Interest in Katherine was sensible and the very reason why he wanted to keep distant. Behind the adorable blue-eyed-with-brown-specks exterior, what he saw was an intriguing soul... kind, intelligent, independent, and talented, and despite the sadness that seemed to hold her in a vice, she had guts. He knew many guys who preferred empty shells the likes of Anne. Someone like Katherine would require too much work. But Steve had nothing but admiration. He wanted to get to know her, to have long conversations with their heads bent together, to be her friend.

Sometimes he dreamed about walking into a darkened room and finding a baby at the breast of a woman. While the image was never clear, the emotion evoked in the dream was overwhelming. He'd wake in a sweat, the feeling of joy and pride and love and possessiveness lingering in the depths of his heart; the only desire to not have been yanked from the dream, but to remain until his dying breath.

Was Katherine that woman?

He felt a great determination to reach into the watery blue of her eyes, to feel their coolness against his skin, to protect them from any storm that mucked them up. And the storm was quite obviously raging. He wanted to learn how to make the waters calm again, and he wanted to drown himself.

On a chilly night in the week following the unexpected tea party they'd shared in his father's backroom, Steve made the decision to take a small, feet-first leap into the mysterious. What she was going through demanded distance and respect. He was prepared to give that to her… but not without grasping the invitation for friendship with both hands. Dinner, anytime, she'd said. Right. He carried a take-away from the Greek's and two bottles of very decent red wine to her place, hoping he wouldn't be turned away. Taking a massive breath for courage, he pushed through the door. Perhaps it worked to his advantage that Katherine was on her knees before the round dais, working with a mother-and-daughter duo clad in fancy dresses. She finished placing a pin in a hem and glanced in the direction of the door.

"Food delivery." He held up the sack and bottles.

Surprise tickled a smile at the corner of her lips. She nodded with no inkling of rejection and he took that as permission to proceed. Without pause, he took the stairs two at a time, his heart racing way ahead. Rafael was asleep in a multicolour basket by the hearth. The room was chilly and dark. Steve carried everything to the kitchen and set the oven to preheat. He returned to the living room, quickly busying himself cleaning cold ashes into the bin beside the wood burner. He built a new fire. The kitten, awakened by the clangour of metal on metal, stretched and yawned.

"Hello Rafael," he said, giving him a good scratch in his tiny neck. "You are one lucky little man, aren't you?"

The kitten rubbed his tiny head gratefully against Steve's outstretched fingers, green eyes barely visible behind large round pupils. Steve grinned. Conversation downstairs continued. The women laughed. An eclectic, modern clock above the double doors showed ten minutes to seven.

He did a turn about the room. Even without having been invited, he felt welcome in the apartment. It was clean, not a speck of dust anywhere, and the rugs showed signs of having been recently hoovered. An aroma of incense blended with a hint of Katherine's perfume. Steve inhaled deeply and decided it smelled vaguely like patchouli. He was curious about the drafting table by the window. Closer inspection showed an unfinished sketch. The mannequin's form seemed incomplete to his untrained eye and a splash of purple paint topped the right-hand corner as if Katherine hadn't wanted to forget the idea. The apartment had the vibe of a comforting cocoon.

Abandoning the urge to further look around, Steve went in search of plates and wineglasses in the kitchen and uncorked a bottle to let it breathe. He set the table, found some candles, and used the small light over the Aga as the only other light source. He searched for an oven dish, and popped the *kotopita* he'd bought into the oven to keep warm. Raf joined him, twirling in and out of Steve's legs in successful seduction for food. He checked the fridge and was shocked to find nothing but half a tin of cat food covered with plastic wrap. He took a whiff of it to verify it hadn't spoiled and turned it over in a small dish on the floor. Raf purred appreciatively.

Katherine joined them just as Steve bent over the chicken pie. Satisfied that it was hot throughout and the pastry was as crispy as it should be, he used oven mitts to remove the dish from the oven, and he left the door at a crack to help heat the kitchen, which wasn't very warm. The pie's fragrant mix of chicken, spices, and phyllo dough added to the inviting atmosphere he had managed to bring about.

"Smells delicious." Katherine smiled timidly. Leaning against the doorway, she looked marvellous in a black turtleneck and a pair of tight jeans tucked into black high-heeled boots, hair pulled back in a ponytail. She was also rather tired. He took note of the dark circles and the smile that didn't quite light her eyes from within. He resisted a kiss. It would probably invoke too much of a scene of domesticity.

"Hungry?"

He didn't wait for the answer but sliced the piece in half with a sharp knife. She nodded in silence, amused by the unanticipated visit and by the nonchalance of his moving about the kitchen as if to dare her to kick him out. Steve had already arranged the salads on the plates, and he grabbed them one at a time to add a slice of pie. She took a seat at the table, taking the open bottle of wine and pouring them each a glass. The flames of two candle stubs danced happily between them, light chasing after its own shadows. Katherine felt shy and had to make a conscious effort for her walls not to go up so thick and so high they became impenetrable. She needed this. She needed people, needed to find some sort of balance within her conscience, to keep guilt from consuming her thoughts. It would have been easier to ask Steve to leave.

"How was your day?" he asked, sensing the awkwardness between them but refusing to go with it.

"Busy."

She added the required amounts of salt and pepper and stabbed at her food, not really tasting it. For the first time since the initial rush at the opening of the business, Katherine deemed her mother's vision a sane one after all. The watery sunshine had finally driven those with a winter's worth of hard-earned pound sterling to the seaside town to chase away cabin fever.

"Dad has been complaining about business being slow, but of course he always does."

"Why am I not surprised?" She had a sip of wine, realized she was thirsty, and got up to fill a glass of water from the tap.

"A woman came in today, loaded with money and airs, demanding that I make a jumpsuit for her from the same material I use for an accent piece in the summer collection. Something her sister-in-law purchased from me a week ago. But, the poor woman is not exactly built to wear a jumpsuit, in any colour, gracefully, let alone bright yellow."

She drained the water in large gulps, filled the glass again, and gave one to Steve before sitting back down.

"But you're doing it anyway?"

"Your father is right. Business has been slow and I need money to pay my bills. So, I charged her a very special rate to design a one-of-a-kind ensemble that will be more figure-friendly even if she'll look like a bloody canary."

Steve laughed out loud. "My father would appreciate that. But didn't you just inherit a small fortune?"

"I will not touch the money until I know more about it." She smiled, taking a sip from the incredible Bordeaux. "My mother would be quite surprised to find that I am no longer a compliant little girl. But she was right about the shop, I think."

They ate. The house was quiet but for the scraping of cutlery against plain white plates. Rafael, having given up hope for chicken morsels, lapped up water from a small bowl in the corner. It sounded like a brook gently making its way around some pebbles, and Katherine liked it. It was one of the few things that brought about some sweet noise in an otherwise very silent little world. She put her fork and knife down, had a sip of wine and then another. Steve paid attention only to his plate, and she took in his hearty appetite before she spoke.

"I haven't had anything to eat since breakfast. What gave you this idea?"

He looked up, swallowed hard when he noted the candlelight reflected back from a pool of vulnerability. He needed a good tug of his wine to make the food travel past his throat. He set the glass down without breaking eye contact and decided honesty would be the path of least resistance.

"I wanted to see you. I thought food might be a good way to get that accomplished."

She studied him, hoping her shyness and discomfort weren't so obvious nor that, brick by brick, she might be building a fortress to protect her heart.

"I like that you're honest," she said finally.

Steve sat back in his chair. "It's the truth."

"I'm not one to kick someone out who has provided a lovely meal that I didn't have to cook, but," she said lightly, trying to smile, "I have a few hours' work to do for this commission."

"Okay."

His heart plummeted and he tried to hide disappointment by topping off their glasses. He didn't want to go, didn't want to leave the cocoon, and yet he had to keep from running away. He'd never been very smooth around women, but in this moment, Steve had never been so tongue-tied.

In a show of appreciation, Katherine finished the rest of her food and pushed the plate back. "You can hang 'round if you want or I can give you a ring later."

"Are you sure?" He stood when she did.

"Not really, but it doesn't mean you should go." With a hand squeezing his arm reassuringly, she planted a kiss on Steve's cheek. She thanked him and left him to the washing up. He got a full, spectacular view of her backside swaddled tightly in her jeans, pony swaying to and fro as she walked away. He sensed Raf's eyes on him.

"What? Don't tell me you don't appreciate a nice ass."

The kitchen tidy, armed with the second wine bottle and some olives from the absolute loneliest jar the inside of a fridge had ever seen, Steve went in search of a book. He perused the shelves, listening to the whirring sound of a sewing machine from a firmly shut door off the landing, and settled on Richard Adams's *Watership Down*. It was a book he'd wanted to reread for ages but never thought to buy at the bookshop. With another log to feed the fire and Rafael settled against his thigh, he opened it to the first chapter.

Katherine found them a couple of hours later, Steve completely engrossed about halfway through the book, wine in hand and Raf softly snoring away in his lap. The sight of them caused her lips to curl into a genuine smile. She checked the fire and poured herself some wine, quietly joining them with her own book. She was still burning her way through *The Hobbit*.

Steve was surprised to see her there. She had changed into the trusted overalls and sat with her legs drawn up, empty glass in hand. He looked at the clock over the door and realized several hours had passed. Lovely that she hadn't disturbed his reading but had in fact joined in the activity. In an instant, his imagination was overwhelmed by something quite the opposite of desire: a snapshot of companionship that fit like a comfortable old slipper. He grinned. The sound of wine being poured tore her attention away from Frodo and his cohorts.

"Done?" he asked as she offered her glass.

"She'll be here first thing for a fitting. I needed to make an adjustment to your grandmother's dress. I'd promised to bring it by before work tomorrow, but would you mind doing that on my behalf?"

"Not at all," Steve said with a voice reflecting endearment for his Gran.

Katherine agreed. "Thank you."

She looked around her place with its small modern lamps dimmed, candles flickering gently, as did the fire in the wood-burning stove. Some part of her wanted there to be a bit of music on the stereo, but the silence had been terrific too. She sighed, feeling as close to content as she had in ages.

"What's the matter?"

"I'm tired. But it's nice to have company. I guess that was a sigh of contentment."

"Another log?"

"Yes, please."

He noticed the silver Box on the bookshelf behind the stove, dull and taunting. It looked as if it belonged there, in that spot. He was quite curious about its contents. Katherine sensed that he was going to ask her about it.

"Have you opened it?"

"I have not," she said.

"Why not?"

She contemplated the answer, and when she spoke it wasn't completely satisfying, even to her own ears.

"I'm not sure," she said simply.

He picked it up, regarded it from all sides. When he lifted it to look at the bottom, he saw the spot that his father had cleaned to be able to read the stamps. There was a small but prominent crack, about an inch-and-a-half long that ran from the corner towards the hallmarks. Knowing it wasn't a good sign, he frowned at it.

"What do you think might be inside?" he asked.

Katherine picked up an olive but only by way of killing time. She turned it over and over between her fingers, the smell of brine seeping into her skin. She wanted the Box back on the shelf, safely, as if it were a life that mustn't be disturbed. As long as it stayed where it was, she could probably deal with it.

As if he could read her thoughts, Steve put it back abruptly. He seemed such a decent man, honest, she thought. When she was by herself, it was easy not to think about it, but with Steve's question hovering between them like a tennis ball waiting to be bounced back over the net, she saw the benefit of talking it through.

"Information about my father," she said quietly.

"Your father?" He regarded her curiously. "Who is he?"

"I don't know."

For lack of wanting to eat it, she put the olive on top of a magazine. She wiped her hands on her overalls without thinking. Steve didn't say anything immediately. He was treading deeply into uncharted territory. But arriving at the most logical of questions, he posed it.

"Do you want to know?"

Katherine didn't have the answer to that either. She shrugged instead, with an air of nonchalance she didn't really feel.

Steve looked at the Box in a different light this time and ran a hand over it as if to touch it one more time might lift some of its mystery.

"Perhaps it's got nothing to do with him at all." He returned to the sofa.

She laughed without pleasure. "That might very well be an even bigger disappointment."

"I see."

Katherine took another sip. Rafael stretched and yawned in her direction. He trotted across the sofa, standing his front paws on her leg to reach Katherine's chin in a spontaneous caress.

"Hello, sweet pet," she said and stroked him lovingly.

Steve smiled. The energy in the room was amicable even if the conversation had gone from zero to heavy.

"I found some old records in a storage box recently. Some sort of ancient-computer-generated things. None of it makes any sense, but of course now I wonder if they might have something to do with the trust."

"How old were you when she died?"

"I'd just turned sixteen."

Steve shook his head in disbelief and said, "I don't understand, under the circumstances, how you cannot open the Box. It might actually be rubbish in there, or just something that has nothing to do with anything."

Katherine buried her face in her hands thinking that very thing for perhaps the thousandth time, but she disagreed entirely and expressed as much.

"I don't think so. It's a beautiful Box that she kept hidden at a solicitor's office for God knows how long. It must have been special in some way, and since she was always vague and… unwavering in secrecy, I've no doubt it has something to do with it. The bloody thing just sits there, sort of vibrating like some ancient thing that's been cursed or something, and I feel quite okay not knowing what's in it."

"What about the computer records? Do you want to look at them together?"

"What, now?"

"If you want to," he said.

"I wouldn't mind help with it, but I'm too knackered."

He nodded. "I will ring you one day next week if that's okay."

"You might be bored to death."

"Hardly. I love a good mystery."

Katherine didn't say anything for a long while. The silence between them was palpable, as it had been at the beginning of the evening. Rafael purred loudly at the scratching bestowed upon him. Being aware of an immense need to be close to another human being, to briefly connect without being afraid of emotional pain, was a luxury Katherine hadn't indulged in for quite some time.

"Steve…" She started struggling to say what she wanted without driving him away. "Before you get that close to me I should probably tell you that as young as I am, I have already lived two lifetimes."

Some moments walked between them before he held out his hand.

"I'm not blind to that."

Her need to feel his arms around her grew too intense. She could almost feel his skin against her skin and knew instinctively that it would be warm and comforting. Her hand filled his as Katherine relented. He drew her close and she snuggled against his shoulder gratefully. To be held was the most wonderful sensation, like slipping into a hot bath.

"I could fall asleep," she whispered after a while.

Steve said nothing. He stroked her hair over and over, the way he would a child's and could only admit to himself that he needed it as much to be held. The moment held nothing sexual, not even the promise of emotion. It was what it was, depth wrapped in a blanket of simplicity.

He simply continued, never wavering his caress even as she became heavier in his arms. Just when he thought that she really was asleep, she spoke again.

"Steve, have you got somewhere to be?" she whispered.

When he realized what he'd heard, he might have gone rigid, but she tightened her grip searching his face.

"I hardly ever sleep well. I'd like to fall asleep with you. Please."

"No, I haven't got anywhere to be," he replied quietly and gently brushed some hair back from her face. "Except the loo. Let me get up a moment."

She moved, reluctantly, but used the opportunity to add the rest of the logs to the fire. When he rejoined Katherine, light from the flames danced frivolously across the sitting room. Dry wood popped and hissed. Katherine removed some cushions to make room for them both and used two throw pillows to rest their heads on.

Steve settled against the back of the sofa. Katherine moulded herself against him. He slipped an arm around her and she turned, nestling against his chest. Raf began the tedious process of making himself a bed between them, purring loudly. When all was quiet but for the beating of Steve's heart, he began to stroke Katherine's hair, neck and her back, rhythmically until her breathing slowed and changed into soft musical snoring. When the fire lost some of its gumption, Steve pulled a small blanket from the back of the sofa to cover them with.

***

WAS IT FRIDAY? No, Thursday. Whatever. There wasn't any need to get up just yet. Not for a couple of hours at least. She settled closer against his rhythmic breathing, finding warmth and strength where a void had curled its tentacles and taken hold.

Norman appeared from the darkness. He appeared from it with confidence. She was happy to see it because it had saddened her to watch him lose the light. He smiled. Her heart filled with happiness, and she threw herself in his arms with a force that would have knocked him over at the height of the illness. But not now. Confidence had brought that sinewy strength back, the kind that could keep him on stage for hours or keep him sketching, filling canvas after canvas with concepts for oil paintings. The power of passion that gave him both selfish and selfless satisfaction.

"Please, not yet," he said.

"What?"

"Not yet. I'm not ready to let you go. I can't bear it."

"But I'm here! I'm right here! I love you!"

A deep need burned its way from the core of her belly to her legs and back. She slipped her leg between his and he ran his hand down her back to her bum, in response. She kissed him, gentle nibbles at first, still afraid that he might be too fragile for the abundance she felt inside. His hair tickled her face. He began to respond to her kisses. Passion flooded between them like the burst of a dam. Too briefly, neither held back in kissing the other. Their mouths moulded together, tongues in a slow dance of pursuit, of promise. They were hot for each other, each kiss flowing into another, more intensely.

"Katherine, stop!" Steve murmured, hovering between realms of what was real and what was too good to be true.
He rolled onto his back without letting go. Unaware, she snuggled against him as she had the night before.

***

STEVE FOUND KATHERINE in the kitchen the next morning, slicing tomatoes. Raf, who sat at her feet, meowed in greeting and continued grooming a paw. Steve couldn't guess how Kath might feel about having asked him to spend the night, and he was almost tentative in joining her. He was surprised to find her showered and dressed for the day and somehow looking better than the day before. Her face was fresh; some of the dark circles beneath her eyes had lifted.

"Good morning!" She smiled openly, inviting reciprocation.

"Morning. Have you been to the supermarket already?"

"I have. Coffee?"

"You look... different," he said, because he was puzzled by the change, "beautiful, actually."

"Do I?"

"Not that you weren't before, don't get me wrong. But there's a radiance about you that wasn't there yesterday. I hope you don't mind my mentioning it."

"I don't. Thanks."

"You're welcome."

Steve poured two cups and set them on the small table that had been laid for breakfast. They consumed toast, slices of sharp cheddar and tomatoes liberally peppered. Katherine took charge of the conversation. The thought struck him that this was their very first breakfast together. He almost willed for time to stand still, wanting to remember every detail, how she looked, how she smelled, what she talked about, that she wore a dress.

But time walked on as it always did, and an empty coffee pot later he had to tear himself away. He needed to drop Katherine's parcel at Gran's house, and his father would be waiting for him to move an old cabinet that he had bought at a London auction into the shop. After that, a shower and a good bit of the day with a guitar and some paper to write lyrics on. He could feel his creative juices beginning to flow. He helped Katherine clean the table before he went to find his jacket.

"Steve?"

"Yes?" He walked back into the kitchen, shrugging into it.

Water clattered loudly into the sink, and she cleared leftovers from the few dishes with vigorous energy, a foot holding the lid to the rubbish bin. It dropped with a bang as she shut the faucet off.

"It probably crossed your mind that I might regret having asked you to spend the night..." She turned to face him. "But I don't. I think I might have caught up on four weeks of sleep overnight, and I suspect that's why I look different to you now."

"That's great. Mission accomplished."

She nodded. "I had a dream about Norman."

"Do you have them often?"

"Sometimes. Always the same dream about when we first met," she confessed quietly. "This time it was different. We kissed. It was quite an intense feeling."

Steve smiled, holding the memory close. "Must have seemed quite real."

"It wasn't as upsetting to find that it was only a dream. Not sure why. Steve..." Katherine took two steps closer. "It was a selfish thing to ask of you to stay. I'm aware of that," she whispered and suddenly her eyes brimmed with tears.

Steve took the three remaining steps between them. He held her.

Chapter XV

Compromise

The pressure of time weighed on Steve to get the band to pre-production rehearsals. Alone in the virtually empty apartment, he poured all of his energy into writing songs. The curtains were drawn because he preferred for it to be dark when he worked. There was enough food in the house to keep him fed and enough caffeine to keep him going. Family and friends, including the rest of the band, knew not to disturb. The telephone remained unplugged, the doorbell unanswered. They and everything else were resolutely banned from his mind.

There was no real order to his creative process. Any notion of an orderly home ceased to exist. The open-plan kitchen and living room were a chaotic mess. Every available surface (mostly the floor) had sheet music, napkins with poetry, random words, but in his mind everything was structured. He played and jotted the notes of riffs down that he liked and, when he tired of that, he wrote poetic sentences. He went back and forth between guitar, sheet music, and scraps of paper. Slowly compositions emerged, poems became lyrics. Riffs became melodies, and then songs that were recorded on demo tapes. Those he felt worked were neatly transferred onto sheet music one last time and then tucked into a plastic sheath, along with the song's corresponding cassette tape.

Anon giant Belfort toll/
Mania and survival roll/
Walls about us built to last/
Running everywhere chaos vast/
War is upon us, time to get mean/
Hatred and killing to the extreme/
Soundless march to the death/
Deafened by a baby's first breath/
Knights and soldiers to the tomb/
There's a new warrior/
Virtue lost in the womb

Composing was the part of being a musician he loved the most. Some would say it should be the act of performing. He did like to perform, but as introverted as he was, bearing his soul on stage was nothing like turning inward. Being on stage was the absolute antithesis of Steve Denison's essence. Writing was the most introspective he could be, letting the energy flow from his mind and heart, through his fingers, out of the guitar. It meant thinking at its most intense, about what he wanted to do artistically, about what he had to say to the audience from the stage.

He used the full two weeks he was given and a few days extra. When his gut told him there were eight songs that were good, he rang the rest of Tornado Wave, packed a duffel bag and the newly purchased Fender Precision bass guitar that he planned to use on the record and during the next tour. They convened at the home of their manager in London's Holland Park, where they usually held team meetings and rehearsals. In the next few days, the songs were polished, arguments were had, and decisions made over pints, arrangements completed. With the final selection for the album made, they were collectively driven to Heathrow for a commercial flight to the Bahamas. It was a whirlwind. Steve could barely remember how he'd gotten from his own living room to the airport. While the delay had annoyed some of the band, they agreed quality ruled over everything else, including postponing the release date by a week or two. The record company was not happy about it, but they were collectively told by the band to fuck off.

During the flight, the rest of Steve's life was allowed back to the fore of his conscience. He remembered the promise to help Katherine solve the mystery of the computer-generated records she'd discovered. He cursed himself aloud, drawing questions from a bandmate, which he waved away. Steve wanted to keep Katherine —and whatever may happen between them—to himself. There was a lot to contemplate. He knew instinctively that he needed to be prepared to spend many a night with her and nothing but a budding friendship in his arms, and if they were fortunate, the possibility of love between them.

So many questions swirled around his mind during the many hours strapped in the airplane seat. Could he combine the complex relationship this one might be with his job? Would he be able to give Katherine the time and the attention she deserved? Would he ever be able to find a balance between true love and music? If the work was manageable now, what it would become in the future was hard to predict. Steve had a *feeling* about this new album. They were all excited about it. Deep down inside there was a sense that life was about to change, that he would either find intense happiness or devastating heartbreak.

Which would it be? Would Katherine trust him? Was he ready to find out?

At this point there were no complaints about the prospect of blue water, boats, lethal drinks with umbrellas, and girls in bikinis, but Steve, knowing how quickly his mates could become entwined in any of these distractions at any given time, let alone all of them in one place, convinced them to hit the ground running as soon as they arrived in the Bahamas. A round-the-clock drive was a side of Steve that was perhaps the most dynamic and also the least liked by the other band members. They forgave him the quiet lifestyle he chose to lead away from them, even on the road. But when Steve had a foot on the pedal in the studio, he could work until well beyond what the rest of the crew deemed endurable.

It was a side of himself he recognized in Katherine. She was driven by the fact that the harder work was to make the dream succeed, than to build it. Could two people with the same disposition, but with two very different schedules, make a relationship work?

Tornado Wave went through three days of intensive rehearsals before Steve saw the inside of his eyelids. He'd been focused in the studio, but distracted otherwise. It was noticed, but the others knew Steve well enough to give him space. He rang International Information as soon as he got to his room but decided to wait to dial the number until after he'd taken a long shower. He used the time to think about what to say.

Three weeks had gone by since having spent the night with her and he was unhappy with himself for not having called. Languishing beneath a powerful beam of purified sea water, he envisioned how her bum had felt in his hand, how her hair had smelled, how their kiss had ignited a fire in his belly that continued to linger. He longed to be there again, with Katherine wakeful and eager to meet him in the blooming heart of passion.

"Hullo, yes?"

"Kath, hi!" Just to hear that distracted tone of voice made his lips curl into a smile.

"Steve!"

The shower did nothing to kill fatigue. He was tired, music ringing incessantly in his ears, and he wanted nothing more than to keel into bed, curl up in a ball, and fall asleep.

"Are you working, still?" he asked.

"No, actually. I know that comes as a surprise. Are you all right? You sound quite distant."

"I'm in a hotel room in Nassau."

"The Bahamas? Are you on holiday?"

"Hardly. What are you doing?"

"Raf and I are curled up with a book. The windows are open. It's quite warm, lots of tourists today."

"Which book?"

"A Tale of Two Cities," she said.

He burst into a spontaneous, throaty laugh. "Trying to fall asleep, are you?"

"I confess." He could hear the smile in her voice.

"Have you opened the Box?" Picking up the telephone, he paced with it as far as the cord would allow, back and forth. Nothing but a towel wrapped around his middle, droplets of water trickled down his fit torso and dripped on the floor like a trail of breadcrumbs. He held the curtain aside for a look at the cerulean-blue ocean sparkling invitingly in the late afternoon sunshine.

"No."

"How can you stand it, sitting there, taunting you?" he teased, dropping the curtain to pace again.

"It's not that difficult. Not when my gut tells me I should proceed with care and protect myself."

"I want to understand and help you if there's a way."

"Thanks. I hope to one day be able to explain it. That is if you can stand to be around me long enough."

The statement silenced him, but only briefly. He said, "If only long enough to know what's in that bloody thing."

Katherine laughed. There was a knock at the hotel room door. He asked her to hang on.

"Do you miss me already?" He asked John, the lead singer of the group. He too had showered and shaved, and he tugged from a bottle of ice-cold island beer. Steve's mouth puckered.

"Three of us need fresh air. We've booked a deep sea fishing boat. There's room if you want to go. They're throwing in a cooler full of beer."

"I'll meet you in the lobby in a few minutes." He said, the view of the ocean too powerful a scenery to say no to just now. He slammed the door shut. "I'm back."

Steve moved about the room more purposefully now, opening a zipper here and a zipper there without closing them again. The conversation would be cut short, and that was something he regretted.

"New plans?" Katherine asked.

"Deep sea fishing, apparently," he said.

"Some time very soon I hope you will tell me exactly what it is that you do."

Steve grinned. "You really don't know, do you?"

"No, how should I, if you haven't told me?"

"If you really wanted to know, you'd be able to find out in any music shop, but if you trust me, I'd rather show you myself when the time is right."

"When the time is right?"

"Yes." He tried to get into a pair of denim shorts with one hand, succeeded and searched for the floppy hat he knew he'd packed. "Whatever you do, don't subject yourself to asking my father."

"Is being shown more interesting?"

He chuckled. "Definitely."

So I trust to leave it up to you... when you think the time is right."

"Okay."

"I think you better go. There must be a fish out there dying to get caught."

"Very funny. I'd rather be in bed but I convinced a few people to work hard for three solid days so I owe them one. The evening will probably end in massive quantities of beer and Pina Coladas on my tab," he scoffed, not at all looking forward to socializing. "Listen, I wanted to apologize for not having called sooner. It was inconsiderate and I certainly won't be back in Blackwell any time soon."

"I'm sure it's not such a great hardship to be where you are. I'm not a bit sorry for you!"

"No, I guess you're right. But if it's okay I'll stop by in a couple of weeks."

"Sure."

Suddenly, Steve felt the distance that lay between them. He didn't want to ring off just yet. He wanted Katherine in his arms again. Here, now, in this anonymous three-star hotel room with its impersonal atmosphere and crisply starched sheets on the bed, the sun sparkling its way to a spectacular sunset. He wanted to open the curtains wide to have the light play across her body like a caress as they made love.

"Katherine…" For what seemed like an eternity, he tried to speak but couldn't get what he wanted to say out. His breathing was fast and shallow, as if in a panic. He wasn't sure that she was ready to hear his innermost confession.

"There is no need for words, Steve. I know you like me. I know you want to spend time with me… that you want more."

He exhaled. She held his heart in such a gentle grip. He shifted the horn from his right hand to the left and rooted around for a t-shirt.

"Listen," Katherine's voice crackled in his ear, "I can't deny that you stir feelings in me, that you're an intriguing man with whom I would love to spend more time." She paused. "But you know, it's really hard for me to confess this to you without some considerable measure of betrayal in my heart. In a way, I suppose you're a bit like the Box."

Steve fell down on the side of the bed as if he'd been kicked. How much of herself had she relinquished in that statement? How could she hold a balance between having hope and orbiting around it? He pressed his fingers against his eyes to keep them from burning. When was the last time he had come close to tears, for goodness's sake? Was this what a real woman did to a man? Was this what true love felt like?

"You're very perceptive for only having lived two lifetimes, Katherine Loch," he said.

***

THE PHONE CALL left Katherine's feelings spinning in uncertainty. It hadn't occurred to her there could be anyone but Norman. Not in this lifetime. She had removed her wedding band and kept it in a box in the bedside table. There was no point wearing it. Instead his, with the six added sapphires, lived on the middle finger of her right hand. He had tried to get her to face a future filled with love and children. But to be with another man Katherine would have to find a way to tuck Norman in the bedside table along with the ring, and however hard she tried, it was difficult to find her way in a world without him in it.

She had even entertained the idea of his and hers lethal doses of heroin. But Norman, ever the philosopher, demanded contemplation about the possibility of life after death. How could they be certain about the outcome of suicide? Would they be together? These things they discussed in the darkest hours, their most private moments. But speculation about the afterlife was never as important to him as the quest for Katherine to move forward. She had relented, to make him happy and for his peace of mind. How could she not? She loved him more than life itself. Even if it meant she had to live it.

As Steve cast a line into the vast blue ocean that only reminded him of Katherine, back home in England she reached into the cupboard beneath the stairs and grabbed Norman's ancient acoustic guitar by the fret board. Wet from the shower, she moved the chair in the middle of the room. The instrument required patient tuning. She played the notes to a song she hadn't played in a while. Like the masterful tattoo that her body reflected in the floor-length mirror, the sound was naked, exposed, loving, wanting, needing, and perhaps more than anything… demanding.

***

A COUPLE OF WEEKS later, Steve's return was announced by a large duffel bag left on her doorstep. Airline labels confirmed it had been to the Bahamas. Daring a glance into her heart, Katherine had to acknowledge she found joy. Genuine joy. It looked like Billie would already be on the beach. She hauled the bag inside and left it.

Away from the heart of the village, the shoreline shortly after six a.m. was quite windy. Waves crashed loudly against the huge boulders jutting treacherously from the sea. The spray composed enjoyable music as it was cast against the horizon and fell back down. Groups of gulls perched lazily atop the rocks, mesmerized by the spectacle. Approaching the castle, Steve was seemingly in conversation with the green door, Billie patiently by his side.

Steve said something to her that caused the large dog's head to turn in Katherine's direction. She took off, teeth bared in an absurd grin. Affection for the beautiful creature had only grown since their first encounter, and Katherine greeted Billie with enthusiasm. She waved at Steve. Dressed for a run, his hair was loosely braided and he sported the shadow of a beard, which furthered the air of mystery about him.

"Can't get enough of the beach, can you?" she asked, taking the stairs to the door where Billie's master lingered in the doorway.

"I need to work on my tan." Steve's teeth sparkled in a tremendous smile and sun-kissed face.

"Hardly. I'm very jealous! Good morning, Gus!"

"Morning Katherine." He nodded. "Looks like you get two for the price of one, Billie."

She looked good. Thin perhaps, but good, and that he was happy to see her was a gross understatement. In his mind's eye, butterflies fluttered about, holding his heart on a string. It was a ridiculous image, and yet, he acknowledged it for what it was. He was in love. More in love than ever and, in fact, never before. The dog made impatient leaps around them, forcing Steve back in the conversation. They chatted a while longer before Gus mentioned porridge, and the three of them walked to the starting point by way of warm-up. When they arrived at the breakwater, they used its surface to stretch. Billie, anxious to run, barked for them to get a move on.

"She's on fire today," Katherine noted.

"She's had to be patient awhile. I rang Gus from the phone box to let him know I was here. We've been talking over a pot of tea."

"He's got a phone in there?"

"Of course. His home is quite nice. Sparse in luxury. It quite suits him."

They used each other's shoulders to balance for leg curls, as had become routine on the occasions they'd run together, and turned for a slow jog along water's edge where the sand was packed hard as concrete and they could easily avoid the pebbles.

"It's a bit creepy if you ask me."

"What? The castle?"

"Yeah."

"Do you mean you've not explored it?"

Billie barked once and bared her teeth as if to confirm a truth she was not pleased about. It made them laugh.

"What happens when neither of us is here to run with her? Does he take her out?"

"No. Gus is quite ill."

"He is?"

"Well, not physically. Nobody knows what happened to him during the War, but from what I understand it's caused him to become a hardcore agoraphobic."

"Agora-what?"

"Agoraphobia is caused by a severely traumatic experience. It's curable in most cases through medication and psychotherapy. But Gus can only feel safe enough to function behind the walls of the castle."

"Forty years after the bloody war?"

"I know. He's a terrific person. Paul and I learned so much by spending time with him when we were boys."

"Like what?" she asked, amused.

"Like how to make a bloody great catapult to shoot wads of paper at the girls!"

Katherine laughed. "He seems kind, but I hardly ever see him."

"When I considered quitting my job, it was Gus I came to see to talk it through. No one else could be objective enough to have a conversation about what I wanted from life without arguing."

"Not even Paul?"

"Especially not Paul. Gus argued that if I had the strength to be a challenge to my own life, that we all, including myself, needed to find trust in that. Of course, very wisely, he suggested I have a backup plan."

"Is that not advice he might follow as well?" Katherine panted.

"Whatever happened makes that impossible, I think."

They chipped away the yards as the sun rose. The wind made for a more strenuous run, and the point came that they were too winded to talk. Billie, bored with the slow pace, ran ahead only to sit and wait for them almost tauntingly.

"Do you have one? A plan?"

"I maintain qualified-teacher status but eventually I plan to go back to University," he breathed, "for a PhD in Education or English."

"Not music?"

"No." Steve coughed into a lopsided grin. "I'm earning that degree in the school of heavy metal."

Katherine chuckled. They continued the rest of the morning's run in silence, and eventually met at the door of Mon Chocolat, Katherine with bakery goods and Steve with several newspapers.

"What's for breakfast?" He was beyond hungry. "And have you got eggs to go with it?"

"I do. The croissants smelled like they should be had. You're welcome to shower first. I'll make breakfast."

"Brilliant."

He ran up two flights of stairs and used Katherine's shampoo liberally as he showered. He'd thought forward enough to have his laundry done at the hotel and dressed in a clean pair of jeans and white tee-shirt. The first thing she said as he fell down on the sofa, where a steaming mug of coffee awaited him alongside the papers, was that he smelled like a girl.

He swatted her bum with *The Times*, making her squeal. "At this point I smell better than you!"

She returned, showered and dressed, before the eggs were ready. With over three hours before work, they spent most of it reading over breakfast. Steve had brought a mango-pineapple-guava-jam gift pack from the Bahamas, and Katherine tore into each of the pots with equal curiosity.

They shared the most comfortable silence two adults can share, interrupted only by the sound of newspapers being folded over to the next page. After the whirlwind recording session locked in a small room with unkempt farting men and assaulted by loud music, the silence was heavenly. He thanked Katherine for it.

"Don't mention it. I quite enjoy it as well." She smiled.

He wanted to kiss her! He wanted to put his hand through her hair and draw her close until their lips met. If he did so now, would she respond to him? He thought it better not to find out just yet.

"Where are the computer prints?" he asked, remembering the reason why he had asked Charlie, the band's driver, to drop him off near High Street instead of his own apartment.

"In the cardboard box underneath the big table."

He stepped over Katherine's legs to retrieve it, and very nearly dropped it on her foot as she moved the newspapers aside. When he fell down again, she curled up by his side, feet tucked underneath her bum. He found the dot-matrix-generated prints and hauled them out.

"I've seen this sort of thing before, years ago at my parents' house," he said ponderously.

"It's probably from the Trust."

"Right. Unless you know of another savings account."

"No. I would have known about it through my mother's will. I knew about the trust; I think I told you that."

Steve frowned. "What happened with your mum?"

Katherine hesitated. She had talked about it with Doctor Ramsey so much in order to try to work it all out, that to drag it all up again when she was so contented, seemed too unnecessary. Steve sensed her hesitation.

"Kath, anything you want to tell me about yourself, I want to hear. If I ask a question that is out of bounds,"—he shrugged—"just tell me. Okay?"

She nodded and gave him a snapshot of her early childhood. "I had no relatives to speak of, which left the care of my mother and myself to me. At first it was little things, the finer work she couldn't do... sewing on small buttons and such. But the more she took to bed, the more I did to keep our life quasi-normal. Eventually, a decision had to be made. Take control or Mum will go into an institution and me into foster care."

"How old were you then?"

"Fifteen at this point. She was vehement about staying home so, with the help of our doctor, we began the process for my being granted legal emancipation when I turned sixteen. He paid for the expenses." She smiled fondly. "Doctor Feldman is a wonderful man. There was such scrutiny in our neighbourhood surrounding him for being gay. So stupid. I would choose him to be my father in a heartbeat."

Katherine shifted position and cleared her throat. "He was an unofficial guardian of sorts and we managed. He spent a lot of time with us. He cooked at least twice a week, thankfully, or we might have starved. He helped me through physics and chemistry. Even,"—she paused to sip from her coffee— "my first period. My mother died, about four months after my sixteenth. I sold the house, put the money in a real estate account and lived in the attic of an old Victorian B&B that belongs my mother's sister. I gave myself an allowance for courses after I graduated and continued sewing and mending to have an income."

"At sixteen?"

"Yes."

"Shouldn't you have received money from the trust a lot sooner?"

"I've requested to see the deed. It appears the trust that my mother set up was an Accumulation and Maintenance Trust. You're right. I could have received the money at her death or else I would have at least received income from the trust when I turned eighteen. There's some sort of law for that. But my mother very *specifically* stipulated that I was to receive it no sooner than my twenty-fifth birthday. There was a note that she felt it would be the right age to have a shop of my own, that I would have gained enough knowledge and apprenticeship then, but not before."

"Now you find yourself with ninety-four thousand pounds without any idea of where that money might have come from."

"Right." With a glance at the clock, she stood from the sofa. "I better get ready for work. It's nine thirty."

"You don't mind if I look at these?"

"No, certainly not. Keeping my ledgers in order is daunting enough as it is." She walked away.

Steve hesitated but saw no point in holding back. "You do realize that what I find here might lead to the Box?"

Katherine had gotten almost to the stairs and stopped. She turned and walked back slowly.

"The thought has crossed my mind," she said, looking deep into Steve's eyes.

The honest vulnerability they reflected, the almost raw fear, caught Steve off guard. He reached for her hand and they remained like that, he on the sofa and she standing beside it, their fingers intertwined. His were warm, hers cold. Sunlight filtered through the windows casting the room in a pleasant light, dust particles floating in search of a place to settle down.

"Have you thought about a compromise?" he asked.

"What do you mean?"

"You could start by simply opening the Box without looking through it. Hold the lid open for one timed minute and then close it again. Just take small steps."

She let go of his eyes and looked at their hands, mulling it over. With a sad smile she bent down to kiss him briefly, tenderly on the lips. It surprised him.

"I'll think about it," she said and disappeared up the stairs.

THE PUB, WRAPPED in the usual comfort of a fire, conversation, and music, had a publican highly distracted by plans to have a show these days. The event was being advertised as "A Charitable Evening with the Blues." The proceeds would help cover legal expenses for a newly set-up charity for children with serious illness aspiring to be musicians. It was an exciting idea to be a part of helping it off the ground, and Paul enlisted the help of the one person in town who seemed in dire need of new challenges. Ned moped about early retirement, and since he made regular trips to London, it was the perfect time to involve him. Paul had ordered supplies via telephone.

"The tablecloths and oil lights are ready to be picked up. It's on your way to the auction house, same sort of vicinity."

"Sure. How many of each am I getting?" Ned made notes.

"Fifty."

"Fifty? Where on earth will you put fifty tables?"

"Smaller round tables will be delivered, and we'll open up the wall to the back room. Most things will be hauled out of here and stored a few days before. We'll need to come up with a way to make it more attractive than it is, but it shouldn't be too difficult. Katherine lent me a book about the Blues clubs in America. There are some inspiring photographs."

"Have you brought this up with the council?"

"On the program for Tuesday's meeting, but it's never been a problem before."

"True. We all wish you'd have them more often."

Paul smiled. "It's a logistical nightmare. But I've been toying with the idea of a house band."

"As long as it's not that clamour my son thinks of as music." Ned saluted Paul with his nearly empty beer glass.

Seated at a table for their meeting, Susan had agreed to tend to the pub. Harry occupied his bar stool, casually ignored by his wife. This late in the day it was likely he didn't realize she was there at all, much less that their children were in the kitchen working on their lessons. The man was like a robot that wasn't aware its chip had shorted out. Susan looked up from a book when Paul laughed. The door opened. It brought with it a draft and Steve Denison.

"Speak of the devil." Paul waved, catching Steve's attention.

Steve stopped at the bar to put in an order and joined them, dropping his leather jacket over the back of the chair. He was dressed to impress with the usual pair of black jeans, a dress shirt, and a staggering amount of hair that made Paul jealous because his was beginning to thin into a widow's peak.

"You need a haircut, son," Ned said by way of greeting.

"Fuck! I keep forgetting to do that," Steve said lightly. "For nine years now. Am I interrupting?" He pointed to the notebook and pen they each had.

"We're having a bit of a meeting." Paul raised two empty glasses, getting Susan's attention.

"What about?"

"Ned's helping me with some of the things for the Blues night."

"Oh, right. When is that again?"

"The twelfth. You better be there."

"Isn't that Gran's birthday dinner?"

"Your Gran doesn't like to be out late. She's made reservations at the Blackwell Tearoom for a proper High Tea. We'll come here immediately after."

"Is someone driving her home?"

"Yeah, Aunt Pauline."

Susan arrived with a full tray. She set three pints on the table and a bowl of tomato soup for Steve. Lettie trailed behind with a basket of sliced French bread.

Steve focused on his former pupil. He liked having her in the classroom. She was a driven student, tenacity making up for having nobody to turn to. Of course, in those days her father had had a proper job and was more or less normal. But she seemed a bit lonely even then, introverted definitely. It was a wonder anger hadn't gotten a hold of her, Steve thought, but there still seemed to be an innocence about her which he found interesting in today's angst-ruled world of teenagers.

"Hi Lettie! How are you?"

"Hello, Mister Denison." She smiled shyly.

That she still adored him was obvious, but she was also awestruck by the fact that he had become somebody famous and that he found unfortunate. Her blond hair was cut in a bob to just below the ears. It made her look younger than fifteen. She wore big earrings that irritated her skin, and just a hint of makeup that set off the yellow in her whiskey-coloured eyes.

"Don't linger, child. You've got work to do." Susan shooed Lettie away.

"What's wrong with her?" Steve asked quietly as Susan, too, removed herself from any chance of small talk.

"Lettie decided to make money for herself. I gave her a job which pissed off her mother. She also made it so that I wouldn't pay her in cash, but directly into a savings, and that pissed Susan off even more which of course proved Lettie right that her mother would have taken the money. They've been at odds ever since."

Paul's eyes followed Lettie as she collected some empty glasses from a table on the way to the loo and deposited them on the bar. She, too, was angry with him. Very angry. On the first day she'd been to his cottage to clean, she had stripped the bed and found what she recognized to be her mother's bra trapped in the sheets. She'd thrown it on his desk where he'd been working on the bookkeeping. Her eyes had been ablaze with fury and something else. Something he couldn't discern. She hadn't asked for an explanation. The hurt in her demeanour said enough to make him want to explain himself to a fifteen-year-old. But she wouldn't have it. She had turned on her heels to finish the chores she'd been asked to do, unabashedly slamming doors as she marched through the house, and hadn't said a word to him since.

Now, as she did the menial things most teenagers would conveniently ignore, he was more than ever aware that sleeping with Susan had been one of the worst mistakes he'd ever made. But the clock couldn't be turned back, and there was nothing to be done for it now. To have lost the trust that Lettie had grown to have in him was the worst feeling, and it was imperative that he gain it back somehow. She pushed the door to the ladies' room open, threw him a glance, and showed surprise to find his pensive gaze on her. He winked, but she only looked away.

Steve, famished after a meeting and a traffic-heavy drive back from London, hungrily attacked the soup. Before the bowl was empty, Susan filled it again. He barely noticed as he talked about the preliminary discussion for Tornado Wave's next world tour.

"The plan is to give the record some time. There will be a few single releases before heading out. Patrick wants us to have small production shows where we get airplay, see which countries go well, and take it from there."

"What do you mean by airplay?" his father asked.

"Radio. The more DJs play our music, the more records we sell. It's marketing. Then we play shows where the market is for ticket sales while trying to keep the expenses down."

"You mean this is an actual *business*?"

Steve was no longer amused by his father's sarcasm. "That's nothing I haven't tried to explain to you before."

"You have the rights to most songs, don't you?" Paul asked. "What are your prospects now?"

"The publishing company we formed has the rights, but I do get royalties for everything I've contributed. It's a win-win as far as I'm concerned."

"How does it get divided?"

"Fifty-fifty. We've got a strong product. It will go bigger than the previous record, but we won't know that for a while." Steve paused, pointing his spoon at Paul. "Your tomato soup is better than my mother's."

"When is the tour being planned?"

"January, beginning in the southern hemisphere. Then we work our way back to Europe by early summer."

"Festival time!" Paul wiggled his eyebrows, rising from the table to collect the dishes.

"Yeah." Steve winked.

"You're speaking in tongues, the both of you!" Ned, frustrated, looked from one to the other.

Paul's eyes sparkled with mischief as he held his hands before his own chest. "*Tits*, Ned," he said, making gestures of roundness.

Ned drew up an eyebrow and glanced at his son, who nodded in confirmation. "It's true. Lots of them."

"Whose tits?"

"Does it bloody matter?" Paul asked, incredulously. "The important thing is, they just appear. Big ones, little ones, tattooed ones... pierced ones." He pointed to his friend. "You've got the best damned job in the world. You better get me in, Steve. I want a spot on stage!"

"It'll cost you."

"Name your charity."

"You two are bloody crazy!" Ned interjected.

Paul left the both of them to argue about Steve's job and carried the tray to the kitchen where Lettie and the oldest of her little brothers were in the middle of homework. He thought of the hours he'd spent upstairs doing that very same thing while his parents ran the pub. Rather, the many hours he had *pretended* to do homework to get out of washing the endless stacks of dishes. Was it regrettable that these children would likely be the only ones to do their homework in this kitchen? Probably not, he thought. He had avowed long ago not to have a family.

Which gave him the freedom to be fond of these, Paul told them to behave themselves or else he would make sausage out of them. It made them laugh hysterically. Even Lettie gave an inkling of being amused by her brothers' reaction to Paul's teasing. He left to check that Susan was okay before returning to spend time with his friends and found Katherine by the bar to place her order for soup and beer.

"Hello, gorgeous," he said as he stopped to kiss her on the cheek.

"Hiya," she said but turned back to Susan. "Let's get a round going, Susan. Whatever they are having."

"I'll bring the usual."

"Thanks." Katherine smiled and joined the others. She kissed Ned and then Steve on the cheeks and took the seat next to Paul.

"Am I interrupting?" she asked, noting the stacks of papers on the table.

"We were talking about Blues Night."

"Oh. How is that going?"

"Slowly. But surely." Paul smiled. "You are coming, I hope," he said.

Katherine hesitated. "I will do my best. If not, you can definitely count on a contribution for the cause."

"Nonsense. You will give me a generous contribution *and* you will be here, and if not, I'll come and get you myself!" Paul said firmly.

"Hear hear!" Ned contributed his opinion.

As the banter flew back and forth, Steve took advantage of the few precious moments to observe her. He had known she would come, of course. They'd agreed to meet for a beer and a chat but stopped short at committing to a time. It would have seemed too much like a date, and he was relieved that his father and Paul were here as well, making the evening more of a social gathering. So intent was he in his observation of Katherine that he didn't notice they had all stopped talking when a couple of men approached them. He was drawn from his thoughts by the grip of a firm hand on his shoulder. He followed the arm that was attached to it, to the face of none other than his former—and sometime—boss who now offered a hand in fond greeting.

"Headmaster Haywood!" Steve rose from his chair and shook it firmly.

"Mister Steve Denison, just the man I was hoping to find. Please, don't get up. Good evening, everybody."

He was introduced to Katherine as the headmaster at the local school while the vicar borrowed two chairs from another table and carried them over. The headmaster was a serious man, someone with a friendly smile but with an air that probably commanded the utmost respect. Steve certainly held him in high regard.

The vicar's gaze on the other hand could penetrate walls, and while he had a wicked sense of humour, he commanded an entirely different kind of reverence. He greeted them all in turn, but his gaze lingered with Katherine just a fraction longer.

"Lovely to finally see you, my dear," he said. "You do have the occasional drink, I see."

Steve noticed Katherine's discomfort under the vicar's scrutinizing curiosity and took note of the wall that she immediately raised around her. He interjected himself by fuelling the conversation with the headmaster, drawing everyone's attention to him. "Have you just come from the school?" he asked.

"Yes. Long night I'm afraid. We had a meeting to discuss some of our more interesting students," he revealed, "which is what led me here."

"You wanted to see me?" Steve asked as Susan brought another tray and divided the order among them six of them.

"Yes, two reasons. Three, if one counts the pint. Cheers."

They laughed. Mr. Haywood nor the vicar hesitated to down their glass. Katherine was surprised by it. At first glance, the headmaster seemed the sort of man who would, in the throes of passion, stop to store his suit away properly and who might prefer a gin and tonic over a menial pint. The vicar, on the other hand, seemed the sort to drink only to gauge the status of the Blackwell flock.

"We need you in the fall, if you can manage. Mrs. Smith is having a baby mid-October."

"For how long?" Steve took a diary out of the inside pocket of his leather jacket and thumbed through page after page filled with appointments.

"Until the Christmas holiday begins."

"I don't have anything scheduled that I can't work around. Consider the position filled."

"Excellent."

"Thanks for the opportunity," Steve said as he drew a line through three months' worth of dates with a pen that was on the table.

"No problem. We're all excited to have you back for a while, not in the least our pupils. Now,"—he took another sip of ale and produced a few sheets of paper that had been folded in half to fit in his inside pocket— "I'd like for you to have a look at this."

"What is it?"

"An essay, fifteen hundred words. The subject was poverty."

Katherine watched Steve discretely as he reviewed the work. He read incredibly fast, something she hadn't noticed before. His level of concentration, despite the music and conversation in the pub, seemed unwavering. The other men discussed the goings-on in the village while Katherine remained focused on her soup, with the occasional glance at Steve. He turned the pages rapidly. At the last page, he inhaled deeply through his nose and rubbed a hand over the barely there stubble on his face. He shifted in his chair.

"Okay," Steve said, looking at Master Haywood. "It's not graded. Why?"

"It was brought to my attention by Mrs. Regis this evening. She was unable to be objective because, she said, it had her blubbering like a baby. The colleagues scoffed, but she challenged us all to give it a proper grade. Nobody could do it. Including myself. I think we all feel that something should be done, and we'll try to work that out. In the meantime…"

"I won't grade it unless she knows I did," Steve said.

"That is highly irregular."

"As is the fact that you're here asking me to. More than being a blubbering baby, Mrs. Regis appears to be a blubbering idiot!"

Paul threw a raised eyebrow in Katherine's direction, the beginnings of a grin suppressed in the corner of his mouth.

"She cares. We all do."

"That's neither here nor there, is it? The work deserves a grade, and if I write anything on this paper, the pupil should know. You can't ask that of me, and nor can Mrs. Regis, without allowing me the opportunity to express that I'm proud. She needs that sort of support from her surroundings, wouldn't you agree?"

"Bloody hell," Mr. Haywood said, causing the vicar to cough in his beer. The impassioned language was quite out of character for a man in a brown three-piece suit. "Does he get this sort of… righteousness from you?" He addressed Ned.

"I know he doesn't get it at church, because I never see him there," the vicar inserted. "Nor Katherine for that matter, and I had high hopes."

Steve turned in his chair. "Susan, would you send Lettie over here, please?"

"She's just putting a clean diaper on Jimmy," Susan replied. "She won't be long."

Katherine had her gaze levelly on the vicar. "Well vicar, I'm not sure what you expect me to say except that had you not harboured such hope, you wouldn't miss me at all."

Paul scratched the side of his nose, exchanging a meaningful glance with Steve. The vicar looked away without a comeback.

Lettie shut the door to the kitchen, drying her hands on a towel, and when she saw who was at the table she threw it atop the bar very quickly. She pushed her hair behind her ears and, touching her earlobe, she winced a little.

Harry was still there, on his perch at the corner of the bar as if it were a piece of real estate he was meant to guard from the rest of the world, clinging to it fiercely. Lettie threw him a sideways glance that held more than a hint of contempt.

"Those children need a father figure." Ned shook his head.

The teen approached with some trepidation. She buried her hands in the pockets of her skirt.

"Hello, Headmaster. Hi, Vicar," she said, returning their greeting.

"Lettie, I've been given the honour by Mrs. Regis and Headmaster to grade this essay of yours," Steve said. "How do you feel about it? Is it weird?"

Lettie nodded, her gaze timidly on the paper in Steve's hand that she had turned in to her teacher the previous week.

"Would you rather I didn't?"

She shrugged her shoulders. "Not as long as I get a fair grade, Mr. Denison," she said.

Katherine smiled in her last spoonful of tomato soup. Paul winked in her direction.

"I do have a few questions if you don't mind. Is that okay?"

"Yes, sir."

"How did you decide on this subject? Poverty in your own nation while everybody is up in arms about children dying in Ethiopia at the moment."

Lettie drew up a shoulder. "That's precisely the issue. Children are innocent in every country including our own. Can Bob Geldof not see that help is needed locally as well? I'm as excited for the Live Aid concert as my peers, but… there ought to be local programs, if not for financial gain of the system, then in activities and education. It's something that I care about."

"Where did you find your research?"

"The newspaper archives at the library. There has been a lot of information given the economic crisis."

"And you decided to make a study about poverty in the UK, within a portrait of your own family. Was it difficult to be objective?"

"Not really. I just reported the truth as I see it."

"Are you interested in a career in journalism?" Mr. Haywood asked.

"Not quite, sir."

"What have you got in mind for your future, Lettie?"

"I'm interested in law, Mr. Denison. International law and children's rights to be specific."

Steve and Mr. Haywood did their best to conceal frustration. Lettie had rightfully pointed out in her essay that education should be a right for every child, not just the privileged. A law degree would be a tall order for someone who had spent life at the poverty level. The best schools in England cost enormously, and the road leading to their front doors was not necessarily paved with scholarships. The essay showed that Lettie had a lot on her fifteen-year-old mind.

"Lettie... this is one of the best essays I've ever read, and before I put a grade down, I thought you should know that. Composition and style are as good as an experienced journalist would have done, vocabulary is excellent. It's well constructed, well researched, and you've cited your references. It's terrific."

A blush crept into Lettie's pretty face. Paul positively beamed, sitting back in his chair. His head bobbed up and down as if to say he had known all along that she was a star. Steve made two quick marks somewhere on the pages and wrote A- in the top left corner.

"That said, you made a couple of spelling mistakes. Even if you think you know the words, look them up in the dictionary to make sure. It's important. You know I would never let you get away with that in my classroom."

Something about the last comment amused her. "No, you wouldn't."

"You are a very clever young lady, Lettie." Steve kept a most serious tone of voice. "You made everybody proud, and you should be proud of your work."

Katherine was in complete admiration for his easy-going demeanour with the youngster. There could be no doubt that he believed in her abilities so much that she'd simply have to believe it herself. She wondered if all children he'd ever encountered adored him the way Lettie did. It was obvious that she did.

"Thanks." She blushed.

"You're welcome."

The girl walked away, and her shoulders slacked in obvious relief, flashing a smile at her mother behind the counter. With business tended to, the headmaster was quick to leave, saying his wife would have supper in the oven. He and the vicar bade them all goodnight, and the headmaster thanked Steve for accepting the temporary job.

"Where were you when I was in school?" Katherine saluted Steve with her pint when they were just the four of them again.

"Fortunately far, far away from you," he said without thinking twice.

He could have kicked himself, but the blush and the smile that crept into Katherine's cheeks were so good to see. He winked, returning the smile. Paul added that she wouldn't have survived the two of them. Ned paid them no attention. He drained his glass.

"I've said it before and I'll say it again," he said. "Capital waste of my hard-earned pounds when you decided to un-become a teacher."

Steve rolled his eyes. "Bloody hell. You'll wear yourself out, man!"

Without warning, the sickening smack of a flaccid human body hitting the floor sounded through the pub. It was accompanied by the loud crash of a barstool. Someone screamed. Heads turned. Most patrons jumped to their feet, chairs scraping across the floor as they were being shoved aside.

Harry lay face down on the floor.

Chapter XVI
Blasted Box

Traffic to London was unusually light when Ned made the journey for auction and the usual supply errands. He accepted this as a mild bonus because the added stops he needed to make for Paul would put him on the very edge of a rush-hour jam on the way home. One never knew. He hated London and disliked its inhabitants migrating to the south coast to get away from the capital city. Ned wanted nothing more than for life in their village to remain a constant, and for real estate to be sold locally. He loved tourists for the simple reason that they spent money in Blackwell and went away again. A terrific concept!

The auction, as always, energized him. He loved the sensation of finding treasure in a room perfumed with wood and varnish cracking with age or neglect; he loved to look for the perfect item that screamed to be fought over by virtually imperceptible nods of the fiercest competitors. It was the one aspect of his profession that he still enjoyed, and he had many friends here with whom he had grown old over the years; their parents had died and they'd had families who had families of their own now. There was always some scrap of news to be shared. When good things happened, it was celebrated with a congratulatory slap on the shoulder and when bad things happened, they shared some words of comfort. Until the hammer came down, niceties were the norm. Then it was each man for himself.

Steve arrived at the auction house in time to witness his father reel in a deal and together they loaded the chest of drawers into the van. Ned insisted on making some introductions. A few remembered Steve as a scrawny kid with short hair, and said as much. As they chatted, a bloke approached him for an autograph. It wasn't his habit to turn people away, and he didn't do so now. Ned didn't say anything. The unrestrained curious stares from his peers made him uncomfortable. Because he was of the opinion that Steve had made a terrible life decision, he rarely spoke about what his son did for a living, and that Ned should be proud but wasn't, Ned knew, hurt Steve's feelings.

They hadn't seen eye to eye since Steve was a teenager, but the rather abrupt career change had made things worse. No amount of reasoning would convince Ned it had been anything but stupid and careless. They were there for each other in moments of need like any family, but refused to meet in a place that held some sort of compromise or a renewed mutual respect; tension between them was mounting.

After leaving the auction, they argued about where to have lunch. Steve wanted a restaurant in a more quiet part of the city where they were not likely to be disturbed; Ned wanted fish and chips in the heart of the West End, within walking distance of where the bulk of his errands would take him. In the end, Steve left him on the sidewalk standing next to the van. He was stumped by his son's angry dismissal. What in bloody hell was wrong with fish and chips in the West End?

What in bloody hell was wrong with Steve—and with Paul for that matter? The episode with Harry crashing on his face at The Wicked Mule was fresh in Ned's memory. It was a sound he wouldn't forget anytime soon. An involuntary shudder ran through him. In the time span of a few minutes, the situation had evolved from alarming to chaotic to utterly bizarre and he'd wanted to buy Steve lunch to discuss it.

Marching to the nearest pub for beer and grub, the images of that night scrolled through his mind like a movie reel. Katherine had quickly gotten a hold of a crying Lettie. It was heart-breaking to see how the young girl clung to Katherine, who both comforted and kept Lettie's gaze averted from the scene by the bar. Someone shouted to call an ambulance but Susan was already on the horn, or so they assumed. Paul had a difficult time bending through his leg so he busied himself getting everybody out of the pub. It was what had caused the most commotion. Nobody wanted to miss *The Harry Show*. Steve was the one to assess Harry's state. He'd loosened the drunk man's shirt and checked his pulse, surprising Ned with very swift action.

"He's not dead," he said, only loud enough for Ned to hear. "His heartbeat seems fairly strong. Perhaps we can wake him."

"Excuse me," a voice said, and Susan towered over them with a pint-sized glass of water in her hand.

As if in slow motion, her wrist turned. Ned and Steve had just enough time to lean out of the way as the liquid clattered into her husband's face from over a yard away. Ned barely had the time to register the look on her face, but now that he thought about it, Susan's state of disconnect should have registered with him then.

Harry sputtered awake and they'd carried him through the kitchen where they were met by the horror of the boys. Katherine and Susan stayed in the kitchen as the two men carried Harry outside between them. They dumped him on a stack of crates where he sat with his back against the wall, quite oblivious but not completely down for the count.

"Harry!" There was nothing but indecipherable moaning in response.

"I've never seen him like this before," Paul said pensively. "It's odd."

They nodded in silent agreement. They had seen the man drunk countless times, and it was true his skin had been yellowing lately, but he seemed more ashen now.

"What's he had to drink?" Steve asked. "It looks like he's had something else, doesn't it?" His voice trailed off, and he threw a dawning look towards Paul.

Paul stiffened visibly. With a grim face, Paul bellowed Susan's name. Ned was oblivious to the meaning of the exchange between them. He had a seat on top of three stacked crates and found the next hour to be one of the most maddening he'd ever witnessed. He was so stunned that all he'd done was to observe, not interfere.

Susan popped her head around the kitchen door. Ned had seen the bruises on her at times and so her lack of interest as to whether her husband lived or died shouldn't have surprised him. But it did. She was absolutely despondent about it, as if she had already accepted the fact.

"A word, Susan."

It wasn't a friendly request or a question. It was a demand, and she stepped just outside. Katherine filled the doorway with her back against the half-open door, holding it to ensure the children stayed where they were.

"Did you call an ambulance, Susan?" Paul asked calmly.

"No."

"There wasn't anybody on the other side of the line, was there?"

"No."

"What did you give him?"

At this point both Katherine and Ned had looked to one another with raised eyebrows. To Ned's further astonishment, it wasn't Paul but Steve whose body went rigid with anger. His hands were balled into fists. When Susan didn't answer right away, it was Steve who repeated the question.

"What did you give him, Susan? Answer the fucking question."

"Just a couple of sleeping pills." She stuck her chin out.

"How many?"

She didn't reply.

"Susan!" Paul bellowed.

"Five. I crushed up five pills in a beer. He's a big man."

Ned stole a dubious glance at Harry, who lived in his clothes as if he'd shrunk back to the size of a teenager lately. Susan must have stopped trying to get a decent meal into him long ago. The man was thin from malnutrition. He had fallen to the side, held up only by a tower of empty kegs.

"We've got to make him vomit," Katherine said from the door and disappeared inside.

Ned was quite possibly the only one who'd heard. The others stood in a triangle where anger, defiance, and unnatural calmness bounced among them like dangerously volatile molecules. Soon after, Katherine emerged with a mug, and Ned stood to offer assistance while the others argued.

"What have you got, love?" Ned asked.

"Warm milk laced with salt," she said.

"Clever girl," Ned said as he looked around for a bucket.

"He's out of it again. Can you rouse him?"

"*Harry! Harry!*" Ned whacked him on the cheeks a few times until the man fought to open his eyes.

"This may come too late," Katherine said.

"It won't hurt as long as we stay with him. Drink up, mate."

Harry fought them. Steve and Paul, attention stolen by the flailing of drunken arms, joined them. The three men held Harry while Katherine pinched his nose shut and poured the milk down his throat, forcing him to swallow. The milk that didn't make it down ran from his chin and soiled his clothes. Susan looked on, her gaze void. The next thirty minutes weren't pretty. What came out of

Harry reeked more than Ned could ever describe. Katherine was the one who held the bucket. She did so without flinching.

It didn't take long before Paul couldn't handle the incessant retching. He said something about looking in on the children and promptly followed suit. Susan tried to grab hold of his arm, but he shook it from her grasp. The gesture broke something in her. She may have been beaten physically and mentally, but for the first time, Ned noted something like real pain in her eyes. It caused him to wonder about the nature of their relationship, but there were more important issues to be dealt with. Katherine calmly set the bucket down by Susan's feet. Susan stared at it.

"This is your responsibility. Do it quickly because if he pukes on this floor it will be you scrubbing it clean. Ask Paul for more milk and bring the salt shaker. Please."

Harry put up more of a fight in the next round, and while they waited for him to empty his stomach again, Steve finally abandoned any attempt at keeping his anger in check.

"How dare you?" Steve asked, silently at first, then louder.

Katherine looked away from bucket duty. The woman had a stomach of steel, Ned remembered thinking. She hadn't turned away once at the sight or stench of Harry's vomit.

"Despite what your life is like, everybody here would help if you were willing to help yourself and your children. You have no right whatsoever to involve Paul in poisoning your husband. Have you no idea… have you no remorse for what it might do to him if this got out? How bloody dare you!"

"Nobody saw it, and anyway, he wasn't even there. I did it while he was talking to you lot."

"So you wanted us to be his alibi for attempted murder, did you?"

Susan looked away. Steve had practically roared. Ned had seldom seen his son this way even in the most heated of arguments between them over the years. Susan turned on her heels and disappeared inside.

"Steve, you're frightening her," Katherine uttered quietly.

"What?" He turned on Katherine, realized who she was, and unclenched his fists.

Harry, looking decidedly green at the gills, began to heave again, and Steve moved to hold him up by the scruff of his clothes but averted his gaze.

"Lettie just told me that Susan does try to help her children by keeping them away from their father, by stepping in the line of fire when he goes after one of them. She takes the punches even when they aren't meant for her."

"Why would you defend her, Katherine? We should call the guards."

Katherine let go of Harry's arm and stepped before Steve as if she were the one facing off with him now. Her temper flared. Ned noticed it by the way her nose narrowed and her eyes widened.

"You would call the coppers for her slipping him a sleeping pill, but not when she's full of bruises for having been beaten?"

"Of course I would call them but I'm never there to witness it, am I? What she did here is wrong!"

"I agree with everything you've said, Steve, but yelling isn't the way to get through to Susan. She's fragile. And she did this because she is desperate. She's scared and without a clear vision of the future until she becomes empowered enough to leave. So if you want to ring anybody, let it be your mum. And hold your bloody temper."

Harry had fallen to his knees at that point, ever vomiting and heaving—there seemed no end to it—and they both returned to focus on making sure he didn't choke to death. Ned, believing Katherine's suggestion a sound one, left them to call Beth from the pub's telephone. She'd arrived quickly but no amount of on-the-spot-psychotherapy could convince Susan to go anywhere but home. With Harry.

Nobody could force her so Steve and Ned half carried Harry to his house. Susan, Lettie, and Katherine each took charge of a younger child and followed. They had propped Harry up in bed where he could sleep off the rest of his unexpected evening cocktail.

Lettie was quiet and withdrawn, her jaw as set in defiance as her eyes emanated uncertainty and fear. Ned took note of the struggle that raged inside of the girl even as the little children clung to her for comfort, and even as she tried her best to provide that for them. Paul was behind Lettie's chair, hands resting reassuringly on narrow shoulders that were rigid with tension. It was clear where his loyalty was in this situation.

Beth had met them there by car and asked Susan for the remainder of the sleeping pills. She had flushed them, while Susan blushed with embarrassment.

"Do that again, and I get social services involved," Steve said to her calmly. "Do you understand?"

"Mind your own business," Susan replied.

"Paul is my business. So are your children. Get them out of this situation before something worse happens."

Katherine took him by the hand and pulled him towards the door where she turned back to Susan.

"Steve is right, you know. This will escalate. No matter how much I care, I will not be the one to stop him from calling the authorities if you mess with Paul's life again. What you did was unfair anyway, but you ought to be ashamed after all he's done for you."

Ned had fallen down in the car next to his wife, feeling older than normal. Katherine and Steve were in the backseat holding hands. On the way to drop them off at their respective homes, little was said. There was tension among them. They reeled from the shock of what might have been had Susan given Harry more than the five pills. Despite them all being torn between empathy, and knowing their loyalty was for Paul, they would have offered Susan and the children a place to stay had she said the word. Beth was a persuasive woman; Katherine had stood by her with sound reasoning, but Susan had had the last declaration.

No was a powerful word.

No means *no*.

That was the last Ned had heard about it. Now he was in London, leaving the pub with a meal that was heavy in his stomach, quite alone after what should have been a rare lunch appointment with his oldest son, whom he loved but didn't quite understand. He worried about Paul. He worried about Katherine and the blasted Box that he couldn't get out of his mind, bringing back the past like an ice-cold mirror that he may or may not be forced to look into.

Armed with lists, Ned drove from shop to shop, the van becoming ever more packed. He had the canvas, paints, turpentine, hides, and the usual things for Gus; an array of items for Paul's

Blues night at the pub; office supplies and medications for Beth; things for his own shop.

It wasn't until he was nearly on the motorway that he remembered the post office box. There hadn't been any letters for years, but he still checked it every month, and never without a fraction of hope. He made a U-turn and drove through the Wandsworth Borough, along a cluster of South-West End's side streets that he was less familiar with. He took a few wrong turns and somehow ended on the wrong side of the train tracks. But eventually he found Shaftesbury Park with its quaint Victorian laborers' cottages, and navigated down Eversleigh Road which would bring him closer to the Battersea post office he'd visited for very nearly thirty years.

Cars were parked on both sides of the street, and an older woman made her way from sidewalk to sidewalk, dragging a shopping trolley with little regard for oncoming motor vehicles. Slowing down gave him the time to look around. The quaint homes with front gardens the size of a napkin were well kept. It was a colourful neighbourhood with lively people chatting to the neighbours from their front doorstep.

A football sprang into his peripheral vision just ten yards in front of the van, followed by a young boy chasing it. Ned slammed a foot on the brake, his heart very nearly popping out of his body against the windshield. He honked the horn with scorn. The boy lavished him with a naughty, toothless smile and disappeared into the very house where Katherine had spent her childhood.

Chapter XVII
Discoveries

Spring popped a myriad of colours into the hundreds of window boxes and planters throughout Blackwell-on-Sea. With the flowers and blossoms came a throng of tourists. Mon Chocolat's first season taught Katherine that the time had arrived to hoard money like nuts for next winter. She hadn't just advertised locally, but as far away as London, and lady visitors seemed to respond to the ads, her tasteful window displays, and there was further business because she and her partners in the village worked harder because they had a small stake in each other's shops.

Customers who understood the construction of clothing admired Katherine's work. Compared to similar shops in the bigger cities, including London, she was an unknown, but the detail in workmanship spoke for her skills in a way no printed advertisements could and word of mouth slowly became a factor as well. That prices were set higher than at any of the high-end boutiques in Brighton or Hastings didn't seem to throw them off.

Katherine was busy with alterations or making garments for customers whose sizes had not been available into the wee hours of the night, but the bookkeeper would not agree to hiring help, and he was right that the cooperative weather was the unpredictable factor. Being confident in her work at least helped her to be swift. Stock was carefully replenished without too great a risk, and she managed to pay herself a salary to cover living expenses and health insurance. The rest of the boutique's gross income was deposited for taxes and bills, and to reinvest into next season's materials. She bought a knitting machine but lacked the time to learn how to use it.

In between customers, she planned for the fall-and-winter season. The change for fall was scheduled to take place in mid-August. She made lists of things to do, checked pricing, scheduled models for a catalogue photo shoot, and stewed over the idea for a small fashion show. In addition, industry standards required being ahead in the game and the research train for next year's spring-and-summer season had departed the station. The catwalks in London, Paris, and New York left Katherine's imagination abuzz with ideas, and a spring sketch was completed for every constructed fall piece, simply to keep everything moving forward somewhat commensurately.

Steve remained close at a distance. With the album now in post-production, the band rehearsed for the gigs that would accompany its release, and work kept him in London. He enjoyed the time with his mates, but he made sure Katherine knew she was never far from his mind. He stole away for an occasional chat, and the workaholic in him marvelled at her ability to have a conversation through the whirring of a sewing machine without surrendering a high level of concentration. The picture of their professional lives became clearer, and so too the need for a greater effort in feeding their friendship to give it a chance to grow. Steve's desire to send flowers and ask her out grew stronger. He made up his mind to invite her on a proper date, and the next time he dialled the number, he skipped the usual small talk for a direct approach.

"I'm coming home this weekend. Will you have dinner with me on Saturday?"

The whirring in the background stopped abruptly. Steve had caught her off guard, and he braced himself for rejection. Was it too soon? It seemed an eternity before she cleared her throat to speak.

"Are you asking me on a date?" The shy smile in her voice sent rivulets of love through him.

"I am."

She cleared her throat again. "Okay, yeah."

"Yeah?" He allowed the butterflies in his belly to take flight. "There's a small Italian restaurant in Brighton where they have candles on the tables and Mario Lanza on the record player."

"I love Mario Lanza."

"I thought you might. See you Saturday."

"See you Saturday."

***

THAT SATURDAY EVENING Katherine was relieved to lock the shop's doors and leave it all behind. She had pulled her hair into a tight bun, dressed in a pair of vintage white bell-bottom jeans, and paired it with a chocolate brown sleeveless top from the summer collection. While plain, the low V-neck did amazing things for boobs, and hers were no exception. She was tired but felt good about the business, and the prospect of a night out filled her with energy. She walked to Steve's place in record time, purse bumping harmoniously against her hips. The front door was unlocked.

"Anybody home?" She knocked at the top of the stairs.

"I'll be done shortly; make yourself at home!"

Rounding the corner to the sitting room, Katherine was met by a small legion of guitars. She stopped abruptly in her tracks and her hand flew to her mouth to keep the surprised squeal inside. There were six electric bass guitars, all Fenders, a gorgeous acoustic six-string bass, and an empty stand. Next to the instruments were three massive Marshall Amplifiers. A door slammed somewhere deeper in the apartment, and she jumped a little, acutely aware that she'd been staring with her mouth open. The piano was within reach, and, unable to resist, she sat down to play. The first thought was always a classical piece but, admittedly nervous to see Steve, especially because of the gear she had her back to now, her fingers found the keys to a boogie-woogie.

Not wearing jeans was out of the question, but Steve made an attempt at ironing a button-down shirt in the bedroom. Lured by the music, he gave up and unplugged the iron. His heart beat like a drum when he laid eyes on her and not merely because the notes seemed to bubble from her effortlessly. Smoky eye shadow made her blue eyes pop as they found him standing ten feet away, buttoning the shirt. She smiled, ending the song with a perfect run across the keys.

He chuckled. "You are full of surprises, Kath!"

"I quite miss having one of these." She swivelled the piano stool around to face him. "And you're one to speak! There are thousands worth of equipment in here!"

"I haven't got much room anywhere else." He smiled, omitting an explanation.

"Tell me, do you play all of them at once?"

The weeks away seemed to have had an effect on them both.

They were getting to know each other even on the phone, yet in the moment it seemed they were nervously meeting for the first time. He held out a hand. She took it. The twinkle that played in Katherine's eyes caused Steve's intentions to keep himself at arm's length to melt like ice cream on a hot summer day. He pulled her to her feet.

"I was aiming for one a day but…," he said, shaking his head.

"A clear underestimation." She snorted and he saw evidence of the naughty twinkle again.

"You are beautiful," Steve smiled, almost shyly. Their fingers entwined loosely together.

"Thanks. You're not half bad yourself! Did you buy the shirt for this occasion?"

"No, but I ironed it. Does it look okay?" he asked, scrutinizing what, for him, was a true accomplishment.

Katherine tried to look impressed but couldn't put her heart in it so she kissed him on the cheek as a reward for the effort and retrieved her purse.

"If we're driving along the coast, I don't want to miss the sunset."

The evening was a glorious one, and the sunset did not disappoint. Steve drove with ease along the road trapped between the coast to the left and fields of grass swaying in the breeze to the right. The sea shone in the reflection of the sun as if dancing with fire opals—a spectacle to enjoy in the company of someone special. When shifting didn't require attention, his hand found Katherine's leg. At the restaurant, there wasn't a boy or a man whose eyes didn't rove over Katherine's body as she strode by the tables. She was seductive and cute, intelligent and sophisticated in one package. That she didn't seem at all aware of it made her even more beautiful and Steve was proud to be seen with her.

They ordered wine and fried calamari for starters and laughed conspiratorially when a few other patrons addressed looks of disgust at the mass of curls pouring freely down Steve's back. Otherwise they paid attention only to the meal and each other, and decompressed from work. Steve couldn't keep his eyes off of Katherine. He'd always thought she had great breasts, but tonight's hint of cleavage caused his fingers to burn with longing. It pleased him when she became aware of it and blushed.

After sharing a pizza and gelato for two, Steve paid cash for the meal, leaving a generous tip for the waiter who had recognized Steve at first glance but graciously hadn't bothered him with it. Steve appreciated this more than ever in that moment. Katherine thanked the young man with a brilliant smile. They held hands to the car. As the last of the light fell behind the horizon, and they left

Brighton, it occurred to Steve that if this were any other woman, the night might end in a shag. With Katherine he harboured the hope that she would sleep soundly in his arms again. Stealing sideways glances as they barrelled down the road, he realized there was something novel and exciting about being with a girl knowing the outcome would not be shallow.

The Triumph approached Blackwell-on-Sea with a fierce engine roar. The moon rose higher in the sky, illuminating the castle's gigantic silhouette, dark and menacing. Katherine shivered. Centuries ago, when enemies prepared to take the fortress in war, the image would have instilled fear. And yet there was no denying there was something magical about the place as well... magical in its ability to awaken the imagination. She thought of Billie and her master, and wondered how they spent their evenings behind the massive perilous walls.

"Nightcap at The Mule?" Steve suggested over the noise of the little car. She nodded.

He parked the Triumph in the garage at his place. The evening was pleasant enough to walk the rest of the way, and they did so with loosely intertwined fingers and hearts filled with probability. Katherine's heels clicked musically on the ancient cobblestones.

The Mule burst at the seams. Paul was surprised to see them out together, with Katherine looking as radiant and relaxed as he had ever seen her. He motioned for them to meet him outside and said he would join them shortly. Steve made for the loo as Katherine opened the door to the kitchen. She was met by a most homely tableau that sent a broad smile of surprise to her face. Susan's children had their hands in a bowl of dough, and an aroma of vanilla and chocolate told her something was imminently ready in the oven.

"Hello, everybody. What's baking?"

"Scones and cookies," the taller boy said, grinning.

"It smells heavenly in here! Are you doing this all by yourselves?"

"Lettie and Mummy helped." He was missing a front tooth and clearly in his element.

All three of the boys were dressed in matching light-blue button-down shirts with short sleeves and a pair of jeans. Each of them wore an apron with his name embroidered on it. They were adorable.

"That's lovely! What you are you making with that?" Katherine pointed to the pile of dough in a bowl, rising beneath a chequered towel.

"I'm not supposed to touch it." The little boy of around two or three pouted.

He had some amount of flour on his perfectly round face, streaked through with tears. "That's right, Jimmy." Susan came in with a tray full of used glasses and set them down next to the sink.

Apparently the dough had posed a matter of some contention between mother and son, and Jimmy had clearly not overcome the argument yet. Katherine smiled. She greeted Susan and Lettie, who was busy at the sink. There was an air of tension between them, though Susan looked remarkably well. She seemed relaxed as she and Lettie, wearing a similar apron as her brothers, worked their way through an endless stream of dishes. The dishwasher noisily did its business at a much slower rate than Lettie did manually working through a load, and as usual, a large pot of soup was kept warm on the Aga.

"May I have a word with you, Katherine?" Susan asked. "Lettie, scones should be done at any time. Don't burn yourself."

"Yes, Mum."

"And where will you lot be when your sister opens the oven door?" Susan asked with her hands on her hips and a no-nonsense look on her face.

The boys pointed to the opposite corner of the kitchen. Katherine hid a smile behind her hand and winked at Lettie. She stepped outside. The Christmas lights were not switched on in the outdoor area, giving the little improvised outdoor room a lack of lustre. Susan shut the door and joined her.

"How are you?" Katherine asked.

"You don't have to ask, you know," Susan replied quietly. "I'm not sure why you would be interested. Nobody else is. My own fault, I suppose."

"I am interested. I wouldn't ask otherwise."

"Oh. Well... I'm okay for now. My kids are okay."

She fiddled with the hem of her apron nervously. Katherine wondered if Susan had ever confided in another woman before. It seemed she had no trust and very little confidence. Was there something that could be done?

"I wanted to thank you for the other night," Susan said. "You've been through your share of vomit."

Katherine hesitated. She didn't know Susan and wasn't one to tell her life story to just anybody. But how could she offer help if she herself showed no trust? Lead by example. Wasn't that one of the golden rules of engagement?

She scuffed her toe against a loose piece of pavement. "You're right. I cared for someone who had severe reactions to chemo."

"Oh," Susan said quietly. "Was it someone close to you?"

Katherine nodded. "My husband."

Susan was astonished. She started to say something, eyes on the opposite wall focused on an invisible image. The apron endured more fidgeting, its hem rolled between Susan's thumb and forefinger again and again, almost rhythmically.

"Did he make it?" she asked quietly.

"I'm afraid not."

A cacophony of noise emanated from the brick wall Katherine leaned against. The pub vibrated with the essence of village life. Katherine realized in that moment that she loved Blackwell. She wondered if Paul or Steve would arrive with something to drink. She was parched for a Schweppes. And she loved Blackwell-on-Sea.

"I want you to know that you mustn't hesitate to give me a ring or to stop by." Katherine sensed the other woman growing tense and quickly continued, "I understand you don't need it right now. But Susan, I just want to hear you acknowledge that someone cares should that need arise. We all do care that nothing happens to you or the children that you can't bounce back from, together. Because you've got a very lovely family in there."

Susan stood and made for the door. She turned.

"I've been told I'm a bad mother for not leaving Harry."

"Are you?"

Susan took some steps towards Katherine. "If it makes me bad for them to see him hit me, wouldn't it also make me bad for leaving their father, whom I vowed before God to care for in sickness and in health?"

"Perhaps it would help to see Doctor Ramsey."

"What, the batty doctor?"

"Do you think I am?"

"What?"

"Crazy."

"Of course not."

"Do you think it's easy for me to figure out the emotional crap I'm going through or... that I've had a posh life so far?"

"Do you see her?"

"I can't do it on my own, Susan. It helps to talk about it with someone who doesn't have an emotional stake in my life."

"She might convince me to leave Harry."

"You're wrong. Only you can convince yourself of that."

"Was he good to you?" she asked, throwing the conversation in a different direction.

Katherine could only nod for the lump in her throat. She realized Susan existed side by side with a breathing cadaver. She didn't envy her that. At least Norman was dead; she could be sure of that.

"Do the good die young, you think?"

Katherine laughed, in spite of their conversation. "I hope not." It came out croaky. She cleared the tears out of her throat.

Suddenly the terrace was bathed in the magic glow of Christmas lights. The big wad beneath the corrugated roof had the improbable semblance of a chandelier. The lights were arranged in a way that the side storing pub things was left in relative darkness. Paul and Steve appeared from the kitchen. Susan unexpectedly embraced Katherine, a brief but heartfelt hug.

"Thank you," she said.

"You're welcome."

Giving his leg a much needed rest, Paul fell down heavily in his comfortable lawn chair. Seeing the painful grimace on his friend's face, Steve expressed his concern.

"The usual, only worse lately," Paul said flippantly. "What's going on with you two? I haven't seen you in ages."

"Work," Katherine and Steve answered in unison.

Susan brought a tray with tea things so quickly it was obvious Lettie must have prepared it. Little Jimmy followed formally and proudly with a basket of scones and cookies. He carried it in both hands as if he were holding a pillow with the crown jewels.

"That's lovely, Jimmy!" Steve said to the little boy. "Did you make these all by yourself?"

Jimmy said "yes" very loudly and promptly hid behind his mother.

He took a bite from a cookie. "Hhmmm, that's very good! This is the best cookie I've ever had."

Jimmy beamed at his mum, earning him a loving rub across the head as they disappeared again. Katherine and Steve spent a half hour with Paul. It took more than one pot of tea for the grimace to relax from his face. Katherine asked for a double shot of espresso at the kitchen door, to keep the evening from sudden collapse.

Steve inquired about Susan, not at all surprised to have found her back in the kitchen and Harry with his head on the bar, oblivious. He knew how Paul's mentality worked. He was like a cat lady, a batty old woman to whom cats flocked like a magnet. Only Paul collected people. If the pub was his mother ship, then his aura was the force field. Paul would never admit to being the nurturing type, but he was actually, albeit in a non-traditional sense.

"One mustn't kick a dog that's already hurt, you know. That's what my father always said."

"One mustn't kick a dog at all! Has she changed her mind?"

"No. Your mother explained there may be a catalyst to bring this all to a head. Which is fucking frightening."

"It must be so lonely for her despite the children," Katherine returned.

"Love does strange things to the brain," Steve said cryptically.

Paul snapped his head 'round. "Since when have you become an expert?"

"Well isn't it true?" Katherine spoke quietly.

Both men turned to her. She finished her coffee. "From what a person would do to be rid of it, to what they would do to hang on to it... and everything in between. It boggles the mind. And in the end, what is it about, really?" She put the cup on the tray. "That's what I wonder."

"Being daft, if you ask me," Paul said so candidly that both Katherine and Steve roared with laughter.

As if on cue, loud laughter came from inside the pub too, and Blackwell-on-Sea's favourite publican remembered he had a job to do.

"You kids want a bottle of wine to take home?" he asked, preparing to stand. With full weight resting on the prosthesis, he grimaced and gave it a minute to acclimate to the pain.

"I won't say no to that," Katherine said. "Are you quite all right, Paul?"

"Nothing I'm not used to, love. Breakfast on Monday?"

"Yes, lovely!"

"Come to my place. If the weather is decent we can sit on the wall."

"See you then." Katherine kissed him lovingly on the cheek.

"Thank you," Paul said, throwing an arm around her neck.

"For what?"

"For being kind. You're a fantastic girl, you know? The best."

***

THEY UNCORKED THE BOTTLE and carried two wine goblets to the living room. Rafael, happy to see them, curled himself around their legs, as if weaving through an obstacle course. Steve and Katherine tucked into the corner of the L-shaped sofa together. The brief Overture to *La Bohème,* Act I, softly filled the room. He reached over to switch off the lamp behind the sofa, leaving only a few small candles for light. With her head against Steve's shoulder, Katherine closed her eyes and sighed. For a while the music was the only voice.

"You enjoy Puccini?" Steve asked quietly, finding her fingers.

"I listen to it often."

"*La Bohème* is rather tragic."

"Sometimes life is like opera. It has helped me to appreciate the music more. It's brilliant." She raised her head for a sip of wine.

Being together was quietly anticipated without discussion. It felt comfortable as much as exciting and unfamiliar. Katherine massaged the enormous calluses that had formed on Steve's fingertips. He closed his eyes, enjoying her gentle touch. When the needle crackled off the record, he volunteered to turn it to Act 2 and smoothly resumed their position. Rafael repositioned himself on Katherine's shoulder.

"I think I was in danger of forgetting what it was like to relax."

Steve snorted. "I've had too many bloody meetings."

"Would you like to spend the night?"

"Only if you let me cook the eggs this time," he said dryly, referring to the scrambled eggs she'd fixed last time.

She laughed. "It wasn't that bad, was it?"

"The eggs were quite dead, you know. Not even a defibrillator could have brought them back."

"Oh my God!" She sat up. Raf roughly awakened from his snooze, ran off with a perturbed yowl. She hit Steve with a pillow. "What an awful thing to say!"

He laughed heartily. "It's the truth!"

Katherine's eyes fell on the box that held the records and she kicked it, spell of relaxation broken for the moment. "Tell me about what you've found out."

"I thought you'd never ask. Are you up for it?"

"They're just numbers. They might not be significant."

"They are just numbers, Katherine, but if there is a possibility of their being insignificant, then why don't you open the bloody Box?"

She chuckled. "Touché."

"I think you should keep an open mind about whether or not the numbers are significant."

"Tell me."

"All right. First, we don't have all the numbers. I looked through everything. The first date on the computer-generated prints is 1964, but when you analyse that money was added like clockwork every month, then the earliest amount is probably not the starting figure. So the trust must have been established earlier, or with a starting sum. I've checked on that type of trust and either is possible."

"What were the individual deposits?"

"They happened on or about the third of the month for one hundred fifty pounds each time."

"Were they my mother's?" she wondered aloud.

"Possibly, but we don't have details about the nature of the deposits. Only that they happened."

"That's nineteen hundred pounds per year!"

"Right, but the total for one year equals more than that."

"It would have to, given the size of the check."

"There were frequent additions around the middle of the month as well, but they didn't add up to much and they were hardly ever the same amount. I would say they averaged around fifty, sometimes less and sometimes more. But Katherine, there is something else…"

Steve didn't refer to the notes she'd seen him jot down as he spent the day on the floor among a mass of paper, a calculator resting on his thigh. Katherine wondered if he had memorized the information.

She was instantly breathless. "What?"

"Are you ready for this?" He took her hand.

"What?"

"Sporadically, there were erratic amounts dropped in the account. I believe it was sometime in 1964 for twenty-two hundred pounds."

"In one go?" Katherine asked in disbelief.

"Yes."

"But how can that be?" She leaped from the sofa and made an agitated turn around the sitting room. "My mother wouldn't have had that kind of money!"

"Only you would know that, but I agree that's a rather substantial sum for that time. It wasn't the highest though, over the years."

"What was that?"

"In 1975. Six thousand."

Katherine looked at him in disbelief. "What?"

Steve shrugged, unable to explain. He'd hoped that Katherine could shed some light on the irregularity of the dates and amounts.

"My mother was bedridden by then, and I certainly didn't know about the trust then. I barely made enough for us to live off."

"The smaller deposits stopped around 1973, about August if I remember correctly."

Katherine thought back. Her eyes grew wide with a significant realization. "Steve, that's when my mother became too ill to leave the house," she said as he put his empty glass on the coffee table.

She went rigid with possibilities beginning to form inside her mind. She moved her hands restlessly across her face.

"What's going through your mind?" he asked, willing the discombobulation out of her.

"I thought the amount was accumulated through good investments… but someone kept spiking the trust," Katherine whispered, almost afraid to speak the words aloud as if the printed numbers weren't proof already. "My mother wasn't the only settlor, yet she was the only one listed on the deed."

Steve could almost see the images flying before her eyes, so intent was she on the past as she disappeared into a faraway gaze.

"It must have been my father," she whispered, more to herself.

Steve agreed. Secretly, he'd arrived at that very same conclusion. Katherine took her glass again and emptied it in one big swig. Her eyes were on the Box now, still in its spot on the shelf where it had pulsed with seduction for weeks. Steve realized what she was about to do and held his breath.

As curious as he was, he could understand a certain amount of reluctance. He recognized the possible implications. Perhaps it meant nothing. Or maybe it would throw Katherine's life onto a completely different path. He wanted to support her every step of the way for as long as she cared to pursue what the Box might have in store.

"One minute?" Katherine turned to him, eyes burning with intensity.

He nodded, holding his watch at the ready. Katherine picked up the Box. She rested it on her left arm and took a breath to draw in courage. At the top of the minute he said "go," and the lid was flipped open. Steve would have liked nothing better than to look over her shoulder, but it was too private a moment and he didn't dare intrude upon it. The minute ticked by as thick as honey. Her head barely moved, but her eyes were never still. She touched things gingerly, as if not wanting to disturb the order within the Box.

"Time!" he said, probably louder than he had intended.

Katherine dropped the lid. She pushed the Box back on the shelf, none too gently, and stared at it with fiercely balled fists. She turned away abruptly.

"I'm ready for bed," she said.

Thundering up the stairs, out of sight, she left him staring after her. Was he meant to follow her? To bed? He drew up a bemused eyebrow, and calmly rose to prepare the house for the night. He went downstairs to check the front door, blew out candles, washed glasses and a few cups… giving her time. Giving himself time.

Katherine was sitting cross-legged on top of the bed, waiting, when Steve joined her upstairs. His heart hammered against his ribcage. He used the loo and found a brand-new package of name-brand pyjamas and a new toothbrush by the washbasin. He recognized the name of the shop on the price sticker. She'd been shopping. For him. Not having worn pyjamas since he was a small child, Steve couldn't help but grin into the mirror. He washed up and brushed his teeth before stepping into the pyjama bottoms. She had guessed his size perfectly.

Raf lounged on the foot end of the bed as if he owned it, which of course if he could speak, he might have said he did. Following Steve's every move with mischievous emerald eyes, the kitten swatted when his belly was tickled.

"Little Riff-Raff!" Steve teased with a fond smile.

Finally, not allowing himself the slightest bit of excitement, he joined Katherine on the bed. Taking Steve's hand, she played with his fingers, regarding his manicured fingernails, touching the bass-player calluses that ran in a line across four fingertips. She looked into his eyes. The intensity of the blue gaze plunged into him freely with a profundity of sadness. It tugged at his heart more than he would have ever thought possible.

Her hair was freshly brushed, face free of makeup, her breath minty with toothpaste. She wore demure black cotton pyjamas and, as adult as her features were, what he saw was the little girl she must have been. He could envision how she might have crawled into bed, tucked in by her mother, and while her eyes stood big, innocent and hurt, they also held a vast amount of wisdom that she probably hadn't wanted to gain the hard way, but accepted nonetheless.

Steve touched her cheek with his free hand, pushed the wayward strand of hair behind a dainty ear, brushed at some freckles on her nose, and kissed her cheek. Even with the windows open, it was fairly warm in the attic bedroom. Without a word they lay down on top of the covers, and Steve drew her close. They switched off the lights, leaving the moon with the task to spill its glowing milky blanket over them.

***

KATHERINE LAY AWAKE for hours, unable to push the mysterious trust from her mind. That and the Box were somehow Tessa's legacy. As much as she hadn't wanted to open it, even wished she hadn't received it at all, there was no logical reason why it should have remained shut. Steve's suggestion to compromise made sense. It was what she had of her mother. It was all that remained that probably meant anything… or everything.

What if it did lead her to her father?

Fear had its ugly claws in her so deeply that she pushed against life consistently and chose to hide from it. As if the mourning process wasn't enough to navigate, she now fought images of meeting her dad. She felt panicked about it. She was angry about everything. There were no more romanticized fantasies about having a real family, a family of her own and a father who cared the way she'd pictured as a child. That picture was replaced by a monster that had not yet shown its ugly face.

But the circumstances had seemingly put her fate directly into Steve's path as if it were he who needed to present life like it was meant to be lived. His presence filled her with new feelings and mixed emotions and budding things and glimpses of things to come. Good things, she thought, hindered by obstacles that begged to be overcome, that lived just beneath the surface of her soul.

Norman had been Katherine's only experience with a man She thought he would mean that to her always. But nearly eight months without him, she was left with a need he had unlocked so gently at first and filled Katherine with a passion that she feared was impossible to find again. Her truest fear was to find it only to have it taken away again, for whatever reason, and this was much more overwhelming than she could control. In that sense, Katherine worried that what Steve did for her might hurt him in the end.

Love, she scoffed to herself. She loved her father as much as she hated him. She hated him out of loyalty to her mother. Perhaps because of their lonely life, it was somehow easier to love a man she didn't know.

What would the Box bring to Katherine's life? Or better yet… whom?

"Katherine?" Steve whispered against the tension in her shoulders.

"Yeah?"

"You've got to believe that you will be okay."

"I can't seem to find the connection between then and now."

He watched her in the moonlight. "You will. Just don't be afraid."

She turned around to face him. His hair was loose even though it was probably hotter than having it in a braid. He was handsome. Incredibly handsome. And alive. She took a deep breath.

"What?" he continued to whisper.

"Have you ever really loved someone?" she asked softly.

"No."

"You haven't?"

"I've been saving myself for the right girl." He grinned.

Katherine chuckled. "Didn't you have a first love?"

Steve laughed softly. Memories danced triumphantly before his eyes.

"Tell me about her."

"She was an older woman, seventeen, I think. On my fourteenth birthday her parents and mine had a function, a ball or something. They bribed us to babysit. When my brother and sister were asleep, mysterious things occurred."

"Was it nice?"

"It was mind-boggling! She gave me a blow job and said it was an experiment so she'd know what to do. I admit, I was rather crushed when I found out she had a real boyfriend."

"Was that the only time?"

"The experimentation on my body went on for a number of months. Easy to do since she lived just across the street. I was rather smitten, I thought, until I discovered there were other fish in the sea that begged further exploration."

"It sounds nice to have had experiences. I've never been with another man."

"You haven't?"

"No."

Steve leaned on his right elbow, regarding Katherine pensively. Her lips were slightly parted, eyes glistening in the dark. She was pretty, just as he imagined she would be beneath a moonlit night.

"How long has it been?"

"Oh, I don't know. Making love used to be so important in our marriage but faded away quickly during Norman's treatments. We slept hand in hand. In the end it mattered to have one more day, one more moment. Another kiss."

He ran a finger gently over her lips. "Do you know...," he started as she took his hand and kissed it, "that you're teaching me that already?"

Steve caressed her cheek, giving her the space to draw back if she chose to. When she showed no sign of timidity, he kissed her, allowing his budding emotions to spread through her like a cup of warm milk laced with honey, until it reached her core where it bloomed into the promise of something infinite, the flower that would never cease to turn its head to the sun and whose colours would always be as bright as they were at its birth. He unbuttoned her shirt and spread the fabric over her breasts, drinking in the image. She watched, fire blazing through her body.

"Katherine..."

Steve drew her close, until her breasts gently touched his bare chest. It was an indulgence. Something he had dreamed about. Her arms slipped around his back. Their mouths met again, tongues twisting in a very slow dance of passion.

He needed to let her go. He kissed her mouth, her cheek. He cupped her breasts one by one. He grew hard against her. God! He wanted her so badly.

"Steve, I want to..." She moaned, reaching for him.

He stopped her, with the utmost gentleness and with complete disregard for her need and for his own.

"I know it would be so lovely to have you, to be inside of you." He touched her face gently and made her look him in the eyes. "But sex is too easy. And you're much too special."

As much as he knew it should stop, he kissed her again, but he buttoned her shirt, one by one, speaking tenderly but firmly some of the most important words he would ever say to her.

"I want nothing more than for us to be together, Kath. But it's important that you want it too, that our need is for each other alone." He drew back, holding her face in his hands. "I think... I feel that you might be the right girl. Do you understand? I want for your heart to be with me, and you're not ready."

Katherine cried softly in his kiss, tears unguarded as their mouths locked once more in a heated dance. Steve took her tears, accepted them, and for that she was so grateful. He drew her securely against his body and stroked her hair until the last teardrop tickled slowly across his chest and her breathing slipped quietly into sleep.

***

DOCTOR RAMSEY WAS terribly intrigued by the notion of the Box. Her patient hadn't been around much lately because of her work. She noted Katherine's difficult time to begin the session and to concentrate. It was a few days after the evening Steve had timed Katherine's first glimpse at the contents of the Box. They hadn't talked about it until the next morning when they'd had brunch over the Sunday papers, and the silence between them was a bit more complicated than it had been before.

"There must have been a deciding factor to have a look finally," Doctor Ramsey said in an effort to bring the session to some sort of a solid starting point.

"It was something a friend said to me. He presented the possibility of having a compromise."

"This friend is the same person you spoke of before, the man you said you'd met?"

"Yes."

"You've allowed him to see a bit of who you are."

"I really like him."

Doctor Ramsey interjected a rather provocative question, with purpose. "Have you become intimate?"

"What's that got to do with my mother's Box?"

"More than you think. The Box represents a very personal dilemma for you. The fact that you have shared this, that he guided you, or rather, that you allowed that to happen, seems to me like a reasonably big step in your healing process."

"I thought about it for a while, you know. The suggestion to have a very quick look seemed quite fair."

"You did it Saturday, you said?"

"Saturday night, yeah. He timed it. One minute. Then I put it back on the shelf."

Doctor Ramsey smiled at that and said, "I can respect that... it's rather brilliant."

"Yes, I thought so."

"You never answered my question, Katherine. Is that hard for you?"

"We haven't had sex if that's what you want to know."

"I doubt sex is your definition of intimacy after what you went through, and nor is it mine, but it certainly is a part of a whole."

Katherine looked away. The memory of Saturday night was still delicate in her heart. There had been moments since that she had grasped Steve's words and his kisses and allowed them to touch her again in a smile on her lips. She touched them now, with her fingers, mesmerized. Their kissing had been amazing, completely surprising in the way every single thought had disappeared, other than Steve himself. Focusing on an invisible spot on the opposite wall, she reached inside to find a way to describe how things were between her and this man who was, at the end of the day, Doctor Ramsey's son.

"We are as close as we allow ourselves to be, perhaps each in our own way and for our own obvious reasons. I think it's safe to say that we enjoy each other's company. There doesn't seem to be a need to say very much. He's comfortable to be with. It's quite nice actually. I find that I look forward to spending time with him. But it isn't any more than that."

"True discussions will have to happen at some point."

"The thing about him is that he doesn't require me to bare my soul and so I feel as if I can trust him with it. In that way, yes, I am beginning to show myself. That's really as much as I can say about it. Except snogging with him is quite exceptional," Katherine added with quite a wicked look in her eyes.

Doctor Ramsey could not contain an approving smile.

"It sounds as if he has a good sense for what you're going through. Do you talk about Norman?"

"Not really. It seems like a violation to do so. To the both of them. They do deserve to have their own private moments with me, don't they?"

Doctor Ramsey made some notes in Katherine's folder.

"Let's talk about the Box."

"It's been opened now. I suppose there is no way back."

"Were you surprised at all by the things you saw? You seem quite resigned about it."

Katherine thought about the little shirt and shorts and the matching little cap. So beautifully made, with tiny, loving stitches. She would have recognized her mother's work blindfolded and in that moment, it filled her with nostalgic longing for her mother.

The morning after opening the Box, she'd removed the outfit for a better look and to show Steve what her mother had been capable of. He'd asked if she was happy to have it.

She forced herself back to Doctor Ramsey's question. "At first glance I'd say I was right about the purpose of the Box."

"Somehow you seem certain this will lead you to your father."

"I am faced with a choice of finding him with all possible consequences. Or to allow him to continue to be the mysterious figure whom I love but who can't hurt me."

"You love your father."

Katherine thought about it, finally pulled her legs beneath her bum. It was a sign to Beth Ramsey that her patient had relaxed into their session. She leaned back in her chair knowing the hour would be productive.

"I love the idea of him. This idyllic vision I had as a child that is still with me."

"Name the consequences for me, if you can."

"The first one that comes to mind is, of course, that he might not want to be found."

"Certainly."

"There must be a reason for him to have wanted to hide, to not be in our lives."

"One hopes." She made a note in Katherine's chart. "What else?"

"He could be dead."

"Would that be devastating?"

"I think I've told you this before. I'd be disappointed probably, or relieved perhaps. Certainly not as devastated as the notion that he didn't want me or that it was somehow my fault that my parents were not together."

"Do you feel it likely that he is deceased?"

"How would I know?"

"I think you do. I think you feel connected to this man enough that you do know. What does your gut tell you?"

Katherine chose not to answer. It was sort of obvious, wasn't it? She believed very deeply that her father was alive. She could sense him. But the little girl who wrote a letter to that man was not ready to come out to face him.

She continued with her list of consequences.

"Of course, he could be alive and loving but old and decrepit."

"And that, Katherine, is what kept you from opening the Box, isn't it?"

For a minute or so, she said nothing. She thought of that fear again. The fear of loving and losing.

"Yes," she said quietly.

"But this friend, this new potential... lover, or whatever your relationship may turn out to be, convinced you to make a step towards any of the possible consequences."

"He makes it so that I don't feel alone in this quest. But I'm afraid that he might be waiting for something I cannot give And my father as well."

"Love." Doctor Ramsey threw the card on the table for Katherine to stare at.

"Perhaps the wall is wobbly in some spots, but it's there nonetheless. What if the only love I can give is from a distance in a way that nobody should have to put up with? It's not fair. So really, why should they... or I, for that matter, even begin to try?"

Beth, excited for Katherine's progress, leaped out of her seat and practically shouted. "Because you need it, my dear Katherine!" She paused. "And because you're *worthy* of it!"

Katherine shook her head in fierce denial. Her eyes pooled with tears.

"What you are putting yourself through now, and yes, Katherine, you could be better if you allowed it. It is keeping you from finding *bloody* anger!"

"But what's the use being angry? *Who* is there to be angry with?" Katherine said, frustrated.

"Whatever you want it to be... the universe! Only you can know that. Being angry, getting it out of you! It's right there." She touched her own sternum to demonstrate. "Anger will allow you to take what is rightfully yours!" Doctor Ramsey exclaimed, spreading her arms with such vigour that the file in her hand spewed its contents through the room. They fluttered to the floor like white doves gently aiming for a place to settle down. Doctor Ramsey left them where they chose to land.

"What?" Katherine was a little astonished at this sudden burst of passion from Doctor Ramsey.

"Happiness, Katherine! Love, children of your own... whatever it is, but happiness ultimately. Don't you want these things for yourself?"

She thought about the tiny outfit again and Steve's question whether she was happy to have it. The truth was that she'd known about the little things her mother had stitched for her. She had begged over the years to see them, to use them for her doll. But it hadn't been possible because every last bit of it had been given away, she'd been told.

Yes, she was happy to see the baby clothes, but Katherine questioned what it would have mattered showing them to her when she was a child? Would it have killed her mother to allow this small request?

"It's funny how I used to be okay about my relationship with my mother. I was always led to believe that she did the best she could and I thought I did the same for her. I found some sort of balance there that I thought I could live with."

There was an odd pause in the conversation, as if something in their universe shifted.

"It has changed in the last few weeks, hasn't it?" Doctor Ramsey said quietly.

Katherine nodded, biting her lip. "It seems she wants me to find my father, but in that process she has become even more of a mystery. A relationship with my father is something that has yet to begin. There's a strong feeling that I will not be able to make amends with my mother until that happens." Something hit the window, or so she thought, but it didn't deter Katherine from her thoughts. "I really don't want to be the kind of mother mine was. It scares me, God... how that frightens me! I'd rather not have children at all."

"I know, child. I do know and believe me, I even understand," Beth said. "You told me once that even as a young girl you sensed being stronger than your mother. We've had many sessions since then." Doctor Ramsey licked her lips, trying to determine how to continue. "It is my firm belief that you will use everything in your arsenal for your children not to grow up the way you did. They will be sure of your love for them. You are a very strong woman, Katherine, even in the face of everything that has happened to you."

Beth crossed the barrier of the coffee table to sit down beside Katherine. They faced each other.

"You are one of very few people I get in my surgery by whom I am absolutely touched." She paused. "I want you out of here. I know it is possible and I think we are almost there but for the one obstacle that stands in your way. Believe me when I say that I so want to bust through that wall of yours, and I've really got to hold myself back not to shake you until you get angry with me!"

Katherine laughed at the mental image and blew her nose loudly. They stood. They had well exceeded the allotted hour.

"Thanks," she said and spontaneously gave Beth a hug, breathing the earthy things like basil and rosemary and lavender that seemed to be a part of her essence.

It suited her. She seemed a true earth mother. It wasn't surprising that Steve was such a level-headed man with a mum like Beth, Katherine thought.

Beth squeezed Katherine's shoulders firmly. "See you next week, Katherine. I would implore you to try to make time."

As Katherine quietly closed the door behind her, Beth Ramsey collected the paper with a smile and a spark of hope in her heart

Chapter XVIII

The Painting

There was something about spending time with Paul that was familiar, like falling into a favourite chair. Several mornings a week they had breakfast, talking about experiences with clients and travels and stupid things. They had formed a habit of buying an uneven amount of scones or croissants or Danish in order to have an absurd contest over who should get the last one. It could be the number of customers that had been in the store compared to the pub—as if Katherine could ever win that one—or they would calculate their average income from four to five on a Tuesday afternoon and whoever made the least amount of money, won.

Katherine found that she was able to let go of her inhibitions the most being with Paul. He could get her to laugh about the most ghastly things. But for all of their banter, they could also be quite serious. It's not that they sought out talk of intensely private things, but it also wasn't something they avoided, although Katherine was certainly more open about her life in the Netherlands than about her friendship with Steve. Paul assumed the situation was both too fragile and too serious to spill the beans about what went on between them. He was of the opinion that as long as they moved forward spending time together, things were as they should be.

Paul believed that Katherine was much stronger than she realized. He believed fear kept her from being freed from her shackles. He knew exactly what she needed and was going to make it happen.

The situation between Lettie and Susan was a source of worry. He confided in Katherine about his tryst with Susan because it wasn't something he could discuss with just anybody. Katherine could envision that a woman with an incredible need to be touched without violence would turn to someone like Paul, though for his sake she thought it best it happened only once. Susan's desperation, however, had manifested in other ways.

"She spends every waking moment in church lately."

"Does she?" Katherine asked curiously. "Well… there's nothing fundamentally wrong with that is there? As far as I'm concerned it's better than having sex with you!"

"*What?!*" Paul reached for a pillow and threw it at her.

Katherine held up her hands. "Okay, yeah, sex with you could be what God is made of for all I know!" She laughed, throwing it back with equal force. "*Sooo sorry* to step on your bloody ego!"

"Fuck off. No, of course there isn't anything wrong with it." He waved her question away as if she weren't seeing the point. "Lettie wanted a job to save money, but reality is that the chances to attend the A-Levels in Brighton are slim. There's no way she'll ever be able to raise enough. But that's neither here nor there."

"What do you mean?"

"Her decisions deserve respect, don't they? With drive and tenacity, who knows what might happen? She is channelling her anger down the right road and that must give her a measure of control." He sighed, running a hand through his hair. "For now anyway. My point is that she's got a lot of studying to do to graduate Secondary with the grades she needs to even be considered... and with Susan at church, who's responsible for the little ones?"

"I see. Does she do it on purpose?"

"I do get that she needs support and the vicar is someone to turn to."

"He stares any time we're around each other. Have you noticed that? Makes me feel bloody uncomfortable."

Paul smiled. "Well, who wouldn't? You're a very striking woman and he's probably curious about you. He's been in this community for a very long time and he cares about it. Susan is probably scared of losing Lettie so much that even school is a threat, though."

"I'm sure we can find a way to diffuse that kind of thinking."

Paul shifted. "I hate that she dusts my house, Katherine. I really bloody hate it." He pointed a finger and said, "I put an extra hundred in the account last week. What do you think happened?"

"I can take a guess." Katherine smiled, having a sip of coffee.

"I found it on my bureau in an envelope, neatly sealed and addressed to me. There was a note... *Thank you but I don't remember earning this.*"

Katherine snorted, amused as much as she was impressed. "Rather cheeky beneath that withdrawn exterior, isn't she? I like her."

"Me too. I want so much to help, but I'm starting to feel perverse that a fifteen-year-old is all I can think about. I've even considered bribing Susan to allow Lettie to study."

"You must be absolutely bloody bonkers!" she said. "I mean, yes help, but you know Lettie would be furious and she'd be right. There are lines that shouldn't be crossed. Clearly she is telling you that."

The private doorbell chimed in the stairwell. Katherine threw a quick gaze at the clock. Just before eight. She had a good idea who it might be. She fetched her keys from the kitchen.

Paul said. "I know. You're right, of course."

Their game for the last chocolate croissant had not yet begun, and with the bell ringing again, she pointed to Paul with a stern warning. "Don't you dare touch it when my back is turned!"

She ignored that he looked hurt and quickly thundered down the stairs to find Steve on the doorstep, dressed for a run but not at all sweaty.

"Hiya," she said.

She threw him the keys and thundered back upstairs two at a time expecting to catch Paul with a mouthful of croissant. But he sat with folded arms, looking every bit the part of innocence. She glanced suspiciously at the coffee table and found everything was in order.

"You actually thought I would do that!" Paul stated with a hand over his heart as if he'd been stabbed.

"You *would* do that." Katherine fell down in her spot, laughing. "There's no point denying it."

"What's going on? Hey, Paul, how are you?"

Steve, who was about to have a seat beside Katherine, noticed the breakfast plate and said, "Oh, can I have that?"

Paul and Katherine each held out a hand in protest, to no avail. Without invitation, Steve swiped the croissant and took a hungry bite, and one look at each other sent Paul and Katherine in a fit of laughter.

"What?" he asked, which made them laugh even harder.

"How was Billie?" Katherine asked, waving away the question.

"She wasn't able to run, so I gave up. Is there more coffee?"

"Why not? Is something wrong?" Katherine raised her voice so that it followed him to the kitchen.

"She growled fiercely when I approached," he said as he joined them again. "You've got to go down there yourself. She is most definitely waiting for you."

"What do you mean?" She frowned.

"I swear, Kath. Go to the sally port."

"The what?" She looked to Paul, but he had a stupid grin on his face. "What's so amusing?"

"I'm just glad you didn't get it. It's almost as good as winning."

Katherine rolled her eyes but couldn't suppress her amusement. She turned back to Steve, who popped the last bit into his mouth and had a tentative sip of coffee.

"The green door. It's high time you learned castle terms if you're going to invest in our great monstrosity as you call it!"

"Invest? What are you talking about?" She frowned.

"That's right, you've turned twenty-five!" Paul snapped his fingers as if she should connect some sort of imaginary dots.

"Right," Steve grinned and pushed against her leg. "Go to Billie. Now. Go."

Katherine left without another word. She wished they hadn't been quite so mysterious but stopped dead at the sight of Billie perfectly perched on the top step by the green door. She was freshly bathed, fluffy like a bear. She looked dapper, as if she knew not only how good she looked but also understood the importance of her task. She sat still with great difficulty as doing so got in the way of wagging her tail. In her mouth she held a large, fully blooming yellow rose, and her eyes stood big and round with a dog's innocent desire to please. Next to her, leaning against the door jamb was a brown-paper-wrapped parcel.

"Is that for me, sweet girl?" Katherine asked with a smile, petting the top of her big head.

She took the rose gently from Billie's mouth. It was indeed for her and had been carefully stripped of its leaves and thorns. Grossed out by the slobber, Katherine held the rose between two fingers. Billie made a monkey noise, poking her nose against the parcel. It was rectangular in shape, fairly thin, with her name in large, gracefully printed letters. Billie danced around, barking excitedly. Drawing it into her lap, she sat down in the spot the dog had vacated. Her task completed, Billie bolted down the steps to the beach and with bared teeth, ran 'round and 'round in ever bigger circles, expelling pent-up energy.

Katherine took a moment to absorb the beach. She became aware of the gulls circling above, voices sweeping down to the beach effectively by the wind. The joy of living by the sea was yet again surprising. The water was grey beneath the cloudy morning sky, and she inhaled the aroma of wet sand, and decaying shellfish. Wind touched her skin with utmost delicacy. She sighed, contented, and focused on the package. The hemp-twine knot holding it together yielded quickly to her fingers. There was a letter, which she tucked into her jeans pocket.

"Oh my…"

The canvas depicted a sunset view from a soaring height's vantage point over steeply pitched Elizabethan rooftops and cobbled streets, in thick layers of oil paint. Glorious colour burst from the town's heart as the sun was reflected by whitewashed buildings and many tiny windows. It was perhaps a snapshot of yesterday or several decades ago, or more. Blackwell-on-Sea, without the sea, yet somehow it could be assumed the artist had listened to the crashing waves as he worked.

Katherine couldn't quite read the signature, but it must have been painted by the keeper of the castle who spent many mornings tethered to palette and easel. She could hardly wait to show Paul and Steve. Taking a few steps down the beach, she sensed being watched and turned slowly. A lone figure stood atop the castle, gazing down with a foot casually resting on top of the low battlement. Moments went by. He brought a hand to his mouth, and suddenly Billie, who had been sniffing around near the water's edge, made a beeline for the green door. Gus didn't move otherwise. His attention was entirely focused on Katherine. She tried to think of a way to thank him from this distance. Finally, she curtsied clumsily with the flower and the painting held wide in each hand. Gus waved and with that, Katherine went home.

Katherine,

Please allow me to congratulate you on your recent twenty-fifth birthday. As Chair of the Foundation responsible for maintaining our magnificent Castle, it is my honour to contact the inhabitants of this village at the beginning of their twenty-fifth year, with the request to become a participating member of the BCF (Blackwell Castle

Foundation). This rather unusual tradition began as a great necessity when it was realized some years ago that centuries of decay, due to both battle and its location by the seaside, had taken its toll on the structure. Regular maintenance is of the utmost importance.

While it is not difficult to have materials donated, expertise and craftsmanship are quite costly. As the castle continues to lure much-needed business to our community, we ask our villagers to become involved either by donating time to work at the entry, the tea stand, or gift shop a few times per annum. Base membership of the BCF costs 50 pounds, but of course, any amount in addition is welcome. As a member you will also be invited to a yearly fundraiser banquet which is held on the day of the Fall Equinox in September.

Enclosed is a form with all pertinent information that you can return to me completed at your earliest convenience if it is indeed your choice to participate. Meanwhile, please accept this birthday gift on behalf of the BCF with our kindest appreciation.

Sincerely,

Gus, BCF Chair and Founding Member

"How did this come about?" Katherine murmured. "Interesting concept."

"A necessary one. The city council and many of the villagers back then decided to do it. I think Gus's father was still alive and the caretaker then. If you but visited, you would be able to read about it at the museum," Steve said.

"Get off my back, will you? My energy is better spent for the future and trust me, that's arduous enough."

Paul and Steve threw each other a knowing glance.

"Katherine, as a merchant, you must realize how much of our revenue is directly related to the castle. Before making a donation, remember to give that some thought," Paul added.

Steve nodded. "It's true. They sold a quarter of a million tickets last year, not counting school groups."

The men each shared the story of their own BCF gift. Steve had received a very old compass, he assumed donated by his father. "The note read for me to always find my way home no matter where I am in the world." He nodded as if to say he had taken the message to heart. "I keep it by my bed as a reminder that it's still the most comfortable place to sleep."

"I was given the carved wooden cognac glass holders, but he had been making them for my dad around the time of his death and Gus told me that finishing them was more about closure," Paul said. "He gave me sea-view sunrise but with a rare distant view of the castle. He does hardly any of those because he never leaves the damn place. But he's a well-known artist around here, and the painting you received is valuable."

Giving the canvas a place of honour on the bookshelf, Katherine offered to make another pot of coffee but Paul declined. He needed to get some things done. He slapped Steve on the shoulder telling him not to be such a stranger and kissed Katherine on the cheek. Steve let him out, using Katherine's bundle of keys to lock the door. He found her in the kitchen with the morning's dishes.

She smiled. "Are you staying a while?"

"I'm afraid I can't. I overslept this morning and I've a lunch date with dad and my brother. I should probably just shower and leave."

Running hot water into the sink, Katherine reached for the dish soap and let a few drops fall into it. Foam formed instantly. Steve leaned back against the counter, looking on as she wiped the counters clean before turning off the tap. She had dark circles under her eyes. He reached out and touched her arm. She smiled but continued the task.

"Are you all right?" he asked.

"I didn't sleep well last night."

"Are you happy with the painting?"

"I am. It's beautiful, don't you think?"

"Not as beautiful as you," he said, longing to kiss her.

"We hardly compare."

"True," he murmured and was unable to resist stepping in behind Katherine for an embrace. He kissed her shoulder. "But I can't kiss a painting."

"You could, but it would look rather silly." She smiled, leaning against his shoulder as he moved her hair aside to kiss her neck.

"Hmm, I can taste the sea on your skin," he said without removing his lips.

She giggled. He suckled her earlobe and she turned her head a little, making her lips invitingly available. Their eyes met—and their lips. Katherine relaxed against his chest. They kissed tenderly. Steve's hands slipped underneath her shirt, fingertips fluttering lightly across silken skin. They found her breasts and Steve cupped them without restraint. Her nipples poked against the lace of her bra and grazed the palms of his hands. When she thrust her chest forward, it drove him mad. He grew rock hard, and not willing to hide, he made sure she felt him. Katherine made to turn around in his arms but he held her close.

"No, don't move," he whispered against Katherine's lips. "It's time you knew how fantastic wearing these overalls can be for you."

Katherine moaned in his mouth when his fingers eased down a flat belly and found her knickers. She was more than ready. He played with her slowly, agonizingly slowly, both the washing up and the lunch meeting quite forgotten. He took the time to probe keeping the fabric between them, curious for her body to reveal its secrets ever so slowly. She bit her lip, spellbound, caught in the game. She threw her head against his shoulder, and her eyes closed as she lost herself in his touch. Her breasts stood full and erect, and he teased to see how far she would let him go. Her breathing became more and more halted. Taking direction from her body, his hand slipped beneath her panties and he was welcomed by buttery softness. She moaned as her flesh swelled to meet his touch and only then did he slip inside. Steve's labour was instantaneously rewarded. She trembled against him hard, and he made it last until she gave her mouth to him again, kissing passionately, and until the trembling became a mere ripple of tiny tremors.

It took the mother of all self-control for Steve not to take her right there in the kitchen. A healthy blush had spread on Katherine's cheeks and it pleased him. She panted against him. Forcing his heartbeat to steady, their eyes met. He grinned wickedly, pulled her panties back in place, tucked the shirt, and whacked her gently on the bum.

"The dishes won't wash themselves, Katherine."

In a daze, she listened to him disappear. He took the stairs two or three at a time to the bathroom where in the next moment he was in the shower. Needing a moment to collect herself, Katherine was glad for the privacy. Her knees were weak with the intensity of the first real orgasm in well over a year. It stirred a panicked feeling in her heart. Was it because it had been so long? Or because it was the first time for a man other than Norman to have touched her that way?

Was it Steve?

Ten minutes later he came back down, and Katherine turned toward the kitchen entry. She regarded him, big cornflower-blues filled with liquid wonder. He leaned against the door pane, comfortable, handsome, smiling, love lights dancing from his eyes without a shred of doubt. And that was her answer. Steve. Steve. She experienced a surge of something not familiar lately. A fragment. Happiness. It was devastating, but she was mesmerized. And open. Steve. Katherine made a decision.

"If you want it..." She took a deep breath. "Steve, if you want it, there's a spare key in that drawer." She nodded towards it. "Please, don't be cross that I ask you to leave, but I need some time to myself."

She tried hard to keep her dignity, and he quite understood that she needed to work through what she had allowed him to do. There were so many firsts in her life, and there would be for a while yet. His heart filled with gratitude. Still weak in the knees, Katherine held out a hand and Steve walked into her embrace. They hugged strongly and she buried her face in his neck.

"That was amazing, Kath," Steve said quietly. "Thank you."

He kissed her cheek and gave her bum a squeeze, opened the drawer, took the key, and left her to ponder the ponytail tucked in its envelope upstairs; a new future with a different cast of characters, among them a cat and a dog; and the cherry red Stratocaster that called to her more strongly every day.

And... Katherine thought as she blew the strand of hair out of her face, there was this wonderful intimacy tingling with possibility to love a man with chocolate eyes whose heart was clearly hers for the taking.

She left the washing up in the sink, climbed the stairs, and hauled the gear out of the closet. She played along with records and tapes until her fingers turned raw. At the first sign of blood, she taped them, and ignoring the pain, continued to play.

PAUL CARRIED A CARDBOARD box with six valuable bottles of cognac to the castle. Lettie had cleaning duty at the pub, giving Paul the opportunity to get through necessary paperwork after the breakfast with Katherine. He had called ahead to let Gus know that he was on his way there. As he made his way from the cottage, he remembered his tenth birthday when he and Steve, their fathers, and Gus had spent the night in the Lord's chambers which had been newly restored. A terrific time for two impressionable boys with imaginations larger than life.

As an adult, Paul hardly ever visited anymore. The big fortress was just a place he walked by twice every day without giving it the consideration it deserved. He took it for granted as probably many people in the village did. As a merchant it was difficult to donate the time, and a check was written in under two minutes. Katherine's letter from the Foundation was a terrific reminder that brought it all back into perspective.

Limping across the narrow but long drawbridge, he noticed that Gus had an eye on him through the small grate in the small door that was set in the main gate door, which was massive. The timber from which they were made was nine inches thick, he remembered, as solid as the day it was heaved into place. As Paul approached, Gus opened the smaller door and stepped aside to let Paul duck through to the gatehouse.

"What's the small door called again?" he asked, holding out his hand in greeting.

Gus was nearly as tall as Paul, slender still but with a small belly hidden beneath a knit sweater that had seen better days or else a few moths. He wore bifocal glasses with thin gold rectangular frames of which the temples looped around his ears. His beard was trimmed but not neatly. The old man had the shabby appearance of a starving artist, which of course, he was.

"A wicket," Gus replied easily, shaking Paul's hand with surprising firmness that belied the impression of fragility. "You look well."

"You've hardly aged since I last saw you." Gus wasn't yet sixty-five, he didn't think, but he had looked the age for as long as Paul could remember.

Gus produced a cigar-steeped rattle that was meant to be laughter as he bolted the door. It was at least ten degrees cooler beneath the protection of the gatehouse, until they stepped into the morning sun caressing the quadrangle with its spring rays.

"Coffee?" Gus pointed to one of the small round cast-iron tables where awaited a thermos, cups, and a tin of biscuits.

"We can make it a *royale*," Paul suggested.

"What have you got there?"

Paul sat down in one of the chairs that looked delicate but were in fact heavy cast-iron affairs with complex patterns. He produced a bottle of *Cognac de Grande Champagne Extra Old* and gave it to Gus, who whistled appreciatively.

"This certainly is too superior to end its life in coffee. How much for the lot?"

"Trade." Paul poured them each a cuppa. He added two lumps and some cream to his.

Gus asked, looking from the bottle to Paul, "For what?"

"I'm having a charity event a week from Saturday. Have you met Katherine Loch? Nice piece you gave her, by the way."

Gus carefully set the bottle on the small table, with the label facing them. The label was as much a work of art as the amber liquid in the bottle. His mouth watered at the prospect, though he wondered if the bottles could be held back another number of years.

"The young lady who runs on the beach with my dog most mornings. We've spoken on occasion."

"Perhaps you know she's a young widow. Her husband's family would like to start a charitable cause in his memory."

Gus squinted at the gulls that circled and squawked overhead. He sighed deeply. "Such hardship for such a young woman hardly seems fair. Or the young man, of course."

"Right." Paul sipped from the strong hot coffee. "I realize it's hardly an even trade, but it is my hope that we can auction one of your paintings that night."

"What's the cause?"

"To bring music and art to children with cancer," Paul said.

"No problem. I would have donated one. There was no need for this."

"I know you'll enjoy it anyway." Paul smiled at the gentle old man who, despite a myriad of eccentricities, was a pillar in the Blackwell-on-Sea community.

"Indeed."

Billie appeared from the shadows of Gus's rock-solid home that had only a tiny window facing the castle's inner courtyard. There was a door, painted bright-green like the sally port on the beach. Paul knew that large windows added in the last thirty years faced

Gus's private, and much smaller, courtyard where he had a patch of grass and a small garden with vegetables and prize roses.

"How is business?" Gus produced a packet of cigarillos and offered one to Paul.

"No, thanks. It's good. Only one person missing from this town, you know?"

Gus lit the cigar with a match. He blew it out and threw it in a small ashtray imprinted with advertisement for Lipton tea. During opening hours tourists could buy a tea, coffee, or a fizzy drink from the window behind them. There was a roll-up awning over the terrace, but it wasn't needed now. The sun warmed Paul's skin in a very pleasant way. He could hear the waves crashing on the beach; though, rather than the sound penetrating the walls, it washed over them.

"I know."

"You're missing out."

"Perhaps not," Gus said. "There's nowhere I'd rather be."

"But you do grasp that the War is over, don't you, Gus? It's okay to have a pint with your friends down the pub."

"I do know, though I must say, it has been a number of months since you've told me."

Paul laughed at the note of sarcasm in the old man's voice. "I should visit more often, I know. Much like you, though, I like to be in my own space."

He studied the inner ward, enjoying the aroma of Gus's thin cigar. Together with Steve, he had encountered numerous locked doors on their adventures of discovery, of course. Some parts of the place were in decay as one would expect of something that was nearly 1000 years old. The battle-scarred walls rising high into the jagged edges of the battlement were blackened with age.

The inner courtyard was a cascade of cobblestones and small manicured lawns beneath which snaked a labyrinth of subterranean passages reeking of dark and damp. The flower-filled gardens were a beautiful contradiction to the scariest hollows and recesses below. If there was one warning they'd heeded as boys, it was never to go down there. Knowing their fathers would allow it, they believed Gus when he said he'd put them over his knee one by one. That and the merest mention of numerous resident ghosts Gus claimed to have seen, bore respect.

The most fascinating portions of the castle were the stunning chapel on the top floor of the gatehouse, from which ran a long corridor around the perimeter of the inner ward to the keep where the Lord's quarters were located. The keep was the tallest portion of the castle, heavily protected by parapets dotted with arrow slits along the dark twisting stairwells. Like the chapel, the keep was kept in pristine condition.

"Do you remember how we used to try to hide after you locked up for the night?" Paul asked, the memory laced into a fond grin.

"Yes, of course. It happens on occasion even now, but you two were really good. You tried to climb up the chimney in the Lord's bedchamber!"

Paul laughed. "Mum scoured my face for a week… quite brutally so, I might add."

"You boys were fun. I had to be stern, but you know, I laughed when you weren't paying attention."

"We're still fun, I hope."

"You've certainly turned out to be very interesting men." Gus grinned, blowing smoke.

"That's probably true." Paul nodded as he poured more coffee. He did it to be polite. His hands were practically shaking with caffeine. Gus liked his brew about three times stronger than Paul did. He supposed it was necessary to keep a place like this running.

"Do you remember the toys my father used to get for me?"

"Your father was a good man. I miss him." He stubbed the remainder of the cigarillo into the ashtray. "You liked playing with the horses and dinosaurs and the knights and blocks. He got them for you in massive quantities. Every birthday, every Christmas." Gus smiled, revealing a good set of dentures. "You were a little spoiled, I think."

"Probably. I still have it all in the attic at the cottage."

"Do you really? That's marvellous." The old man bobbed his head up and down, clearly pleased.

"Do you still make them, the little dragons and catapults and things?"

"I do sometimes."

"I'd like to buy a small chest full. Enough for three boys to play with."

"Is there something I should know?" Gus drew up an eyebrow behind his spectacles.

Paul grimaced. "Good God. That would be the day! It's for Harry and Susan's boys."

"Yes. I heard about what happened at the pub. Sad business."

"They probably haven't seen a birthday or Christmas in some time. I'll have to get something for Lettie, but she's too old for this sort of thing. Maybe throw in one of those small maiden dolls for her though."

"You're a kind man, Paul. You make your father proud, I'm sure of it. Why don't you give them your old things?"

"No." Paul shook his head. "That's one thing I'll never part with. It reminds me too much of him."

Gus said something in the affirmative.

"I'm the only publican in town who still feeds Harry's habit, without him having the money to pay for it. I admit to feeling guilty. Not sure it's the right thing to do; in fact, I know it isn't. I'm just not really sure what to do. I wish Dad were here to guide me."

Gus regarded Paul pensively, as if he were trying to summon the thoughts that his old friend might have about the situation.

"Time will reveal the answer. It always does, you know," he said finally. "Mind you, sometimes it comes too late, but even that is meant to be. Things tend to domino through the lives of people."

There were times, even after so many years, that Paul missed his parents intensely. Gus's words moved him and he swallowed hard, unable to speak. No wonder Gus and his father got on so well, he thought. It was probably right in line with Dad's philosophical view of life. He nodded and stood, waiting for Gus to follow him to the door within a door.

"It was good of you to stop by, Paul," Gus said. "I will send everything 'round to the pub."

"Thank you."

"Next time, don't hesitate to ask. But thanks for the cognac. Stop by anytime you've the need for a nightcap of superior dimensions. I'm usually up past midnight anyway."

"I'll stop in on my way home one of these days."

"I look forward to it." They shook on it with great fondness for one another.

Paul stepped over the threshold and limped away.

***

STEVE DROVE TO HIS parents' thatch-roof Elizabethan cottage on the outskirts of Blackwell. David was in school, and with it being the shop's weekly closing day, he knew that his father would be in the garden. Their family had grown vegetables for as long as he could remember. Over the years, Steve had learned a lot about it, and gardening was a tradition he hoped to continue with his own family when the time came.

They hadn't spoken since parting ways outside of the auction house in London. There was no point in putting off facing the music. Granny's birthday affair was on Saturday, and Steve intended not to have to deal with tension around the dinner table. Being a chip off the old block, he knew how stubborn his father could be.

The Triumph came to a roaring halt in the driveway, announcing his presence. There was no sign of his father in the garden, though it looked like some of his tools were there. Birds sang their lyrical songs and frolicked in a puddle of water nearby. One narrowly flew by his head with a collection of nesting material in its beak, preparing to mate. It made him smile. Today was an excellent day to make amends, because after what had just happened in Katherine's little kitchen, he was in such an excellent mood that nothing could possibly ruin it… not even the old man.

Katherine. He could barely contain the joy flying exuberantly through his heart. Katherine. There was progress. Small steps were steps nonetheless, weren't they? What happened this morning hadn't been the intention at all. He simply hadn't been able to resist, and good that he didn't stop from expressing it. She was delicious. It was not difficult to imagine that making love to her would be like an intense stream of warm water pouring over his body on a cold winter's day, or equally like a cool shower in the heat of summer, a pleasure that wouldn't end until they turned off the faucet. He had seen that in the way Katherine had opened herself to him.

A noise from the direction of the garage forced him out of a dreamlike state. The door to the storage space, attached to the building as an afterthought years ago, stood wide open, and the sound of Ned's cursing met him on the garden path. The room was in greater disarray than normal, as if a bomb had exploded, papers and receipts and empty boxes strewn everywhere.

"Dad! What's going on?"

"What are you doing here?" Ned retorted curtly.

Steve breathed before he replied. "It's a beautiful day, Dad. I thought you could use some help in the garden."

Box in hand, Ned stopped what he was doing to regard his son. He was indeed dressed for getting dirty, that bloody hair of his tied together and wearing a floppy bush hat he'd picked up in Australia from the looks of it. Gloves were tucked in the back pocket of his jeans. Ned swallowed away the lump in his throat.

"What's all this about? Are you getting rid of it?" Steve pointed to the mess.

Ned swung around as if he noticed the ravage for the first time. He dropped the box by his feet, by a hair's breadth avoiding a broken toe. It made a dull, flat sound as it landed on the floor, sending some papers to float back in the air only to settle down again in a different spot.

"I'm trying to find something," he said.

Steve frowned. His father appeared to be out of sorts. He was dressed for gardening, yet seemed to have been distracted from it when clearly there was a lot to be done out there if they wanted a harvest in a few months' time.

"What are you looking for?"

"Ah, I'm not quite sure. A receipt, I think."

"Why?"

"Oh, don't mind me. I'll find it eventually. I'm just a bit… overwhelmed with the way things are in here, that's all," he laughed nervously. "I thought I might as well sort everything. More retirement preparation, you see."

"I see," Steve said, not believing a word of it. "What about the garden?"

"There is that too."

"So why don't you take a break from this and walk outside with me? Show me what needs to be done and where everything is supposed to go this season. I assume you've laid out a plan?"

They discussed the garden, and his father continued to sort things, noises of frustration occasionally drifting through the open door. Steve got to work. Nothing spoke of spring more than preparing the soil to plant seeds, to till the earth and enrich it, to bring the garden to the point where nature could take over. There was nothing more satisfying than to walk outdoors, harvest a cauliflower, and have it for supper.

Before long, the structure for green beans was hammered solidly into the ground with seeds planted all around its poles, and he moved on to the next task and the next until his father brought sandwiches and two large bottles of ale for them to share. They sat on the ground with their backs against the garage wall, sun on their faces. It was well after the noon hour. Steve wiped his brow with the sleeve of his sweatshirt.

"David should be here any minute now," Ned said, taking a bite from his roast beef and cheddar. Mustard oozed from slices of homemade bread.

Steve smiled. Some things never changed, and he was grateful for it. His father was the bread baker in their family. The best bread to come out of any oven anywhere, he would stake his life on it. And Dad would put mustard on strawberries if Mum would allow him to.

"Speak of the devil," he said as David biked his way up the drive towards them.

The teenager leaped off his bicycle and threw it down, shaking off his rucksack in the process.

"Hey! Put your bike away proper!" Ned raised his voice, but his mouth was too full to make any impact.

"Why? It's bloody rubbish!"

"David!"

"Well it's true, isn't it? You're too stingy to buy a new one for me." David picked up the bike and tried to put it on the kickstand but it wouldn't hold. It tipped over as if in slow motion. When the right handle met with the ground, it gave the bell a jolt and the top popped off. The three of them watched it roll beneath a budding elderberry bush.

David gave his father a dirty look. "See?"

"That's really pathetic, Dad," Steve mumbled, winking at David.

"I'm famished. Is there any for me?"

"Kitchen table, son."

When he'd turned to retrieve his lunch, Ned leaned closer to Steve and whispered that a new bicycle had been purchased for

David's upcoming birthday and stashed in the garage attic. Steve laughed.

"Mum and I are having a bit of fun with him. He probably unscrewed the kickstand and the bell this morning, knowing I'd be here when he came home from school today. I'd put money on it."

Steve laughed out loud. "That's just what I would have done."

"Thank God we had you before him. He's absolutely predictable, doesn't have a clue! He rather thinks he's reinvented the wheel."

"He's bloody adorable," Steve said, and meant it.

After lunch, Ned went back to the shed looking grim but determined. He seemed in a better mood. Somewhat. Steve convinced David to help him in the garden as there was so much to be done and he wanted a chance to hear him out.

"What's he up to in there, do you know?" he asked quietly as they sat side by side on their knees, pulling weeds out by the root.

David looked at the door where their father worked and whispered, "I don't know. He's been acting really weird lately."

"How?"

"He's been in the shed all the time. He says he wants to clean it up. But when have you ever seen him clean anything, and does it look any cleaner to you?"

Steve laughed quietly. "Hardly."

"He's bloody short-tempered. Even with Mummy," he continued.

"Really? Have they been fighting?"

"They never really fight, do they, but she's been complaining that he's not getting the garden done because he's always in there. Shit like that."

They moved backwards little by little, a pail in between them for the weeds they removed from the ground. Every once in a while, Steve wiped his forehead until he gave up and removed his sweatshirt, streaked with dirt, to work bare-chested. He aimed it for the garden bench but missed. It landed on the path where it was left.

"He's looking for something but he won't say what it is."

"Why do you say that?"

"Not sure. Why else would he bother? I wish he'd just torch the lot. I offered to help for money. I really need a new bike. I could buy it myself if he'd let me make some money off him, but if I even go near that bloody mess it's 'don't go in there.'"

"Your mouth is beginning to outgrow your head. Stop it." Steve fussed. "Can't you get a paper route?"

"It's already taken, and besides I've got too much football practice to take on a job. Mummy doesn't want me to do anything else."

"Do you want to do something else? Are you tired of football?"

"God, no! Are you *mad*?" David suddenly turned to Steve with a vigorously accusatory stare. "You haven't been to any of my matches lately."

"I know, David. I'm sorry. I'm busy."

"Are you making a new record?"

"Yes."

"Oh. Is it a lot of work?"

"It's a bit like playing football." Steve smiled. "Once you've got it all pieced together and mapped out, you've got to practice like mad to make it all seamless."

"Can I come with you some time?"

"We've got a show in a few weeks. I could talk to Mum and Dad."

"Is it in London?"

"Yeah, it's at the Hammersmith."

"Are you joking? That would be terrific! It's famous, isn't it?"

"It's a monstrosity with really cool acoustics. We've never played there before. I'm excited."

"That's bloody fantastic. I can't wait to tell my friends."

"Perhaps you can do it without cursing so much," Steve said, chiding.

David shrugged and Steve knocked him over.

Just moments later an explosive "Bloody hell!" erupted from the shed's door. David motioned to Steve as if to say, "And you wonder where I pick it up." He grinned smugly, opening his mouth to speak.

"Don't get smart with me," Steve cut him off. "I'm still bigger than you."

"Which makes me much faster than you."

Ned watched his boys as they rolled around in the dirt, play-fighting. Their laughter was music to his ears and eased his mind a little. He'd been so obsessed about that bloody Box and the implication of what he might or might not know about Katherine's parentage, that he was losing ground. Everything else in his life had been put on hold. He'd claimed to have to sort through forty years' worth of sales slips and bits to begin retirement preparation, but it was clear nobody believed him. Daily, he chided himself for having been too cheap to buy a new banker's box each year. Over the years he'd simply continued to fill receipts and copies of invoices until a box was full. Nothing was stapled, organized, or labelled. He heaved a sigh of desperation and called out to Steve from the doorway.

"Have you seen Katherine?"

The slowly sprawling grin on his son's face spoke louder than any confession could have.

"This morning over breakfast. Paul too."

"Is that all you kids ever do is have breakfast?"

"It's when they have time, Dad. What do you need Kath for?" he added as he made a futile attempt to brush dirt from his arms. "She got a letter and painting from the Foundation this morning, by the way. I hope you thought to buy her a pint for her birthday."

Bloody hell!

Ned was in dire need of a plan. He was fairly certain of the year he'd bid on a similar box. That particular auction had taken place in 1959. It was now 1984.

Just over twenty-five years ago.

Chapter XIX
The Blues

Katherine struggled with the idea of *Blues Night at The Wicked Mule*, but the cause was one she and Norman would have supported wholeheartedly, and that was difficult to resist. Paul had sent private invitations without announcing a band, claiming he didn't want fans; he wanted people with check books. Clever man. She'd accepted in return mail, but had yet to decide to attend. Time was running short. The Blues was so near to her heart. It had encompassed Norman, dominated their lives in good ways as well as bad. Countless songs held intense memories. When lonely nights kept her from sleeping, when she missed Norman the most, or lately when the fear of forgetting what it was like to be with him struck with powerful desperation, she had but to play along with him to bring him into the room, and when she sensed him, she lost all sense of time or place.

The ringing of the telephone pierced through her musings. She looked at the clock. Lunch time. It was Steve.

"You sound sleepy." Katherine checked the sky through the windows.

"I just woke up and realized what time it was," he yawned. "It was after two when I got to Blackwell. Bloody monstrous traffic down to Brighton for the weekend."

"Apparently. I've had a good crowd so far."

"Terrific. I've thought to ring a thousand times to ask you to be my date for high tea tonight, but I thought it was too soon."

"With your gigantic family? Very clever of you not to have asked."

"You're welcome."

"What have you been up to?"

"Aside from working? I've been thinking about you, of course. I can't seem to get the feeling of you, trembling in my arms, out of my mind."

The breath caught in her throat, and her heart made a small jump. She closed her eyes. Similar thoughts had haunted her throughout the week and it made her smile as much as conflicted.

"Are you blushing, Katherine?"

"Probably."

"Good."

"I, eh… haven't had a chance to thank you for that. I'm sorry for not… reciprocating."

"I wasn't in it for myself. There is no need to rush."

"Well then, I hope you enjoyed your shower afterward," she said cheerfully.

He chuckled. "It was quick and explosive. And I appreciate the thought but let's talk about something else."

"Okay, well… I suppose I'll never be able to look at my shower in quite the same way," she said, and through his laughter added, "I have a question for you, actually."

"What's that?"

"Have you been seeing anyone? I mean, since Anne."

"Was I not clear when we were in bed the other week? Of co—" he started, but she cut him off.

"You're away a lot of the time and that's fine because we're just getting to know each other. Honestly, when I think about this past week it makes me all warm inside, and I catch myself smiling even though I haven't given the intimacy between us a space just yet." She paused, regarding the mess on her desk without seeing it.

Steve remained silent on the other side of the line, not even a half mile away from Mon Chocolat.

"There are so many things that I seem to have to experience before you can even get to me, and I'm sorry for that." She kept an eye on a couple who were on a discovery tour of the shop's window displays. She hoped they would not come in just yet. "But you see, a few days ago I wanted to say thank you for that sweet little bouquet which, I assume, you left on my doorstep?"

"How many admirers have you got?" Steve teased.

"Admirers? What I'm getting at, Steve, is that I don't have a way to contact you when you're not at home, and I was rather hoping there wasn't something you forgot to tell me."

"You're quite right. I'll have a phone number for you tonight for when I'm in London. And you should never hesitate to call 'round my parents' or Gran's either, you know. I'm not hiding. I just don't want to overwhelm you with attention you're not ready for, and I don't want you to feel any pressure."

"At the very least, I can admit that I long to see you and that is… something, isn't it?"

"That's music to my ears, Kath. Will you go to The Mule with me tonight?"

"As your date?"

"Yes. You're at the top of my dance card," he flirted.

"Am I? I'd love to go out with you again, but I'm not sure about tonight." The doorbell chimed and the couple entered the shop. "Listen, I'm just not sure if I can make it, but use the key and call 'round if you want, after. I've got customers."

She rang off.

At day's end Katherine counted the till and locked the money in the safe upstairs. She made some notes in her day book to order more accessories and to ask her jewellery artist to bring new stock. Someone had inquired about one of the pieces of furniture as well. Whether the interested party would return was a different story, but it seemed hopeful. Any thoughts of the gig were firmly kept at bay even an hour before the start. She took a long hot shower and, with the water streaming down her body, concentrated on finding what was really important more than her own apprehension. The answer was simply to accept having a good time, see Steve, and very much to support Paul.

She dried her hair, applied smoky makeup and stood in front of her wardrobe, unable to decide what to wear. The invitation said the occasion was formal, but she wasn't in the mood for it. She wanted sultry and provocative, perhaps more as a shield of defiance against inevitable emotion than to show something Blackwell hadn't seen before. There was a white box at the bottom of the closet. With a pang of excitement, spreading into a delighted smile, she threw the box on the bed where Rafael lounged sleepily. Norman's leathers!

"I just might fit into them, Riff-Raff," she told the cat. "Grief is good for the waistline if nothing else."

Joining Rafael on the bed, Katherine opened the box to a pair of tissue-wrapped black leather trousers and a wide belt with a big brushed-silver buckle in the form of a guitar. She touched the belt tenderly, remembering all the times she'd unhooked the bloody thing, sometimes with teasing patience, and at others in a heated rush. Katherine lifted the trousers against her cheek. They had been fashioned after Norman's button-up Levi's jeans, and they were brilliant even if she said so herself.

Because they were men's, they would ride very low on her hips, but she'd be able to pull it off. It wasn't something that followed the norm of what was fashionable for women, but Katherine couldn't care less. It was in her nature to be different and innovative, the very traits that made her good at selling an idea to customers. It was how she lived and what made her successful even as a neighbourhood seamstress.

Norman had been a slender man, only slightly taller than Katherine. While her hips had been wider than his, she was able to slide in and button them up effortlessly. Standing in the middle of the room with a black lace brassiere and her bum hugged tightly in black leather, she caught a glimpse in the mirror of the colour splashed on her back.

Just then the telephone rang. She answered, expecting Steve but it was Ned who invited her to join their table for a celebration: he and Beth were to be grandparents! She conceded and rang off on the promise of a celebratory bottle on her tab. Smiling now, she returned to the wardrobe in search of a top, settling on a tight-fitting halter top designed to look like a tuxedo vest, made of a lovely charcoal taffeta.

She slipped the top over her head and hooked it at the back. It had almost no material but for the front buttoned panels, a strap around the neck, and one around the waist. Double-sided tape held everything securely in place. She'd built a bra into the halter to give her breasts a gentle lift. The shirt was meant to shock. It was a prototype for the collection she would release before the holidays, and tonight seemed an appropriate time for its test debut. An elegant black Victorian-style choker topped it off. Eyeliner smudged to create a sultry bedroom look set her eyes ablaze, and her hair she left for the mess it was. It fell in large waves down her back. Finally, she stepped into her favourite black boots.

One last look in the mirror revealed a woman who was a mixture of sophistication and sexy carelessness. She dabbed some Anais-Anais perfume behind each ear, and at just before eight, Katherine snatched her purse and a black tuxedo dinner jacket from the table and said goodbye to Rafael.

***

PAUL HAD BEEN on pins and needles all day. While Susan continually brewed pots of tea for him, he barked orders and checked every single detail three times. She would be in charge of the till and the silent auction as he worked the room. Paul had sprung for the little ones to spend the night at a babysitter's. Harry had been persuaded to stay home with an ample supply of beer and the cheapest whiskey money could buy.

A full house was expected and he'd engaged three professional bartenders and a few servers, the lot of them dressed in black trousers, white shirts, and black bow ties. Susan wore a black dress that she'd made for herself. Lettie and another girl from the village were charged with washing dishes but had been promised they could watch the show every once in a while, if they could keep up. There was an air of excitement between Lettie and her mum that hadn't been present in some time.

The band had arrived earlier in the day and arranged their gear. With the sound check done before opening, they were outside having sandwiches and coffee, waiting for Paul's signal.

Everything was in place, the setting perfect. Paul all but burst with anticipation, standing by the door to welcome guests, shaking hands, but in fact anxious only for Katherine to arrive. When finally he witnessed her confident approach, he did a double-take. She looked so very stunning, so hot that it sent fire through his body. She trotted up the stairs, surprised to see him away from the bar and dressed in a tuxedo.

"Look at you!" She smiled.

"Leather? Really, Katherine?" he replied as they hugged. "Steve is going to flip when he sees you! Good God, woman, your arse looks amazing!"

She giggled appreciatively. He led her inside by the hand, beaming and a little more relaxed, if only for the fact that she was here. He turned to see her reaction to the pub's astonishing transformation. It had the desired effect. Katherine's jaw dropped.

BB King poured from the stereo system with the volume turned low. Strings of white Christmas lights kept the lighting dim but festive. They were everywhere: the ceiling, the walls, over the stage. With all the sofas removed and smaller round tables with two to eight chairs around them, there were more seats than usual. The tables were dressed with red-and-white-chequered tablecloths, and small oil lamps collectively scattered soft, dancing light about the room. The stairs were roped off for the night, but the large fold-away wall to the rarely used back room had been opened. It looked rough and uncared for back there, but somehow it made the look complete.

The Mule had become a real Blues bar. This was America in the Deep South where cotton had made hearts as well as hands bleed; where yearning for the traditions of the African homeland and being humiliated by caretakers had resonated through the sounds of agony and fearful shouts of warning across the fields, into song.

Today, many cultures across the world shared a common truth about humanity that they responded to, whether it be Jazz or Rock 'n Roll or Metal or another form of music that pushed the boundaries away from the origins called "the Blues." Unfortunately, time had moved people so far away from history, they failed to realize that what they listened to had a beginning so profound.

"Toto, we're not in England anymore," Katherine said, taking it all in.

"I thought you might like it. I sort of tried to mirror a photograph out of that book you lent me."

"Mission accomplished. It's like being in Memphis all over again."

"Yeah?"

"Yeah!" She assured him with a squeeze of the arm. "Where is the Denison table? I'm to join them."

"Just there. Do you want a drink?"

"Yes, of course." She marched to the bar.

"Cognac?"

"No, I'll have some wine. Hiya, Susan. You look lovely!"

Susan smiled shyly. "Hi, Katherine. I'll have one of the waiters bring a bottle to your table."

"Oh," she remembered, "a couple of bottles of champagne and some glasses when the Denison crew arrives, please. Put that on my tab as well. Thanks."

Katherine found the reserved table quickly, two tables back from a stage that had been built over the much smaller permanent one by the hearth. A painting was put in place on an easel, and a large group of people had gathered around it, making it impossible to catch even a glimpse.

The baker and his wife had come out for the occasion. Katherine wondered if Sean might fall head first into his dough with fatigue when the time came to bake for Sunday morning. They were seated at the next table together with the butcher and his wife and the lady from the shoes shop with whom Katherine had an agreement. She had a conversation with them while rooting around her purse to check that she had enough money to pay for the booze she'd just ordered.

Suddenly, a chair was scraped back and, startled, Katherine whirled around. Rick took a seat beside her. He put a bottle of wine and a glass down on the table. She was so surprised that, for a moment, she didn't know what to say and stupidly studied the bottle as if it held some sort of explanation. She read the label. It was a 1977 *Château Cos d'Estournel, St Estephe*. Bordeaux.

Out of nowhere, Noah appeared; then Steven and Charlie and Jon. For an absurd moment Katherine thought they were waiters because they were dressed as if they'd been lifted from the 50s in black trousers, white shirts, and skinny black ties. But they had this look on their faces, a look of excited apprehension.

A sick feeling grew in her stomach. Realization struck with the force of a brick through a window. She said nothing. Everything slowed around her. Sound faded to the background. Time suspended. Her gaze moved to the stage in slow motion.

Every instrument there was familiar. Rick's black tubs. Steven's upright bass. Jon's guitar. Charlie's Korg piano labelled with a cacophony of stickers. Noah didn't have an instrument, if you didn't count his voice, but his microphone was electric blue and it was there as well. Amps were at the ready, lights aglow, connected to two short towers of speakers.

And there, featured in a single spotlight, was Norman's Gibson guitar.

Waiting.

For her.

She heard a wounded cry. Probably from her own soul. She hadn't wanted the instrument. She'd left it with her sisters-in-law as a memory of their brother. To see it now choked her up, as if

Norman himself stared back from the grave, beckoning to fill his shoes again.

The past fast-forwarded and crashed into the present.

"You can't be serious," was all she could say.

"*Hallo Rientje*," Rick said with a smile that died a quick death when he saw the storm develop in Katherine's eyes.

Hearing Norman's nickname for her ignited Katherine's temper, though all she did was to hold a finger out to him. Rick held up his hands in apology. Inside, his heart pounded with fear. He was aware; they were all aware of the magnitude of the moment. It wasn't taken lightly. The last thing they wanted to do was to hurt her. They missed Norman tremendously, and because she was their friend and they had come to rely on her support quite heavily, they missed Katherine too. The band members had unanimously agreed that the only person who could replace Norman was Katherine. The alternative was to form a new band which they were not keen on doing. But her reaction to the sight of Norman's guitar brought it all home. They wouldn't be able to continue. She wasn't going to do it.

"You can't be serious," she said again.

She was cold to the bone and shivered.

Paul observed the moment from a short distance away. He was struck by the look of sheer panic on Katherine's face, which probably had nothing to do with performing. He had heard her perform and she was not afraid. The guitar frightened her—the memories of songs the instrument hadn't known since Norman's death. She didn't want its sacred silence ripped open.

He limped over and sat down in a chair borrowed from another table. "You're not angry with me, are you?" he asked.

Katherine turned to him. Disbelief at once made way for fury. "I need air," she said, pushing back from the table.

They followed her, Paul bringing up the rear. A steady stream of people entered the premises now, many of whom hovered by the bar. She weaved her way through them, irritated because they blocked a smooth exit. Paul urged his customers to find a seat and place their orders with a waiter who would come to their table.

Steve and his family pushed through the door just as Katherine made her way to the kitchen, her face bearing emotions that caused Steve to recognize immediately something was very wrong.

"Kath…?" He started over the clamour of voices and Muddy Waters.

"Get out of my way." She pushed him aside.

Steve drew up a curious eyebrow and stopped short of a reply, puzzled by the stream of men who followed her through the kitchen door.

"Get on with it, Steve. You're holding up the queue," Ned said behind him.

"Why don't you all have a seat?" Paul said to them in passing. He wasn't smiling in welcome as he had with other guests before. "Table's got a card with your name on it."

"Like hell. I'm coming with you," Steve said, but Paul had already gone, bum leg carrying him faster than seen in recent history, making his limp more pronounced.

***

STEVE STEPPED OUTSIDE in the courtyard followed by his mother and Susan. Katherine stood by the covered portion facing all six of the men. Her eyes were ablaze with anger. Steve sensed that it was her against the rest of the world; only she was the firing squad and executioner. Judging from her rigid posture and fiery eyes, he thought they should get ready to dodge the bullets. Together with the two women, he watched the arduous scene unfold.

"What in God's name have you done?" Katherine, fairly in control, addressed Paul.

"Some time ago Rick gave me a tape that was recorded during one of your gigs. It really bowled me over. I learned they were considering a foundation in honour of your Norman and that initial funding was needed. We spoke several times at length and came up with this plan. I wanted to help."

"Whose idea was the charity?"

"Ramona and the girls. They want it to be called the Norman Loch Foundation," Jon chimed in. "The idea is to have it all set up by August for the first anniversary and to have another benefit then, at home. They wanted to ask you in person to be the charity's patron but Marlies broke her shoulder blade and had surgery yesterday. They stayed with her."

Katherine aimed at him, eyebrows raised in question, but she
didn't say anything. How could she shoot down an idea that would
give meaning to all that Norman had suffered? Diffuser. Paul was
probably safe, but this was far from over, and Steve was still in the
dark.

One of your gigs?

"I've wanted to host a gig here for a while now, but I could
never get the right band. So here we are," Paul continued.

"And you think this is the right band?"

"Without doubt!"

"It may be the right band, Paul, but I'm *not the right fucking lead
guitarist!*" Her voice raised an octave or two with that shot.

Steve gaped. He shook his head thinking he'd misheard. Had she
said lead guitarist? He looked at his mum, but she showed no
surprise at all, only deep concern.

"You do everything well, Katherine. You're quite an infuriating
person actually." Paul's second attempt to diffuse the situation
failed.

Katherine took a step towards him and lashed out. "For weeks
and weeks you've been going behind my back to plan this, all the
while pretending that you care about me, that you are my friend?
Why didn't you talk to me?"

Steve suspected that shot went right in the balls. Paul actually
cringed a bit and sighed, realizing he'd made a mistake. He wiped a
hand over his mouth in a show of frustration.

"It appears you wouldn't have done it," he said quietly.

"How dare you judge what I can and cannot handle emotionally?
And your second mistake was to assume I could ever *in my lifetime*
play that fucking guitar again!" She paused, looking at each of them
in turn. "*He died with it in his arms!*"

She spat the words and let them fall where they may. Her friends
regarded one another uncomfortably, shuffling their feet. They
hadn't known. Only Katherine had been present in Norman's final
moments.

"As for performing," Katherine continued, "it was one thing to
be a stand-in for him when he was ill. There were obligations. God
knows half of us needed bread on our tables. But that was then, and
this is now, and I will not be Norman's replacement."

Steve whispered to Susan to get some shots for everybody. He had a feeling Katherine could probably use one, and for that matter, so could he.

"Katherine, I've heard you play. You're very good. I wanted this for you and your friends. We've made over two thousand quid so far, and the evening hasn't even started. Gus has donated a painting to auction. That will really bring in some cash."

"*Oh God!*" Katherine shook her head now, vigorously.

The others in the band chimed in with Paul, speaking words of encouragement. She exhaled and inhaled deeply, pushing against her eyelids.

"You know it happened to them too, Katherine. This isn't just about you," Paul said.

The comment struck Katherine hard. She actually bent over a little, holding her stomach.

"Enough, Paul!" Steve bellowed, taking a step forward as every ounce of defensiveness struck at once.

Paul's head whipped around, surprised to find him there at all and with balled fists, at that. He took note of Beth's and Susan's presence as well before facing Katherine again.

"Katherine, darling, please, let me have it tomorrow. You can yell at me for hours. But tonight…" He hesitated but continued. "It's probably selfish of me but it would be such an honour to hear you play here, in my pub."

"*Shut up!*" Steve's anger built as he noted how Katherine's chin trembled, how her hands trembled. She was really very hurt. Paul had gone too far. He stepped in front of Katherine.

"I said enough, man! One more word to make Katherine feel as if she owes anybody anything and I will kick your bloody arse."

Paul knew from experience just how angry Steve could be when provoked and he braced himself against it. They faced off, thinking the same thought at the same time. Quite unexpectedly it had finally happened that a woman had come between them. It wasn't a matter of jealousy. It was a matter of love. Of friendship.

Lettie brought a tray with not one, but a dozen, shot glasses filled to the brim. Steve took one and knocked it back, not caring what it was. Swallowing the harsh liquor, he looked at Katherine and found her eyes on him. Something had softened in her gaze.

"*Bloody hell, Susan*," Paul barked. "She's not supposed to handle alcohol! Take the fucking tray from her!"

Katherine knew the aftermath of Steve's decision to stand up for her wasn't a battle she could fight for the two of them. She was still in defensive mode, and her gaze leveled on Paul once more.

"I came here tonight against my better judgment. I thought I could put any emotional ties I have with this music aside for an hour or so, to support you. I respect what you're trying to do here, and I appreciate your help on behalf of Norman's family." She took a step until they were almost nose to nose. "But listen to me very carefully. When I play tonight, it will not be to please you, and what's more, *fuck off*!"

To Steve's detriment, Paul laughed, which only added insult to injury, and he wondered how long it would be before Katherine would set foot in The Wicked Mule again. She toyed with the ring on her right hand. Susan had the tray. All but Katherine had accepted a shot. She left the tray on a crate nearby and turned to go back inside. Paul followed with one last look at Katherine. Lettie lingered in the courtyard a little longer. That she adored Katherine and worried for her was quite obvious.

Relief among the band was palpable. They kissed her one by one, and she allowed it, reciprocated even.

"We have about twenty more minutes. We've got a set put together that you know inside and out," Noah said.

"I'm not at all prepared. We haven't rehearsed," she said.

"Can you honestly say you haven't been practicing? That you haven't thought about it or even missed it?" Rick asked, suspecting the answer.

Her eyes found Steve again. The fear in them nearly made him say that she didn't have to do it, that it was okay not to, but it went against his beliefs. An audience should never be let down, no matter what. He held her eyes and waited.

"Have you got your key?" she asked.

Twelve pairs of eyes turned to Steve, including his mother's. He didn't let it distract him. He nodded once.

"There's an amplifier and a guitar in the cupboard off the bedroom. Will you get them for me?"

Steve nodded again and disappeared.

"I need some breathing room," she said to everybody else.

"We'll get on stage when your gear is hooked up. We can go through an introductory song or two to give you a little bit more time. That will be your sign?" Rick asked.

Katherine acknowledged the idea with a curt "fine."

Only Doctor Ramsey remained. As soon as they made eye contact, Katherine fell down on a stack of crates, as if deflating. Beth bent down to retrieve two shots and handed one to her. They knocked them back. Katherine took another.

"Are you angry, Katherine?"

"I feel a tremendous sense of pressure that I've been dreading. Like some sort of life-altering, explosive menstrual episode gone terribly, terribly wrong."

"I am sorry they made this decision for you," Beth said pensively. "At the same time, it could be useful."

Katherine followed Steve's mother as she paced slowly back and forth, in obvious counsellor mode.

"Sorrow is the root of this music, is it not?" she asked.

Katherine nodded. "Among other things."

"Then try to let it guide you through, try to channel your feelings outward." She made a pushing motion, away from her torso. "You may not be aware of this, but you do know how. You must believe that you do. It's one of the final obstacles." Doctor Ramsey placed her hands on Katherine's shoulders. "I will not leave you, Katherine. When this is over, we simply go to your place and we work it out. However it comes out. I think this is an excellent opportunity."

Katherine laughed bitterly. "I'd hate to ask your after-hours fee."

"That's my girl." She chuckled but grew immediately serious again and squeezed her shoulders in reassurance. "This is not okay, Katherine, but you will get through it. We will make sure of that."

"My purse is beneath your table. My keys are inside. I owe for a bottle of wine and two bottles of champagne. I think there is enough cash in my wallet."

"I think Paul..."

Katherine's nostrils flared. "No!"

Beth nodded and looked away. "You will forgive him for this eventually, I should think. I hope that you do. He is like a son to me and he means well."

Katherine scoffed. Beth smiled and caressed her cheek. She went inside. Cold to the bone, Katherine buried her hands in the pockets of the trousers. There was something small and hard in the right one: a pick, left by Norman. Katherine sighed and threw an accusatory glance at the brightly sparkling sky.

"You had this in mind all along, didn't you?" she said, but there was no reply. "Damn you."

She shivered and pulled her jacket closer. Damn Paul. Bastard. As if she could in good conscience say no to a pub full of people, and a moral obligation to honour Norman. The neighbours and colleague merchants were certainly in for a surprise. Tuesday should be interesting at the shop, as word spread around the village. She supposed it would either be empty or packed.

It wasn't long before the crowd began to shout and applaud. Just moments after the band began to play, sending Katherine's anxiety into overdrive. Steve returned with two glasses of champagne and a sheet of paper. He was dressed in a tuxedo, his shirt open at the neck, and she vaguely remembered him ripping off the tie in a moment of frustration.

"Are you okay?"

She shrugged, shaking her head, not knowing the answer.

"My family sent this. They said to thank you."

Taking a glass, she managed a little smile that was genuine. "Congratulations."

They toasted and drank.

Steve nodded. "Bloody brilliant news. I thought my old man would expire on the spot. Then they said they wouldn't move back to England at all. He was terribly disappointed." He pointed to the wall. "My sister is in there, and my brother-in-law."

"How is your grandmother?"

"Happy. She loved the flowers you sent and said she'd be in touch. She was the belle of the ball tonight, thanks to you."

"And the good news, I'm sure."

"Yeah, that too."

The music emanating from the pub was upbeat and smooth. The boys were very good. The part of Katherine that would always feel strange, ached to be on stage. It was an absolutely startling feeling, like a dual personality kept very secret and suppressed; the seamstress hadn't a clue how to play guitar, and the guitarist didn't know the first thing about threading a needle.

"Did you see the painting?" Steve asked.

"No."

"It caught me off guard."

"Why?"

"It's a sunrise on the beach with a man, a woman, and a dog running together down below. It's quite stunning. Just like you are tonight."

She laughed bitterly. "My two worlds appear to be on a collision course this evening."

"Will you be all right?"

"I suppose so."

"I'd bail you out but…"

"I know, wrong instrument."

"Yeah." He smiled. "Give me your hands."

"What's that you've got there?" She reached for the choker and took it off. "Would you tie this around my wrist?"

"Your set list. Rick asked me to give it to you." He put it down beside her and took the choker from her ice-cold fingers. She read through it.

"It's a good one," he said, tying a double knot. He massaged her fingers and felt the rough spots. "These are whoppers of calluses. You have been practicing."

She admitted to it. "Yeah. I'm sorry you had to find out this way, Steve. It's a part of that life I haven't made decisions about. It's important but… not as important as my own work."

"Don't apologize, Kath," he said in earnest as the heat from his hands seeped into hers. He kissed them, one by one.

She smiled a little. "Which one of these covers do you like?"

"'Stormy Monday,'" he replied without hesitation.

She smiled, almost shyly. "I love playing it."

As the band navigated through to the end of the first song of the evening, one that they would play again later accompanied by guitar and vocals, Katherine stood, claiming her hands back gratefully. "I think I've got to get up there now." She finished off the champagne. "Will you bring me another?"

"Sure."

They embraced affectionately and, taking Steve's hand, Katherine preceded him through the kitchen where Susan stopped them.

"Are you quite all right, Katherine?" she asked, concerned.

"I will be," she said. "Thanks."

"Do you really play guitar, Katherine?" Lettie asked, a bit awestruck.

She smiled at the young girl. "I'm afraid so, Lettie, though my talents with a needle far exceed it."

"That's amazing. I wish I could do that."

"You can, sweetheart. You can do anything you want to do," Katherine kissed her on the cheek and squeezed her hands. Lettie nodded, wanting to believe it.

"Susan, can I have a word?" Steve asked as Katherine disappeared through the gaping mouth of Pandora's Box.

Slowly winding her way towards the stage, Katherine's heart pounded with fear as much as anticipation. She acknowledged Daniel, the band's trusted sound guy, by putting a hand on his shoulder. He gave it a good squeeze. Twisting her hair up in an untidy bun, she caught Rick's eyes and stepped up on stage. Her back to the audience, outside of the limelight, she took the Stratocaster by the neck and lifted the strap over her head. The feeling the pub had invoked earlier had lost some of its magic. She noticed the painting and her new life depicted within it and took in her old one on stage. Suddenly, the guitar weighed a ton.

Noah, perched on a barstool, gave her a few picks, and she put them in her pocket, thinking how ironic it was that she had chosen to wear Norman's leathers. She shook her head in disbelief. How could they have done this without discussion? Noah, too excited to feel contrite, gently smiled. It wasn't difficult to read how happy they all were to be back on stage. It made the situation more tolerable. Katherine kissed his cheek.

"I've a message for you. Before her surgery, my girlfriend asked to say hello. She's sorry to miss the show."

Katherine frowned, and as the intended implication dawned on her, drew up her eyebrows in amusement. "You and Marlies?"

"Yes."

"Does Ramona know?"

"She's very unhappy!"

"Well done." She nodded, impressed, but otherwise paid attention to her instrument, making sure it was tuned and that the amp settings were as she wanted them to be.

Steve appeared. Katherine accepted the glass with that smile that was all braveness but belied the fear in her eyes. She was good at taking one under the belt, he thought. She lifted her glass in salute to his family who had all eyes on the stage. They raised their glasses warmly in response.

"My eyes will be on you," he whispered quickly in her ear, "but only because you take my breath away."

He didn't wait for her to respond but went to join his party. There were puzzled faces in the audience and surprised whispers buzzed around the room at the sight of Katherine ready to play with the band. If he could see himself, he would probably find that he was one of them.

"You're in for a treat, my friend," Paul said as he appeared by Steve's side.

"Sod off!" His smile froze, and he turned a glare of disapproval on his best friend, hoping the sting of disdain would be felt. In that moment it was an all-consuming, terrible feeling to have. Words like that had never been exchanged between them unless they were in jest.

Paul became upset now. The music came to an end. He held Steve's eyes for a long moment. This wasn't a jest. His heart sank a little bit further than it already had, but he wouldn't admit to it. He merely shook his head in disbelief.

"I understand she's cross with me now. I understand it is... unexpected. But I'm not stupid," he said, adding, "She needs this."

Steve stabbed Paul with eyes like daggers a moment longer before he turned away. Paul awkwardly got on stage and took the microphone. Katherine tested her sound. It reverberated around the room in a short burst of notes. It surprised Steve somehow, even though he was expecting it.

"Thanks for coming, everybody. You all know why we're here and we'll talk about it more a bit later, but without further ado we've got a special treat for you tonight." Paul looked at Katherine and for form's sake, she smiled. "All the way from Holland, and also just down the street at Mon Chocolat, put your hands together for The Blues Delirium!"

Katherine, heart absolutely hammering, started them off with "Reconsider Baby," a Lowell Fulson song that could normally get her in the groove immediately. But tonight she kept her eyes on the boys and her guitar, because they were the familiar, and only when the solo came did she throw herself out there. Her inhibitions flowed away. The band sensed it in her and quickly melded into the solid unit that The Blues Delirium was known to be around the pub circuit in the Low Countries.

Steve could hardly believe it. He had read the set list with some trepidation. Most of the songs were quite complicated covers. It actually shocked him to hear "Reconsider Baby" from her strings, so unexpected. Katherine had confessed that technically, she was not up to Norman's level, but Steve figured for him to have allowed Kath to take his place probably meant she could keep up. She did that and more. The band was remarkably tuned in to Katherine for not having played together in such a long while. He was surprised, again, when she sang harmony. She handled the guitar at the same time which was not always a given for musicians.

Steve realized after a couple of songs he was rigid with tension. He was nervous, willed her to do well, needed to tell himself to stop being a musician, to stop analysing, and to enjoy the music. They were really good. The crowd's reaction, even in their formal wear, evolved quickly from curious enthusiasm to complete immersion. "Driftin' Blues," a twelve-bar West Coast Blues song from 1945, reverberated through the crowd in a really big way.

Just when he relaxed, two things happened. Katherine removed her jacket between songs and the only person to see her backside was Rick, on drums. His reaction was one of bewilderment, so much so that he halfway rose from his stool, and a tub crashed into the ground. The singer, Noah, who was in the midst of announcing the next song, an Otis Rush tune named "Double Trouble," frowned. Katherine turned to pick up the tub. Steve and his parents and, he felt, everybody in the pub, collectively gasped.

"Good God!" his father exclaimed next to him.

"Whoa, bloody cool!" David said, earning him a smack against the arm from their father.

Some whooped and shouted. Others whistled their admiration. And to his own surprise, Steve joined them. Katherine's back was utterly and completely covered with an explosion of Japanese art.

All of it. He wasn't one for tattoos, however popular they were among his generation and peers. For a woman he definitely preferred the beauty of her natural skin. It was yet another side of him that leaned towards the traditional. But this... had to be the sexiest back he'd ever seen, and that he had been in bed with her without having seen it was almost unthinkable.

Noah counted and the band played, Katherine quite focused. "Double Trouble" was an intense song with an incredibly long solo, he knew. As she played rhythm, she walked the two or three steps off the stage and slowly began a turn around the room followed by the sound person who fed her power cord. The crowd was on its feet. At times she barely picked at the strings, producing a sweet mesmerizing sound, while at others what she drew from the Strat was too big for The Wicked Mule. Musically he was filled with joy and his heart bursting with love, Steve's mind was in danger of a system overload.

"Your mouth is hanging open, son," his father said, with an arm around Steve's shoulders.

It was impossible to follow her through the dense crowd. But she ended her solo for their group, and across the table Katherine's eyes reached for him. Steve received a jolt. The door to her soul was quite open. The pain he saw there took him aback. As if reaching from the life that was before, the life with Norman, with a need for reassurance that there would be new normality, with Steve in it. She turned away and with a smile for anybody in her path, calmly walked back to the stage where she signalled to the band, and they ended in perfect unison.

Taking the microphone, she thanked the audience. The band grinned from ear to ear, giving into the feeling of having succeeded in something only they were privy to. They got a full-minute standing ovation. Katherine, in a moment of surrender, smiled at her mates. She shared the feeling that what they had delivered was pretty awesome work. She introduced them one by one, wiping away perspiration.

"The next song is a very old one by T-Bone Walker." She paused to give the audience time to settle down a bit. "There's someone here tonight who means very much to me," she said, adjusting the microphone. "I would like to dedicate this song to that person and say how much..."—she inhaled as the words became stuck in her throat— "how very much our friendship has captured my heart."

Her eyes lingered on Steve briefly. "I don't always know how to express myself," she said to the audience's amusement, and she held up a hand. "All right, tonight I'm probably not doing too badly but,"—she paused again— "I think 'Stormy Monday' pretty much sums it up."

It was a long song with heavy gospel influences. Katherine sang the prayer solo, stepping up to the microphone, gingerly strumming the guitar. Their eyes locked, didn't let go.

And I say, Lord have mercy/
Won't you please have mercy on me/

It was a moment that they might later in life look back on as the one when they had connected for the first time on an emotional plane that, even in a room full of people, would never be shared. She laid her pain bare to him, and through an act of vulnerability, made a pledge to him personally to find a way to move on, to find a way to her new love through being denied the old. While the audience applauded, Steve remained her captive. The pub and everybody in it had faded away. His only reply was to put his hand over his heart. She acknowledged it with a nod before turning away.

"It was you?" Beth asked her son by his ear.

Steve didn't have to answer. The sincerity in his eyes when he turned her way, struck Beth through the heart. Understanding Katherine's struggles, she was unsure if her son wasn't in for the biggest disappointment and heartbreak he might ever experience. Her first instinct was one of protection. But having been witness to the life of her beautiful son unfolding, she knew that nothing she said would have an impact. He would always choose to live through what life chucked his way.

Beth could be certain of the level-headed way in which Katherine meant to live her life, especially in the face of the adversities she had already experienced. She and Steve were much alike in that regard. Nothing would stop them from being driven, from pushing forward. She nodded, but Steve had turned his attention back to the stage.

She patted his arm for attention. He leaned in to hear her over the boisterous noise.

"I've seen you smitten, before. But this is new," she said against his ear.

Steve should not have been surprised by her perceptiveness. It was one thing his father teased him about this girl or that, although he had a pretty good feeling that he would approve of Katherine, but that his mother could read his love life like an open book, was disconcerting every time.

"I think what I am, is the definition of captivated."

***

THE BOYS ASKED IF she wanted a break, but Katherine declined. She was hot, sweaty, and dying for something cold to drink, but wanted to get the gig over with. They indicated to Susan behind the bar that they wanted a tray full of drinks. Paul mostly sat on a barstool, in smug satisfaction over the evening's obvious success. He'd bet his money and his horse was coming in with room to spare. Eventually, the gig came to its conclusion.

"Thank you, everybody. Before we bring things to an end, there is something we need to talk about," Noah said. "About eight months ago, this band lost its founder and lead guitarist to an evil fucking disease called cancer. His name was Norman Loch. He was thirty-three years young. This is the first time we've played since shortly before his death."

He waited for the applause to die down again before continuing. "We miss him more than we could ever express in words, but... when you know his band is here, when you know his guitar is here,"—he pointed to it sitting in a spotlight— "and also the lovely Katherine who was not only his love but in many ways an inspiration... then it is our hope that we've managed to bring his spirit to your hearts as it lives on in ours. It's the next best feeling, and we thank you all for being here."

Katherine turned to the band and registered their emotion. Half of them had longing eyes on the Gibson and somewhere deep down it occurred to her that she should have called them once in a while.

"Please put a bid on this beautiful painting donated by a local artist. You can do so at the bar, and we'd like to take the opportunity to thank Paul for being our host."

People applauded, hooped, and hollered. Paul acknowledged them. Katherine fidgeted with her guitar strap. She kept her back turned away, leaving no room for forgiveness.

"And last but not least, we must thank Katherine for having graciously agreed to be Norman's stand-in once again as she did so many times when he was too ill to perform. I'd like to take a poll actually. I'd like to know if she quite blew your minds away." The crowd appropriately roared. "That's right. And to think she grew up playing classical piano," he laughed. "Now, it's an honour to play for you lot but I see in this audience someone who's been making quite a name for himself in the world of metal, and..."

Katherine looked at Noah in surprise. What?

"... for our last three songs we would love the honour of your presence on stage, Mr. Steve Denison."

Steve, silently cursing, got up from his chair to another roar. David, proudly leaped from his chair. Paul, meanwhile, limped through the crowd and met Steve with his own bass guitar. Steve looked surprised and Paul said something that made him laugh despite his anger. He stepped on stage and walked to the mike.

"Did you steal my amp too, Paul?"

Everybody, including Katherine, laughed, although she had no idea what the hell was going on, except that perhaps it was time for her to find out exactly what Steve did for a living. Her heart pounded wildly at the idea of sharing the stage with him. He shook everybody's hands and he kissed her cheek. He plugged in, playing a couple of bars to test the sound.

"What are we doing?" he asked.

"'Born Under a Bad Sign,' immediately flowing into 'Voodoo Chile' and then 'Little Wing,'" Noah said.

"No!" Katherine stepped closer. "We stop with 'Voodoo Chile' tonight!"

"We always end with 'Little Wing.'"

"I just... can't." Katherine's eyes were ablaze.

Rick stood up from his chair. "Yes, you can, Katherine. You will get through it somehow. You've been on fire all night."

Katherine, feeling more and more defeated, blew air out of her lungs as if she wanted her life to end on the spot. Steve looked at her with concern, not understanding her trepidation. Behind them the audience clapped impatiently.

Steve bent closer to her so only she could hear what he had to say. "I'll be right beside you. Find my eyes and we'll get through it."

"Hendrix was Norman's idol, his entire reason for playing guitar at all," Noah explained to the audience. "Probably like many of the youngsters who will benefit from this charitable cause."

Katherine's chin trembled, and Steve gave her neck a squeeze in a show of support, to guide her focus find the strength. Her skin was wet with perspiration.

"It has always been this band's commitment to end each gig with the same songs in commemoration to the Master. Tonight will be no different."

Noah paused to look at Katherine, who still had her back turned to the audience. They had gotten through the night with complete abandon, so much so that he'd almost forgotten having sprung this on her. His heart went out to her. If this was the last time they ever played together, he wouldn't be in the least surprised. She turned around and nodded slightly, indicating readiness.

"*Born Under a Bad Sign*, ladies and gentlemen."

Katherine, aware of Steve's presence, trembled. She might not have made it through the evening if it weren't for keeping him in her peripheral vision. He started the introduction bass riff. She'd never seen nor heard him play before, and how ironically weird that they were on stage. The brilliance of Jimi Hendrix's music drove Katherine into the mind of Norman. She remembered his definition of "The Zone." As a guitar player, he'd taught her, carrying the solo work during gigs, The Zone was the reward for everything, even life itself.

> "*The goal is to please the audience, Rientje,*" he'd said, "*but the reward is mutual. Your energy will send the audience to its feet, but you won't realize it until the song is over. When you've managed to pour yourself back into your own soul, is when you should be confident that you've reached a level of performance that will have changed someone's life.*"

She was aware that what her fingers did came from within, and yet she was an innocent bystander, a puppet on six guitar strings. She was alone in the room. It was perhaps that very notion that allowed for zero inhibitions. Her performance soared to peaks she'd never reached before.

When "Born" came to an end, Katherine immediately ripped into the beginning riff of "Voodoo Chile," sending the audience to its feet. She sensed people coming closer to the stage and let her eyes fly over them, aware again and aware of Steve. For the fun of it, she stopped and waited; made them shout for it, making a slight adjustment to her amp and on the guitar. Then she ripped the beginning of the song with a ferocity that grounded people's attention directly on the roaring Strat, a blazing red contrast to Norman's virgin-white Gibson looking on in silence.

She found Paul's eyes. Steve, standing beside her, watched how her intensity grew into anger, grew into despair, and flew out in a terrific assault on the strings. It left The Wicked Mule in quite a state. Paul was on his feet whistling and shouting along with everybody else. Lettie stood beside her mother, clapping her hands raw. Susan carried a relaxed smile. Steve's family was proud. Even Ned, to his own surprise, found himself moved by the music.

"Thanks, ladies and gentlemen. Thanks. She's pretty good, isn't she? Yes, indeed."

Two bar stools were lifted on stage. Katherine took a seat. Steve did as well, positioning himself to face her. Noah held his hands up to get the pub to calm down. With his next words, emotion caught in his throat. Katherine, unable to look at Noah or anybody, held her head down waiting for him to finish—waiting for the applause to recede. People shushed others to be quiet.

"'Little Wing' was Norman's favourite song ever." He picked up the microphone stand and carried it to the side of the stage, not to obstruct the view of what he was certain would be the crowning moment of tonight's show. "I would like to ask for your patience," Noah said. "Norman Loch, tonight it's not for Hendrix. Tonight, it's for you."

There was silence in the audience, aware of the burden of the moment. Katherine took her time to begin. Her shoulders were rigid. She breathed deeply in attempt to steady her heartbeat and loosen up. Steve held his breath. He couldn't even begin to fathom what this was like for her. What had the song meant for them together? It was probably a minute or more, an eternity. He willed her to get through it, intuiting that it might be a turning point.

Finally, Katherine threw her head back. Two fat tears rolled from her eyes in slow motion, taking with it some of her so carefully smudged eyeliner. She placed her fingers on the fret board, rolled the pick between her fingers into position.

One could hear a pin drop.

And then she began the first notes of the song, by herself. Rick chimed in on drums. Steve followed, completing the three layers of sound. Everything ceased to exist for Katherine. She could feel Norman, could even see him look at her not from the corner of the room, not from the other side of the stage, but from within. She felt his hand on her neck as he had done many times while she played, he said, to feel the reverberation as she manipulated the strings and interpreted what the song meant for her.

She played with great tenderness at times, only to let her anger rip through and pick up the pace with harsh emotion, and then let it cool down again in desperation, ending with the sweetest strokes of the Fender's strings as she had Norman's cheeks in the last moment of his life. Begging, begging. And releasing.

"Katherine Loch, ladies and gentlemen!"

She emerged through her tears, slowly. The audience was on their feet in deafening appreciation. Katherine removed the guitar. Her attempts at stopping the tears had ceased. Her soul lay bare for all of the village to see. She hated Paul for it. He stood by the stage, and she drilled her eyes into him until he stopped clapping and whistling altogether. Steve put the guitars away. Rick came to the front and lifted Katherine in his arms. He laughed. She had just given a ten-minute performance of a lifetime, one that Norman himself couldn't have done any better. He wiped her tears with his thumbs, to no avail, and pulled her forehead against his own.

"*Was je van de duivel bezeten dan?* Were you possessed by the devil?"

The band surrounded Katherine for a group hug that she didn't reciprocate. She was about to lose it completely and needed to get out quickly. She bowed with them just once and jumped down from the stage, through people who touched her, tried to speak with her. She pushed against them blindly until she was freed from The Wicked Mule.

Beth Ramsey stood in the doorway of Mon Chocolat, waiting.

Chapter XX

Rock Bottom

The door of The Wicked Mule fell shut. The exuberant pub was muted against the virtually empty streets of Blackwell-on-Sea. Steve stood at the edge of the sidewalk. Sometime in the last two and a half hours, the temperature had turned from pleasant to cold. He shivered. Having left his jacket, his dress shirt was soaked through quickly, but he didn't notice. The abrupt silence amplified exponentially in Steve's mind. He stood in a drizzling rain, hands buried in his trouser pockets, slowly emerging from an experience so surreal it felt he had been part of it from the farthest seat in a 60,000 capacity stadium.

Time, he considered. Time had stopped with the first strike of Kath's pick against the strings, and now, in the abrupt quiet of the night, in the rain, it cranked up again. It resounded in his mind like a metronome drawing him back into reality's rhythm. With the dread of defeat making his legs feel like they were filled with gravel, he turned in the direction of Mon Chocolat, and for the second time that night, he used the key to let himself into Katherine's place.

To be continued…

Acknowledgements

I am so grateful to my first reader, my beloved friend Mimi Roberts. Her encouragement, advice, and belief that Rhythms and Blues is a great story were instrumental in my not throwing it into the trash. She was the first person to tell me to write the first chapter, last. Her passing has left a tremendous void in my life and I'll miss her forever.

Editors, proof-readers, and test readers are indispensable to an Indie author, and I've been so fortunate to have been surrounded by an awesome crew. My sincere gratitude goes out to Kelley Kennedy, Terra Shute, Brenda Hall, and Madeleine Passerini, who spent precious vacation days hungrily tearing through the pages to catch the little things that are often the most tedious.

Thank you to Michelle Winton for editing and formatting, and for always being there. My awesome full-copy editor Teri Sullivan-Elmore, whose comments throughout the manuscript sometimes had me laughing aloud: it's an honour to know you. My most heartfelt thanks.

Maggie Worth, author and friend, made me feel it was okay to be a beginner, and was invaluable in helping me to find confidence in my writer's voice. I can't thank her enough for reading and for sharing her passion.

Thanks to my father-in-law Jerry for the wisdom and the discussions in psychology and reading parts of the manuscript before he wanted to read it.

I'm indebted to Gill Steel of LawSkills in the UK whom I contacted out of the blue for information about trusts, and not knowing who I was, still took a moment out of her day—as she said, "for the arts"—to respond to my questions. That's an act to always pay forward and I'll never forget it.

To Grzegorz Kosinski for sharing his incredible knowledge about bass guitars and also, his beautiful talent. Find him on YouTube.

Thanks to Michel Goessens, photographer/ singer/songwriter, for the awesome author photograph. Find Michel's music and schedule at www.goesendegasten.be

Choosing the cover was difficult but in Saturn99, I found the right person to work with. As readers do actually judge a book by its cover, I'm immensely grateful for his patience, excellent design skills, artistic eye, and input. Find Saturn99 through 99designs.com.

To my friends Judy and Kelley, with whom I shared the most outrageous moments at the best blues gigs we could find in and around Memphis, I hope you know how inspiring it all was.

To my parents for teaching me to be fiercely independent and to go after the things that I want with tenacity and on my own merit. Those life lessons are impossible to appreciate in words. For this and for their love and support, thank you.

I can't find words to describe what my husband's loving support means to me. His patience—and willingness to repeat everything five times before I ever notice he's trying to get my attention—and putting food in front of my face when I forget to eat are more than a girl could ever dream of. I'm humbled you made me yours.

And finally, to the artists who inspire me whether I'm writing, dusting the house, or thinking... To all the Blues, Rock 'n' Roll, and Heavy Metal greats, both living and dead...

...thanks for the music.

A Blues Playlist

"You Never Really Loved Me" by Trampled Under Foot

"I Love You More than You'll Ever Know" by Beth Hart & Joe Bonamassa (Seesaw)

"Born Under a Bad Sign" by Gary Clark Jr

"Make It Rain" by Ed Sheeran

"Red House" by Jimi Hendrix

"Hootchie Cootchie Man" by Muddy Waters

"Didn't it Rain" by Rosetta Tharpe

"Dance for Me Girl" by Buddy Flett and Kenny Wayne Shepherd Band (KWS) (Live in Chicago)

"Stormy Monday" Eric Clapton (Blues Live)

"Tin Pan Alley" by SRV with Johnnie Copeland (Blues at Sunrise)

"Damn Right I Got the Blues" by Buddy Guy

"The Stinger" by Rod Piazza and the Mighty Flyers

"I Put a Spell on You" performed by Annie Lennox

"We the People" by Guitar Shorty

"I'm a King Bee" performed by Kenny Wayne Shepherd (Live in Chicago)

"Eye to Eye" KWS and Willie "Big Eyes" Smith (Live in Chicago)

"Double Trouble" by Eric Clapton (Just One Night)

"Little Wing" Eric Clapton and Steve Winwood (Live Madison Square Gardens)

"Voodoo Chile" Eric Clapton and Steve Winwood (Live Madison Square Gardens)

"Catfish Blues" by Gary Clark Jr

NOW AVAILABLE Rhythms and Blues, Vol.2

1985

Hardworking seamstress and Blues woman, Katherine Loch is emerging from the tentacles of grief and bracing herself to explore the mysterious Box she believes may contain clues to the identity of her father. Former schoolteacher Steve, who has fallen for Katherine like a ton of bricks, helps her to pursue the quest even as the ups and downs of his own life threaten their budding love.

Fate is asserting itself in more than one Blackwell-on-Sea household and Katherine, knowingly or not, is caught in the fire of many hearts. Meanwhile, everybody's favorite publican, Paul, quietly fosters the balance of it all from behind the bar at The Wicked Mule.

In the second volume of the captivating Rhythms and Blues trilogy, love, friendship and laughter are strung like beacons of light between the secrets of the past, and an unpredictable future.

RHYTHMS AND BLUES, VOL.3
... IN PROGRESS

About The Author

A perpetual expat, Belgian-born Brenda Faucon has spent a lifetime being curious, exploring endless bucket lists, reading books, and appreciating music, especially the Blues. Newly returned to Europe after 23 years abroad, she currently roams the French countryside on a scooter with her husband, a slew of notebooks, and a fountain pen in tow.

For an in depth interview with the author about the *Rhythms and Blues* series, how she became inspired to write the books, her writing habits and also a titbit about what's coming down the pipeline, please visit her website at brendafaucon.com.